PENGUIN CLASSICS

THE DEATH OF IVAN ILYICH AND OTHER STORIES

COUNT LEO TOLSTOY was born in 1828 at Yasnaya Polyana in central Russia, and educated privately. He studied Oriental languages and law (unsuccessfully) at the University of Kazan, then led a life of dissipation until 1851, when he went to the Caucasus and joined an artillery regiment. He took part in the Crimean War, and on the basis of this experience wrote *The Sevastopol Stories* (1855–6), which confirmed his tenuous reputation as a writer. After a period in St Petersburg and abroad, where he studied educational methods for use in his school for peasant children at Yasnaya Polyana, he married Sofya (Sonya) Behrs in 1862. The next fifteen years was a period of great happiness. The couple had thirteen children; Tolstoy managed his estates, one in the Volga steppeland, continued his educational projects, cared for his peasants and wrote *War and Peace* (1869) and *Anna Karenina* (1878). A *Confession* (1884) marked a spiritual crisis in his life; he became an extreme moralist and in a series of pamphlets after 1880 expressed his rejection of state and church, indictment of the weaknesses of the flesh and denunciation of private property. His last novel, *Resurrection* (1900), was written to earn money for the pacifist Dukhobor sect. His teaching earned him many followers at home and abroad, but also much opposition, and in 1901 he was excommunicated by the Russian Orthodox Church. He died in 1910, in the course of a dramatic flight from home, at the small railway station of Astapovo.

ANTHONY BRIGGS, Senior Research Fellow at Bristol University and Professor Emeritus at Birmingham, has written, translated or edited many books and articles on Russian and English literature. A leading authority on Aleksandr Pushkin, he has also edited five volumes of English poetry. His recent translation of *War and Peace* for Penguin has been widely acclaimed.

DAVID MCDUFF was born in 1945 and was educated at the University of Edinburgh. His publications comprise a large number of translations of foreign verse and prose, including twentieth-century Russian and Scandinavian works. He has translated a number of nineteenth-century Russian prose works for the Penguin Classics series. These include Fyodor Dostoyevsky's *Crime and Punishment*, *The Brothers Karamazov*, *The Idiot*, *The House of the Dead* and *Poor Folk*, Leo Tolstoy's *The Cossacks*, and Nikolay Leskov's 'Lady Macbeth of Mtsensk'. He has also translated Isaak Babel's *Red Cavalry* and Andrey Bely's *Petersburg* for Penguin.

RONALD WILKS studied Russian language and literature at Trinity College, Cambridge, after training as a Naval interpreter, and later Russian literature at London University, where he received his Ph.D. in 1972. Among his translations for Penguin Classics are *My Childhood*, *My Apprenticeship* and *My Universities* by Gorky, *Diary of a Madman* by Gogol, filmed for Irish Television, *The Golovlyov Family* by Saltykov-Shchedrin, *How Much Land Does a Man Need?* by Tolstoy, *Tales of Belkin and Other Prose Writings* by Pushkin, and six other volumes of stories by Chekhov: *The Party and Other Stories*, *The Kiss and Other Stories*, *The Fiancée and Other Stories*, *The Duel and Other Stories*, *The Steppe and Other Stories* and *Ward No. 6 and Other Stories*. He has also translated *The Little Demon* by Sologub for Penguin.

LEO TOLSTOY

The Death of Ivan Ilyich and Other Stories

Translated by
RONALD WILKS, ANTHONY BRIGGS *and* DAVID MCDUFF
With an Introduction by
ANTHONY BRIGGS

PENGUIN BOOKS

PENGUIN CLASSICS

Published by the Penguin Group
Penguin Books Ltd, 80 Strand, London WC2R 0RL, England
Penguin Group (USA) Inc., 375 Hudson Street, New York, New York 10014, USA
Penguin Group (Canada), 90 Eglinton Avenue East, Suite 700, Toronto, Ontario, Canada M4P 2Y3
(a division of Pearson Penguin Canada Inc.)
Penguin Ireland, 25 St Stephen's Green, Dublin 2, Ireland (a division of Penguin Books Ltd)
Penguin Group (Australia), 250 Camberwell Road, Camberwell, Victoria 3124, Australia
(a division of Pearson Australia Group Pty Ltd)
Penguin Books India Pvt Ltd, 11 Community Centre, Panchsheel Park, New Delhi – 110 017, India
Penguin Group (NZ), 67 Apollo Drive, Rosedale, North Shore 0632, New Zealand
(a division of Pearson New Zealand Ltd)
Penguin Books (South Africa) (Pty) Ltd, 24 Sturdee Avenue, Rosebank, Johannesburg 2196, South Africa

Penguin Books Ltd, Registered Offices: 80 Strand, London WC2R 0RL, England

www.penguin.com

This collection first published in Penguin Classics 2008
6

Set in 10.25/12.25 pt PostScript Adobe Sabon
Typeset by Rowland Phototypesetting Ltd, Bury St Edmunds, Suffolk
Printed in England by Clays Ltd, St Ives plc

ISBN: 978-0-140-44961-7

www.greenpenguin.co.uk

Contents

Chronology

1724 Pyotr Tolstoy (great-great-great-grandfather) given hereditary title of Count by Tsar Peter the Great
1821 Death of Prince Nikolay Volkonsky, Tolstoy's grandfather, at Yasnaya Polyana, Tula Province, 130 miles south-west of Moscow
1822 Marriage of Count Nikolay Tolstoy and Princess Marya Volkonskaya
1828 28 August (Old Style). Birth of fourth son, Leo Nikolayevich Tolstoy, at Yasnaya Polyana
1830 Death of mother
1832 The eldest son, Nikolay, informs his brothers that the secret of earthly happiness is inscribed on a green stick buried at Yasnaya Polyana (Tolstoy later buried there)
1836 Nikolay Gogol's *The Government Inspector*
1837 Death of Aleksandr Pushkin in duel
Death of father
1840 Mikhail Lermontov's *A Hero of Our Time*
1841 Death of Lermontov in duel
Death of first guardian Alexandra Osten-Saken, an aunt. The Tolstoy children move to Kazan to live with another aunt, Pelageya Yushkova
1842 Gogol's *Dead Souls*
1844 Enters Kazan University, reads Oriental languages
1845 Transfers to Law after failing examinations. Dissolute lifestyle: drinking, visits to prostitutes
1846 Fyodor Dostoyevsky's 'Poor Folk'
1847 Inherits estate of Yasnaya Polyana. Recovering from

gonorrhoea, draws up scheme for self-perfection. Leaves university without completing studies 'on grounds of ill health and domestic circumstances'

1848–50 In Moscow and St Petersburg, debauchery and gambling, large debts. Studies music

1850 Ivan Turgenev's *A Month in the Country*

1851 Travels to the Caucasus with Nikolay, who is serving in the army there. Reads Laurence Sterne: starts translating his *Sentimental Journey* (1768) (not completed). Writes 'A History of Yesterday' (unfinished, first evidence of his powers of psychological analysis). Begins writing *Childhood*

1852 Death of Gogol. Turgenev's *Sketches from a Hunter's Album*

Enters the army as a cadet (*Junker*); based mainly in the Cossack station of Starogladkovskaya. Sees action against the Chechens, and narrowly escapes capture

Childhood

1853 Turkey declares war on Russia

'The Raid'

1854 France and England declare war on Russia. Crimean War starts

Commissioned, serves on Danube front. November: transferred at own request to Sevastopol, then under siege by allied forces

Boyhood

1855 Death of Nicholas I; accession of Alexander II

In action until the fall of Sevastopol in August. Gains celebrity with 'Sevastopol in December' and further sketches, 'Sevastopol in May', 'Sevastopol in August 1855' (1856), 'Memoirs of a Billiard Marker', 'The Woodfelling'

1856 Peace signed between Russia, Turkey, France and England

Turgenev's *Rudin*

In St Petersburg, moves in literary circles; associates with Turgenev, Ivan Goncharov, Nikolay Nekrasov, Afanasy Fet and others. Leaves the army. Death of brother Dmitry

'The Snowstorm', 'Two Hussars', 'A Landowner's Morning'

1857 February–August. First trip abroad, to Paris (lasting

impression of witnessing an execution by guillotine), Geneva and Baden-Baden

Youth, 'Lucerne'

1858 Long-term relationship with peasant woman on estate, Aksinya Bazykina, begins

'Albert'

1859 Goncharov's *Oblomov*; Turgenev's *The Home of the Gentry*

Founds primary school at Yasnaya Polyana

'Three Deaths', *Family Happiness*

1860 Death of brother Nikolay from tuberculosis

Dostoyevsky's *Notes from the House of the Dead* (1860–61). Turgenev's *On the Eve*

1860–61 Emancipation of serfs (1861). Other reforms follow: Elective District Councils (*zemstvos*) set up (1864); judicial reform (1865). Formation of revolutionary Land and Liberty movement. Commencement of intensive industrialization; spread of railways

Serves as Arbiter of the Peace, dealing with post-Emancipation land settlements. Quarrels with Turgenev and challenges him (no duel). Travels in France, Germany, Italy and England. Loses great deal of money through gambling. Meets Pierre-Joseph Proudhon in Brussels

1862 Turgenev's *Fathers and Sons*

Starts a magazine at Yasnaya Polyana on education for the peasants; abandons it after less than a year. Police raid on Yasnaya Polyana. Considers emigrating to England and writes protest to the Tsar. Marries Sofya Andreyevna Behrs (b. 1844)

1863 Polish rebellion

Birth of first child, Sergey (Tolstoy and his wife were to have thirteen children – nine boys and four girls – of whom five die in childhood). Begins work on a novel, 'The Decembrists', which is later abandoned, but develops into *War and Peace*

'Polikushka', *The Cossacks*

1865 Nikolay Leskov's 'Lady Macbeth of Mtsensk'

First part of *War and Peace* (titled *1805*)

1866 Attempted assassination of Tsar Alexander II
Dostoyevsky's *Crime and Punishment*
1867 Turgenev's *Smoke*
Visits Borodino in search of material for battle scene in *War and Peace*
1868 Dostoyevsky's *The Idiot*
1869 Publication of *War and Peace* completed
1870–71 Franco-Prussian War. Municipal government reform
Dostoyevsky's *Devils*
Studies ancient Greek. Illness; convalesces in Samara (Bashkiriya). Begins work on primer for children. First mention of *Anna Karenina*. Reads Arthur Schopenhauer and other philosophers. Starts work on novel about Peter the Great (later abandoned)
1872 'God Sees the Truth but Waits', 'A Prisoner of the Caucasus'
1873 Begins *Anna Karenina*. Raises funds during famine in Bashkiriya, where he has bought an estate. Growing obsession with problems of death and religion; temptation to commit suicide
1874 Much occupied with educational theory
1875 Beginning of active revolutionary movement
1875–7 Instalments of *Anna Karenina* published
1877 Turgenev's *Virgin Soil*
Journal publication of *Anna Karenina* completed (published in book form in 1878)
1877–8 Russo-Turkish War
1878 Reconciliation with Turgenev, who visits him at Yasnaya Polyana. Works on 'The Decembrists' and again abandons it. Works on *A Confession* (completed 1882, but banned by the religious censor and published in Geneva in 1884)
1879 Dostoyevsky's *The Brothers Karamazov*
1880 Works on *A Critique of Dogmatic Theology*
1881 Assassination of Tsar Alexander II. With accession of Alexander III, the government returns to reactionary policies
Death of Dostoyevsky
Writes to Tsar Alexander III asking him to pardon his father's assassins

1882 Student riots in St Petersburg and Kazan Universities. Jewish pogroms and repressive measures against minorities

Religious works, including new translation of the Gospels. Begins 'The Death of Ivan Ilyich' and *What Then Must We Do?*

Studies Hebrew

1883 Deathbed letter from Turgenev urging Tolstoy not to abandon his art

1884 Family relations strained; first attempt to leave home.

'What I Believe' banned. *Collected Works* published by his wife

1885 Tension with his wife over new beliefs. Works closely with Vladimir Chertkov, with whom (and others) he founds a publishing house, The Intermediary, to produce edifying literature for the common folk. Many popular stories written 1885–6, including 'What Men Live By', 'Where Love Is, God Is', 'Strider'

1886 Walks from Moscow to Yasnaya Polyana in five days. Works on land during the summer. Denounced as a heretic by Archbishop of Kherson

'The Death of Ivan Ilyich', 'How Much Land Does a Man Need?', *What Then Must We Do?*

1887 Meets Leskov

'On Life'

1888 Anton Chekhov's *The Steppe*

Renounces meat, alcohol and tobacco. Growing friction between his wife and Chertkov. *The Power of Darkness*, banned in 1886, performed in Paris

1889 Finishes *The Kreutzer Sonata*. Begins *Resurrection* (works on it for ten years)

1890 *The Kreutzer Sonata* banned, though, following an appeal by his wife to the Tsar, publication is permitted in *Collected Works*

1891 Convinced that personal profits from writing are immoral, renounces copyright on all works published after 1881 and all future works. His family thus suffers financially, though his wife retains copyright in all the earlier works. Helps to organize famine relief in Ryazan province. Attacks smoking and alcohol in 'Why Do Men Stupefy Themselves?'

1892 Organizes famine relief. *The Fruits of Enlightenment* (published 1891) produced at Maly theatre, Moscow

1893 Finishes 'The Kingdom of God is Within You'

1894 Accession of Tsar Nicholas II. Strikes in St Petersburg

Writes preface to a collection of stories by Guy de Maupassant. Criticizes *Crime and Punishment*

1895 Meets Chekhov. *The Power of Darkness* produced at Maly theatre, Moscow

'Master and Man'

1896 Chekhov's *The Seagull*

Sees production of *Hamlet* and *King Lear* at Hermitage theatre, severely critical of William Shakespeare

1897 Appeals to authorities on behalf of Dukhobors, a pacifist religious sect, to whom permission is granted to emigrate to Canada

What is Art?

1898 Formation of Social Democratic Party. Dreyfus Affair in France

Works for famine relief

1899 Widespread student riots

Serial publication of *Resurrection* (in book form in 1900)

1900 Meets Maxim Gorky, whom he calls a 'real man of the people'

1901 Foundation of Socialist Revolutionary Party

Excommunicated from Orthodox Church for writing works 'repugnant to Christ and the Church'. Seriously ill, convalesces in Crimea; visitors include Chekhov and Gorky

1902 Finishes 'What is Religion?' Writes to Tsar Nicholas II on evils of autocracy and ownership of property

1903 Protests against Jewish pogroms in Kishinev

'After the Ball'

1904 Russo-Japanese War. Russian fleet destroyed in Tsushima Straits. Assassination of V. K. Plehve, Minister of the Interior Death of Chekhov

Death of second eldest brother Sergey. Pamphlet on Russo-Japanese War published in England

'Shakespeare and the Drama'

1905 Attempted revolution in Russia (attacks all sides involved). *Potemkin* mutiny. S. Yu. Witte becomes prime minister
Anarchical publicist pamphlets
Introduction to Chekhov's 'Darling'
1908 Tolstoy's secretary, N. N. Gusev exiled
'I Cannot be Silent', a protest against capital punishment
1909 Increased animosity between his wife and Chertkov; she threatens suicide
1910 Corresponds with Mahatma Gandhi concerning the doctrine of non-violent resistance to evil. His wife threatens suicide; demands all her husband's diaries for past ten years, but Tolstoy puts them in bank vault. Final breakdown of relationship with her. 28 October: leaves home. 7 November: dies at Astapovo railway station. Buried at Yasnaya Polyana
1912 First publication of 'The Devil', 'Father Sergius', *Hadji Murat*, 'The Forged Coupon'

Introduction

Men must endure
Their going hence, even as their coming hither:
Ripeness is all.

King Lear V ii

THE VOICE OF DEATH

One of Leo Tolstoy's distant ancestors is likely to have been a large man; the family surname is an adjective implying bulk. Generations later, Leo came into the sturdily named dynasty having inherited every last tendency to massiveness. He turned out to have a big, strong body – he could lift 180lb (82 kilos) with one hand – a large ego, and a colossal appetite for life and learning, along with a formidable intellect. He lived a long life, fathering thirteen children and dying in his eighty-third year, famous for having written, by common acknowledgement, the biggest and best novel in the world. By then he was also recognized across the globe as a titan of moral and spiritual leadership. His *Collected Works* run to ninety large volumes; there isn't a delicate lyric among them. For Leo Tolstoy the only scale was gargantuan. It comes as no surprise, therefore, to learn that when, at the age of forty-one, he was afflicted with what we might now call a mid-life crisis, it was an acute one.

The trouble started in the late 1860s as he finished *War and Peace* (1869). Now, in his full maturity, at the zenith of his physical and intellectual powers, bursting with vitality and nurtured by success, Tolstoy should have been a happy man. But on the contrary, the sheer goodness of living seems to have made him all the more obsessed with the inevitability of death. What he had could be taken away, *would* be taken away, and soon. His wife describes how he felt at this time: 'Often he said his brain hurt, some painful process was going on inside it, everything was over for him, it was time for him to die.'[1] Some of the pain came from what he was reading; during the summer of 1869 he was immersed in the work of the German philosopher Arthur Schopenhauer, whose poisonous pessimism was enough to make a happy man sad, and a sad man suicidal.

In August Tolstoy set off for the distant province of Penza in the hope of buying some land, and broke his journey in the small town of Arzamas. During a sleepless night he was suddenly seized with dread. He described the feeling to his wife as follows:

> It was two o'clock in the morning. I was exhausted. I wanted to go to sleep, and I felt perfectly well. But suddenly I was overwhelmed by despair, fear and terror, the like of which I have never experienced before . . . such an agonizing feeling . . . God preserve anyone else from experiencing it.[2]

Eleven years later he recalled the occasion in an unfinished work of fiction, *Notes of a Madman*:

> I had hoped to get rid of the thing that was tormenting me in the room. But it came out behind me and everything turned black. I became more and more frightened. 'This is ridiculous,' I told myself. 'What am I afraid of?'
>
> 'Me,' answered Death. 'I am here.'[3]

Tolstoy's spiritual agony at this time cannot be overstated. He never fully recovered from this shocking encounter with death. His dark thoughts on suffering, death and the meaningless of life itself stayed with him and were reflected in much of his subsequent work, particularly the last sections of *Anna Karenina* (1878) and the whole of *A Confession* (1884). The multiple irony in the distressing circumstances of 1869 is striking. First: within a few months of completing the world's most life-affirming novel he becomes obsessed with dying and death. Second: Schopenhauer's philosophy is so black that it sees life as nothing but suffering, a constant striving without any satisfaction; death, then, should be warmly anticipated as a welcome release. Yet the knowledge of death, far from providing a soothing promise of relief, ruins what small happiness can be found in living. Third: although Tolstoy couldn't have known it, at the time when he was being addressed so ominously by the voice of death, his life was actually at its meridian. He had lived for forty-one years, and had another forty-one still ahead of him. At that time, incidentally, the expectation of life in Russia stood at forty-one years.

DEATH IN THE MIDST OF LIFE

The Book of Common Prayer reminds us solemnly that 'in the midst of life we are in death', and until recent times that used to be true in a literal sense: all families experienced death repeatedly at first hand. Tolstoy's was one such. Death visited his home at regular intervals; for instance, five of his children did not survive childhood, and in one short period, 1873–5, five family members died. He saw men shot or blown up on the battlefield, watched a man die under the guillotine blade in France, and sat with his brother until he died from consumption. All of this must have been very painful, but it is probably more significant that Tolstoy's own childhood was badly affected by the death of his mother when he was two, his father when he was nine, a devoted grandmother when he was ten, and his doting Auntie Tatyana when he was thirteen. True, he was loved and protected throughout by family members, but perhaps the early loss, one after the other, of four parental figures instilled into him a particular sense of the fragility of human life and a sharper than normal fear of death. Mortality would become one of this writer's most persistent themes, as he worked against the idea attributed to Samuel Johnson that our fear of death is so great that the whole of life is but keeping away the thought of it. All of the stories in this volume are connected by this preoccupation, along with the author's simultaneous attempts to help us improve our lives. However, far from being overt morality pieces, they are all gripping narratives, and should be enjoyed as such before being examined for lessons in living and dying.

But this volume is only a representative selection of Tolstoy's writing on the subject. The idea of death haunts his work from *Childhood* in 1852 to *Hadji Murat* in 1904 and *Alyosha the Pot* in 1905. *The Sevastopol Stories* (1855–6), transmitted straight from the Crimean warfront, necessarily pile up the corpses of soldiers, many of which Tolstoy saw with his own eyes on the battlefield. The vitality of *The Cossacks* (1863) is undermined by the suffering of the story's mortally wounded hero, Lukashka. In *War and Peace* the deaths of old Count Bezukhov, Lise, Hélène, Andrey, Count Rostov, Petya Rostov and Platon Karatayev bring particular poignancy to the subject that has been generalized in thousands on the field of war. And in *Anna Karenina* the famous suicide of the heroine is hardly more moving than the death of Nikolay, brother of the novel's other protagonist Konstantin Levin, which is itself a transcription from the real-life demise of Tolstoy's own brother. This occurs in Part Five, Chapter 21, the only one out of the 734 chapters that make up the three longest novels of this author to be given a title, *Death*. *The Kreutzer Sonata* (1889) examines sexual passion that has culminated in a gruesome murder. 'Master and Man' (1893) ends in the self-sacrificing death of a man who has hitherto been the epitome of calculating egoism. In *Resurrection* (1899) the story hinges around another murder, the poisoning of a prostitute's client. In a play of 1886, *The Power of Darkness*, there is another poisoning, though this is transcended in awfulness by a rare example of nothing less than infanticide on stage. It is all there – death in every conceivable guise: murder, accident, suicide and natural causes, finishing off the young, the old and everyone in between. Even from this kind of brief overview it is clear that Tolstoy's obsession with death and dying is something out of the ordinary; few serious writers come near him in persisting with this difficult subject and presenting it from so many different angles.

THE LIFE OF IVAN ILYICH

It is ironical that *The Death of Ivan Ilyich*, one of the world's most penetrating fictional examinations of the sick room and the deathbed, was handed to the author's wife as a pleasant surprise on her birthday. Far from being disturbed by the shocking content of the story, Sonya was delighted. First, she welcomed this new work, handed to her when she returned from a stay in Moscow, in 1882, because of its symbolic value. According to her perceptions, her husband had been indulging himself ever since *Anna Karenina* three years earlier by fiddling around with second-rate works of philosophy, morality and religion that no one wanted to read. The appearance of a new work of fiction, even if it had death in its title, seemed more like a resurrection to her. Second, she was a sensitive critic of her husband's work, and she knew a masterpiece when she saw it. Her husband may have been in his sixth decade, but he was obviously not written out or even declining in literary ability. Third, this piece would nicely enhance the *Collected Works* that she was working on. Finally, practical woman as she was, Sonya could hardly have been indifferent to the prospect of new royalties coming in.

There is something unusual about this story from the outset. The title of the tale announces its ending. To emphasize this, we are barely a hundred words into the narrative when we are told, 'Gentlemen, Ivan Ilyich is dead.' So much for suspense. At no stage in the succeeding pages are we going to entertain doubts about the protagonist's fate, which has been settled and sealed. Clearly, no time will be lost worrying about whether a sick man is going to die or survive; the interest must be elsewhere – in the process of dying, and the life that is being left behind. And that is how things turn out; what is at stake is the life of Ivan Ilyich. And by shifting the emphasis of his story like this Tolstoy lays down a benefit for himself as narrator; he can now allow himself to get right into the nasty details of dying, death and decomposition without facing a charge of prurience. An author who has renounced suspense cannot be said to be gratuitously milking gruesome material for every last drop of horror.

The idea for this story came from real life. In Tula, the nearest town to Tolstoy's estate, a judge by the name of Ivan Ilyich Mechnikov had died from stomach cancer the previous year (July 1881), young and in mid-career. Tolstoy had been used to meeting some of the wretches sentenced by him to long years in Siberia, sometimes for fairly trivial reasons, and he had wondered about the kind of man who could sit in judgement over them, dispatch them and then return to his family and continue his happy lifestyle. Mechnikov's brother told Tolstoy about the judge's death in some detail, and the general shape of the narrative seemed obvious. A man of privileged background and good education, accustomed to sentencing others, would find himself under sentence of death; the reader would follow his struggle and be persuaded to look with contempt at the empty life of the declining man. An early idea to put this in diary form under the title *Death of a Judge* was abandoned as too shallow a vessel for all the ideas that the author wanted to include. In other respects there was no reason to depart from what had happened in real life. For instance, even the man's first names could be kept, since they had a kind of Jack Robinson ring to them, suggesting ordinariness and general applicability. The surname of Tolstoy's Ivan Ilyich is Golovin, from the Russian word *golova*, meaning head, a rather obvious indication of the man's cerebral rather than spiritual attitude to life and death.

Ordinariness is the currency Tolstoy chooses to deal in. We are invited to see this man as unfortunately typical of most people – small-minded, self-centred, materialistic. He has gone through law school, drifted into marriage, acquired two children almost incidentally and developed his career successfully, using every decent contact and opportunity to better himself. Like many of the upwardly mobile, he continually overreaches himself, but each promotion brings more money and he reaches a stage where he can manage fairly well. As his family life declines into indifference, because he and his wife are unsuited to each other and their small stock of affection is soon used up,

Ivan Ilyich turns for satisfaction to his professional duties and to a small circle of male friends who like to play cards for small stakes. And now, on the brink of middle age, he is struck down by an illness that starts out as something trivial, though we know from the title and the opening that it is going to prove fatal.

Before looking at the illness itself it is worth considering the lifestyle of Ivan Ilyich, which Tolstoy depicts, subtly but insistently, as arid, unimaginative and useless, a matter for retrospective regret and for contempt if viewed from outside by a thinking person. Many people would object to this charge if it were put to them more directly. The judge is a successful man rather than a nonentity, and he is scrupulous in his dealings. He likes the feeling of power that he wields over the miserable people who come before him, but he never exploits or misuses it. He has made no serious mistakes and has no hidden crimes on his conscience. He is good to his children and faithful to his wife. Even his one besetting peccadillo, a penchant for cards, is kept under control; only small amounts of money are at stake, and there is no danger of addiction because the pleasure comes more from playing skilfully and exploiting any good luck than from significant winnings. This 'weakness' in the character of Ivan Ilyich is no worse than, say, watching too much television in the present era, except that it has the advantage of getting him out of the house and enjoying the company of other people. All in all, there is nothing much for this man to be ashamed of. No wonder he has few regrets when illness begins to make him review his life. He knows that it has not worked out too well, but when he starts to consider the reasons for this he cannot blame himself for having got things seriously wrong. 'How can that be when I did everything properly?' It is true that at the very end Ivan Ilyich appears to grasp Tolstoy's truth that a life lived wrongly is an obstacle to an easy death. He does conclude that his only real happiness was in childhood and just afterwards, and that there was something disgustingly unsatisfactory about the second half of his life. Finally he sees the light, and is permitted to die. But the purity of this vision of an unhappy adulthood is subject to some doubt. Is this not a fairly common experience, even without the promptings of severe illness? Did not the author himself see his life as pointless at precisely the same age (Ivan is also forty-one)? And, in any case, is he not suffering from blurred perceptions because of the pain he has suffered and the opium he is now being treated with?

This is to say that there is something amiss with Tolstoy's moral purpose here. But there is one thing we can be reasonably sure of: if a miracle had occurred and he had survived, Ivan Ilyich would probably not have gone on to live his life differently, soulfully, newly inspired by his close encounter with death. He would have been more likely to return to his fractious family life and his cards. The life of this man has been trivial rather than despicable, and it is unfair of the author to adopt such a disparaging attitude towards his protagonist. To accept Tolstoy's implied disparagement would be to condemn and dismiss the lives of millions of people carrying on as best they can in a difficult world without doing much harm to others. The idea implicit in this story that we should emerge from reading it determined to reshape our misguided lives is rather unrealistic.

THE DEATH OF IVAN ILYICH

Yet there is no doubt about the devastating power of this harrowing narrative. Its literary quality, founded on grim descriptive realism and remarkable psychological insight, stands beyond dispute. Many people have claimed this as Tolstoy's finest work apart from the big novels, and it has gained an international reputation. To take a well-known example, among its many admirers was the French writer Guy de Maupassant, for whom this was the last work of literature that he read before he died, and after reading it he is reported to have signed off with these unhappy words: 'I realize that everything I have done was to no purpose and that my ten volumes are worthless.'[4] The reasons behind this widely acknowledged success are not far to seek.

The Death of Ivan Ilyich is an object lesson in style, construction and the sensitive use of language (much of which is apparent even in translation). The author has abandoned the rich, descriptive and discursive style of his long novels. Here the pace and tone throughout are brisk and businesslike; once the funeral is over (Chapter 1) there is nothing digressive, leisurely or poetic. The narrative process is one of relentless compression, a steady tightening of resources until the pressure becomes all but unbearable. Like life itself, the story begins expansively, gradually narrows and then ends in small sections rapidly falling away. The first six chapters decrease in size one by one, then Chapters 7 and 8 open out again to slightly greater length, before issuing in a swift succession of the very shortest chapters to end the story. Even the paragraphs and sentences get shorter and shorter; time shrinks, and the sense of gathering urgency is unmistakable.

Increasingly, as the illness progresses and Ivan's understanding of it develops, the author grinds out his agonizing story with forensic efficiency. This is directed not at the illness itself, which remains a mystery to us. One day, hanging curtains in his new flat, Ivan has a bit of a fall and bumps his side. From this trivial accident he sustains an illness that most commentators have taken to be cancer, though in our era it is considered rare for physical trauma to have any such result, just as some of the symptoms (such as a bad taste in the mouth) do not seem particularly relevant. But the details do not matter, and in any case Tolstoy held the medical profession in such contempt that he would have been delighted to defy any of their theories or pronouncements. This story loses no opportunity to excoriate the doctors with bitter satire. Tolstoy's clinical exactitude is directed at the progress of Ivan's condition and its effect on the sufferer, an inexorable progression from bemusement through panic to a crescendo of intolerable pain as this terrible affliction crushes the sufferer simultaneously in body and mind.

Terrible contrasts sharpen our perception of what is going on: the wholesome past versus the unhealthy present; young flesh compared with an ageing and decaying body; large swathes of hypocrisy and indifference set against spontaneous love emanating (rather unrealistically) from only two people, Ivan's servant Gerasim and his son Vasya; the turning of the tables as Ivan Ilyich Golovin changes from arbiter to supplicant when faced with a doctor:

> It was just like being in court. The way he looked at the accused in court was exactly the way he was being looked at now by the famous doctor.

The judge is judged; the sentencer is being sentenced. The power of such writing does justice to the awful importance of its theme. This story stands as one of the most effective *memento mori* statements in world literature. And the real reason for this is that, for all his implicit condemnation of Ivan Ilyich's way of living, Tolstoy warms to his man as he dies. Far from transmitting a sense of individual *schadenfreude*, he writes with the kind of compassion that unites us all in confronting the terrible predicament of our mortality.

THREE DEATHS AND MORE

The reason for the success of *The Death of Ivan Ilyich* is that its didactic purpose (an instruction for us to reappraise our lives and to promote love as the only standard to live by) is thoroughly integrated into a compelling narrative. Tolstoy varies in his ability to pull off this trick, as is demonstrated by the other stories in this collection. All of them are strong in narrative interest, all of them have an inner message to convey, but the emphasis changes from story to story. An early tale, 'Three Deaths' (1859), has very little purpose other than to tell us how to die. An aristocratic lady, an old peasant and a tree perform this deed for us, and the message is clear: stay close to nature and the dying will be easy; deathbed agony awaits the educated sophisticates of modern society who have left nature behind. This is Tolstoy at his most simplistic, but the tale has its positive qualities – striking portraiture, natural dialogue, touching descriptions of the natural world, a succinct style of writing – and they make for a half hour of pleasurable reading.

Two other early stories, 'The Raid' (1853) and 'The Wood-felling' (1855), foreshadow later works by Tolstoy that will look realistically at warfare and cast doubts on its glory; the former is particularly strong in its depiction of soldiers doing what they are paid to do, which includes killing and being killed. These tales have a painfully enduring relevance because they describe military events in an area on the border between Europe and Asia which for generations has known nothing but a feuding and tribal conflict that is still alive today. The region was then, and is now, also at the interface been two great religions, Islam and Christianity. We are speaking of Chechnya, that arid, mountainous enclave which could be a beautiful homeland to take pride in, but for the warring antagonism that no one seems able to transcend or dispel. The military town of Grozny, a fearful name even in today's newspapers, was at the centre of things in Tolstoy's two stories, though they both take place in the same nearby countryside. In each case an order is received by a military detachment, which marches off to do its duty, taking with it a shrewd and articulate observer who will give us the atmosphere and tell us what happens. The assignment is achieved, but at severe cost; lives are lost on both sides, and particularly poignant are the deaths of two young men, Alanin in the former story and Velenchuk in the latter. The individualized tragedies of these youngsters, so poignantly described, are more eloquent than the piles of corpses littering the field on Tolstoy's broader military canvases (*The Sevastopol Stories* and *War and Peace*). These small narratives are among his masterpieces. They both tell a compelling story, filling it out with topographical detail from mountains to midges, warm portraiture based on close psychological observation, and a modicum of gently delivered moral instruction. There are strong underlying contrasts between brutality and civilization, youth and maturity, simple local people and more sophisticated intruders, the beauty of the natural scene and the horrors of soldiery, but these are not pressed upon us by too earnest a teacher. You will take pleasure from the telling of the story, but you will probably also be persuaded to think over some serious ideas, about honour and glory, self-dramatization and sincerity, egoism and courage – the whole meaning of going to war, and how it affects both the guiding political minds and the lads who do the fighting and dying. Our present-day war correspondents still tell the same tales, some of them set in the same region.

The preoccupation with violence and death shown in these early stories is still in Tolstoy's mind half a century later, as we can see in two very late works, 'After the Ball' (1903) and 'The Forged Coupon' (1905). The first of these is a remarkable story that was written in a single day. The critic A. N. Wilson ranks it with the very greatest things Tolstoy ever wrote.[5] Its power is drawn from the shocking contrast between two opposite personalities displayed by an elderly colonel, seen first at a ball dancing serenely with his daughter and charming the company, and then, the following morning, enthusiastically directing a gruesome ceremony in which an army deserter is made to run the gauntlet, and beaten so viciously that his death seems certain. Needless to say, the narrator's love for the colonel's daughter does not long survive this ghastly experience. 'The Forged Coupon' is a morality piece with strong narrative interest, in which a small transgression – the forging of a banknote – leads inexorably to a series of much more serious crimes, including multiple murder, and then, less convincingly, to salvation for the main characters. The neatness of construction and the simplicity of Tolstoy's writing are strong features of this work; it has been disregarded not for any real faults, but because its posthumous publication went largely unnoticed.

One of Tolstoy's most accomplished and moving novellas is *Polikushka*, written in 1863, at the end of the long literary apprenticeship that was about to produce two of the world's greatest novels. It tells the story of Polikey (also known as Polikushka), a peasant horse doctor given to drunkenness and petty crime, who reforms himself with great effort and is rewarded by his mistress when she excuses him from the military conscription that he seems to deserve. But he then loses a large sum of money entrusted to him, and the results are catastrophic. The build-up of suspense in this tale is painful because there is so much at stake for so many people. The village is required to provide men for military service, and

Polikey ought to be sent because he has a bad record. But the mistress supports him, so they must send someone else. The choice is an agonizing one: conscripts could be retained for long periods, up to twenty years, and many never returned. So we have two things to worry about: whether Polikey will continue to withstand temptation and become a good member of the community, and how the conscription problem will be solved. The stakes are high, the characters – mostly from the peasant class – are among Tolstoy's most memorable portraits, and the undeserved outcome has a terrible twist of ironic inevitability. Best of all, Tolstoy has built up a powerful case against warfare, conscription and violence, without our really noticing what he has been up to. This is one of his short masterpieces.

THE DEATH OF LEO NIKOLAYEVICH

Considering the time and effort expended by this famous man in an effort to confront death and prepare himself for the end, the death of Leo Nikolayevich Tolstoy was a disastrous shambles. The apostle of love and charity ran away from his devoted wife in a spirit of bitter malevolence and fell ill at a railway station, where he died a few days later, surrounded by six doctors, a police chief, government officials and an elder from the nearby monastery, even though he had rejected all the institutions they represented. His wife was excluded from the company until the very end, when he was unconscious. One or two of his hardline disciples were present, but they failed to carry through an experiment which Tolstoy had thought up in anticipation of a lingering death. Ten years before, he had written in his diary, 'When I am dying I should like to be asked whether I still see life as . . . a progression towards God, an increase of love. If I should not have the strength to speak, and the answer is yes, I shall close my eyes. If it is no I shall look up.'[6] They knew of this, but no one asked him.

The sad truth is that, throughout his life, Tolstoy wanted to tell us all how we should conduct our lives, how we should love other people as a first priority, and how we should learn to die well. But the only way to do any of this would be to treat his life story like one of his cautionary tales, as an object lesson in how not to love and how not to prepare for death. On the subject of love, he behaved like Ivan Karamazov, Dostoyevsky's rationalist ideologue who found it easy to love the whole of humanity but had great difficulty in loving his next-door neighbour. Tolstoy's uncharitable treatment, over many years, of his wife and of all those close to him (except a few devoted disciples) remains as a stain on his reputation. On the subject of death, his oblique and unintended lessons are that we should not become obsessed with dying and death as he did, and that there is little point in raging incessantly against the dying of the light.

However, his art is so powerful that it frequently achieves a didactic purpose by dispersing it in a strong solution of distracting entertainment. At its (frequent) best, Tolstoy's writing sharpens our sense of being alive, even if our lives are rather ordinary ones. This accords with his claim (in a letter of 1865) that the first aim of art is to make people love life in its countless manifestations, which applies even when the subject matter is death. At the same time he persuades us also to consider the deeper issues that interest him, thus raising our perceptions and aspirations. It may not be quite what the master wanted, but we remain thankful for his existence and achievement, first because of the wonderful storytelling and portraiture, and then the thoughtful provocation and the inspiring affirmation of the life spirit as presented in *War and Peace*, *Anna Karenina* and a broad range of Tolstoy's stories, some of the best of which are represented in this volume.

NOTES

1. Diary of Countess S. A. Tolstoy, 14 February 1870, cited in Henri Troyat, *Tolstoy* (London: W. H. Allen, 1968), pp. 317, 726.
2. Letter to S. A. Tolstoy, 4 September 1869, cited in A. N. Wilson, *Tolstoy* (London: Penguin Books, 1988), pp. 249–50.

3. Troyat, p. 319.
4. See L. N. Tolstoy, *Smert' Ivana Ilyicha* (Letchworth: Bradda Books, 1966), introduction by Michael Beresford, p. 14.
5. See Wilson, p. 471.
6. See Troyat, p. 691.

Further Reading

Bayley, John, *Tolstoy and the Novel* (London: Chatto & Windus, 1966).

Benson, Ruth Crego, *Women in Tolstoy: The Ideal and the Erotic* (London: Weidenfeld & Nicolson, and Urbana, Illinois: University of Illinois Press, 1973).

Berlin, Isaiah, *The Hedgehog and the Fox: An Essay on Tolstoy's View of History* (1953; reprinted, New York: Simon & Schuster, 1966).

Bloom, Harold, ed., *Leo Tolstoy: Modern Critical Views* (New York: Chelsea House, 1986).

Christian, R. F., *Tolstoy: A Critical Introduction* (Cambridge: Cambridge University Press, 1969).

Donskov, Andrew, ed., *Lev Tolstoy and the Concept of Brotherhood* (Ottawa: Legas, 1996).

Egan, David R., and Melinda A. Egan, eds., *Leo Tolstoy: An Annotated Bibliography of English Language Sources to 1978* (Netuchen, New Jersey and London: Scarecrow Press, 1979).

—, *Leo Tolstoy: An Annotated Bibliography of English Language Sources from 1978 to 2003* (Lanham, Toronto and Oxford: Scarecrow Press, 2005).

Eykhenbaum, Boris, *The Young Tolstoi*, trans. and ed. Gary Kern (Ann Arbor, Michigan: Ardis, 1972).

Gifford, Henry, ed., *Leo Tolstoy: A Critical Anthology* (Harmondsworth: Penguin Books, 1971).

Gustafson, Richard F., *Leo Tolstoy, Resident and Stranger: A Study in Fiction and Theology* (Princeton: Princeton University Press, 1986).

Jones, Malcolm, ed., *New Essays on Tolstoy* (Cambridge: Cambridge University Press, 1978).

Knowles, A. V., ed., *Tolstoy: The Critical Heritage* (London and Boston: Routledge & Kegan Paul, 1978).

McLean, Hugh, ed., *In the Shade of the Giant: Essays on Tolstoy*, California Slavic Studies (Berkeley: University of California Press, 1989).

Matlaw, Ralph E., ed., *Tolstoy: A Collection of Critical Essays* (Englewood Cliffs, New Jersey: Prentice-Hall, 1967).

Maude, Aylmer, *The Life of Tolstoy*, 2 vols. (London: Constable, 1908–10; reprinted in 1 vol., Oxford: Oxford University Press, 1987).

Mjøor, Johan Kare, *Desire, Death, and Imitation: Narrative Patterns in the Late Tolstoy*, *Slavica Bergensia* 4 (Bergen: University of Bergen Press, 2002).

Orwin, Donna Tussing, *Tolstoy's Art and Thought, 1847–1880* (Princeton: Princeton University Press, 1993).

—, ed., *The Cambridge Companion to Tolstoy* (Cambridge: Cambridge University Press, 2002).

Rancour-Laferriere, Daniel, *Tolstoy on the Couch: Misogyny, Masochism and the Absent Mother* (New York: New York University Press, 1998).

Rowe, William W., *Leo Tolstoy* (Boston: Twayne Publishers, 1986).

Sankovitch, Natasha, *Creating and Recovering Experience: Repetition in Tolstoy* (Stanford: Stanford University Press, 1998).

Shestov, Lev, *Dostoevsky, Tolstoy and Nietzsche* (Athens, Ohio: Ohio University Press, 1969).

Shklovsky, Victor, *Lev Tolstoy*, trans. Olga Shartse (Moscow: Progress Publishers, 1978).

Silbajoris, Rimvydas, *Tolstoy's Aesthetics and His Art* (Columbus, Ohio: Slavica Publishers, 1991).

Simmons, Ernest J., *Leo Tolstoy* (New York: Vintage, 1960).

Sorokin, Boris, *Tolstoy in Prerevolutionary Russian Criticism* (Columbus, Ohio: Ohio State University Press, 1979).

Steiner, George, *Tolstoy or Dostoevsky: An Essay in the Old Criticism*, 2nd edition (New Haven: Yale University Press, 1996).

Tolstoy Studies Journal, 1988–present. In addition to many articles, the journal (published annually) contains an annotated bibliography. For a list of the articles published in *TSJ*, see its website at www.tolstoystudies.org, which also contains many other materials related to Tolstoy, including a list of film versions of his works.

Wasiolek, Edward, *Tolstoy's Major Fiction* (Chicago: University of Chicago Press, 1978).

—, ed., *Critical Essays on Tolstoy* (Boston: G. K. Hall, 1986).

Wilson, A. N., *Tolstoy* (London: Penguin, and New York: W. W. Norton, 1988).

THE RAID

A Volunteer's Story

I

On July 12th Captain Khlopov came through the low door of my mud hut, complete with epaulettes and sabre. This was the first time I had seen him in full dress uniform since my arrival in the Caucasus.

'I've come straight from the colonel's,' he said in reply to my quizzical look. 'Our battalion is moving out tomorrow.'

'Where to?' I asked.

'To N—. All the forces are to assemble there.'

'And from there they'll make some sort of attack, will they?'

'I think so.'

'But in which direction? What do you think?'

'What should I think? I'm telling you what I know. Last night a Tartar galloped over from the general with orders for the battalion to move out with two days' biscuit rations. As to where, why and for how long – well, we don't ask such questions, my friend. Orders are orders and that's that.'

'But if you are taking rations for only two days, that means the troops won't be away longer than that, doesn't it?'

'No, it doesn't mean a thing . . .'

'Why not?' I asked, very surprised.

'Because that's how it is here. When we went to Dargo we took a week's rations, but we were there almost a month!'

'Can I go with you?' I asked, after a brief silence.

'Yes, you can, but I wouldn't advise it. Why run risks?'

'Well, please allow me to ignore your advice. I've been waiting here a whole month just for the chance of seeing some action and you want me to miss it!'

'You must do as you think fit, but in my opinion you should stay behind. You could do a spot of hunting while you're waiting for us, while we would go and do what we have to. That would be splendid for you!'

He spoke with such conviction that for a moment I really did think it would be splendid. But then I bluntly told him that nothing would induce me to stay behind.

'But what do you expect to see there?' the captain went on, still trying to dissuade me. 'If you really want to know what battles are like, read Mikhaylovsky-Danilevsky's *Description of War*[1] – it's a fine book and you'll find all you want there, where each corps was positioned, how battles are fought.'

'But it's just that kind of thing that doesn't interest me!' I replied.

'What *does* interest you, then? Want to see how people are killed? In 1832 there was a civilian here, like you . . . I think he was a Spaniard. He accompanied us on two expeditions and wore a kind of blue cloak . . . well, the poor fellow got killed. But that's nothing new here, my friend.'

However humiliated I felt at the captain's misinterpretation of my motives I did not start arguing with him.

'Was he a brave man?' I asked.

'God knows! He was always riding out in front and where the fighting was, there he'd be!'

'So he must have been brave,' I said.

'No. Poking your nose in where you're not wanted isn't what I'd call brave.'

'Then what would you call brave?'

'Brave? Brave?' the captain repeated with the air of someone asking the question for the very first time. 'The man who behaves as he ought to is brave,' he replied after some thought.

I remembered that Plato had defined bravery as *the knowledge of what should and what should not be feared* and, despite the looseness and vagueness of the captain's definition, I felt that in their basic ideas the two definitions were not so different as they might appear and that the captain's was even more accurate than the Greek philosopher's since, had he been able to express himself as well as Plato, he would most probably have said that the brave man is the one who fears only what *ought* to be feared, and not what *should* not be feared.

I wanted to explain my idea to the captain. 'Yes,' I said, 'it seems to me that in every danger there is a choice, and the choice that springs from a sense of duty, for example, is courage, while a choice made under the influence of base feelings is cowardice. Therefore, the man who risks his life from vanity, curiosity or greed cannot be called brave. Conversely, the man who avoids danger from an honest sense of responsibility to his family, or simply out of conviction, cannot be called a coward.'

The captain looked at me with rather a strange expression as I spoke. 'Well, I'm not much good at arguing about such things,' he said, filling his pipe, 'but there's a cadet here who's fond of philosophizing. Go and have a chat with him. He writes poetry too.'

It was only when I was in the Caucasus that I got to know the captain, but I had heard about him before I left Russia. His mother, Marya, has a small estate less than two miles from mine. Before I left for the Caucasus I visited her. The old lady was absolutely delighted that I would be seeing her Pashenka (her pet name for the elderly, grey-haired captain) and that, like a 'talking letter', I could tell him all about her and deliver a small parcel. After treating me to some excellent pie and smoked duck, she went to her bedroom and returned with a rather large black leather pouch containing an amulet with a black silk ribbon attached to it.

'This is the icon of our Lady of the Burning Bush,' she said, crossing herself and kissing the icon as she handed it to me. 'Please give it to him. You see, when he left for the Caucasus I said prayers for him and vowed if he remained alive and unharmed I would have this icon of the Mother of God made for him. For eighteen years Our Lady and the saints have been merciful to him: not once has he been injured – and when I think of the battles he's taken part in! What Mikhailo, who was with him, told me was enough to make one's hair stand on end! You understand – all I know about him is only through others. The dear boy never writes back about his campaigns for fear of frightening me.'

(Later in the Caucasus I found out – not through the captain, however – that he had been severely wounded four times but, needless to say, had not written one word to his mother either about wounds or campaigns.)

'So, let him wear this holy image now,' she continued. 'My blessing goes with it. May the Holy Mother of God protect him! Especially in battles – that's when he must never forget to wear it. Please tell him, dear sir, that those are his mother's wishes.'

I promised to do exactly as she asked.

'I know you'll like my Pashenka,' the old lady went on. 'He's a wonderful man. Why, he never lets a year go by without sending me money. And he's a great help to my daughter Annushka, too. And all he has is his army pay! I shall always be so thankful to God for giving me such a son,' she concluded with tears in her eyes.

'Does he write often?' I asked.

'Rarely. Perhaps a few words once a year, when he sends me money, but not otherwise. "If you don't hear from me," he writes, "that means I'm alive and well. But should anything happen to me, God forbid, they'll be sure to let you know!"'

When I gave the captain his mother's present (it was in my quarters) he asked me for some paper, carefully wrapped it and put it away. I told him a great deal about his mother's life, but he said nothing. When I had finished, he retired to one corner of the room and took what appeared to be ages to fill his pipe.

'Yes, she's a fine old lady,' he said from over there in a rather muffled voice. 'Will God ever let me see her again?'

In those simple words there was much affection and sadness.

'Why do you serve here?' I asked.

'One has to,' he replied with conviction. 'The double pay means a lot for poor devils like me.'

The captain lived frugally: he did not play cards, rarely went out drinking, and he smoked very cheap tobacco which, for some reason, he was too proud to call shag, giving it some obscure brand name instead. I had taken to the captain from the start: he had one of those simple, calm Russian faces that are easy and pleasant to look straight in the eye. After this conversation I felt deep respect for him.

2

Next morning at four o'clock the captain came for me. He wore an old threadbare coat without epaulettes, wide Caucasian trousers, a sheepskin cap which once had been white but which was now yellow and tattered; a rather inferior Asiatic sabre was strapped around his shoulder. His small white horse ambled along, its head hung low and its thin tail swinging. Although the good captain's appearance had nothing particularly martial or handsome about it, it expressed such equanimity towards everything around that it could only inspire respect.

I did not keep him waiting, but immediately mounted my horse and together we rode out of the fortress gates.

The battalion was about five hundred yards ahead of us and resembled some dense swaying black mass. One could tell that it was the infantry only from the bayonets, which looked like a bunch of tightly packed needles, and from the snatches of songs, the beating of a drum and the delightful voice of the Sixth Company's second tenor (I had often admired it back in the fortress) which occasionally reached us. The road ran along a deep and wide ravine by the side of a small stream in full spate. Flocks of wild pigeons circled over it, settling on its rocky banks or turning, swiftly wheeling and disappearing from sight. The sun was not yet visible, but the top of the right slope of the ravine was just beginning to brighten. Grey and whitish pebbles, yellow-green moss, dew-covered Christ's Thorn bushes, dogwood and dwarf elm could all be seen with extraordinary clarity in the limpid, golden light of dawn. But the other side of the ravine and the valley, which was shrouded in drifting, smoky layers of dense mist, were damp and gloomy and presented an elusive medley of colours – pale lilac, shades of black, dark green and white. Directly in front of us rose the dazzling white masses of snowy mountains, strikingly clear against the deep azure of the horizon, their shadows and outlines fantastic but graceful in every detail. Crickets, dragonflies and myriads of other insects awoke in the tall grass and filled the air with their clear incessant sounds: it was as if countless numbers of tiny bells were ringing in our ears. The air smelled of water, grass, mist – all the scents of a beautiful early summer's morning. The captain struck a flint and lit his pipe. I found the smell of his cheap tobacco and tinder extremely pleasant.

We rode along the side of the road to catch up more quickly with the infantry. The captain seemed more pensive than usual, never took his Daghestan pipe from his mouth and at every step prodded his little horse with his heels. Swaying from side to side, the horse left barely perceptible, dark green tracks in the tall wet grass. A pheasant flew out from under its hoofs with that cry and whirr of wings that makes every huntsman involuntarily start, and then slowly rose into the sky. The captain didn't take the slightest notice of it.

We had almost caught up with the infantry when we heard the thud of hoofs behind us and a very handsome young man in officer's uniform and tall white sheepskin cap galloped past, nodding at the captain and flourishing his whip . . . I only had time to notice the unique grace with which he sat in the saddle and held the reins, his beautiful black eyes, his fine nose and the first signs of a moustache. What I particularly liked about him was the way he could not stop smiling when he saw us admiring him. The smile alone showed that he was indeed very young.

'Where does he think he's dashing off to?' the captain muttered with a dissatisfied look, his pipe still in his mouth.

'Who is he?' I asked.

'Ensign Alanin, a subaltern from my company. He arrived from the Cadet Corps only last month.'

'So this is the first time he's seen action, is it?'

'Yes – that's why he's so pleased!' the captain replied, thoughtfully shaking his head. 'Youth!'

'But why shouldn't he be pleased? I can imagine how interesting it must be for a young officer.'

For a couple of minutes the captain did not reply.

'That's just what I mean by *youth*!' the captain continued in his deep voice. 'Why be pleased when you haven't even seen the real thing? When you've seen it a few times you're not so pleased! Now, I reckon there's about twenty officers going into action today and you can bet your life that someone or other will be killed or wounded. Today it might be me, and him the day after. So what's there to be pleased about?'

3

The moment the bright sun appeared above the hill and began to light up the valley through which we were passing, the rolling layers of mist lifted and it grew hot. The infantry, rifles and kitbags on their backs, slowly marched along the dusty road. Now and then laughter and the sound of Ukrainian could be heard in their ranks. A few old campaigners in white tunics – mostly non-commissioned officers – were walking by the roadside smoking their pipes and in solemn conversation. Heavily laden wagons, each drawn by three horses, trundled along, raising clouds of dust that hung motionless in the air. The officers rode in front. Some of them were dhzigiting,[2] as they say in the Caucasus. That is, they kept whipping their horses to make them perform three or four leaps and then jerked their heads backwards to bring them to an abrupt halt. Others were busy with the singers who untiringly sang song after song, in spite of the stifling heat.

About two hundred yards ahead of the infantry a tall handsome officer in Caucasian costume rode with the mounted Tartars on a white stallion. Renowned in the regiment for his reckless daring, he was not afraid to tell anyone what he thought of them, no matter who that person was. He wore a black quilted jacket trimmed with gold lace, leggings to match, new tight-fitting soft Caucasian boots that were also trimmed with gold, a yellow Circassian coat and a tall sheepskin cap that was tilted backwards. Over his chest and back were silver straps, to which a powder flask and pistol were fastened.

Another pistol and a silver-mounted dagger hung from his belt. Above them was a sword in a red morocco sheath and a rifle in a black case was slung over his shoulder. From the way he dressed, his posture in the saddle, his general bearing and movements, it was obvious that he was trying to look like a Tartar. He even said something to the Tartars with whom he was riding in a language I did not understand and I gathered from the bewildered mocking looks the Tartars gave each other that they did not understand either. He was one of those young, daredevil officers who model themselves on Marlinsky's or Lermontov's heroes. These young men view the Caucasus only through the prism of these Mullah Nurs[3] and Heroes of Our Time[4] and in everything they do are guided by the example of these models and not by their own inclinations.

The lieutenant, for example, may well have liked the company of well-bred women, of high-ranking men such as generals, colonels, aides-de-camp, and I do not doubt for one moment that he doted on such company, for he was extremely conceited. Nevertheless, he considered that it was his solemn duty to show all important people his rough side, although always in moderation. For example, whenever a lady appeared at the fortress he considered it his duty to parade beneath her window with his Tartar friends, wearing only a red shirt and slippers over his bare feet, shouting and swearing at the top of his voice. But his intention was not so much to cause offence as to show the lady what fine white legs he had and how easy it would be for her to fall in love with him, had he so wished. He would make frequent excursions into the hills with two or three of his Tartar friends to lie in ambush by the roadside and kill a few hostile passing Tartars. And although his heart told him more than once that there was nothing very daring in this, he felt that he must cause suffering to those who disappointed him for some reason, or whom he professed to hate or despise. There were two things he always carried – a large icon which hung round his neck and a dagger which he wore over his shirt, even in bed. He genuinely believed that he had enemies and convincing himself that he must take revenge on someone and wash away some insult with blood brought him the greatest pleasure. He was quite certain that hatred, vengeance and contempt for the human race were the noblest and most poetic of emotions. But his mistress (a Circassian girl, of course), whom I happened to meet later, maintained that he was the kindest and gentlest of men, and that every evening he would enter his melancholy thoughts in a diary, draw up his accounts on ruled paper, and then go down on his knees to pray. And how that man suffered, just to appear in his own eyes the way he wanted to appear, for his fellow officers and the soldiers could never see him the way he wanted to be seen.

Once, during one of those nocturnal expeditions on the road with his Tartar friends, he happened to wound a hostile Chechen in the leg with a bullet and took him prisoner. For seven weeks after that incident the Chechen lived with the lieutenant, who nursed and looked after him as though he were a bosom friend and then, when he had recovered, loaded him with presents and let him go. Not long afterwards, during an engagement, when the lieutenant was retreating with his men, firing as he went, he heard an enemy soldier call out his name and the Chechen he had wounded rode out and motioned to him to do the same. The lieutenant rode out to his Chechen friend and shook hands. The other Chechens kept their distance and did not shoot, but the moment the lieutenant turned his horse several of them fired at him and one bullet grazed the small of his back. Another time, at night, when a fire broke out in the fortress and two companies of soldiers tried to put it out, I suddenly saw the tall figure of a man on a black horse, lit up by the red glow, appear in the crowd. Forcing his way through, he rode right up to the fire, leapt from his horse and ran into a house, one side of which was burning. Five minutes later he emerged with singed hair and his arm badly burnt around the elbow, carrying in his bosom two pigeons he had rescued from the flames.

His name was Rosenkrantz, but he would often speak of his ancestry, somehow tracing his origins back to the Varangians,[5] thus clearly proving that he and his ancestors were pure Russians.

4

The sun had run half its course and cast its fiery rays through the glowing air on to the dry earth. The dark blue sky was perfectly clear; only the foot of the snowy mountains was beginning to be cloaked by pale, lilac clouds. The motionless air seemed filled with a kind of transparent dust and the heat was becoming unbearable. When the troops reached a small stream – the halfway stage – they halted. The soldiers stacked rifles and rushed to the water. The battalion commander sat down on a drum in the shade. Demonstrating the importance of his rank by the expression on his face, he prepared to have a snack with his fellow officers. The captain lay down on the grass under his company's wagon. The intrepid Lieutenant Rosenkrantz and some other young officers sat on their outspread cloaks, intending to make merry, judging from all the bottles and flasks around them and from the peculiar animation of the singers who stood before them in a semicircle, whistling and singing a Caucasian dance-song:

Shamil thought he would rebel,
In bygone years . . .
Tra-ra, ra-ta-tai . . .
In bygone years.

Among these young officers was the young ensign who had overtaken us that morning. He was extremely amusing – his eyes sparkled, his speech was rather muddled and he wanted to kiss and declare his love for everyone . . . Poor young man! As yet he had no idea that he might look ridiculous or that the frankness and affection which he lavished on everyone might arouse only ridicule, and not the affection he greatly yearned for. Nor did he realize how exceptionally appealing he looked when, with flushed face, he threw himself at last on to his cloak, rested on one elbow and tossed back his thick black hair.

Filled with curiosity, I listened to the soldiers' and officers' conversations and closely studied their expressions. But I could find absolutely no trace in any of them of the nervousness I was feeling: their jokes and laughter, the stories they told – all this was indicative of their high spirits and their indifference to impending danger. It was as though it was unthinkable that some of them were fated never to return by that road.

5

After six o'clock that evening, dusty and tired, we passed through the wide fortified gates of the fortress at N—. The sun was setting and cast slanting rosy rays on the picturesque batteries, on the gardens surrounding the fortress, with their tall poplars, on yellow wheat fields and on the white clouds that hung low over the snow-covered mountains: as if imitating them, they formed a range that was no less fantastic and beautiful. On the horizon the new moon was like a tiny translucent cloud. A Tartar was calling the faithful to prayer from the roof of a hut in the village just by the fortress gates. Our singers burst into song again with renewed vigour and energy.

When I had rested and tidied myself up I went to see an aide-de-camp I knew to ask if he would convey my intentions to the general. On the way from the suburb where I was billeted I saw things in the fortress of N— that I had not at all been expecting to see. I was overtaken by a handsome two-seater carriage in which I caught sight of a fashionable bonnet and from which I could hear the sound of French. The strains of some 'Liza' or 'Katenka' polka played on an out-of-tune piano came from the open window of the commandant's house. I passed a tavern where some clerks with cigarettes in their hands were sitting over glasses of wine and I could hear one saying to the other, 'Look here, old chap, when it comes to politics, Marya Grigorevna is first and foremost amongst the ladies here.' A hunchbacked sickly faced Jew in a threadbare coat was dragging a wheezy old barrel-organ and the whole suburb echoed to the finale from *Lucia*. Two women in rustling dresses with silk kerchiefs on their heads and brightly coloured parasols in their hands glided past me on the wooden pavement. Two young girls, one in a pink dress, the other in a blue, stood bareheaded outside a low-roofed cottage and broke into shrill, forced laughter, evidently to attract the attention of passing officers. As for the officers, they swaggered up and down the street in new uniforms, with white gloves and glittering epaulettes.

I found my acquaintance on the ground floor of the general's house. I scarcely had time to explain my wish and to hear that there was no problem in carrying it out when the same handsome carriage I had seen earlier rattled past the window where we were sitting and stopped at the entrance. A tall, well-built man in an infantry major's uniform climbed out and went into the house.

'Please excuse me,' said the aide, getting up. 'I must go and announce them to the general immediately.'

'Who is it?' I asked.

'The countess,' he replied, buttoning his uniform as he rushed upstairs. A few minutes later a short but extremely good-looking man in a frock-coat without epaulettes and with a white cross in his buttonhole went out on to the front steps, accompanied by two other officers. The general's gait, his voice, his every movement, showed that here was a man fully conscious of his own worth.

'*Bonsoir, Madame la Comtesse*,' he said, offering his hand through the carriage window.

A small hand in a kid glove pressed his and a pretty, smiling face in a yellow bonnet appeared at the window. All I could hear of their conversation, which lasted several minutes, was the smiling general saying as I passed, '*Vous savez que j'ai fait voeu de combattre les infidèles; prenez donc garde de le devenir*.'

Laughter came from the carriage.

'*Adieu donc, cher Général*.'

'*Non, au revoir*,' said the general as he went up the steps. '*N'oubliez pas que je m'invite pour la soirée de demain*.'

The carriage clattered off down the street.

Now there's a man, I thought as I walked home, who possesses all that Russians strive after: rank, wealth, family. And the day before a battle that could finish God knows how, he can joke with a pretty woman and promise to have tea with her the next day, just as if they had met at a ball!

Later, at the aide-de-camp's house, I met someone who surprised me even more. He was a young lieutenant from K— Regiment, a man of almost feminine gentleness and timidity, who had called on the aide to give vent to his bitterness and annoyance towards certain people who had apparently intrigued against him to stop him taking part in the forthcoming action. He maintained that it was very caddish of them, not the decent thing at all, that he would not forget it, and so on. The more I scrutinized his face and listened to his voice, the more convinced I became that he was not play-acting, that he was deeply resentful and distressed at not being allowed to go and shoot Circassians and expose himself to their fire. He was as upset as an unfairly beaten child . . . I was completely mystified by it all.

6

The troops were to move out at ten that night. At half-past eight I mounted my horse and rode to the general's house, but on the assumption that the general and his aide would be busy I stopped in the street, tied my horse to a fence and waited for him to come out.

The heat and glare of the sun had already given way to the coolness of night and the soft light of the new moon which was just setting – a pale, shimmering crescent against the dark, starry sky. Lights appeared in the windows of the houses and shone through chinks in the shutters of the mud huts. Beyond those whitewashed moonlit huts with their rush-thatched roofs, the graceful poplars seemed even taller and darker on the horizon.

The long shadows of houses, trees and fences formed pretty patterns on the bright, dusty road . . . From the river came the incessant, resonant call of frogs.[6] In the streets I could hear hurried footsteps and voices, a galloping horse. Now and then the sound of the barrel-organ playing the song 'The Winds are

Gently Blowing' or some 'Aurora' waltz drifted over from the suburb.

I shall not say what I was thinking about then, firstly because I am too ashamed to admit to the succession of gloomy thoughts that kept nagging at me while all around there was only joy and gaiety, and secondly because they would be quite irrelevant to my narrative. I was so deep in thought that I did not even notice when the bell struck eleven and the general rode past me with his suite. I hurriedly mounted my horse and raced off to catch up with the detachment.

The rearguard was still inside the fortress and I had great difficulty crossing the bridge, with all those guns, ammunition wagons, supply carts, and officers shouting out orders. Once through the gates I trotted past the line of soldiers which stretched in a line almost a mile long and who were silently moving through the darkness, and finally I caught up with the general. As I passed the guns drawn out in single file and the officers riding between them I suddenly heard a voice call in a German accent, 'A linshtock, you *schwein*!' which struck a jarring, discordant note amid the quiet solemn harmony, followed by a soldier hurriedly shouting, 'Shevchenko! The lieutenant wants a light!'

Most of the sky was overcast with long, dark grey clouds, with only a few dim stars twinkling here and there. The moon had disappeared behind the black mountains on the near horizon to the right and shed a faint, trembling light on their peaks, in sharp contrast to the impenetrable gloom enveloping their foothills. The air was so warm and still that not one blade of grass, not one cloud moved. It was so dark that it was impossible to make out even the closest objects: by the side of the road I thought I could see rocks, animals, strange people and it was only when I heard them rustle and smelled the fresh dew that lay on them that I realized they were only bushes.

Before me I could see a dense, heaving black wall, followed by several dark spots: this was the cavalry vanguard, and the general and his suite. Behind us was a similar dark mass, lower than the first: this was the infantry.

The whole detachment was so quiet that I could distinctly

hear all the mingling sounds of night, so full of enchanting mystery: the mournful howling of distant jackals, now like a despairing lament, now like laughter; the sonorous, monotonous song of crickets, frogs, quails; a rumbling noise whose cause baffled me and which seemed to be coming ever nearer; and all of Nature's barely audible nocturnal sounds that defy explanation or definition and merge into one rich, beautiful harmony that we call the stillness of night. And now that stillness was broken by – or rather, blended with – the dull thud of hoofs and the rustle of the tall grass as the detachment slowly advanced.

Only occasionally did I hear the clang of a heavy gun, the clatter of clashing bayonets, hushed voices, or a horse snorting. Nature seemed to breathe with pacifying beauty and power.

Can it be that there is not enough space for man in this beautiful world, under those immeasurable, starry heavens? Is it possible that man's heart can harbour, amid such ravishing natural beauty, feelings of hatred, vengeance, or the desire to destroy his fellows? All the evil in man, one would think, should disappear on contact with Nature, the most spontaneous expression of beauty and goodness.

7

We had been on the move for more than two hours. I began to feel shivery and drowsy. In the darkness I could still catch glimpses of vague shapes: not far ahead was that same black wall and those same little moving dots. Close by I could make out the rump of a white horse swishing its tail, with its hind legs wide apart; the back of a white Circassian coat with a rifle in a black case swinging against it and a white pistol butt in an embroidered holster; the glow of a cigarette lighting up a fair moustache, a beaver collar and a hand in a kid glove. Every now and then I leant forward over my horse's neck, closed my eyes and forgot myself for a few minutes. But then the familiar tramping of hoofs and rustling would suddenly bring me to my senses and I would glance round, feeling that I was standing still and that the black wall in front was moving towards me, or had stopped and I was about to ride straight into it. At one such moment I was even more conscious of the unbroken rumbling that I had been unable to explain and which was drawing nearer. What I had heard was in fact the sound of water. We were entering a deep gorge and approaching a mountain torrent that was in full spate at this time of year.[7]

The roar grew louder, the damp grass became thicker and taller; there were more bushes and the horizon gradually closed in. Now and then bright lights flared up here and there in the dark mountains and immediately vanished.

'Please tell me what those lights are,' I whispered to a Tartar riding beside me.

'Don't you know?' he replied.

'No.'

'It's the mountain tribesmen. They tie bundles of straw to poles, light them and wave them around.'

'Why are they doing that?'

'To warn everyone the Russians are coming. They must be running around like mad in the villages now,' he added, laughing. 'Everyone will be dragging his belongings down into the gorge.'

'Surely they can't already know from right up there, in the mountains, that a detachment is coming?' I asked.

'Oh yes, they know all right! They always know. We Tartars are like that!'

'So Shamil[8] too is preparing for action?' I asked.

'No,' he replied, shaking his head. 'Shamil himself won't be taking part – he'll send his henchmen while he watches from up there through a telescope.'

'Does he live far away?'

'No, not very far. About eight miles away, over to the left.'

'How do you know?' I asked. 'Have you been there?'

'Yes. All our people have been there.'

'And did you see Shamil?'

'No! It's not for the likes of us to see Shamil! He's always surrounded by his bodyguards – a hundred, three hundred, perhaps a thousand of them, with Shamil himself somewhere in the middle!' he added with an expression of servile respect.

When I looked up I saw that the sky had cleared and it was growing brighter in the east, while the Pleiades were sinking towards the horizon. But it was damp and gloomy in the gorge through which we were advancing.

Suddenly, not far ahead, several lights flashed in the darkness and almost instantaneously some bullets whistled past. The shots rang out in the silence, together with a loud shrill cry from the enemy's advance picket, made up of Tartars, who whooped, fired at random and scattered.

When all was quiet again, the general summoned his interpreter. The Tartar in the white Circassian coat rode up and had a long talk with him, gesticulating and whispering.

'Colonel Khasanov! Tell the men to advance in open order,' the general drawled, softly but audibly.

The detachment advanced towards the river, leaving the towering dark sides of the gorge behind. It began to grow light. The sky immediately above the horizon, where a few pale stars could just be seen, seemed higher. The dawn glowed brightly in the east, while from the west blew a fresh, piercing breeze; shimmering mist rose like steam over the rushing river.

8

Our scout showed us the ford and the cavalry vanguard, followed by the general and his suite, started crossing the river. The water, which came up to the horses' chests, rushed with tremendous force between the white boulders which appeared here and there above the surface, and foamed and eddied around the animals' legs. Startled by the noise, the horses lifted their heads and pricked up their ears, but they stepped carefully and steadily against the current, over the uneven riverbed. The riders lifted their feet and weapons; the infantry, in literally nothing but their shirts, and holding above the water their rifles, to which their clothes were tied in bundles, linked arms in groups of twenty and struggled bravely against the current, the enormous strain clearly showing in their faces. The mounted artillerymen gave a loud shout and drove their horses into the water at a trot. Now and then the water splashed over the guns and green ammunition wagons whose wheels rang against the bottom. But the sturdy little horses all pulled together, churning the water, until finally they clambered up on to the opposite bank with dripping manes and tails.

Immediately the crossing was completed, the general's face suddenly became thoughtful and serious. He turned his horse and trotted off with his cavalry down the broad glade which opened out in the middle of the forest before us; a cordon of Cossacks spread out around the edges.

In the forest we spotted a man on foot dressed in a Circassian coat and a tall sheepskin cap . . . then a second . . . and a third . . . One of the officers said, 'They're Tartars', and at that moment a puff of smoke appeared from behind a tree, followed by the report, then another. Our rapid fire drowned the enemy's and only occasionally did a bullet come flying past with a sound like the slow buzz of a bee, as if to show us that not all the shots were ours. First the infantry, at the double, followed by the field guns at a trot, joined the cordon. I could hear the guns booming, then the metallic sound of flying grapeshot, the hiss of rockets, the crackle of rifles. All over the broad glade could be seen cavalry, infantry and artillery. Puffs of smoke from the guns, rockets and rifles mingled with the dewy verdure and the mist. Colonel Khasanov galloped over to the general and sharply reined in his horse.

'Your Excellency,' he said, touching his cap, 'shall I order the cavalry to charge? The enemy's colours are in sight.' And he pointed with his whip at some mounted Tartars headed by two men on white horses bearing poles decorated with bits of red and blue cloth.

'Carry on – and good luck!' the general replied.

The colonel turned his horse on the spot, drew his sabre and shouted, 'Hurrah!'

'Hurrah! Hurrah! Hurrah!' echoed from the troops and the cavalry flew after him.

Everyone watched with great enthusiasm as one colour appeared, then a second, a third, fourth, fifth . . .

Without waiting for us to attack, the enemy hid in the forest from where they opened fire with their rifles. The bullets flew thicker.

'*Quel charmant coup d'oeil!*' the general remarked, rising slightly, English-style, in the saddle of his slim-legged black horse.

'*Charrmant*,' replied the major, rolling his r's and striking his horse as he rode over to the general. '*C'est un vrrai plaisirr que la guerre dans un aussi beau pays*,' he said.

'*Et surtout en bonne compagnie*,' the general added, pleasantly smiling. The major bowed.

Just then, an enemy cannon ball flew past with a nasty hiss and struck something. Behind us we heard the moan of a wounded soldier. This moan had such a peculiar effect on me that the spectacle immediately lost all its charm. However, I seemed to be the only one to notice it – the major was laughing with great gusto; another officer was repeating with the utmost composure what he had just been saying; and the general was looking the other way and saying something in French with the most tranquil of smiles.

'Shall we return their fire?' the artillery commander asked, galloping up.

'Yes, let's give them a fright!' the general replied nonchalantly, lighting a cigar.

The battery took up position and the firing began. The earth groaned under the shots, lights continually flashed and my eyes were blinded by the clouds of smoke through which it was almost impossible to make out the gun crews at work.

The village was bombarded and Colonel Khasanov galloped up once more and then rode off to it at the general's command. The war cry rang out again and the cavalry disappeared in clouds of dust. It was a truly magnificent scene. But the one thing that spoilt the general impression for me, an inexperienced onlooker, who had not taken part, was all that movement, animation and shouting, which seemed quite superfluous. I could not help comparing it to a man swinging an axe to cut only thin air.

9

Our troops had occupied the village, in which not one of the enemy was left by the time the general arrived with his suite, to which I had attached myself. The long clean huts with their flat earthen roofs and pretty chimneys were scattered over small stony hillocks, through which flowed a stream. On one side were green sunlit gardens with enormous pear and plum trees, while on the other were the strange shadows cast by the tall, erect headstones in the cemetery and the long poles with balls and multicoloured flags fixed to their ends which marked the graves of the dhzigits, the bravest warriors.

The troops were drawn up outside the gates.

A few moments later dragoons, Cossacks and infantrymen poured down the crooked lanes with evident delight and the deserted village immediately sprang to life. Somewhere a roof came crashing down, an axe rang out against a strong wooden door. Somewhere else a haystack, a fence and a hut were set on fire and a thick column of smoke rose into the clear air. A Cossack dragged a sack of flour and a carpet along; a soldier emerged from a hut, gleefully carrying a tin basin and some bits of old cloth. Another, with outstretched arms, was trying to catch two hens that were cackling and beating their wings by a fence. A third soldier, who had found a huge pot of milk, drank some and then threw it down with loud guffaws.

The battalion with which I had left N— fortress was also in the village. The captain sat on the roof of a hut smoking his cheap tobacco and sending streams of smoke from his short pipe with such a casual air that when I saw him I forgot that I was in an enemy village and felt quite at home.

'Ah, so you're here, too,' he said when he saw me.

The tall figure of Lieutenant Rosenkrantz flitted around the village. He gave one order after the other and seemed to have a lot to do. I saw him emerge from one hut with a triumphant expression, followed by two soldiers leading an old Tartar whose hands were tied. This old man, whose only clothing was a gaily coloured but ragged coat and much-patched trousers, looked so frail that his bony arms, tightly bound behind his hunched back, seemed about to part company with his shoulders, and he could hardly drag his bare crooked feet along. His face, and even part of his shaven head, was deeply furrowed; his misshapen, toothless mouth with a close-cut grey moustache and beard around it, was always moving, as if he were chewing. But there was still a gleam in those red, lashless eyes which quite clearly expressed an old man's indifference to life.

Rosenkrantz asked him, through the interpreter, why he had not gone with the others.

'Where could I have gone?' he replied, quietly looking away.

'Where the others have gone,' someone suggested.

'The dhzigits have gone off to fight the Russians, but I'm an old man.'

'Aren't you afraid of the Russians?'

'What can they do to me? I'm an old man,' he repeated, nonchalantly surveying the circle that had formed around him.

Later, when I was returning, I saw that same old man bumping along behind a Cossack's saddle, bound and bareheaded, still looking around with the same indifferent expression. They needed him for an exchange with Russian prisoners.

I climbed up on to the roof and sat beside the captain.

'It seems there weren't very many of the enemy,' I told him, wishing to find out his opinion of the raid.

'The enemy?' he repeated in surprise. 'But there wasn't any enemy! Do you call that the enemy? Just you wait until this evening when we leave – they'll be simply pouring out from over there to speed us on our way!'

He pointed with his pipe at the small wood through which we had passed that morning.

'What's that?' I asked anxiously, interrupting the captain and pointing to a group of Don Cossacks who had gathered around something not far from us.

Something like a baby's cry came from there and the words, 'Hey, stop . . . don't cut it . . . they'll see. Got a knife, Yevstigneich? Give it me . . .'

'They're up to something, the devils,' the captain calmly remarked. But just then the handsome ensign, his face flushed and frightened, ran out. Waving his arms he dashed over to the Cossacks.

'Don't touch it! Don't hurt it!' he cried in a childlike voice. The moment they saw the officer, the Cossacks stepped aside and released a little white kid. The young ensign seemed quite confused, kept muttering something and stood before them with an embarrassed look. When he saw the captain and myself on the roof he blushed even deeper and skipped over to us. 'I thought they were killing a child,' he said with a timid smile.

10

The general and the cavalry left the village, while the battalion with which I had come from the fortress formed the rearguard. Captain Khlopov's and Lieutenant Rosenkrantz's companies withdrew together.

The captain's prediction proved perfectly correct: the moment we entered the narrow strip of woodland he had mentioned, hostile hillsmen suddenly appeared everywhere, on both sides of us, mounted and on foot, and they were so close that I could quite plainly see some of them running from tree to tree, stooping and with rifles in their hands. The captain took off his cap, piously crossed himself and some of the older soldiers followed suit. From the woods we could hear them whooping and calling, 'Watch out, Russkies!' Short, dry rifle shots rang out in quick succession and bullets whizzed past on both sides. Our men silently volleyed back at them – only occasionally did I hear shouts from their ranks such as, 'It's all right for *him*[9] in the trees. We ought to use a gun . . .'

Finally the guns were brought out and after a few salvoes of grapeshot the enemy seemed to weaken. But a moment later, with every step our men advanced, the firing and whooping intensified.

We had withdrawn barely six hundred yards from the village when enemy cannon balls began to whistle overhead. I saw a soldier killed by one. But why go into detail over a terrible scene I would give anything to forget?

Lieutenant Rosenkrantz kept firing incessantly, shouting hoarsely at his men and galloping at top speed from one end of the line to the other. He looked rather pale, which perfectly suited his belligerent face. 'We'll beat them back,' he said convincingly. 'Oh yes, no doubt about it!'

'It's not necessary,' the captain replied softly. 'What we must do is retreat.'

The captain's company was holding the edge of the forest and his men were firing at the enemy in lying position. The captain, in his shabby coat and crumpled cap, sat on his white horse, the reins held loosely, his knees bent in the short stirrups. He stayed silent and still: the soldiers knew their job too well to need any orders. Only now and then did he raise his voice to shout at anyone who exposed his head.

There was nothing very martial about the captain's appearance, but it had much in it that was sincere and natural, which greatly impressed me. 'Now, there's a truly brave man,' I couldn't help thinking.

He was exactly the same as I had always seen him: those calm movements, the same even voice, that same ingenuous expression on his plain but honest face. Only his eyes, which were brighter than usual, showed the concentration of a man quietly doing his job. It is easy enough to write that he was 'the same as always', but how many different shades of character had I observed in the others – one trying to appear calmer than usual, another sterner, a third more cheerful. But the captain's face showed that he did not see why he should appear other than his normal self.

The Frenchman who said at Waterloo, '*La garde meurt, mais ne se rend pas*', along with other – particularly French – heroes who uttered such memorable sayings, were brave and did in fact produce unforgettable phrases. But there was this difference between their courage and the captain's: even if a memorable phrase had stirred in my hero's heart, whatever the circumstances, I am quite convinced that he would never have uttered it. Firstly, because by uttering some memorable phrase he would have been afraid of spoiling some great deed; and secondly, because when a man feels he has the strength to perform a great deed, there is no need for words. In my opinion, this is the distinctive and noble characteristic of Russian valour. If this is so, then how can a Russian heart help aching when our young warriors utter trite phrases that claim to imitate antiquated French chivalry?

Suddenly a rather disjointed and weak 'Hurrah!' came from the side where our handsome young ensign was standing with his platoon. When I looked round I saw about thirty soldiers with kitbags over their shoulders and rifles in their hands running over a ploughed field with very great difficulty. They kept stumbling, but still they ran on, shouting as they went. In front galloped the young ensign, sabre in hand. They all disappeared into the forest . . .

After a few minutes' whooping and crackling, a frightened horse ran out of the forest and some soldiers appeared bearing the dead and wounded. Among the latter was the young ensign. Two soldiers supported him under the arms. He was as white as a sheet and his handsome face now showed only a faint shadow of that eagerness for the fray which had enlivened it a minute earlier. His head had sunk horribly between the shoulders and dropped on his chest. There was a small bloodstain on the white shirt beneath his unbuttoned coat.

'Oh, what a pity!' I could not help saying as I turned away from that sad sight.

'Of course it's a pity,' said an old soldier who was standing near me, mournfully leaning on his rifle. 'He's not afraid of anything – how can anyone go on like that?' he added, staring at the wounded officer. 'He's stupid, too – and now he's paid for it.'

'Aren't you afraid?'

'What do you think?'

II

Four soldiers bore the ensign on a stretcher. Behind them a medical orderly led a thin, broken-down horse with two green cases of medical equipment on its back. As they waited for the doctor, a few officers rode over to the stretcher and tried to comfort and cheer up their wounded comrade.

'Well, Alanin old man, it'll be some time before you go dancing again!' Lieutenant Rosenkrantz said with a smile.

He probably thought that these words would help to raise the ensign's spirits, but they did not have the desired effect, judging from the latter's cold sad look.

Then the captain rode up. He took a close look at the wounded man and his normally icily indifferent face took on a expression of genuine sympathy.

'Well, dear Anatoly,' he said in a voice of tender concern that I never expected from him, 'it seems it was God's will.'

The wounded man looked round and a sad smile passed over his pale face. 'Yes, I disobeyed you.'

'Let's say it was God's will,' the captain repeated.

The doctor, who had now arrived, took some bandages, a probe and another instrument from the orderly. Then he rolled up his sleeves and went over to the ensign with an encouraging smile.

'Well, it seems they've given you a hole where you didn't have one before!' he said in a light-hearted, jocular tone. 'Let's have a look.'

The ensign let the doctor examine him, but the look he gave that cheery man was of surprise and reproach, which the latter did not notice. The doctor probed and examined the wound from every angle, but then the wounded man could stand no more and he pushed the doctor's hand away with a deep groan.

'Leave me,' he said, barely audibly. 'I'm going to die anyway.'

With these words, he fell back and five minutes later, when I went over to the group standing around him and asked one of them, 'How's the ensign?' the reply was, 'Passing away.'

12

It was late when the detachment, drawn up in a wide column and singing as it went, approached the fortress.

The sun was hidden behind the snowy mountain ridge and

cast its dying pink rays on a long thin cloud that hung motionless over the clear horizon. The snow-covered mountains were becoming enveloped in a lilac mist and only the highest peaks stood out, amazingly distinct against the crimson glow of sunset. A transparent moon, long risen, was growing pale against the deep azure of the sky. The green of the grass and the trees darkened and became covered with dew. Dark masses of troops marched with measured tread over the lush meadow. The sound of tambourines, drums and cheerful songs came from various directions. The second tenor of the Sixth Company was singing vigorously, and the sound of his pure, sonorous voice, full of power and feeling, carried far and wide in the limpid air of evening.

THE WOODFELLING

A Cadet's Story

I

In the midwinter of 185–, a section of our battery was stationed with an advance detachment in the Great Chechnya District.[1] On the evening of February 14th, when I learnt that the platoon I was commanding in the absence of a regular officer had been detailed to fell wood the following day, I retired earlier than usual to my tent after I had received and transmitted all necessary orders. Since I did not have the bad habit of heating my tent with charcoal, I lay down without undressing on my bed, which stood on small pegs above the ground, pulled my fur cap over my eyes, wrapped myself in my fur coat and fell into that mysterious, deep and heavy sleep that usually comes over one in the anxious, nerve-racking hours before imminent danger. Anticipation of tomorrow's action had put me in this state of mind.

At three o'clock in the morning, when it was still pitch dark, someone pulled away my warm sheepskin coat and a candle's crimson flame glared unpleasantly in my sleepy eyes.

'Please get up, sir,' a voice said.

I closed my eyes again, half-consciously pulled up my sheepskin coat again and fell asleep. '*Please* get up, sir!' Dmitry repeated, cruelly shaking my shoulder. 'The infantry's leaving.'

I suddenly came to my senses, shuddered and leapt to my feet. After a hurried glass of tea and a wash in icy water I crept out of my tent and went to the artillery park. It was dark, misty and cold. The faint crimson light of the bonfires, glowing here and there in the camp and illuminating the figures of drowsy soldiers sitting around them only seemed to intensify the darkness. Nearby I could hear a regular, gentle snoring and from further off came the voices and clatter of the bustling infantrymen's rifles as they prepared to move. There was a smell of smoke, dung, fuses and mist; the early morning cold sent shivers down my spine and my teeth chattered involuntarily.

Only from the snorting and occasional stamping of hoofs was it possible to tell the position of the limbers to which the horses were harnessed and the ammunition boxes in the impenetrable darkness, and only from the shining points of linstocks where the guns were. To the words 'God be with us' the first gun moved off with a clang, an ammunition wagon rumbled after it and the platoon followed. We all doffed our caps and crossed ourselves. After taking up a position between the ranks of infantry, the platoon halted and waited a quarter of an hour for the whole column to assemble and for the commanding officer to ride out.

'One man's missing, Nikolay Petrovich,' said a black figure coming up to me and whom I recognized as Artillery-Sergeant Maximov only from the voice.

'Who?'

'Velenchuk, sir. He was there all right when they were harnessing – saw him with my own eyes, I did. Now he's disappeared.'

Since the column was not likely to move off immediately, we decided to send Lance-Corporal Antonov to look for him. Shortly after, a few officers trotted past in the dark – the commander and his suite. Then the head of the column stirred and moved off, until finally it was our turn. But still there was no Antonov or Velenchuk. However, we had hardly gone a hundred paces when both of them caught up with us.

'Where was he?' I asked Antonov.

'Sleeping in the artillery park.'

'Oh – had he been drinking?'

'No, sir.'

'Then why did he fall asleep?'

'Don't know, sir.'

For about three hours we slowly advanced, in silence and

darkness, over unploughed, snowless fields and through clumps of low bushes that crackled under the gun-carriage wheels. Finally, after crossing a shallow but extremely fast-flowing stream, we were ordered to halt and bursts of rifle fire came from the vanguard. As always, these sounds had a most stimulating effect on everyone. The whole detachment seemed to wake up; the ranks were full of voices, movement, laughter. Two soldiers wrestled with each other; another hopped from foot to foot; others chewed dry biscuits or shouldered and grounded arms to while away the time. Meanwhile, the mist was growing noticeably whiter in the west. One could feel the damp more now and surrounding objects gradually began to emerge from the gloom. I could already distinguish the green gun carriages and ammunition boxes, the brass of guns wet with mist, the familiar figures of my men whom I could not help studying down to the last detail, bay horses and ranks of infantrymen with gleaming bayonets, kitbags, ramrods and mess tins on their backs.

We were soon moved on again and were led to a spot a few hundred yards off the road. To the right we could see the steep bank of a meandering stream and the tall wooden posts of a Tartar cemetery; to the left and in front a black strip showed through the mist. The platoon unlimbered. The Eighth Company, which was covering us, stacked arms, and a battalion with rifles and axes marched into the forest.

Within five minutes fires were crackling and smoking all around. The soldiers spread out to bring up branches and logs and then fanned the fires with their hands and feet. The forest echoed incessantly to the sound of hundreds of axes and falling trees.

The artillerymen, with a certain feeling of rivalry towards the infantry, made their fire, and although it was already blazing so fiercely that it was impossible to come within two paces of it, and dense black smoke was pouring through the frozen branches which hissed as they were piled on to the fire by the soldiers, and although the wood underneath was turning to charcoal and the deathly pale grass was thawing all around, this still did not satisfy them. They dragged great logs up, pushed weeds under them and fanned the flames even higher.

When I went to the fire to light a cigarette, Velenchuk, who was the bustling type and who now, having a guilty conscience, was busying himself more than the others around the fire, pulled a burning coal from the heart of the fire in a fit of zeal, with his bare hand, tossed it a couple of times from one hand to the other and then let it fall to the ground.

'Light one of them twigs for him,' said one of the soldiers.

'Get him a linstock, lads!' said another.

I finally managed to light my cigarette without the assistance of Velenchuk, who was again attempting to pick out a live coal. He rubbed his burnt fingers on the flaps of his sheepskin coat and, most probably for want of something to do, lifted a huge piece of plane-tree wood and with a mighty swing hurled it on to the fire. When at last he felt that he was entitled to a rest, he went right up to the fire, flung open his coat, which he wore like a cloak, parted his legs, thrust out his big black hands, twisted his mouth slightly and frowned. 'Damn! I've forgotten my pipe. What a nuisance, lads!' he said after a brief silence, not addressing anyone in particular.

2

There are three main types of soldier in Russia according to which men from all the armed forces can be classified, whether they serve in the line, in the Caucasus, the Guards, infantry, cavalry, artillery and so on.

These three main types (with many subdivisions and permutations) are:

(1) the submissive
(2) the domineering
(3) the reckless

The submissive can be further subdivided into:

(a) the coolly submissive
(b) the fussily submissive

The domineering can be subdivided into:

(a) the sternly domineering
(b) the diplomatically domineering

The reckless can be subdivided into:

(a) reckless humorists
(b) reckless libertines

The commonest type in the army – the most likeable and, for the most part, endowed with the noblest Christian virtues, meekness, piety, patience and devotion to God's will – is, broadly speaking, the submissive. The distinctive trait of the coolly submissive type is imperturbable calmness and contempt for all the reverses of fortune that might befall him. The distinctive trait of the submissive drunkard is his gentle romantic nature and sensibility; that of the fussily submissive is his limited mental capacity, combined with undirected zeal and industry.

The domineering type is most commonly found in the higher ranks of ordinary soldiers – lance-corporals, non-commissioned officers and so forth. In the first subdivision of the sternly domineering we find exceptionally high-minded, energetic, pre-eminently military types who, nevertheless, are not lacking in lofty romantic impulses (Lance-Corporal Antonov, with whom I intend acquainting the reader, was this type). The second subdivision comprises the diplomatically domineering, whose numbers have been increasing considerably of late. The diplomatically domineering type is invariably highly articulate, literate, wears pink shirts, does not eat from the common bowl, occasionally smokes expensive Musatov tobacco, considers himself immeasurably superior to the rank and file and is rarely such a good soldier as the sternly domineering type of the first subdivision.

The reckless, like the domineering types, are good soldiers if they belong to the first subdivision – the humorists, characterized by unshakeable cheerfulness, tremendous versatility, rich personality and daring – but in the second subdivision (the libertines) tend to be thoroughly disreputable. However, to the glory of the Russian army, they are very rare and where they do appear are usually ostracized by the soldiers themselves. The main characteristics of this section are godlessness and a certain bravado in their debauchery.

Velenchuk was the fussily submissive type. He was Ukrainian, had already served for fifteen years and, although he was a rather insignificant-looking, blundering soldier, he was simple-hearted, kind, extremely zealous (although this zeal tended at times to be misdirected) and extraordinarily honest. I say extraordinarily honest, because something happened the previous year where he showed this characteristic very clearly. Here I must point out that almost every soldier knows a trade, the most common being tailoring and boot-making. Velenchuk had learnt the first of these and, judging by the fact that none other than Sergeant-Major Mikhail Dorofeich ordered clothes from him, had attained a certain degree of skill. The previous year, in camp, Velenchuk had undertaken to make a fine coat for Mikhail Dorofeich but, on the very night he cut the cloth, measured the trimmings and hid everything under his pillow in his tent, disaster struck: the cloth, which had cost *seven roubles*, vanished during the night. With tears in his eyes and pale, trembling lips, suppressing his sobs, Velenchuk reported the theft to the sergeant-major. Mikhail Dorofeich was furious. In the first moments of anger he issued the tailor with dire threats. But then, as he was well off and a reasonable man, he forgot all about it and did not ask Velenchuk to pay for the material. No matter how much fuss that busy Velenchuk made, no matter how many tears he shed as he told of his woes, the thief was not found. Although a certain Chernov (one of the reckless libertines) who slept in the same tent was strongly suspected, there was no conclusive evidence. As Mikhail Dorofeich (the diplomatically domineering type) was well off, being engaged in various business activities with the quartermaster and mess caterer – the aristocrats of the battery – he soon completely forgot the loss of his civilian coat. Velenchuk, however, could not forget his misfortune. The soldiers said at the time that they feared he might do away with himself or run off into the mountains, so shattering was the effect of the disaster on him. He would not drink or eat, could not even work and was always crying. Three days later he went to see Mikhail Dorofeich. White as a sheet and with trembling hands he took a gold rouble from under his cuff and handed it to him. 'I swear that's all I have, Mikhail Dorofeich, and I even had to borrow that from Zhdanov,' he sobbed. 'But I promise to pay back the other two roubles as soon as I've earned them, I swear by God I will! *He* [who "he" was even Velenchuk did not know] made me a crook in your eyes. *He*, the rotten bastard, has squeezed the last breath out of his own comrade . . . and I've been fifteen years in the army . . .' But it should be said, to Mikhail Dorofeich's credit, that he would not accept the two roubles, although Velenchuk brought them two months later.

3

Besides Velenchuk, five other soldiers from my platoon were warming themselves by the fire.

Maximov, the platoon gun-sergeant, was sitting on a wooden bucket in the best place, protected from the wind, smoking his pipe. His posture, his whole bearing and expression – not to mention the wooden bucket on which he was sitting, an emblem of authority at stopping places, and his nankeen-covered coat – clearly showed that he was used to giving orders and highly conscious of his own dignity.

When I went up to him he turned his head, but his eyes remained fixed on the fire and only followed his head movement much later. Maximov came from a family of small landowners, had money and had been given a rating at military training school where he had acquired a great deal of knowledge. He was awfully well off and awfully learned, in the words of the soldiers. I remember how once, as we were practising plunging fire with a quadrant, he explained to a group of soldiers around him that a spirit level is 'nothing other as it occurs, than atmospheric mercury possessing its own motion'. In actual fact, Maximov was far from stupid and really knew his job. But he had the unfortunate habit of sometimes deliberately speaking in such a way that it was impossible to understand him. I am convinced that he himself did not understand what he was saying either. He had a particular passion for the words 'occurs' and 'continuing', and whenever he said either of them I knew in advance that I would be unable to understand anything of what followed. On the other hand, the soldiers, as far as I could make out, loved to hear those 'occurs' and were convinced that this word had some profound significance, although, like me, they did not understand a word he said. However, they ascribed their lack of comprehension to their own stupidity and respected Fyodor Maximov all the more. In brief, Maximov was the diplomatically domineering type.

The second soldier by the fire, who was putting his sinewy red feet into a pair of boots, was Antonov – that same Bombardier Antonov who, in 1837, when he was one of three left to man an exposed gun, had fired back at a powerful enemy and had continued to stand by his gun and reload it – with two bullets in his thigh. 'He would have been made a sergeant long ago if it weren't for that temper of his,' the soldiers used to say. And he really did have a strange character. When he was sober there was no one more docile, quiet and well behaved, but after a few drinks he became a completely different person. He would defy all authority, fight and brawl and become a useless soldier. Only a week before, on Shrove Tuesday, he had got drunk and, despite all manner of threats and warnings – even being tied to a gun – he had persisted in his drunken brawling until the following Monday. Throughout Lent, although the entire detachment was under orders to eat meat as normal, he ate nothing but dry rusks and in the first week even refused the regulation cup of vodka. However, one just had to see his short, steely, bandy-legged figure, his shiny, whiskered face when, under the influence, he would take a balalaika in his sinewy hands, casually glance round and strike up 'The Young Maiden'; or when he strolled down the street, his coat thrown over his shoulders, his medals dangling, his hands in the pockets of his blue nankeen trousers; one only had to see that expression of soldierly pride and contempt for all things non-soldierly to realize how impossible it was for him to resist a fight with any batman, Cossack, infantryman, settler – with anyone, in fact, who was not an artilleryman, who had been rude to him or had just happened to cross his path. He fought and brawled not so much for personal satisfaction as for the morale of all the soldiers, whose representative he considered himself to be.

The third soldier squatting by the fire, with one earring, bristly whiskers, a bird-like face and a clay pipe between his teeth was Chikin, a driver. 'Old Chikin', as the soldiers called him, was a humorist. Wherever he was – in a biting frost, up to his knees in mud and having gone two days without food, marching, on parade or at drill, that dear man would always pull funny faces, twist his legs comically or crack jokes that had the whole platoon rolling with laughter. The young soldiers would always crowd round Chikin at stopping places or in the camp, and he would play filka[2] with them, tell them stories about the crafty soldier and the English lord, mimic Tartars and Germans, or simply say funny things which had them splitting their sides. In fact, his reputation as the battery humorist was so firmly established that he had only to open his mouth or wink to produce guffaws from everyone. But that man really had a flair for the unexpected. He was able to discover something unusual in everything, that others would never dream of. But, most of all, this ability to see the funny side of everything was never affected by any kind of ordeal or misfortune.

The fourth soldier was an unattractive young lad, recruited the previous year and on active service for the first time. He was standing in the middle of the smoke, so close to the fire it seemed his shabby sheepskin coat would burst into flames at any moment, but, judging from the way his coat was flung open, his calm, complacent pose with thighs out-thrust, he was obviously deriving a great deal of pleasure from it.

The fifth and last soldier, who was sitting some way from the fire, whittling away at a stick, was 'Grandpa' Zhdanov. He had served longer than any other soldier in the battery and had known all the others as young recruits, all of whom called him 'Grandpa' out of force of habit. It was said that he never drank or smoked, never played cards or used foul language. He spent all his free time making boots, went to church on holidays, whenever he could, or would light a cheap candle before his icon and open his psalm book – the only book he could read. He rarely mixed with the other soldiers and to those who were his senior in rank but junior in years he was icily polite. As he never drank, he had little chance of keeping company with his equals. But he had a particular liking for recruits and young soldiers, always taking them under his wing, admonishing them when necessary and frequently helping them. The whole battery considered him a capitalist, as he had about twenty-five roubles which he would willingly lend to anyone in real need. That same Maximov who was now a gun-sergeant told me that when he first arrived as a recruit ten years before and had drunk away all his money with the old, hardened drinkers, Zhdanov saw the dreadful mess he was in, called him over, severely reprimanded him for his behaviour, even beat him, lectured him on the good soldier's life and sent him away with a shirt on his back (Maximov had none left by then) and a half-rouble. 'He made a man of me,' Maximov always said of him with respect and gratitude. He also helped Velenchuk, whom he had protected ever since he was a recruit, at the time of the stolen cloth disaster. And there were so many others whom he had helped during his twenty-five years in the army.

One could not have wished for a soldier who knew his job better, who was braver or more conscientious. But he was too meek and self-effacing to be promoted to gun-sergeant, although he had been a bombardier for fifteen years. Zhdanov's sole joy, his passion even, was singing, although he himself didn't sing. There were a few songs he particularly loved and he was always collecting a choir from the young soldiers. He would stand with them, stuff his hands in his coat pockets, screw up his eyes and show how deeply affected he was. I cannot explain why, but for me there was something extraordinarily expressive about that regular movement of his jawbones just beneath the ears which seemed uniquely his. His snow-white hair, blackened moustache and wrinkled, bronzed face gave him at first sight a stern, forbidding look. But if one inspected his big eyes more closely, especially when they smiled (he never smiled with his lips), one was immediately struck by something exceptionally meek and almost childlike.

4

'Blow, I've forgotten my pipe. What a nuisance, lads!' Velenchuk repeated.

'Then you should smoke siggars, old chap,' Chikin said, twisting his mouth and winking. 'When I'm at home I always smoke siggars – they're sweeter!'

Naturally, everyone burst out laughing.

'So you forgot your pipe, did you?' Maximov chimed in, ignoring the general mirth and imperiously knocking his pipe against the palm of his left hand. 'Where did you get to this morning, Velenchuk? Tell me.'

Velenchuk half-turned towards him and was about to raise his hand to his cap but let it drop.

'It seems like you had a lot to sleep off if you couldn't keep awake standing up! Your comrades won't thank you for that.'

'You can strike me down dead, Fyodor Maximovich, if one drop passed my lips. I just don't know what came over me,' Velenchuk replied. 'What do you think *I* could have had to celebrate?'

'That may well be, but one of us has to carry the can for you and it's a real disgrace the way you go on,' remarked the eloquent Maximov, in a calmer voice.

'It was a miracle, lads,' Velenchuk continued after a moment's pause, scratching the back of his neck and addressing no one in particular. 'It was like a miracle. I've been sixteen years in the army and nothing like this has ever happened to me. When we were ordered to form up, I formed up and felt fine. But when I was in the artillery park *it* suddenly grabbed me and threw me to the ground, and that was that! I didn't even know what was happening. I just dropped off, lads! Must have been the sleeping sickness,' he concluded.

'I had a terrible job waking you up, I can tell you!' Antonov said, pulling on his boot. 'I had to shake you, push you, but you were sleeping like a log.'

'Yes,' observed Velenchuk, 'but it would have been different if I'd been drunk . . .'

'Reminds me of an old woman back home,' Chikin joined in. 'She didn't budge from over the stove for two years. One day they tried to wake her, thinking she was just asleep. But she was dead! She was always dropping off – just like you, old chap!'

'Come on, Chikin, tell us about the time you started cutting a dash when you were on leave,' Maximov said, smiling and glancing at me as if to say, 'Would *you* like to hear what this clown has to say?'

'What d'ye mean, cutting a dash?' Chikin replied, giving me a fleeting, sidelong glance. 'Well, I naturally told them exactly what the Corkersuss is like.'

'Come on, don't be so modest . . . tell us how you *instructed* them.'

'You know very well how I instructed them. They asked me what life's like here,' Chikin replied in a rapid patter, like a man who has told the same story many times. 'I told them we live well here. Loads of grub – a cup of chockolad morning and night for every soldier and barley broth fit for a lord at midday. And instead of vodka a glass of Modeera – to cheer us all up!'

'That's a good one, Modeera!' Velenchuk exclaimed, roaring with laughter louder than anyone else. 'I'll give you Modeera!'

'What did you tell them about the Hazians?' Maximov asked when the general laughter had somewhat subsided.

Chikin leant over the fire, fished out a small piece of charcoal with his stick, put it to his pipe and for a long time silently puffed at his cheap shag, as if completely unaware of the mute curiosity he had aroused in his audience. When at last he had worked up enough smoke he threw the charcoal away, pushed his cap even further back and after a slight twitch and a faint smile continued. 'They also asked what the Circassians and Turks were like down here in the Corkersuss, if they were fierce warriors. So I told 'em there's different sorts of Circassians, that they come in all shapes and sizes. There's the Daghestanians who live up in the mountains and eat stones instead of bread. They're as big, I told 'em, as tree trunks, with one eye in their forehead and they wear red caps – flaming red like yours, me lad!' he added, turning to the young recruit, who was in fact wearing an extremely comical cap with a red top.

At this unexpected remark the recruit suddenly squatted, slapped his knees and laughed and coughed so violently he was barely able to gasp, 'So that's what the Daghestanians are really like!'

'And there's the Gapers,' Chikin went on, shaking his cap on to his forehead with a toss of the head. 'They're different – they're little people, always going around in pairs, hand in hand, and they run so fast you couldn't even catch 'em up on a horse.' Then, in a deep throaty voice, attempting to imitate a country yokel, he continued, 'So they ask me, "Is those Gapers born loike that, hand in hand?" Why yes, I say, they go round like that from the day they were born. And if you try and cut 'em apart the blood just gushes out, same as a Chinaman – if you take his hat off he'll start bleeding. And then they ask, "Are they fierce fighters?" Well, I say, when they catch you they slit yer belly open and twist yer guts round yer arm. There they are, twisting away and you can't stop laughing – yes, you laugh yourself to death, you do!'

'Did they really believe all that, Chikin?' Maximov said with a faint smile, while the others were splitting their sides.

'That strange lot'd believe anything, Fyodor Maximov. Oh yes! But when I told 'em that the snow doesn't melt all summer on Mount Kizbeck[3] they laughed their heads off! "What's so special about that?" they say. "It's a high mountain, so of course the snow never melts! When there's a thaw here the snow on any little hillock melts first, but it lingers on in the hollows." Now, who would have thought there were such folk!' Chikin winked in conclusion.

5

The bright orb of the sun shining through the milky-white mist was now quite high. The violet-grey horizon was gradually widening and, although now much further away, was marked just as sharply by a deceptive white wall of mist.

Beyond the felled trees quite a large clearing opened up before us. Smoke from the fires – black, milky-white or violet – spread over the clearing from all sides and white layers of mist drifted past in the weirdest shapes. In the far distance groups of Tartars on horseback appeared now and then, and the occasional sound of fire from our rifles and guns could be heard.

'That wasn't what you call action, only a bit of fun!' as good Captain Khlopov would say.

The commander of the Ninth Company of Chasseurs, which had been escorting us, came up to our guns and pointed to three Tartar horsemen riding along the edge of the forest about a mile away, and with that love of artillery fire so typical of infantry officers he asked me to fire a ball or shell at them.

'Can you see that?' he asked with a kind, persuasive smile as he stretched his arm over my shoulder. 'There's one of them in front of those two large trees on a white horse and in a black cloak. The other two are behind. Can you see them? Couldn't you? . . . please . . .'

'And there's another three skirting the forest,' added Antonov, who was renowned for his astonishingly keen eyesight, as he came up to us and hid the pipe he had been smoking behind his back. 'The one in front has drawn his rifle – you can see them clear as daylight, sir!'

'Look – he's fired, lads! There's the white smoke,' remarked Velenchuk, who was standing in a group of soldiers just behind us.

'He must have been firing at our line, the devil!' another observed.

'Just look at all that lot pouring out of the forest. They must be looking for somewhere to put a gun,' added a third.

'If we dropped a shell in the middle they wouldn't like it!'

'Yes, we could just about reach them from here, couldn't we?' Chikin asked.

'It's only about twelve or thirteen hundred yards,' Maximov replied coolly, as though talking to himself, although, like the others, he was obviously dying to open fire. 'At an angle of forty-five degrees our Unicorn[4] could hit them plumb in the middle!'

'Well, you really couldn't miss if you sent a shell into that crowd! Yes, now's the moment, while they're all bunched.

Please give the order to fire at once,' the company commander kept begging me.

'Shall we take aim?' Antonov suddenly asked in a jerky bass voice and with a rather sullen, spiteful look.

I must confess I was longing to fire, so I gave orders for them to aim number two gun.

Hardly had I given the order when the shell was ready charged and loaded into the gun, while Antonov, clinging to the side-plate of the gun carriage and holding his chubby fingers to the back-plate, was already aligning the trail.

'A trifle to the left . . . a fraction to the right . . . a bit more . . . that's it!' he said, proudly walking away from the gun.

One by one, the infantry officer, Maximov and I peered through the sights and each of us gave our different opinions.

'I'm positive it will overshoot!' Velenchuk said, clicking his tongue, although he had only just looked over Antonov's shoulder and therefore did not have the slightest grounds for this assumption. 'God, I bet you'll overshoot, lads, and hit that tree!'

'Fire number two!' I ordered.

The crew moved away to the guns. Antonov ran to one side to watch the flight of the shell. There was a flash and the sound of ringing brass. At that moment we were enveloped in gunpowder smoke and the resounding boom was followed by the metallic hum of the shell receding at the speed of lightning and dying away in the distance.

Just behind the group of riders a puff of white smoke appeared and the Tartars galloped away in all directions. Then the sound of the explosion reached us.

'Great! That made 'em gallop all right. Those devils don't like it!' Chuckles and murmurs of approval came from the ranks of artillery and infantry.

'If only we'd aimed a fraction lower we'd have hit them,' Velenchuk remarked. 'I told you we'd hit a tree and that's what we've done – it carried too far to the right.'

6

After I had left the soldiers to discuss how the Tartars had galloped away when they saw the shell, what they were doing there in the first place and whether there were many still left in the forest, I took a few steps with the company commander and sat down under a tree waiting while the meatballs he had offered me were warmed up. Company Commander Bolkhov was one of the officers nicknamed 'Bonjour' in the regiment. He was well off, had served in the Guards and spoke French. Despite this, his comrades were fond of him. He was quite intelligent and had sufficient tact to wear a St Petersburg-style frock-coat, to dine well and to speak French without causing too much offence to his fellow officers. After we had chatted about the weather, military operations and mutual officer friends and had satisfied ourselves, by means of question and answer, that each other's ideas were acceptable, we involuntarily turned to more intimate topics. When people from the same social circle meet in the Caucasus, the question 'Why are you here?' even if unspoken, invariably arises, and I had the feeling that my companion wanted to reply to this unasked question.

'When will this action ever finish?' he said lazily. 'I find it so boring.'

'I don't,' I replied. 'After all, it's even worse at headquarters.'

'Oh yes, it's ten thousand times worse at headquarters,' he said irritably. 'No, I mean, when will all *this* be over for good?'

'What do you want to be over?' I asked.

'Everything. And for good! . . . Well now, are those meatballs ready, Nikolayev!?' he asked.

'Then why did you come here in the first place if you dislike the Caucasus so much?' I asked.

'I'll tell you why,' he replied with uncompromising candour. 'It's all because of some tradition. In Russia they really do believe that the Caucasus is some kind of Promised Land for all sorts of unfortunate people.'

'I'd say that's true, roughly. Most of us . . .'

'Yes, but the main thing is, all of us who follow tradition and come to the Caucasus are terribly mistaken in our calculations. For the life of me I cannot see why, because of some unhappy love affair or financial trouble one should opt for the Caucasus rather than Kazan or Kaluga. In Russia, you know, people visualize the Caucasus as such a magnificent place, with eternal virgin ice, raging torrents, daggers, felt cloaks, Circassian maidens, but basically there's nothing very cheerful about it. If only these people at least knew that we never go anywhere near virgin ice, and if we did we wouldn't be very amused by it, and that the Caucasus is divided into many different provinces – Stavropol, Tiflis and so on.'

'Yes,' I laughed. 'Living in Russia we view the Caucasus quite differently. Have *you* ever felt that? It's really like reading poetry in a language you don't know very well – you imagine it's much better than it really is –'

'I don't know, to tell you the truth,' he interrupted, 'but I detest the Caucasus.'

'Well, I like it here now, but in a different way . . .'

'Oh, perhaps it's all right,' he continued rather irritably, 'but all I know is, I don't like it.'

'Why is that?' I asked, for the sake of saying something.

'Firstly, because it's deceived me. All that I came to the Caucasus (following tradition) to be cured of has followed me here and the only difference is that previously it was all on the grand scale and here it is on a small and pretty sordid one. Wherever I go I'm besieged with millions of trivial worries, dirty tricks and insults at every step. Secondly, because I feel myself declining morally every day. But the main reason is that I don't consider myself fit to serve here: I cannot endure danger . . . to put it in a nutshell, I'm not brave . . .' He stopped to look at me. 'I'm not joking.'

Although I was startled by this unsolicited confession, I did not contradict my companion, as that was what he apparently wanted. Instead, I waited for him to retract his words, as always happens in such cases.

'Do you know,' he continued, 'this is my first taste of action and you just cannot imagine how I felt yesterday. When the sergeant-major came with the order that my company was to join the main column I went as white as a sheet and was too nervous to speak. And what a night I had – if you only knew! If it's true that people go grey from fear, then my hair should be completely white now, since no condemned prisoner can have suffered as much as I did in one night. Even now, although I'm rather more relaxed than during the night, this is what happens inside me,' he added, twisting his fist in front of his chest. 'And the funny thing is,' he continued, 'that the most awful tragedy is being enacted while here we sit scoffing meatballs and onions, persuading ourselves that it's all very jolly. Is there any wine, Nikolayev?' he said, yawning.

Just then we heard a soldier cry out in alarm, 'They're there, lads!' whereupon all eyes turned to the edge of the distant forest.

Far off a bluish cloud of smoke was growing ever larger, drifting upwards as the wind carried it. When I realized that the enemy was firing at us, everything before me suddenly took on a new and majestic character. The stacks of rifles, the bonfire smoke, the blue sky, the green gun carriages, Nikolayev's sunburnt, whiskered face – all this seemed to be telling me that the ball which had now left the muzzle and was flying through space at that very moment could well be aimed straight at my chest.

'Where did you get that wine?' I lazily asked Bolkhov, while deep down inside me two equally distinct voices were speaking: one was saying, 'Lord receive my soul in peace,' and the other, 'I hope I won't duck and will keep smiling when that ball comes flying over.' And that instant something terribly nasty whistled over my head and a cannon ball fell with a thud about two paces from where we were standing.

'Now, if I had been Napoleon or Frederick the Great,' Bolkhov said, turning to me with the greatest composure, 'I would doubtless have paid you a compliment.'

'But you just have,' I replied, finding it difficult to conceal the panic that the danger (now past) had stirred in me.

'Well, so what? No one will write it down.'

'*I* will, though.'

'But if you write it down it will only be to criticize, as Mishchenkov says,' he added, smiling.

'Damn and blast you!' Antonov called out behind us, angrily spitting. 'Within a whisker of grazing my leg!'

After this ingenuous remark all my efforts to appear calm and collected, all our smart talk, struck me as impossibly stupid.

7

The enemy had in fact positioned two guns just where the Tartars had been riding around and every twenty or thirty minutes fired at our woodfellers. My platoon was moved forward into the clearing and ordered to return their fire. A puff of smoke appeared at the edge of the forest, then we would hear a report and a whistling sound and then a cannon ball would fall behind or in front of us. The enemy's shots were very much off target and no losses were sustained.

As always, our artillerymen were splendid, swiftly loading and diligently aiming whenever they saw puffs of smoke and calmly joking among themselves. Nearby, awaiting its turn in silent inactivity, was our infantry escort. The woodfellers carried on with their work and the forest was filled more and more with the sound of axes. Only when a cannon ball whistled overhead did everything go quiet and in the deathly silence rather anxious voices would ring out, 'Watch it, lads!' and all eyes would be fixed on the ball ricocheting among the fires and lopped branches.

By now the mist had completely cleared and was turning into clouds that gradually disappeared in the dark blue sky. The sun came out and shone brightly, gleaming cheerfully on the steel bayonets, the brass guns and the thawing earth spangled with hoar frost. In the air one could feel both the freshness of the morning frost and the warmth of the spring sun. Thousands of different shades and colours mingled in the dry forest leaves and the tracks of wagon wheels and horseshoe nails could be seen quite distinctly on the even, shiny path.

The exchanges between the two forces were growing fiercer and louder on all sides. Puffs of bluish smoke appeared more often now. The dragoons rode on, the pennants on their lances streaming; songs came from the infantry companies and a train of carts laden with firewood was drawn up in the rear. A general rode over to our platoon and ordered us to withdraw. The enemy had positioned himself in the bushes opposite our left flank and was harassing us with heavy rifle fire. A bullet came humming out of the forest to the left and struck a gun carriage, followed by another, and a third . . . The infantry who were nearby covering us noisily got up, took their rifles and formed a line. The firing intensified and more and more bullets began to fly. The withdrawal began, which meant (as is always the case in the Caucasus) that the real action had begun.

It was obvious that the artillerymen disliked bullets just as much as the infantry disliked cannon balls. Antonov frowned. Chikin mimicked the bullets and cracked jokes about them – but he clearly did not like them. 'That one's in a hurry!' he said of one, calling another 'little bee'. A third, which screeched slowly and plaintively over our heads, he called 'poor little orphan', which made everyone laugh.

Unused to bullets, the young recruit leant his head to one side and bent his neck every time a bullet flew past, which also made the soldiers laugh. 'Bowing because they're friends of yours?' they asked. Velenchuk, usually so indifferent to danger, was now quite agitated. Evidently he was annoyed that we weren't firing case shot in the direction of the bullets. Several times he remarked in a disgruntled voice, 'Why do we let them fire and get away with it? If we turned a gun on them and peppered them with case shot that would soon quieten them down!'

It was in fact high time we did this, so I ordered the men to fire a last shell and then load the gun with case shot.

'Case shot!' Antonov shouted, jauntily walking through the smoke to his gun with his linstock as soon as the shell had been fired.

Just then, not far behind me, I heard the rapid hum of a bullet suddenly end in a dull thud. My heart sank. 'One of ours has been hit,' I thought, too afraid to look around, from a feeling of grim foreboding. And in fact the thud was followed by the sound of a body falling heavily and the heart-rending

'O-oh!' of a wounded soldier. 'They've got me, lads!' a familiar voice just managed to say. It was Velenchuk. He was lying on his back between limber and gun. The bag he had been carrying was thrown to one side. His forehead was covered with blood and over his right eye and his nose flowed a thick, red stream. He had been wounded in the stomach, but there was hardly any blood there – he had smashed his forehead against a tree stump in falling.

I only discovered all this much later and at first I could only make out some vague heap and what appeared to be a dreadful amount of blood.

None of the soldiers who had loaded the gun said a word, except for the young recruit, who kept muttering something that sounded like 'God, just look at all that blood!' while Antonov frowned and grunted angrily. But it was clear that the thought of death had run through everyone's mind. Everyone got on with their work with renewed energy. The gun was charged in a moment and the gunner, who brought up some case shot, walked about two feet away from the spot where the wounded Velenchuk lay, still moaning.

8

Anyone who has seen action must surely have experienced that strange, illogical but none the less powerful feeling of revulsion for the place where a soldier has been killed or wounded. The soldiers under my command evidently yielded to this feeling when they should have lifted Velenchuk and carried him to a cart which had come up. Zhdanov angrily went over to the wounded man and, although it made him scream all the more, lifted him by the armpits.

'What are you standing there for? Get hold of him!' he shouted. Velenchuk was immediately surrounded by about ten helpers – more than was needed. But the moment he was moved, Velenchuk started struggling and screaming horribly.

'Why are you screaming like a hare?' Antonov said gruffly as he held his leg. 'If you don't stop we'll leave you here.'

And the wounded soldier in fact quietened down, only muttering occasionally, 'Oh, I'm dying! I'm dying, lads!'

When he was placed in the cart he even stopped groaning and I could hear him telling one of his comrades something in a soft, but audible voice: no doubt words of farewell . . .

No soldier likes to see a wounded comrade and as I instinctively hurried to escape that sight I gave orders for him to be immediately rushed to the dressing station and then returned to the guns. But a few minutes later I was told that Velenchuk was calling for me, so I went back to the cart.

The wounded man was lying at the bottom of the cart, gripping the sides with both hands. Within a few minutes his broad, healthy face had completely changed: he seemed to have grown thinner and to have aged several years. His pale, thin lips were pressed together with obvious strain. A bright, serene glow had replaced the dull restless look of his eyes and the stamp of death already lay on his bloody forehead and nose.

Although the slightest movement caused him the most appalling pain, he asked for the small purse that was tied like a garter around his left leg to be removed. The sight of that bare, white and healthy leg when they took off his boot and untied the purse aroused the most oppressive feeling in me.

'There's three and a half roubles in it,' he told me as I took the purse. 'Look after them.'

The cart was about to move off when he told them to stop.

'I was making an overcoat for Lieutenant Sulimovsky. He . . . he gave me two roubles. I spent one and a half on buttons and there's another half rouble with the buttons in my kitbag. Give them to him.'

'Of course, of course,' I said. 'Now you get better, old man.' He did not answer, the cart moved off and he started groaning and moaning in the most dreadful heart-rending way. It was as though, having tidied up his earthly affairs, he could find no more reason to exercise any self-control and considered it quite permissible to let himself go now.

9

'Where do you think you're going? Come back!' I shouted at the young recruit who, as calmly as could be, with his spare linstock under one arm and some sort of stick in his hands, set off after the cart bearing the wounded soldier. But the recruit merely glanced back lazily, muttered something and carried on, so that I had to send someone after him.

He doffed his red cap and smiled stupidly at me.

'Where were you going?'

'Back to camp.'

'Why?'

'Because Velenchuk's been wounded, of course,' he said, smiling again.

'And what's that got to do with you? You must stay here.'

He looked at me in amazement, then nonchalantly turned round, put on his cap and went back to his post.

On the whole, the operation was successful. We heard that the Cossacks had carried out a glorious attack and returned with three dead Tartars; that the infantry had stocked up with firewood and had only six wounded; that in the artillery only Velenchuk and two horses had been put out of action. But then about two square miles of forest had been felled and the area cleared beyond recognition: in place of the dense row of trees of before, a vast clearing had now opened up along the forest edge, covered with smoking fires, and cavalry and infantry returning to camp. Although the enemy continued pursuing us with artillery and rifle fire right up to the graveyard and the stream we had crossed in the morning, the withdrawal was successfully carried out. I was already beginning to dream of the cabbage stew and side of mutton with buckwheat porridge that were waiting for me in the camp when news came that the general had ordered a redoubt to be built by the side of the stream and that the Third Battalion of K— Regiment and a platoon from the Fourth Battery were to stay there until morning. Carts laden with firewood and wounded, Cossacks, artillery, infantry bearing rifles and with firewood on their backs, all passed us with a great deal of noise and singing. Everyone's face expressed animation and contentment, stimulated by the thought that the danger was past and by the prospect of a rest. Only we and the Third Battalion would have to wait until morning before we could entertain such pleasant thoughts.

10

While we artillerymen were busy with the guns, parking the limbers and ammunition wagons and tethering the horses, the infantry had already stacked their rifles, made fires, built small shelters from branches and maize straw and were now cooking their buckwheat porridge.

It was getting dark. Bluish rain clouds drifted across the sky. The mist had turned into a fine drizzle, soaking the earth and the soldiers' coats. The horizon seemed to contract and the whole area took on a sombre hue. The damp, which I could feel through my boots and on my neck, the incessant motion and conversations in which I took no part, the sticky mud over which my feet slid and my empty stomach all put me in a thoroughly miserable mood after a day of physical and moral exhaustion. I could not get Velenchuk out of my mind. The whole simple story of his soldier's life kept haunting my imagination.

His last moments had been as bright and calm as his whole life. He had lived too honestly, too simply, for his unquestioning faith in the heavenly life to come to falter at the moment of truth.

'Your Honour,' Nikolayev said, coming up, 'the captain would like you to have tea with him.'

Somehow I managed to pick my way through stacks of rifles and bonfires and followed Nikolayev to Bolkhov's quarters, relishing the prospect of a glass of hot tea and some cheerful conversation to dispel my gloomy thoughts.

'Well, did you find him?' came Bolkhov's voice from a straw hut where a small light was burning.

'Yes, I've brought him, Your Honour,' Nikolayev replied in his deep voice.

Bolkhov was sitting on his dry felt cloak, his coat unbuttoned, and without his fur cap. By his side a samovar was on the boil and there was a drum with food on it. A bayonet with a candle on the end was stuck into the ground. 'Well, what do you think?' he proudly asked, casting his eye over his comfortable quarters. In fact it was so pleasant in the hut that as we drank our tea I completely forgot the damp, the darkness and Velenchuk's wound. We talked about Moscow and things that had nothing at all to do with the war and the Caucasus.

After one of those silent moments which occasionally punctuate even the most lively conversations, Bolkhov smiled at me.

'I think our talk this morning must have seemed very odd to you,' he said.

'No, why should it? Only I felt that you were rather too frank – there are things all of us know but which we should never divulge.'

'Why not? No! If I had the slightest chance of exchanging this life for the poorest, most wretched existence – as long as there was no danger of military service – I wouldn't hesitate for one moment.'

'Then why don't you return to Russia?' I asked.

'Why?' he asked. 'Oh, I've been thinking about it for a long time now, but I can't go to Russia until I receive the Anna or Vladimir medal[5] – an Anna round my neck and a major's rank were precisely why I came here in the first place.'

'But why don't you go back if, as you say, you feel unfit for service here?'

'I feel even more incapable of returning to Russia the same as when I left it. It's just one more of those legends in Russia, confirmed by Passek,[6] Sleptsov[7] and others, that one only has to come to the Caucasus to be showered with decorations. Everyone expects it of us, demands it of us. But I've been here two years, taken part in two expeditions and received nothing. For all that, I've so much pride that I won't leave this place until I'm a major, with an Anna or a Vladimir round my neck. I've reached the point where it really rankles when some Gnilokishkin is decorated and I'm not. What's more, how could I look my elder in the face again, or merchant Kotel'nikov to whom I sell grain, or my aunt in Moscow and all those fine gentlemen in Russia, if I return after two years in the Caucasus with nothing to show for it? No, I don't want to know those gentlemen and I'm sure that they couldn't care less about me. But such is man's nature that although I couldn't give a damn about them they're the reason why I'm ruining the best years of my life, my happiness and whole future.'

II

At that moment the battalion commander called from outside, 'Who's that you're talking to, Nikolay Fyodorych?'

Bolkhov told him my name, whereupon three officers came into the hut: Major Kirsanov, a battalion adjutant and Company Commander Trosenko.

Kirsanov was a shortish, stout man with a black moustache, red cheeks and sensuous little eyes. These eyes were his outstanding feature and when he laughed all that remained of them was two moist little stars. These, together with his tight lips and arched neck, sometimes made him look extraordinarily stupid. Kirsanov behaved and bore himself better than anyone else in the regiment: his subordinates never said a bad word about him and his superiors respected him, although he was generally thought to be very dense. He knew the army, was industrious, diligent, always had money, kept a carriage and cook and was good at pretending to be proud with great naturalness.

'What are you discussing, Nikolay?' he asked as he entered.

'Oh, only the pleasures of army life here.'

Just then Kirsanov spotted me, a mere cadet, and to make me aware of his importance he stared at the drum and asked, 'What's wrong, Nikolay? Tired?' as if he hadn't heard Bolkhov's reply.

'No, we were just – ' Bolkhov began.

But again it was probably the sense of self-importance of a battalion commander that made him interrupt and ask another question: 'A splendid engagement today, wasn't it?'

The battalion adjutant was a young ensign, recently promoted from the cadets. He was a modest, quiet lad with a shy, good-natured expression. I had seen him at Bolkhov's before and he often dropped in on him. He would bow, sit in one corner without saying a word for several hours, roll cigarettes and smoke them, after which he would get up, bow and leave. He was a typical poor Russian gentleman's son who had chosen a military career as the only possible one for someone with his education and who considered an officer's rank the most precious thing in the world. He was the simple-hearted and likeable type, despite those comical accessories invariably associated with it – the tobacco pouch, the dressing-gown, the guitar, the toothbrush moustache. In the regiment he was said to have boasted that he was fair but strict with his batman. 'I rarely punish him,' he had claimed, 'but when I'm driven to it, then God help him!' Once, when his batman was drunk and had robbed him, even sworn at him, he had taken him to the guardhouse and ordered him to be flogged, but when he saw the necessary preparations he was so upset that he could only murmur, 'Well, you see, I can if I want to . . .' and then he lost his head, ran back to his quarters and ever since was afraid to look Batman Chernov in the eye. His fellow officers did not give him a moment's peace, teased him unmercifully and more than once I heard that simple-hearted youth make excuses, blushing furiously as he assured them that what they had heard was not true, but in fact quite the contrary.

The third officer, Captain Trosenko, was an old Caucasian in every sense of the word: that is, he was a man for whom the company he commanded had become his family, the fortress where the headquarters were his home and the songs sung by the soldiers his only pleasure. He was a man for whom everything that was not the Caucasus was beneath contempt and almost inconceivable. He really thought that everything that was the Caucasus was divided into halves – 'ours' and 'theirs'. He loved the first and hated the second with all his heart. Above all, he was a coolly courageous, battle-hardened soldier, exceptionally kind to his comrades and inferiors, but dreadfully brusque and even downright rude towards adjutants and

'Bonjours', whom he detested for some reason. As he entered the straw hut he nearly put his head through the roof, suddenly sank down and sat on the ground.

'Well, what's new?' he asked, suddenly stopping when he saw my unfamiliar face and fixing his dull, staring eyes on me.

'What were you talking about?' the major asked, taking out his watch and looking at it, although I was quite sure there was no need to do this.

'Well, this gentleman's been asking why I'm serving here.'

'Nikolay obviously wants to distinguish himself and then make tracks for home.'

'Come on, Abram Ilich, you tell us why you want to serve in the Caucasus.'

'Firstly, you know, because each of us must do his duty . . . *What*?' he added, although no one had said anything. 'Yesterday I had a letter from Russia, Nikolay Fyodorych,' he continued, obviously wanting to change the subject. 'They write that . . . well, they ask such peculiar questions.'

'What kind of questions?' asked Bolkhov.

He burst out laughing.

'Very strange questions . . . They ask if there can be jealousy without love . . . *What*?' he asked, looking at all of us.

'You don't say!' Bolkhov laughed.

'Yes, you know life is good in Russia,' he went on, as if everything he said followed quite logically from the previous remark. 'In 1852, when I was in Tambov, everyone received me as if I was the Tsar's aide-de-camp. Would you believe it – at the governor's ball – I was given a very warm reception when I went in. The governor's wife herself, you know, talked to me and asked about the Caucasus, and they were all so . . . I don't know what . . . They looked at my gold sabre as if it were some rarity and asked why I had been awarded it – and the Order of Anna and the Vladimir, and I told them . . . *What*? That's what the Caucasus is good for, Nikolay Fyodorych!' he continued, without waiting for a reply. 'In Russia they have a high opinion of us Caucasians. A young man, you know, a staff officer with the Orders of Anna and Vladimir – it all carries a lot of weight in Russia . . . *What*?'

'I really think you did a little bit of boasting there, Abram Ilich!' Bolkhov said.

'Hee-hee!' Kirsanov laughed his stupid laugh. 'It was necessary, you know! How superbly I dined for those two months!'

'So, life is good up north in Russia, is it?' Trosenko asked, as if he were talking about China or Japan.

'I should say so! When I think of the champagne we drank in those two months – gallons of the stuff!'

'Come off it! It was probably lemonade,' Trosenko said. 'Now I'd have shown them how we can knock it back here and made myself famous! I'd have showed them – eh, Bolkhov?'

'But *you've* been in the Caucasus more than ten years, old man,' Bolkhov said. 'And you remember what Yermolov[8] said. Abram Ilich has been here only six . . .'

'I'll give you ten – it will soon be sixteen!'

'Bolkhov, let's have some sage vodka. Brrr! It's damp in here!' he added, smiling. 'Let's have a drink, Major!'

But the major, already unhappy with the way the old captain had first addressed him, now winced visibly and sought refuge in his own grandeur. He hummed something as he again looked at his watch.

'So, I'll never go back there,' Trosenko continued, ignoring the frowning major. 'What's more, I've lost the habit of walking and speaking as they do in Russia. They'd ask, "What kind of freak is this? Something that blew in from Asia!" Isn't that so, Nikolay Fyodorych? And what is there for me in Russia? Anyway, some day I'll be shot here and then they'll ask, "Where's old Trosenko?" "Shot," will be the answer. And what would you do with the Eighth Company then, eh?' he added, addressing all these remarks to the major.

'Send the battalion officer on duty!' Kirsanov shouted, without replying to the captain, although once again I was convinced that there was no need for any orders.

'As for you, young man, I bet you're pleased to be on double pay now,' the major told the adjutant after a few minutes' silence.

'Yes, sir. Very pleased.'

'I think the pay's very good these days, Nikolay Fyodorych,' he continued. 'A young man can live quite decently on it and even permit himself a few small luxuries.'

'No, Abram Ilich!' the adjutant replied timidly. 'Although it's double I can only just make ends meet . . . One has to keep a horse . . .'

'What's this you're telling me, young man? I was an ensign once myself and *I* know. Believe me, you can live very well on it. Go on, add it up,' he said, crooking the little finger of his left hand.

'We're always paid in advance, so that's all you need to count,' Trosenko commented, emptying a glass of vodka.

'That may well be . . . but . . . *What*?'

Just then a head with white hair and a flat nose poked through an opening in the hut and a shrill voice said in a German accent, 'Are you there, Abram Ilich? The duty officer's looking for you.'

'Come in, Kraft,' Bolkhov said.

A tall figure wearing a general staff officer's coat squeezed through the door and shook everyone's hand with the utmost fervour. 'Ah, my dear Captain, so you're here, too,' he said, turning to Trosenko.

In spite of the gloom the new guest managed to find his way over to him and, to the captain's extreme amazement and displeasure (or so it seemed to me), kissed him on the lips.

'Just a German trying to be a really good chap,' I thought.

12

My assumption was immediately confirmed. Captain Kraft asked for vodka and gave a dreadful grunt as he tossed back his head and emptied the glass.

'Well, gentlemen, we had a very pleasant outing today, cavorting over the plains of Chechnya,' he began, but when he spotted the duty officer he immediately stopped so that the major could give his orders.

'Did you go round the lines?'

'Yes, sir.'

'Have the listening posts been set up?'

'Yes, sir.'

'Then go and order the company commanders to be on the alert.'

'Yes, sir.'

The major screwed up his eyes and thought deeply.

'And tell the men they can make their porridge now.'

'They already are.'

'Good. You may go.'

Turning to us with a condescending smile, the major continued, 'Well, now, we were trying to work out how much an officer needs. Let's see. There's your uniform and a pair of trousers – right?'

'Yes, sir.'

'Let's say that comes to fifty roubles over two years, which makes twenty-five per annum on clothes. Then about fifty kopecks a day for food – right?'

'Perhaps not as much as that.'

'Well, let's just suppose, for the moment. You need thirty roubles for a horse, there's saddle repairs – that's all. So, that makes twenty-five, plus one hundred and twenty, plus thirty – one hundred and seventy-five. So you're left with about twenty for luxuries such as tea, sugar, tobacco. There – do you see? Aren't I right, Nikolay Fyodorych?'

'I'm afraid not, Abram Ilich!' the adjutant timidly replied. 'You wouldn't have enough for tea or sugar. You can reckon a uniform will last you two years, but with all these campaigns you'll never have enough trousers to see you through. And what about boots? I wear out a pair almost every month. Then there's underclothes, shirts, towels, leggings – all that has to be paid for, sir. Add it up and you'll find you won't have a kopeck left. It's true, Abram Ilich!'

'Yes, it's lovely wearing leggings,' Kraft suddenly remarked after a minute's silence, pronouncing 'leggings' with particular affection. 'All this is so very Russian!'

'Let me tell you,' Trosenko said, 'however you add it up you'll find that we should all really be starving. But in actual fact we manage to survive, smoke our tobacco and drink our vodka. If you've been serving in the army as long as I have,' he continued, turning to the ensign, 'then you'll learn how to get by. Do you know how this officer treats his batman, gentlemen?'

Trosenko almost died with laughter as he told us the whole story of the ensign and his batman, although we had heard it a thousand times.

'And why are you sitting there looking like a rosebud, old chap?' he continued, still addressing his remarks to the ensign who could not stop blushing, sweating and smiling – so much so, one felt really sorry for him. 'Don't worry, lad, I was like you once, but you can see for yourself what a fine fellow I am now! When those young hotheads first come here from Russia – we know their sort all right – they get spasms and rheumatism. But here am I, snug as a bug. This place is my house, my bed – *everything*! You see . . .'

He downed another glass of vodka.

'*What*?' he said, staring right into Kraft's eyes.

'Now, there's a man I respect! A real Caucasian! Allow me to shake your hand.' Kraft pushed us all aside as he made his way over to Trosenko, grasped his hand and shook it with deep feeling.

'Yes, we can rightly say we've gone through everything here,' he continued. 'In '45 – yes, you were there, Captain, weren't you? Do you remember the night of the twelfth, when we were knee-deep in mud and then attacked the enemy next morning? In those days I was attached to the commander-in-chief and we captured twenty enemy positions in one day. Do you remember, Captain?'

Trosenko nodded, stuck out his lower lip and screwed up his eyes.

'You see,' Kraft went on, extremely excited and making quite inappropriate gestures as he turned to the major. But the major, who must have heard the story many times, suddenly gave the other such a dull, glazed look that Kraft turned away and addressed Bolkhov and me, looking at each of us in turn. He did not look at Trosenko once during the whole narrative.

'So, you see, when we came out that morning the commander-in-chief told me, "Kraft! Capture those barricades!" Well, you know how it is in the army – no arguing. You salute and get on with it. "Yes, Your Excellency!" I said – and off I went. The moment we reached the first defences I turned round and told my men, "Now, lads, no retreating. Keep your eyes open. If anyone lags behind I'll chop him to pieces myself!" Well, you can't mince words with Russian soldiers. And then, suddenly, a shell landed . . . and I could see one soldier, a second, a third . . . then bullets . . . Eeee-eeee-eeee! I called out, "Come on, lads, follow me!" But the moment we got there I saw a . . . you know what it's called . . . ?' At this point the narrator waved his arms as he tried to find the right word.

'A ditch?' Bolkhov ventured.

'No . . . Ach, what on earth is it called? Why yes . . . a ditch!' he said quickly. 'So, rifles at the ready . . . Hoorah! Ta-ra-ta-ta! But there wasn't a soul to be seen. We were all surprised, you know. So far so good! On we went towards the second position. Now, that was quite a different proposition. All of us were burning for action! We moved closer, you know, and I took a good look at the second position and saw it was impossible to go on – there was a . . . what do you call it? Ach, what's it called?'

'Another ditch?' I suggested.

'No, nothing like it,' he continued irritably. 'No, not a ditch . . . oh, what do you call it?' And he made an inane gesture with his hand. 'Ach, what on earth is it called?'

He was obviously suffering so much that one could not help prompting him.

'A river, perhaps?' Bolkhov said.

'No, just a ditch. We were about to go over when, would you believe it, they opened up with such intense fire it was sheer hell!'

At that moment someone outside the hut asked for me. It was Maximov. As I had heard the eventful story before and knew that there were still thirteen barricades to go, I eagerly seized the opportunity of returning to my platoon. Trosenko came out with me.

'What a load of rot!' he said when we were a few yards from

the hut. 'He was never anywhere near any barricades,' he added, laughing so heartily that I too had to laugh.

13

The dark night had closed in and only dim bonfires lit the camp when I finished my duties and went off to join my men. A large stump was smouldering on the coals and only three soldiers were sitting around it: Antonov, who was turning a tin of *riabko*[9] on the fire; Zhdanov, who was pensively raking the embers with a long dry branch; and Chikin with his pipe that was always out. The others had already lain down to sleep, some under the ammunition wagons, some in the hay, some by the fires. In the feeble light of the coals I could distinguish familiar backs, legs, heads. Among those around the fire was the young recruit, who lay very close and seemed asleep already. The all-pervading smell of mist and the smoke from the damp firewood made my eyes smart and the same fine drizzle fell from the dreary sky.

Nearby could be heard the regular sound of snoring, the crackle of twigs in the fire, soft voices and the occasional rattle of infantry rifles. All around fires were burning, lighting up the dark shapes of the soldiers within a small radius. Just by the nearest fires, where the light was strongest, I could make out the bare figures of soldiers waving their shirts right over the flames. Many soldiers were still awake, moving around and talking within an area of about sixty square yards. But that melancholy, deathly night lent a peculiar, mysterious air to every movement, as if the men were affected by the dismal silence and were afraid to disturb its peace and harmony. Whenever I spoke I felt that my voice sounded different and I could read the same mood on the face of every soldier sitting by the fire. Before I arrived I thought that they had been discussing their wounded comrade. Not a bit of it: Chikin was telling everyone about receiving goods in Tiflis and about the schoolboys there.

Everywhere I have been, and especially the Caucasus, I have

always noted the peculiar tact shown by the Russian soldier, who, in times of danger, passes over in silence anything that could have a bad effect on his comrades' morale. The spirit of the Russian soldier, unlike that of southern nations, is not based on easily inflammable but rapidly waning enthusiasm: it is as difficult to rouse him to action as to demoralize him. He needs no special effects – speeches, war-cries, songs or drums. On the contrary: he needs order, and calm, and a complete lack of pressure. In the Russian – the *true* Russian – soldier, one will never encounter boasting, any kind of bravado or the desire to stupefy or excite himself in times of danger. On the contrary: humility, modesty and the ability to see in danger something quite different from danger are the distinctive features of his character. I once saw a soldier with a leg wound, whose first thoughts were of the hole in his sheepskin coat, and a cavalryman who crawled out from under his horse that had just been killed and unbuckled the girths to save the saddle. Who can ever forget that incident during the siege of Gergebil, when the fuse of a live bomb caught fire in a laboratory and the gun-sergeant ordered two soldiers to run and throw it into a ravine. But they did not get rid of it at the nearest point, which was just by the colonel's tent, on the edge of the ravine, but ran further away with it lest they wake the gentlemen asleep in the tent and as a result were both blown to bits. I can still remember the time when, during the campaign of 1852, a young soldier happened to comment, during some action, that the platoon didn't have a hope in hell of getting out alive, whereupon the entire platoon furiously attacked him for such a cowardly remark, which they could not even bring themselves to repeat. And now, when everyone's thoughts must have been of Velenchuk, when Tartars might creep up on us and fire a volley any moment, everyone listened to Chikin's lively tale and no one mentioned either the day's action, or the impending danger, or the wounded comrade, just as if it had all happened God knows how long ago, or not at all. But it did strike me that their faces were somewhat gloomier than usual: they did not pay much attention to Chikin's story and even Chikin felt that they were not listening. All the same, he carried on.

Maximov came over to the fire and sat beside me. Chikin made room for him, stopped talking and started sucking his pipe again.

'The infantry have sent to the camp for some vodka,' Maximov said after a rather long silence. 'The sergeant said that he saw our Velenchuk there.'

'Well, is he alive?' Antonov asked, turning his mess tin.

'No, he died.'

The young recruit suddenly raised his small head with its red cap above the fire, stared at Maximov and me for a minute or so and then quickly lowered it again and wrapped himself tighter in his greatcoat.

'So, you see, death didn't call on him for nothing this morning when I had to wake him up in the artillery park,' Antonov remarked.

'Rubbish!' Zhdanov retorted, turning a smouldering log; everyone fell silent.

Amidst the general silence a shot rang out behind us in the camp. Our drummers replied by beating the tattoo. When the last drum rolls had died away, Zhdanov was first to get to his feet and take off his cap.

We all followed his example.

A harmonious chorus of manly voices echoed in the deep silence of the night.

'Our Father, which art in heaven, hallowed be Thy name. Thy kingdom come. Thy will be done on earth, as it is in heaven. Give us this day our daily bread and forgive us our debts as we forgive our debtors. Lead us not into temptation, but deliver us from evil . . .'

'In '45 a soldier was struck by a shell just here,' Antonov said after we had put our caps on and sat down again by the fire. 'We carted him around for two days on a gun carriage – do you remember Shevchenko, Zhdanov? – and then we had to leave him under that tree over there.'

Just then an infantryman with enormous sidewhiskers and a moustache, carrying a rifle and cartridges pouch, came over to our fire.

'Give us a light for my pipe, lads,' he asked.

'Help yourself, there's plenty of fire!' Chikin said.

'I suppose it's Dargo[10] you're talking about?' the infantryman asked Antonov.

'Yes, Dargo in '45,' Antonov replied.

The infantryman shook his head, screwed up his eyes and squatted beside us.

'Yes, we had a rough time of it there,' he remarked.

'Why did you leave him?' I asked Antonov.

'He was suffering terribly from a stomach wound. Whenever we stopped he was all right, but he screamed his head off the moment we moved. He begged us to leave him, but we didn't have the heart. Well, then *they* started letting us have it. Three of our gun crew were killed and one of the officers, and somehow we got cut off from our battery. We were in a right mess and didn't think we'd ever get our guns out, what with all that mud.'

'It was muddiest of all by the Indian Mountain,'[11] a soldier said.

'Yes, that's where he got worse. Anoshenko – the old gun-sergeant – and me thought about it and decided he didn't have a dog's chance of getting out of it alive and he kept begging us in God's name to leave him there. So that's what we did. There was a tree, a kind of willow. We put some soaked rusks down in front of him – Zhdanov had a few – propped him up against that tree there, put a clean shirt on him, said a proper goodbye and left him.'

'Was he much of a soldier?'

'He was all right,' Zhdanov said.

'God only knows what became of him,' Antonov continued. 'We lost a lot of our lads there.'

'At Dargo?' the infantryman asked, rising to his feet, scraping his pipe and again screwing up his eyes and shaking his head. 'It was really tough.' And he walked away.

'Were there many from our battery at Dargo?' I asked.

'Oh yes, Zhdanov was there, myself, Patsan, who's on leave just now, and about another six – no more.'

'Has old Patsan gone on a spree? He's been away for so long now,' Chikin said, stretching his legs and laying his head on a log. 'I reckon he's been gone nearly a year now.'

'And what about you – have you had your year's leave yet?' I asked Zhdanov.

'No, not yet,' he replied reluctantly.

'But it's good to go, you know,' Antonov said. 'If you're from a rich family, or if you're able to work, it's good to go. Everyone at home's usually so pleased to see you.'

'But what if you have two brothers, like me?' Zhdanov continued. 'They have to worry about finding enough food for themselves without having to feed a soldier as well. You can't be much good after twenty-five years in the army. And who knows if they're still alive?'

'Didn't you write to them?' I asked.

'Of course I did. I sent two letters but didn't get a reply. Either they're dead or they don't write because they're living from hand to mouth themselves. So what can I do?'

'Was it long ago that you wrote?'

'The last time was when I came back from Dargo. Come on, sing us "The Little Birch Tree",' Zhdanov asked Antonov, who was sitting with his elbows on his knees, humming some tune. Antonov started singing.

'It's Grandpa Zhdanov's favourite song,' Chikin whispered to me, tugging at my coat. 'Sometimes, when Filipp Antonych sings it, he fair cries his heart out.'

At first Zhdanov sat quite still, his eyes fixed on the smouldering coals and his face extremely gloomy in the reddish glow. Then his jaws started moving faster and faster beneath the ears and finally he got up, spread his coat out and lay down in the shadows behind the fire. It was either his tossing and groaning as he settled down to sleep, or it may have been the effect of Velenchuk's death and the miserable weather on me, but I really had the impression he was crying.

The bottom of the stump that had now turned to charcoal occasionally flared up, illuminating Antonov's figure with his grey whiskers, red face and medals on the coat slung over his shoulders, or someone's boots, head or back. The same mournful drizzle was falling and that same smell of damp and smoke was in the air. All around I could see the bright dots of dying camp-fires and the plaintive sounds of Antonov's song broke the general silence. Whenever he stopped for a moment the faint, nocturnal noises of the camp – the snoring, the clash of sentries' rifles and those soft voices – seemed to take up the tune.

'Second watch! Makatyuk and Zhdanov!' shouted Maximov.

Antonov stopped singing, Zhdanov got up, sighed, stepped across a log and slowly made his way to the guns.

[15 *June* 1855]

THREE DEATHS

I

It was autumn. Two carriages were bowling along the highway at a fast trot. In the first carriage there were two women. One was a lady, thin and pale. The other was her maid, with a shiny red face and a stout figure; her short, dry hair kept straggling out from under her faded bonnet, and she pushed it back fitfully with a red hand in a torn glove. Her full bosom, covered by a thick cloth of carpet material, exuded good health, and her black eyes were busy; one moment they were peering through the window at the fields flashing by, then they would glance across diffidently at the mistress, or watch the corners of the carriage with some concern. In front of the maid's nose dangled her mistress's bonnet, hanging from the rack, and on her knees lay a puppy. Her feet, raised up on boxes standing on the floor, could just about be heard drumming along with the creaking springs and the rattling of the window-panes.

With her hands folded on her lap and her eyes shut the lady rocked feebly against the cushions placed behind her back, frowned slightly and gave a little cough from time to time. She wore a white nightcap on her head, and a light blue scarf was wound round her delicate white neck. A straight parting disappeared under her nightcap, dividing her remarkably sleek, pomaded, light brown hair, and there was something deathly and desiccated in the white skin that formed the parting. The withered, yellowing skin hung loosely over the thin but beautiful contours of her face, with crimson on her prominent cheekbones. Her lips were dry and restless, her thinning eyelashes had no curl in them, and a cloth travelling cloak lay in straight folds across her sunken chest. Even though her eyes were shut, the lady's face gave an impression of weariness, irritation and continual suffering.

A footman, wedged into his seat with his elbows on the sides, was dozing on the box. The coach driver drove his four big, sweating horses, yelling them on and glancing back now and then at another driver calling to him from a little open carriage behind them. Broad tyre tracks spread themselves evenly in speeding parallel lines along the limy, muddy road. The sky was grey and cold, and a damp mist was settling on the fields. Inside the carriage it was stuffy, smelling of eau-de-Cologne and dust. The invalid lady put her head back and opened her eyes. Her eyes were splendidly dark, and glittering.

'Again,' she said, and her beautiful thin hand nervously pushed away the hem of her maid's cloak which was brushing lightly against her leg, and her mouth was contorted with pain. Matryosha gathered up her cloak with both hands, half-rose on her strong legs and shifted away. Her fresh face was flushed bright red. The splendidly dark eyes of the invalid lady followed the maid's every movement. Her mistress gripped the seat with both hands and also tried to lift herself and sit up higher, but she couldn't manage it. Her mouth contracted and her whole face twisted itself into an expression of impotent, malevolent irony. 'A fat lot of help you are! Oh, don't bother! I can do it myself, and you needn't shove all your bags behind me. Please don't! No, don't touch me. You've no idea!' The lady closed her eyes, then raised her eyelids again sharply and glared at her maid. Matryosha looked back at her, biting her red lower lip. A heavy sigh arose in the invalid's bosom, but it was a sigh that cut itself short as it turned into a cough. She looked away, scowling, and clutched at her chest with both hands. When the coughing spasm was over she closed her eyes again and sat there without moving. The two carriages, one large and one small, drove into the village. Matryosha reached out from under her cover and made the sign of the cross.

'What is it?' asked her mistress.

'A post station, madam.'

'Why are you crossing yourself? That's what I'm asking you.'

'There's a church, madam.'

The invalid turned towards the window and began crossing herself slowly, her eyes widening at the sight of the country church that her carriage was driving past.

The two carriages stopped together by the church. From the small one two men emerged: the invalid lady's husband and a doctor. They walked over to the large carriage.

'How are you feeling?' asked the doctor, taking her pulse.

'How are you, darling? Not too tired?' asked her husband, in French. 'Would you like to get out?'

Matryosha had scraped up her belongings and was squeezing back into the corner so as not to interfere with their conversation.

'Not too bad. Just the same,' the sick woman replied. 'I'm not getting out.'

The husband stood there for a short while, then went into the station building.

Matryosha skipped down from the carriage and ran tiptoeing in through the gateway.

'If I feel bad, that's no reason for you to miss lunch.' The sick lady gave a feeble smile as she spoke to the doctor, who was standing by her window.

'They're not bothered about me, any of them,' she added, talking to herself, as soon as the doctor had walked gently away and trotted up the steps into the station house. 'They're all right, and that's all that matters. Oh! My God!'

'Well then, Edward Ivanovich,' said the husband, rubbing his hands with a cheerful smile as he welcomed the doctor in. 'I've told them to bring the lunch basket in. How does that strike you?'

'Not a bad idea,' replied the doctor.

'How is she doing, then?' the husband asked with a sigh, lowering his voice and raising his eyebrows.

'I've told you. She won't make it, not to Italy. She'll need God's grace to get to Moscow. Especially in this weather.'

'What can we do, then? Oh, my God! My God!' The husband

buried his face in one hand. 'Put it down here,' he said to the man who was bringing in the lunch basket.

'She should have stayed put,' answered the doctor with a shrug.

'Oh yes, but what could I have done?' the husband protested. 'Look, I did all I could to stop her. I told her how about the money involved, leaving the children behind, my work. She just wouldn't listen. She was planning her life abroad as if she was well again. And telling her about her condition – well, that would have been the same as killing her off.'

'She's already been killed off. That's what you must realize, Vasily Dmitrich. A person cannot live without lungs, and lungs won't grow back. It's sad, it's hard to bear, but what can you do? Only one thing matters for you and me – to give her the most peaceful ending we can. And for that we need a priest.'

'Oh, my God! You can imagine my situation, having to remind her about her last wishes. Whatever happens, I'm not going to talk to her about that. You know how good she is . . .'

'Well, try and persuade her to wait until the roads are frozen over,' said the doctor, with a meaningful shake of his head. 'Otherwise something nasty might happen out on the road . . .'

'Aksyusha! Hey, Aksyusha!' yelled the stationmaster's daughter, throwing a jacket over her head and stamping on the dirty back porch. 'Let's go and have a look at that Shirkin lady. She's supposed to be goin' abroad with that disease in her chest. I ain't never seen how it is with them consumptives.'

Aksyusha skipped out on to the threshold, and both girls ran out through the gate, linking hands. They slowed down, walked past the carriage and took a look in through the lowered window. The sick lady turned to face them, but when she saw their curiosity she scowled and looked away.

'Gosh!' said the stationmaster's daughter, whirling her head round. 'She must have been a real beauty – and now look what's happened to her. It's horrible. Did you see her, Aksyusha? Did you see her?'

'Yes, all thin, wasn't she?' said Aksyusha, eager to back her up. 'Let's go and have another look, as if we're going to the well. She looked away, see, and I never got a good look. It's such a pity, Masha.'

'Yes, but look at all this mud!' said Masha, and they both ran back in through the gate.

'I must be a terrible sight,' thought the invalid lady. 'Must get going, as soon as we can, go abroad. I'll soon get better there.'

'Now then, how are you feeling, my dear?' said her husband, coming over to the carriage and chewing as he came.

'Always the same question,' thought the sick woman, 'but he's eating.'

'So-so,' she managed to get out, through clenched teeth.

'Do you know what, my dear, I'm afraid you're going to feel worse out on the road in this weather, and Edward says the same. Don't you think we should go back home?'

Furious with him, she said nothing.

'The weather might improve, the road could harden up, and you might feel better. Then we could all travel together.'

'I'm sorry. If I had stopped listening to you ages ago I'd be in Berlin by now, and I'd be better again.'

'We can't help it, my angel. It just wasn't possible, as you know. And now, if you would just stay on for another month, you'd feel so much better, I could get my business finished and we could bring the children . . .'

'The children are well. I'm not.'

'Darling, you must understand. In this kind of weather, if you take a turn for the worse out on the road . . . I mean, when you're at home, at least . . .'

'What? What could I do at home? . . . Die there?' The sick woman's response was venomous. But the word 'die' had clearly shaken her; she looked at her husband imploringly, her eyes questioning. He looked down, saying nothing. The woman's mouth crumpled like a child's, and tears streamed from her eyes. The husband buried his face in a handkerchief, and he walked away from the carriage without a word.

'No, I'm going on,' she said, raising her eyes to the heavens and folding her arms. She began to whisper incoherently. 'Oh my God, what's it all for?' she said, her tears flowing faster than ever. For some time she prayed, fervently, but her chest felt so painful and tight, the sky, the fields and the road looked so steeped in their gloomy grey, and the autumn mist never thickened and never thinned as it drizzled down in the same old way on to the muddy road, the roofs, the carriage and the thick coats of the drivers chatting to each other in ringing, cheerful voices while they greased the wheels and got the horses ready for the carriage.

2

The carriage was ready, but the driver was in no hurry. He had disappeared into the drivers' cabin. Inside it was hot and stuffy, dark and oppressive, smelling of people, newly baked bread, cabbage and sheepskins. There were one or two drivers there, a cook was fussing over the stove, and on the stove-top itself a sick man lay stretched out on some sheepskins.

'Uncle Fedya! Hey, Uncle Fedya!' said the young driver, still wearing his top-coat and a whip in his belt, as he came in and spoke to the sick man.

'What'm you doin' hangin' about here askin' after Fedya?' responded another driver. 'Look, they'm waitin' for you out in the carriage.'

'I want to ask him about his boots. Mine are worn out,' answered the young man, tossing his hair back and straightening the mittens in his belt. 'Maybe he's asleep. Hey, Uncle Fedya!' he repeated, walking over to the stove.

'You what?' came a feeble voice, and a thin, ruddy face bent down from the stove-top. A broad, skinny, pale and hairy arm jerked a coat up over a bony shoulder in a dirty shirt. 'Give us something to drink, me lad. What was you saying?'

The lad offered him some water in a dipper.

'Well, Fedya, it's . . . er . . . like this,' he said, shifting from one foot to the other, 'I don't imagine you needs new boots now. You could let me 'ave 'em. Seems as if you won't be doing no walking.'

The sick man brought his weary head down to the shiny dipper, wetting his thin, straggling whiskers in the dark water as he drank feebly but thirstily. His matted beard was dirty, and his sunken clouded eyes didn't find it easy to look up at the young man's face. Finishing with the water, he tried to lift one hand to wipe his wet lips, but he couldn't manage it and he wiped himself on the coat sleeve. Saying nothing, he breathed in heavily through his nose and looked the young man straight in the eye, getting his strength up.

'Maybe they're already spoken for,' said the young man. 'If they are, it doesn't matter. The thing is – it's wet out there, and I've got my work to do, and I just thought I'd ask old Fedya about his boots – maybe he don't need them any more. Perhaps you do need them. Just tell me . . .'

There was a rumbling and a gurgling in the sick man's chest. He bent double and started choking on a throaty cough that never really got going.

'How can he need them?' the cook snapped unexpectedly, speaking angrily to the whole cabin. 'He ain't been down off that stove for a couple of months. You can hear him. Gives you a pain inside just to listen to him. Can't be needing no boots, can he? They're not going to bury him with new boots on. His time's up, God forgive me, I'm a sinner. You can see he's cracking up. He ought be taken away into another hut or somewhere else. What I'm saying is, there's hospitals in town. And what right has he got taking up all that corner? No two ways about it. Some of us don't have no room at all. And they keeps telling you to keep the place clean.'

'Hey, Sergey! Get yourself on board. The master and mistress is waiting,' called the post-controller from outside.

Sergey made as if to go, without waiting for a response, but the sick man's eyes signalled while he was coughing that he wanted to give him an answer.

'You can have my boots, Sergey,' he said, stifling his cough. 'But listen,' he added wheezily, 'you buy me a stone when I'm dead.'

'Thanks, Uncle. All right, I'll take them. And I really will get you a stone.'

'That's it, then. You heard that, lads.' The sick man was finding it hard to speak, and he bent double again, choking.

'Sure, we heard,' said one of the drivers. 'Get going, Sergey, or the boss'll be back. That Shirkin lady's not well, you know.'

Sergey slipped off his worn-out boots – they were too big for him – and chucked them under the bench. Uncle Fyodor's new boots fitted him nicely, and Sergey looked down at them as he walked out to the carriage.

'Nice pair of boots! Let me grease them for you,' said a driver with a handful of axle grease as Sergey got up on his box and gathered the reins. 'Got 'em for nothing?'

'Not jealous, are you?' Sergey replied, half-rising and tucking the bottom of his coat round his legs. 'Forget it! Come on, me beauties!' he cried to the horses, cracking the whip, and the two carriages – one large and one small, with their drivers, bags and baggage – disappeared into the grey autumn mist, rocking as they sped away down the wet road.

The sick driver was left behind on his stove in the stuffy hut. Unable to stifle his coughing, he made a big effort, turned on to his other side and lay there still and quiet.

The hut was busy until late in the day with people coming and going and having their supper. Not a sound came from the sick man. As night drew on, the cook climbed up on to the stove and reached across his legs to get at her long coat.

'Don't moan at me, Nastasya,' said the sick man. 'I'll soon make room for you in this corner.'

'All right. All right. Don't go on about it. 'Taint nothing,' muttered Nastasya. 'Where's it hurt, Uncle? You can tell me.'

'It's me insides. All gone wrong. God knows what.'

'Throat giving you trouble, with all that coughing?'

'It all hurts. Time for me to die – and that's it. Oh, oh, oh . . .' moaned the sick man.

'Cover your feet up. 'Ere, like this,' said Natasha, clambering down and pulling his coat over him as she did so.

A night light burned feebly in the hut. Nastasya and a dozen drivers were asleep on the floor or on benches, snoring loudly. Only the sick man could be heard wheezing and coughing as he tossed and turned on the stove. When morning came he was completely quiet.

'I've had a fantastic dream,' said the cook, stretching herself in the half-light of a new morning. 'Uncle Fyodor got down from the stove and went out to chop some wood. "Come on, Nastasya," he says. "Let me give you some help." And I says to him, "How can you go out chopping wood?" but off he goes with the axe, chopping away like mad and the chips flying everywhere. "What's all this?" I says. "I thought you was ill." He says, "No, I'm all right now", and he swings that axe round – scared me stiff, he did. I shouted out and woke up. He's not dead, is he? Uncle Fyodor. Hey, Uncle!'

Fyodor didn't answer.

'I wonder if he has died. Ought to go and have a look,' said one of the drivers, who had just woken up.

The scrawny arm dangling down from the stove, covered in reddish hair, was cold and pale.

'Go and tell the boss it looks like he's dead,' said the driver.

Fyodor didn't have any relatives – he came from miles away. They buried him the next day in the new cemetery beyond the wood, and for several days Nastasya went around telling everybody about her dream and how she had been the first to find out Uncle Fyodor was dead.

3

It was now spring. Gurgling rivulets of water ran down the wet city streets, scurrying between frozen chunks of manure; people bustled about in a bright display of colour and sound given off by their clothing and their chatter. In little fenced-off gardens the buds had begun to swell on the trees, and you could just catch the murmur of branches rocking in the breeze. Limpid droplets dripped and trickled everywhere . . . Sparrows squawked and twittered amidst a fluttering of tiny wings. On the sunny side, on fences, houses and trees, everything shimmered and shone. Joy and youth shone in the sky, and on earth and in the heart of man.

One of the main streets, outside a large house belonging to a member of the gentry, had been strewn with fresh straw; inside, the lady who had been rushing to travel abroad lay dying.

The sick lady's husband and an elderly woman stood by the

closed doors of her room. On the sofa sat a priest with downcast eyes, holding on to something wrapped in his stole. In one corner an old woman reclined in a high-backed armchair – the sick lady's mother – weeping bitter tears. At her side, holding a clean handkerchief, stood a maid waiting to be called; another maid was using some sort of cloth to massage the old woman's temples while she blew upon her grey head under her cap.

'Christ be with you, my dear,' said the husband of an elderly lady standing with him by the door. 'She has so much faith in you, and you know exactly how to talk to her. Try and persuade her, as nicely as you can. Go in and see her.'

He was about to open the door for her, but she, a cousin of the invalid, stopped him, pressed a handkerchief to her eyes several times, and shook her head.

'Now I don't look as if I've been crying,' she said, opening the door herself and walking through.

The husband was in a state of extreme agitation; he looked distraught. He set off towards the old woman, but within a few strides he turned away and headed for the priest. The priest looked at him, raised his eyebrows to Heaven and sighed. His thick beard, shot through with grey, also raised and lowered itself.

'My God, my God!' said the husband.

'What can we do?' said the priest with another sigh, and once again his eyebrows and his short beard were raised and lowered.

'And her mother's here!' said the husband, on the verge of despair. 'That will finish her off. So much love, so much love for her, and she . . . oh, I don't know. Maybe you could comfort her, Father, and get her to go away.'

The priest got up and went to the old lady.

'Quite so,' he said. 'No one can appreciate a mother's heart. But God is merciful.'

The old lady's face suddenly started to twitch all over, and she was retching with hysteria.

'God is merciful,' continued the priest once she was a little calmer. 'I can tell you this. In my parish there was a man who was ill – much worse than Marya Dmitrievna – and – do you know what? – he was cured in no time by a tradesman with some herbs. And you'll find that tradesman alive in Moscow today. I was just saying to Vasily Dmitrievich that we might give him a try. At least it would bring some comfort to the poor woman. For God, all things are possible.'

'No, she's not going to live,' put in the old woman. 'It should be me, but God's taking her.' And her hysterical retching came on so strongly that she fell into a faint.

The invalid's husband buried his face in his hands and rushed out of the room.

Out in the passage the first person he ran into was a six-year-old boy chasing a younger girl as fast as his legs would carry him.

'What would you like me to do? Should I take the children in to see their mother?' asked the nanny.

'No, she doesn't want to see them. It will upset her.'

The boy stopped for a moment, looked his father straight in the face, lashed out with his foot and ran off again yelling with delight.

'She's being a black horse, Daddy!' cried the little boy, pointing to his sister.

Meanwhile, in the next room the invalid's cousin was sitting at her side, conducting a forced conversation in which she was trying to prepare her for death. The doctor stood by another window, stirring his drink.

The sick woman was sitting up in bed, clad in a white dressing-gown and beset with pillows on every side, watching her cousin in silence.

'Oh, my dear friend,' she said, suddenly interrupting, 'don't prepare me. Don't treat me like a child. I'm a Christian. I know it all. I know I haven't got long to live, and I know that if only my husband had listened to me I'd have been in Italy by now, and I might have been better – I probably *would* have been. Everybody told him. But there's nothing we can do. It seems to have been God's will. We all bear many sins, I know that, but I trust in God's mercy that all will be forgiven. It must surely be that all will be forgiven. I am trying to come to terms with myself. I too have borne many sins, my dear. But think how much I have suffered. I've tried to bear my sufferings with patience . . .'

'So, should I tell the priest to come in? You'll feel better when you've taken communion,' said her cousin.

The invalid inclined her head in agreement.

'God forgive me, sinner that I am,' she whispered.

Her cousin went out and winked at the holy father.

'She's an angel!' she said to the husband with tears in her eyes.

The husband burst into tears, the priest walked in through the door, the old woman was still lost to the world, and in the room itself all was completely quiet. Five minutes later the priest emerged from the room, took off his stole and ran a hand through his hair.

'Thank God she's calmer now,' he said. 'She wants to see you.'

The cousin and the husband went in. The invalid was weeping softly, looking at an icon.

'Well done, my darling,' said her husband.

'Thank you! I feel so well now. I feel a kind of sweetness,' said the invalid, a gentle smile playing on her thin lips. 'God is so merciful! Isn't that right? So merciful, and omnipotent.' And she looked at the icon again, her eyes brimming with tears and eager with supplication.

Then suddenly she seemed to remember something. She beckoned her husband closer. 'You never want to do what I ask,' she said in a feeble and petulant voice.

Her husband craned his neck, listening submissively. 'What's that, darling?'

'How many times have I told you the doctors are ignorant? There are folk healers, and they can cure people . . . The priest was telling me just now . . . about a tradesman . . . Send for him.'

'Who?'

'Oh God! You're determined not to understand! . . .' The invalid scowled and closed her eyes.

The doctor came over and took her hand. Her pulse was getting noticeably weaker and weaker. He winked at the husband. The invalid noticed the gesture and looked round in alarm.

'Don't cry, and torment yourself or me,' said the patient. 'You're taking away my last consolation.'

'You're an angel!' said her cousin, kissing her hand.

'No. Kiss me here. Only dead people get kissed on the hand. Oh God! Oh God!'

By that evening the patient had become a body, and the body lay in its coffin in the biggest room in the large house. A deacon sat alone in that great room with the doors wide open, intoning the Psalms in a nasal voice. A bright waxy light fell from the tall silver candlesticks on to the pallid face of the dead lady, the heavy waxen hands and the frozen folds of her pall, which stuck up horribly at her knees and toes. The deacon droned on, with no understanding of his words – words which rang out and died away horribly. Now and then the sounds of children's voices and their rumpus floated in from a distant room.

'Thou hidest Thy face, they are troubled,' ran the psalter. 'Thou takest away their breath, they die and return to their dust. Thou sendest forth Thy spirit, they are created, and Thou renewest the face of the earth. The glory of the Lord shall endure for ever.'

The face of the dead lady was stern, tranquil and majestic. Neither on her clear cold brow nor on her tightly closed lips was there any movement. She was all ears. But was she even now understanding those solemn words?

4

A month later a stone chapel had been erected above the dead lady's grave. Above the driver's grave the stone had yet to appear; nothing more than bright green grass came up from the mound that served as the only indication of the past existence of a man.

'It'll be a sin on your conscience,' said the cook one day at the post station, 'if you don't buy a stone for Fyodor. You kept on saying, "It's winter. It's winter," but now it's different – why don't you keep your promise? You know I witnessed it. He's been back once to ask why you haven't bought it. Next time he'll throttle you.'

'What are you on about? Have I gone back on my word?' Sergey answered. 'I'm going to buy him a stone, like I said, and I will. I'll shell out one and a half roubles. I haven't forgotten, but it's got to be fetched. When I'm in town I'll go and buy it.'

'At least you ought to stick a cross up, that's what I says,' put in an old driver. ' 'Tis just plain wrong if you don't. You'm wearing his boots.'

'Where am I going to get a cross from? I can't chop one out of a log.'

'Can't chop one out of a log – what are you talking about? Take your axe, get yourself out in the forest first thing, and you can cut one there. Go on, cut a little ash tree down . . . and there's your cross. Either that or buy the forester a few drinks. Doesn't mean you've got to treat him for any old bit of rubbish. Couple of days ago when I broke me splinter bar I cut meself a smashing new one, and nobody said nothing about it.'

Early next morning at the crack of dawn Sergey took his axe and went into the woods.

Everything was covered with a cold blanket of dew that was still settling, untouched by the sun. The east was getting imperceptibly brighter, reflecting its feeble light on the vault of heaven that was still thinly veiled with clouds. Not a blade of grass below, not a leaf on the topmost branches stirred. Only now and then the disturbing sounds of wings flapping in the brushwood or a rustling on the ground intruded on the silence of the forest. Then suddenly a strange noise, alien to the world of nature, rang out and died away on the edge of the forest. But the noise came again and repeated itself rhythmically at the bottom of the trunk of one of the motionless trees. One of the treetops gave an unusual shudder, its sappy leaves whispering, and a little robin who had been sitting on one of its branches gave a chirrup and flitted about a couple of times before cocking its tail and transferring to another tree.

Down below, the ring of the axe sounded more and more muffled, sappy white splinters flew down on to the dewy grass, and through the chopping came a slight creaking sound. The tree shook throughout its whole body, lurched over and quickly straightened up, wobbling with alarm upon its roots. Everything was quiet for a moment, but then the tree lurched again, another creak came from its trunk, and with its branches snapping and its boughs dangling it crashed down crown first on to the damp ground. The sounds of chopping and the footsteps stopped. The robin gave a chirrup and fluttered up higher. Its wings snagged against a twig, which shook for a moment or two before settling its leaves like all the others. The trees revelled in the beauty of their branches all the more joyously in the newly created space.

The first rays of the sun found their way through the thinning clouds, shone out against the sky and ran across the ground and sky together. Mist rolled down the valleys in waves, the dew glittered as it toyed with the greenery, and limpid whitening cloudlets sped across the azure firmament. Birds stirred in the thickets, twittering their happy song for all they were worth. On high, the succulent leaves whispered in peace and joy, and the boughs of the living trees slowly stirred themselves, looking down in majesty on the dead tree that lay flat out on the ground.

POLIKUSHKA

I

'You'll have to give the order, madam. It is a pity about the Dutlovs, though. They're all good lads, but one of them will have to go unless we send a house serf,' said the steward. 'As things stand, though, everybody's pointing in their direction. Anyway, it's your decision.'

And he placed his right hand over his left, holding them together over his stomach as he tilted his head away from her and sucked in his thin lips, almost tut-tutting; meanwhile he rolled his eyes, said nothing more and made it clear that he was going to keep quiet for some time to come while he listened without interrupting to the utter nonsense that his mistress was about to come out with.

He was a steward who had come up through the servant ranks. Clean-shaven and sporting the long coat that is the distinguishing feature of a steward, he stood before his mistress on an autumn evening, having come to report. For the mistress the concept of reporting meant listening to his account of estate business past and future. For Yegor Mikhaylovich, the steward, it meant standing ceremoniously in a corner with his toes turned out, eyes on the sofa, listening to all sorts of irrelevant chatter and using every trick in the book to bring his mistress to the point where her patience would run out and she would snap, 'Go on then' to everything Yegor Mikhaylovich was proposing.

Today's topic was conscription for military service.[1] The village of Pokrovskoye was required to provide three men. Two were settled beyond doubt, ordained by fate through a combination of family circumstances, morality and economics. As far as they were concerned there could be no shilly-shallying, no arguing of their case by the commune, the mistress or public opinion. The third place was open to question. The steward wanted to exempt Dutlov, even though he came from a three-man family, and send a married house serf called Polikey (or Polikushka) who had an extremely bad reputation, more than once having been caught stealing sacks, tackle and corn. But the mistress, who had often cosseted his ragged children and was using biblical precepts to improve his moral condition, did not want to give him up. At the same time, however, she wished no ill on the Dutlovs, whom she did not know and had never set eyes on. Somehow she couldn't get it into her head, and the steward couldn't bring himself to tell her straight out, that if Polikushka didn't go, a Dutlov would. 'No, I don't want the Dutlovs to suffer,' she would say, with feeling. 'If you won't do it, just cough up three hundred roubles for somebody else,' is what she should have been told in response. But that would have been impolitic.

And so Yegor Mikhaylovich took up an easy stance, even leaning surreptitiously against the doorpost, though a look of servility never left his face as he watched his mistress's lips moving and her cap frills dancing with matching shadows under the picture on the wall. But he felt no need whatsoever to grapple with the meaning of what she was saying. A spasm of yawning caught him behind the ears, but he was smart enough to convert the trembling into a cough, covering up with one hand and pretending to have a frog in his throat. Not long ago I was watching as Lord Palmerston sat there with a hat over his face while a member of the opposition was fulminating against the government, only for him to rise suddenly and launch into a three-hour oration, rebutting his opponent's every last point. I watched this and was not surprised because I had seen the like of it a thousand times between Yegor Mikhaylovich and his mistress. He may have been afraid of nodding off, or perhaps he felt that she was getting carried away, but now he simply transferred his bulk from his right foot to his left and spoke, beginning as always with an unctuous preamble.

'May it please you, madam . . . it's just that, er . . . it's just that there's a meeting being held now outside my office, and we must bring things to a conclusion. The order says we have to get the recruits into town before the Feast of Pokrov.[2] The Dutlovs are being put forward, and nobody else. And the commune doesn't take your interests into account. They don't mind us ruining the Dutlovs. But I know what a struggle they've had. They've been living in poverty ever since I took over. The old man's just finished waiting for his youngest nephew to grow up, and now they're going be ruined again. You know me. As I'm sure you're kind enough to acknowledge, I look after your property as if it was my own. It's a pity, madam, whatever you may think. They're not my kith and kin, and they haven't slipped me anything –'

'I'm sure I never thought they had, Yegor,' the mistress cut in, and immediately it occurred to her that he had been bribed by the Dutlovs.

'And there's no better farmstead in the whole of the village. God-fearing, hard-working peasants they are. The old man's been a church elder for thirty years, he doesn't drink and he doesn't use bad language. He is a church-going man.' (The steward knew how to get round people.) 'But I'm telling you – the most important thing is this. He only has two sons. The others are nephews. The commune points to them, but the truth is they ought to count as a two-man family in the ballot. Other families, some with three sons, have split up because they are so feckless, and now they're all right, while these have to suffer because they're good-living people.'

By this time the mistress was taking nothing in. She was not taking in the meaning of 'a two-man family in the ballot' or 'good-living people', she was just hearing words and studying the nankeen buttons on the steward's coat: the top one was probably not buttoned very often because it looked firm, whereas the middle one had come away and was hanging loose – it should have been sewn back on long before now. But, for the purposes of conversation, especially business conversation, everyone knows that you don't have to take in what is being said to you, you just have to remember what you wanted to say. That is how the mistress was proceeding.

'You don't seem to get it into your head, Yegor Mikhaylovich,' she said. 'I certainly don't want one of the Dutlovs to go for a soldier. I'm sure you can judge from what you know of me that I do what I can to help my peasants, and I do not wish them any harm. You know I would sacrifice everything to avoid this grievous necessity and make sure that neither Dutlov nor Khoryushkin goes.' (I cannot say whether the thought occurred to the steward that to avoid this grievous necessity it wasn't necessary to sacrifice *everything* – three hundred roubles would have been enough – but it may well have done.) 'But I have only one thing to say to you: nothing will make me send Polikey. After that business with the clock, when he came and made a clean breast of it and he wept and swore to go straight, I had a long talk to him, and I could see he was moved and truly repentant.' (That's it. She's off again, thought Yegor Mikhaylovich, and he turned his attention to the syrup she had dropped into her glass of water – was it orange or lemon? Must be something bitter, he thought.) 'That was seven months ago and in all that time he's never been drunk and his behaviour has been impeccable. His wife has told me he's not the same man. How can you possibly want me to punish him just when he's reformed? And wouldn't it be inhuman to send a man with five children and only him to look after them? No, you'd better not say any more about it, Yegor . . .'

And the mistress drank from her glass.

Yegor Mikhaylovich followed the water as it went down her throat. His response was sharp and succinct.

'So, you want me to send Dutlov?'

'Don't you understand what I'm saying? Do I wish Dutlov any harm? Have I got it in for him? As God's my witness, I'm ready to do anything for them.' (She glanced at the picture in the corner, but suddenly realized it wasn't a holy one.) 'Never mind,' she thought. 'That's not the point.' (Again, it was curious that the idea of three hundred roubles never occurred to her.) 'Well, what do I do? Do you think I know the ins and outs of this? I can't possibly know. I rely on you, and you know what I want. Just do something that will leave everybody happy, without breaking the law. They're not the only ones – everybody has a bad time now and then. But Polikey cannot be sent. You must understand – it would be terrible coming from me.'

She would have said more – she was in full flight – but at that moment a maid came into the room.

'What do want, Dunyasha?'

'A peasant has come and told me to ask Yegor Mikhaylovich whether the meeting should wait for him to come back,' said Dunyasha, with an angry look at Yegor Mikhaylovich. (Oh, that steward, he's gone and upset the mistress, she was thinking. Now it'll be two in the morning before we get to sleep.)

'You must go, Yegor,' said the mistress. 'Just do the best you can.'

'Yes, ma'am.' (He said nothing more about Dutlov.) 'But who shall I send to fetch the money from the market gardener?'

'Is Petrusha not back from town?'

'No, ma'am.'

'Can't Nikolay go?'

'His dad's laid up with a bad back.'

'Would you like me to go tomorrow?' asked the steward.

'No. I need you here, Yegor.' (The mistress had a sudden thought.) 'How much is involved?'

'Four hundred and sixty-two roubles, madam.'

'Send Polikey,' said the mistress decisively, looking Yegor Mikhaylovich straight in the face.

Yegor Mikhaylovich twisted his lips into something resembling a smile, without showing his teeth. His face did not change.

'Yes, madam.'

'Send him to me.'

'Yes, madam.'

And Yegor Mikhaylovich walked off to his office.

2

Polikey, as a person of no standing and with a tarnished reputation, born in another village, had no one to look after his interests, neither housekeeper, butler, steward nor maid, and his *corner* was the worst one, even though he had a wife and family to support. The *corners* had been set up by the late master in the following way: in the middle of a stone-built house, about twenty-three feet square, stood a Russian stove with a passage around it that the house serfs called a 'cóllidor', and each *corner* was boarded off. This meant there was very little space, especially in Polikey's *corner* right next to the door. The entire *corner* was taken up by the conjugal bed with its quilt and cotton-print pillows, a cradle with a baby in it, a small three-legged table used for preparing meals, doing the washing and accommodating all the household bits and pieces, and also for Polikey to work on (he was a horse doctor), little tubs, clothing, chickens, a calf and the family of seven, and there wouldn't have been room to turn round if it hadn't been for the communal stove, a quarter of which presented itself as a place for things and people to lie on, and also the chance of going out on to the porch. And even that was not always possible; October was a cold month and the only item of warm clothing was one sheepskin coat between the seven of them. Still, the little ones kept warm by running about and the older ones by working, and both lots by climbing up on to the stove, which could get up to forty degrees. It may seem too ghastly for people to live in conditions like these, but they didn't think so; you could get by. Akulina washed and mended for the children and her husband, did some spinning and weaving, and bleached the linen, and she quarrelled and gossiped with her neighbours while she did the cooking on the communal stove. The monthly rations fed the children, with a pinch or two left over for the cow. The firewood was free, and also the cattle fodder, and a little hay from the stables sometimes came their way. They had their own small patch in the vegetable garden. Their little cow had calved; they kept their own chickens.

Polikey worked in the stables looking after two stallions. He bled the horses and cattle, cleaned their hooves, drained their swellings and treated them with an ointment of his own making, for which he was paid in money or in kind. Some of the mistress's oats were always going spare, and for a couple of portions a peasant in the village would let them have twenty pounds of mutton a month. It would have been a decent living if it hadn't been for certain troubles of the spirit, real troubles that affected the whole family. Polikey had grown up on a stud farm in a nearby village. He fell into the hands of a groom who was the biggest crook in the district, and eventually got himself sent to Siberia. Polikey received his first lessons from this groom and by the time he became a young man he was so set in this man's *silly ways* that he couldn't stop, even though he wanted to. He was young and feckless, he had no mother or father, no one to teach him. Polikey liked a drink or two, and he couldn't bear to see things lying around. Strap or saddle, lock or bolt, or something worth a bit more – it all ended up in Polikey's hands. There were always people willing to take these things and pay for them in wine or money, by agreement. People say this is the easiest way to earn a living; no training, no effort, nothing needed, and once you've tried it you won't want any other kind of work. There's only one thing wrong with this: everything comes cheap and the living is easy, but suddenly some lousy devils will knock the bottom out of the trade, you have to stump up and life isn't fun any more.

This is what happened to Polikey. Polikey had got married, and God had looked after him. His wife, a cowherd's daughter, turned out to be a healthy, intelligent woman and a hard worker, who bore him one fine baby after another. Polikey kept on at his trade, and all was well. Then suddenly it all went wrong, and he was in trouble. He was in trouble over nothing at all – just some peasant's reins he had hidden away. But he was found out, given a thrashing and taken before the mistress, and from then on he was under observation. He was soon in trouble again, and then a third time. The people despised him, the steward threatened him with military service, the mistress rebuked him, his wife wept with a broken heart – everything was inside out. He was a nice man rather than a bad one, but he was weak, he loved his drink and he had got so used to it that he couldn't stop. His wife would shout at him and even beat him when he came home drunk, but he would collapse in tears. 'I'm a dead loss,' he would say. 'What can I do? Poke my eyes out, I'm packing it in. I won't do it again.' But lo, a month has gone by, he's away from home for a couple of days again, and he's drunk. 'Where does he get the money from to go on a drunken spree?' people wondered. His last exploit concerned the office clock. In the office there was an old-fashioned wall clock that had long since stopped working. The office was unlocked one day and he happened to go in alone. Tempted by the clock, he took it away with him, went down town and sold it. Inevitably, it would seem, the shopkeeper who took the clock off his hands happened to be related to one of the house serfs; he came to visit them in the country and told them about the clock. An investigation was conducted, though it was hardly necessary. The steward had it in for Polikey. They caught him. They told the mistress. The mistress summoned Polikey. Immediately he fell at her feet, full of emotion, movingly confessed everything, just as his wife had told him to. He played his part well. The mistress reasoned with him, she went on and on, moaning away about God and living a good life and the life to come and his wife and children until she reduced him to tears.

The mistress said, 'I forgive you. But you must promise never to do it again.'

'Never again. Cross my heart and hope to die. May my guts be torn out!' said Polikey, moving her with his tears.

Polikey went home and for a whole day he lay on the stove bellowing like a young calf. Since then Polikey had never been seen doing anything wrong. But his life had become a misery. He was looked on as a thief and, now that the time for conscription was upon them, all fingers pointed at him.

Polikey, as has been said, was a horse doctor. How he had suddenly become a horse doctor nobody knew, least of all Polikey. At the stables, working with the groom who was sent to Siberia, his only job, apart from a little grooming and carrying water, was mucking out the boxes. He couldn't have learned his trade here. Then he worked as a weaver and a gardener, clearing paths. Then he spent some time as a convict smashing bricks. Then, paying his mistress a tax for leave of absence, he hired himself out as a porter to a merchant. So, he received no training there. But during his latest spell at home he began to get something of a reputation for exceptional, almost supernatural skill with horses. He bled one horse, then another, then dragged one down, fiddled about with one of its haunches, told them to put it into a stall, and cut into its hoof frog until it bled and the horse whinnied and thrashed about, which he ignored, saying it was a question of 'draining the sub-hoof blood'. He then explained to a peasant that it was necessary to bleed both veins 'for greater ease', and he began to hit the blunt lancet with a mallet, then he bandaged the belly of the yardman's horse with a piece of selvage from his wife's headscarf. Finally, he took to splashing all sorts of sores with vitriol, treating horses with liquid from a little bottle and sometimes giving them medicine made from anything that came to hand. And the more horses he tortured to death, the more faith people had in him and the more horses they brought to him.

My feeling is that we gentlemen are hardly in a position to laugh at Polikey. The tricks he used to inspire confidence are the same ones that worked for our fathers, still work for us and will continue to work for our children. The peasant who lies with his belly pressing down on the head of his only mare – which not only constitutes his only source of wealth but is also virtually a member of the family – and whose eyes are full of trust and terror as he watches Polikey's frowning, purposeful face, his rolled-up sleeves and skinny hands as they go to work deliberately probing the very spot that hurts and cutting boldly into the living flesh (while the peasant thinks to himself, 'Bandy old girl, she'll come through it'), with the air of one who knows where to find blood, and where to find pus, and can tell a tendon from a vein, as he holds a healing swab or a bottle of vitriol between his teeth – this peasant couldn't imagine that Polikey might raise his hand to make a cut without knowing what he was doing. *He* couldn't do such a thing. And once the cut had been made he wasn't going to reproach himself for letting it go ahead when it wasn't necessary. I don't know about you, but I've experienced precisely the same thing with a doctor tormenting my nearest and dearest at my behest. The lancet, the mystery of the little white bottle of mercuric chloride, and words like *staggers*, *glanders*, *bleeding*, *draining the pus*, and so on – are they not the same as *nerves*, *rheumatism*, *organism*, and so on? 'Be bold enough to risk mistakes and dreams,' as the German saying goes, but this applies less to poets than to doctors of horses and of men.

3

On that cold, dark October evening, when the village was holding its noisy meeting outside the office to decide on the conscripts, Polikey was sitting on the edge of his bed working at the table, using a bottle to grind up some horse medicine without knowing what was in it. It contained some corrosive sublimate, some sulphur, Glauber's salt[3] and a herb that Polikey liked to pick, having got hold of the idea that it was effective with broken-winded horses and might come in handy for treating other ailments. The children were in bed, two on the stove, two on the bed itself and the baby in its cradle, next to which Akulina sat with her spinning. A candle end that had been left lying around in the mistress's house stood burning on the windowsill in its wooden holder, and Akulina would get up now and then to trim it so that her husband didn't have to interrupt his important work. Some free-thinking people considered Polikey a nonentity as a horse doctor, and as a man. Others – the majority – considered him a bad man but a great master of his trade. Akulina, though, despite all her shouting at him and even hitting him, had no doubts – he was the best horse doctor and the best man in the world. Polikey sprinkled another ingredient into the palm of his hand. (He didn't use scales, and spoke scathingly of the Germans, who did, saying, 'This isn't a chemist's shop.') Polikey threw in his handful and shook it up, but there didn't seem to be enough of it so he poured out ten times as much again. 'Chuck it all in, it'll give them more of a lift,' he mumbled to himself. Akulina looked round sharply at the words of her lord and master, anticipating some instructions, but when she saw it was nothing to do with her she gave a shrug. 'Look how clever he is! I don't know where he gets it from,' she thought as she went back to her spinning. The piece of paper which the last ingredient had been poured from fell down on to the floor. This did not escape Akulina's attention.

'Anyutka,' she called out, 'look, Daddy's dropped something on the floor. Pick it up for him.'

Anyutka put her thin little bare legs out from under the cloak that was covering her and slid down under the table like a kitten to get the piece of paper.

'Here you are, Daddy,' she said, and slipped her little cold feet back into bed.

'Don't puth me,' lisped her little sister, whining sleepily.

'I'll be after you two!' said Akulina, and both heads disappeared under the cloak.

'He'll give me three roubles,' said Polikey, corking the bottle. 'I'll put his horse right. He's getting it cheap,' he added. 'Hard on the brain, though. Akulina, slip over and get some baccy from Nikita. I'll pay him back tomorrow.'

And Polikey went through his trousers, pulled out a limewood pipe that had once been painted and now had sealing wax instead of a proper stem, and started to fiddle with it.

Akulina left her spindle and eased her way out without snagging anything, which was no mean achievement. Polikey opened a little cupboard and put the medicine bottle inside. He took down an empty little glass container and tilted it into his mouth, but there was no vodka in it. He scowled, but once his wife had brought him the tobacco and he had filled his pipe, lit up and sat back on the bed, his face took on the proud and satisfied glow of a man with a good day's work behind him. Whether or not he was thinking about tomorrow, when he would take hold of a horse by the tongue and pour his amazing mixture into its mouth, or reflecting that a man who is needed never meets with refusal – hadn't Nikita sent him some tobacco? –

he was feeling fine. Then suddenly the door, which hung on a single hinge, was flung open and into their *corner* came a girl from 'up there', not the second maid, but the third one, a slip of a girl who was kept on to run errands. ('Up there', as everyone knows, means the master's house, even if it is situated on lower ground.) Aksyuta – that was the girl's name – flew everywhere like a bullet and, as she did so, instead of bending her arms she swung them, not at her sides but out in front of her body, like two pendulums keeping time with her running speed. Her cheeks were always redder than her pink dress; her tongue always moved at the same speed as her legs. She flew into the room, grabbed hold of the stove for no apparent reason and began rocking forwards and backwards. She seemed to want to speak no more than two or three words at a time, but suddenly she turned to Akulina and gasped out the following message:

'The mistress wants Polikey up at the house this minute, she does . . .' (She stopped and took a deep breath.) 'Yegor Mikhaylovich has been talking to the mistress about the constription . . . and Polikey's name come up . . . Avdotya Nikolayevna wants him up there this minute . . . Avdotya Nikolayevna wants him' (another gasp) 'up there this minute.'

For half a minute or so Aksyuta looked at Polikey, Akulina and the children, who had stuck their heads out from under the blanket, then she grabbed a nutshell lying on the stove and threw it at Anyutka, said 'This minute' once last time and whirled out of the room. The pendulums were soon swinging at their normal speed across the line of her flight.

Akulina got to her feet again and found Polikey's boots. The boots were dreadful, all holes, a soldier's boots. She took his coat down from the stove and handed it over without looking at him.

'Aren't you going to change your shirt, Polikey?'

'Nay, I'm not,' said Polikey.

Akulina never once looked at him as he silently put on his boots and his coat, and it was as well she didn't. Polikey's face was pale, his jaw trembled and his eyes held the kind of tearful, submissive and deeply unhappy expression that belongs only to those who are good-natured but weak and guilty. He ran a comb through his hair, and was about to walk out, but his wife stopped him and tucked in a bit of his shirt braid that was hanging down outside his coat, and put the cap on his head for him.

'What's all this, Polikey? Mistress sent for you?' called the carpenter's wife through the partition.

Only that morning the carpenter's wife had exchanged sharp words with Akulina over a pot of lye[4] that Polikey's children had knocked over in her *corner*, and her immediate reaction, on hearing that the mistress was calling for Polikey, was to be pleased – it couldn't mean anything good. Besides, she was a shrewd, politically minded woman with a sharp tongue. There was nobody better with a cutting word, or at least that was how she saw herself on the quiet.

'They must want somebody to go into town for some shopping,' she went on. 'I'm sure they'll choose somebody reliable. They'll be sending you. If they do, get me a quarter of tea, Polikey.'

Akulina was struggling with tears, and she screwed her lips into a bitter expression. She felt like grabbing that bitch of a carpenter's wife by her mangy hair, but one look at her children made her think of them as fatherless, and herself as a war widow, and she forgot the carpenter's wife with the sharp tongue, buried her face in her hands, sat on the bed and let her head fall back into the pillows.

'Mummy, you're thquashing me!' whined the lisping little girl, jerking her cloak cover out from under her mother's elbow.

'I wish you were all dead and buried. I've brought you into the world for nothing but suffering,' cried Akulina, and the whole *corner* rang to her sobbing, to the delight of the carpenter's wife, who had not forgotten that morning and the spilt lye.

4

Half an hour went by. The baby started crying. Akulina got up and fed him. She had stopped weeping, but her eyes were staring on the guttering candle and, with her thin but still beautiful face propped on one hand, she was thinking about why she had got married, why they needed so many soldiers, and also about how to get her own back on the carpenter's wife.

She heard her husband's footsteps. She wiped away the traces of her tears and stood up to let him through. Polikey walked in triumphant, tossed his cap on to the bed, breathed out noisily and started to take his belt off.

'Well? What did she want?'

'Ha. Everybody knows Polikushka's the lowest of the low. But when a job needs doing, who do they send? Polikushka.'

'What job?'

Polikey was in no hurry to reply. He lit his pipe and spat.

'I've been told to go and fetch some money from a merchant.'

'You, carrying money?'

Polikey gave a chuckle and a wag of his head.

'Right good with words, she is! "You've been under observation," says she, "what with you not bein' reliable, only I trust you more than anybody else."' (Polikey's voice was raised so the neighbours could hear.) '"You promised me you would reform," she says, "and here you are, here's the first proof that I trust you. Go and see the merchant, get the money and bring it back to me." And I says, "Madam," I says, "we'm your serfs, all of us, and we must serve you as we serve God, we must, therefore I feels I can do anything for your sake and I can't refuse no duties. Whatever you tells me, I'll do it, because I am your slave."' (He gave another chuckle, smiling that special smile, the one that belongs to those who are good-natured but weak and guilty.) '"Anyway," she says, "can you do the job properly? Do you understand," she says, "that your fate depends on this?" "How could I not understand that there ain't nothing I couldn't do? And if they've been saying things about me, well accusin' people's easy enough, but I ain't never done nothin', I tell you, nothin' that goes against you, and I wouldn't think of it." Anyway, I sweet-talked the mistress until she went all soft. "You're goin' to be my top man," she says.' (He stopped for a while, with the same smile on his face.) 'I knows a bit about sweet-talkin'. Sometimes when I was out workin' on my own I used to run straight into trouble. But just let me have a few words with the bloke an' I could smooth 'im down like silk.'

'How much money?' Akulina got in at last.

'Fifteen hundred roubles,' said Polikushka casually.

She shook her head.

'When are you going?'

'She's told me to go tomorrow. "Take any horse you want," she says. "Call in at the office, and God go with you."'

'The Lord be praised!' said Akulina, getting to her feet and making the sign of the cross. 'God help you, Polikey,' she added in a whisper so as not to be heard through the partition, holding him by the shirtsleeve. 'And you listen, Polikey. I'm asking you in the name of Jesus – when you get going, swear on the cross you won't touch a drop.'

'As if I'd have a drink when I'm riding with that kind of money!' he snorted. 'Do you know, there were somebody up there playin' the piano ever so nice. It were lovely. Must've been the young lady. I was stood there in front of her – the mistress, I mean – next to that cabinet, and the young lady, she were tinklin' away behind the door. Tinklin' away she were, tinklin' away while she got it right. What a treat! Mind you, I could've played, you know. I'd have mastered it. Wouldn't have taken me long. Good at things like that, I am. I'll need a clean shirt tomorrow.'

And they went to bed happy.

5

Meanwhile, outside the office, the noisy meeting was under way. It was no joking matter. Almost all the peasants were there and, while Yegor Mikhaylovich was away seeing the mistress, they kept their caps on. More and more voices were heard in the general clamour and they got louder and louder. The murmur of deep voices, punctuated now and then by hoarse cries and loud shouting, hovered in the air and, eventually, like the sound of a roaring ocean, it reached the windows of the mistress, where its agitating effect on her nerves was like the feeling brought on by a heavy thunderstorm. It was a mixture of discomfort and fear. She had the feeling that at any moment the voices would get louder and more insistent, and something would happen. 'As if it couldn't all be done in peace and quiet, with no arguments and no shouting,' she thought, 'in a Christian spirit of brotherly love and meekness.'

Suddenly there was an outburst of many voices, but the loudest of them belonged to Fyodor Rezun, the carpenter. Coming from a two-male family, he was attacking the Dutlovs. Old Dutlov was defending himself. Having started at the back, he had worked his way out in front of the crowd. Gesticulating frantically and pulling at his short beard, he coughed and spluttered so much as he spoke that even he would have had difficulty in understanding his own speech. His children and nephews, fine young lads all of them, clung together behind him, while old Dutlov looked like a mother hen in a game of hawk-and-chickens. The hawk was Rezun, but other people as well – all the two-male families, and those with only one male, nearly everybody there – were attacking Dutlov. The argument went as follows: Dutlov's brother had been sent as a soldier about thirty years ago, so he was claiming exemption from the list of three-male families; he wanted his brother's service to be taken into consideration, which would mean putting him into the ballot along with the *two*-male families and choosing the third recruit from the lot of them. There were four other three-male families apart from the Dutlovs, but one of them was headed by the village elder, and the mistress had granted him exemption; one of the other families had supplied a conscript last time round, and each of the other two was doing so now, with one of them absent from the meeting, though his wife cut a pathetic figure right at the back hoping vaguely for the wheel of fate to turn in her favour. The second of the two nominated young men, red-haired Roman, dressed in a tattered coat (though he was not a poor man), stood there in silence leaning against the porch with his head bowed, glancing up now and then to look closely at anyone who spoke up a little louder, only to lower his head again. This made his whole figure look a picture of misery. Old Semyon Dutlov was the sort of man that would have been entrusted with hundreds or even thousands of roubles by anyone who had the slightest knowledge of him. He was a steady, God-fearing man of no little substance, and moreover an elder of the church. Thus it was all the more striking to see him as worked up as he was now.

Rezun the carpenter was, by contrast, a tall, dark and assertive man with a stormy temperament, a drinker, good in an argument, a strong performer at public meetings, or in the market-place, and a good match for anybody – workers and tradesmen, peasants and gentry. Self-possessed but viciously effective, he now used his full height and all the power of his strong voice and rhetorical skill to bear down on the spluttering church elder, who had been completely put out and lost his composure. Others were also involved in the argument. Garaska Kopylov, a stocky, round-faced, youthful-looking, thick-set man with a square head and a curly beard – one of the speakers from the younger generation who was following on from Rezun – had a sharp turn of phrase and what he said was beginning to carry weight at village meetings. Then there was Fyodor Melnichny, a thin and lanky, round-shouldered and sallow-skinned peasant, another young man, with tiny eyes and not much of a beard; always sarcastic and sardonic, he could be relied on to see the dark side of things and he often shocked the meeting with sudden volleys of comments and questions. Both of these speakers sided with Rezun. There were also a couple of men who liked the sound of their own voices, and had to chip in now and then. One of them, Khrapkov, a man with the kindest of faces and a flowing brown beard, would keep saying, 'Oh, my dearest friend . . .' The other, a little chap by the name of Zhidkov, with a face like a small bird's, kept on saying, 'There we have it, my brothers . . .' – words that were well spoken and clearly addressed, but completely irrelevant. They kept changing sides in the argument, but no one was listening. There were others like them, but these two strutted through the crowd shouting loudest, and they frightened the mistress, though no one was listened to less than they were; carried away by the noise and shouting, they were having a wonderful time letting their tongues run free. There were all sorts of villagers there, sullen, respectable, indifferent, downtrodden; there were peasant women with sticks in their hands standing behind their men – but, God willing, I'll tell you about them some other time. Overall, though, the meeting consisted of peasants standing as they did in church, whispering at the back about day-to-day things like the best time to cut faggots in the woods, or waiting and wondering how long it would be before all the jabbering stopped. There were also some rich peasants whose prosperity couldn't have been added to or diminished by the village meeting. One such was Yermil, a man with a broad shiny face; the peasants called him 'big-belly' because he was rich. Another was Starostin, whose face exuded the self-satisfaction that comes from power, and seemed to be saying, 'Say what you like, nobody can touch me. My four lads, none of them's going.' These two were sometimes set on by free-thinking men like Kopylov and Rezun, but they spoke back calmly and firmly, knowing they were untouchable. If Dutlov was like the mother hen in the hawk-and-chickens game, his lads were not like the chickens. They stood quietly behind him without a flutter or a squawk. The eldest of them, Ignat, was thirty years old and married, as was the second son, Vasily, who was unfit for service; the third lad, Ilyusha, Dutlov's nephew, had also recently got married. Fair-haired and rosy-cheeked, dressed in a smart sheepskin coat (he worked as a driver), he stood there glancing at the crowd from time to time, occasionally scratching the back of his head under his hat as if it was nothing to do with him, whereas he was the one the hawks were after.

'Well, my grandad was a soldier,' said Rezun, 'so I'm not going in the ballot. But there ain't no such law, my friend. Last recruitment, Mikheyevich was sent, and his uncle was still away serving.'

'Your father and your uncle never served the Tsar,' Dutlov was saying at the same time. 'And you've never served the masters or the village. You've spent all your time boozing, and your kids have all gone away. Nobody can live with you, yet you go on about other people and sending them for service. Me, I've done ten years with the police and I've served as an elder. Been burnt out twice, I have, and got help from nobody, and now, just because everything's right and proper in my house, I'm facing ruin, am I? Give me my brother back, then. He's probably died out there. You should decide according to the law, and in God's name. This is a Christian village, not somewhere where they listen to a ranting drunk.'

Also at the same time Gerasim was saying to Dutlov, 'You talk about your brother, but he wasn't sent by the village, he was sent by the masters for all them things he did. You can't talk your way out of it with him.'

The words were scarcely out of Gerasim's mouth when the sallow and lanky Melnichny stepped forward and spoke gloomily.

'That's the way it is. The masters send who they want and the village has to sort it out. The village decides to send your son, but if you don't like it, go and ask the mistress. She'll maybe order me to go and get my head shaved and leave my kids behind, and I'm the only man in the family. That's what the law does,' he said bitterly before waving at them and going back to his place.

Red-haired Roman, whose son had been chosen, looked up and said, 'That's it. That's what it's all about!' and sat down furiously on the step.

But these were not the only voices to be heard all speaking at once. Apart from those at the back who were chatting about things that mattered to them, those who liked the sound of their own voices were not neglecting their duty.

' 'E's right, you know. 'Tis a Christian village,' said the diminutive Zhidkov, parroting Dutlov's words. 'We should decide like Christians. Christians, that's what we should decide like, brothers.'

'We should let conscience decide, my dearest friend,' said the kind-hearted Khrapkov, parroting Kopylov's words and catching Dutlov by his coat. 'That was the masters' will, not the village's.'

'Dead right! That's what it's all about!' said others.

'Who are you calling a ranting drunk?' Rezun protested. 'Did you pay for my drinks? And that son of yours – gets picked up at the side of the road – is he going to accuse me of drinking? Come on, brothers, we've got to decide. If you want to let the Dutlovs off you'll have to choose from families with two men, or even one, and he'll be laughing at us.'

'A Dutlov's got to go! Nothing more to be said!'

'It's obvious! Families with three have to draw lots first!' came the various voices.

'Depends what the mistress says. Yegor was saying she might send a house serf.'

This comment put a dampener on the argument for a while, but it soon flared up again, and once more it came round to personalities.

Then Ignat, the man Rezun had accused of being picked up at the roadside, laid into Rezun, saying that he had stolen a saw from the jobbing carpenters, and he had got drunk and beaten his wife to within an inch of her life.

Rezun replied that he didn't have to be drunk to beat his wife, he did it when he was sober, and she still didn't get enough of it, which made them all laugh. But when it came to the saw he suddenly took offence, stepped up closer to Ignat and asked him, 'Who are you calling a thief?'

'You,' said the sturdy Ignat brazenly, stepping closer still.

'Who was the thief? It was you, wasn't it?' roared Rezun.

'No, you!' roared Ignat.

Moving on from the saw they brought up a stolen horse, a bag of oats, an allotment that was common ground, and a dead body. And the pair of them laid such dreadful things at each other's door that if a hundredth part of the accusations had been true both men would have been exiled to Siberia – at the very least.

Old man Dutlov meanwhile had hit on a new form of defence. He didn't like all this shouting from his son. He stopped him by saying, 'That's enough. It's a sin, I tell you,' and he went on to point out that three-man families were not only those with three sons at home but also those who had split up, and he pointed to Starostin.

Starostin gave a half-smile, cleared his throat and stroked his beard with the air of a well-to-do peasant, replying that what counted was the mistress's will. His son must be a deserving case, because he had been given exemption. Gerasim also confuted Dutlov's argument by claiming that the separated families ought not to have been allowed to split up – it wouldn't have happened under the old master. But it was no good bolting the stable door when the horse had gone. And this was no time to start sending men from one-man families.

'Do you think they enjoyed being split up? Why should we ruin them now?' came voices from the separated families, and those who loved the sound of their own voices came in on that side of the argument.

'Buy your way out if you don't like it. You can afford it!' Rezun said to Dutlov.

Dutlov wrapped his coat round himself in a despairing gesture and stepped back behind the other peasants.

'You've obviously been counting my money,' he said venomously. 'Let's see what Yegor Mikhaylovich says when he gets back from seeing the mistress.'

6

And sure enough, Yegor Mikhaylovich came out of the house at that very moment. One by one caps were raised and, as the steward came forward, one by one all the heads revealed themselves, bald down the middle and at the sides, grey or grizzled, red, black or mousy, and gradually, little by little, the voices died down until eventually they had died out completely. Yegor climbed on to the verandah with the air of a man who wishes to speak. In his long coat, with his hands thrust awkwardly into the front pockets, and his factory-made cap tipped forward, standing there with his legs firmly planted and feet well apart, fully in command of the heads that were raised towards him, most of them old ones, most of them bearded and handsome, Yegor cut quite a different figure from the one that had been standing in front of the mistress. He was imperious.

'This is what the mistress has decided, lads. She can't see her way to sending one of the house serfs. The man who goes will be the one you decide on amongst yourselves. Three men are wanted – today. By rights it should be two and a half, but the half will be taken into account next time. Makes no difference – if it's not today, it'll have to be tomorrow.'

'I knew it. That's it then,' came the voices.

'As I see it,' Yegor went on, 'Khoryushkin and Vaska Mityukhin will have to go. 'Tis the Lord's will.'

'Yes, sir. 'Tis only right,' came the voices.

'The third one will have to be either one of the Dutlovs or somebody from a two-man family. What do you think?'

'One of the Dutlovs!' shouted some of the voices. 'There's three in their family!'

And now, steadily, little by little, the shouting started up again, with recriminations about the stolen saw, the strip of kitchen garden and sacks stolen from the mistress's yard. Yegor Mikhaylovich had been managing the estate for twenty years; he was an intelligent man with much experience. He stood there listening for a quarter of an hour or so, and then suddenly asked for silence and told the Dutlovs to decide who had to go by drawing lots. Straws were cut, placed in a hat and shaken up. Ilyushkin lost. No one spoke.

'Is that mine? Show me,' said Ilyushkin in a faltering voice.

Still no one spoke. Yegor Mikhaylovich told them all to bring the recruitment money tomorrow – seven kopecks from each household – and, with all the business completed, brought the meeting to a close. The crowd dispersed, caps went on heads as they rounded the corner to the murmur of voices and the shuffling of feet. The steward stood on the verandah watching them go. When the younger Dutlovs had disappeared round the corner he called to the old man, who had remained behind and now followed him into the office.

'I'm sorry for you,' said Yegor Mikhaylovich, sinking into the armchair in front of the desk, 'but it was your turn. Are you going to buy him out, that nephew of yours, or not?'

The old man gave him a meaningful look, but said nothing.

'Can't do nothing about it,' said Yegor Mikhaylovich by way of a reply to that look.

'I'd be glad to buy him out, but I can't afford it, Yegor

Mikhaylovich. Lost two horses this summer. Paid for my nephew's wedding. It's obvious, isn't it? This is what you get for being honest. It's all right for him to talk.' (He was thinking of Rezun.)

Yegor Mikhaylovich wiped his face with one hand and yawned. He had clearly had enough. It was time for a cup of tea.

'Hey, you tight-fisted old sinner,' he said, 'go and have a little look under your floor. I bet you'll turn up a good four hundred in old notes. I'll buy you a marvellous volunteer. Only the other day there was this man offering himself.'

'Where, in the *government*?' asked Dutlov, meaning the big town.

'Are you buying, then?'

'Oh, I'd love to, I swear to God, but er –'

Yegor Mikhaylovich cut him short with a stern look.

'Right. You listen to me, old man. You make sure Ilyushka don't come to no harm.[5] And when I gives the word, today or tomorrow, you bring him in. You're bringing him, and you're responsible. And if anything happens to him – God forbid – I'm sending your eldest son. Do you hear what I'm saying?'

'But aren't there any two-man families who could send somebody, Yegor Mikhaylovich? It's not fair!' he said, after saying nothing for a while. 'My brother died soldiering, so now they're taking my son. Why are they getting at me again like this?' As he spoke he was almost in tears and on the point of dropping to his knees.

'Go on. Off you go,' said Yegor Mikhaylovich. 'Can't do nothing about it. It's the way things are. Keep an eye on Ilyushka. You're responsible.'

Dutlov set off home, thoughtfully tapping with his stick at the ruts along the road.

7

Early next morning the little cart usually driven by the steward himself stood by the steps leading up into the house serfs' quarters (or 'quartels' as they called them); harnessed to it was the chunky bay gelding known for some reason as Drum. Braving the cold wind and sleet, Polikey's eldest daughter, Anyutka, stood there in her bare feet some little way ahead of the gelding, obviously frightened of him as she held on to his reins with one hand and used the other to keep her head covered by the yellow-green jacket which functioned in her family as blanket, cloak, hood, carpet, overcoat and many other things as well. It was all go in Polikey's *corner*. It was still dark, though the early-morning light of a rainy day was just beginning to force its way in through the window with its paper patches. For the time being Akulina was ignoring the cooking in the oven and the children – her youngest were still in bed, freezing because their blanket had been taken away to be used as clothing and they had been given their mother's headscarf instead. Akulina was getting her husband ready for the road. He had a clean shirt on. She was particularly concerned with his boots, which were, as the saying goes, 'asking for porridge'. To begin with she had stripped off her only pair of thick woollen stockings and lent them to her husband, then she had taken the saddlecloth that had been left lying about in the stables and had been brought home by Polikey a couple of days before, and managed to fashion a pair of insoles in such a way that they plugged the holes in his boots and kept his feet dry. Polikey himself was sitting with his feet up on the bed, rebraiding his belt so that it wouldn't look like a piece of dirty string. The irritable little girl with the lisp, wrapped in a sheepskin that trailed under her feet even though it was thrown over her head, had been sent round to Nikita's to ask for the loan of his cap. The fuss got worse as the house serfs kept calling in to ask Polikey to pick things up for them in town – a packet of needles, some tea, olive oil, baccy, and some sugar for the carpenter's wife who at that early hour had managed to get the samovar going and brought Polikey a mug of what she called tea, just to get round him. Even though Nikita wouldn't lend him his cap, which meant that Polikey had to bring his own up to standard by shoving some straggling bits of wadding back in and sewing the hole up with the help of a vet's needle, even though the boots with the saddlecloth insoles wouldn't fit at first, even though Anyutka was frozen stiff and almost let go of Drum, and Masha put the sheepskin on and went to take over from her, but then Masha had to take the sheepskin off and Akulina had to go and hold Drum herself – it all ended well: Polikey dressed himself in virtually the entire family wardrobe, leaving behind nothing but the jacket and a pair of slippers ('slippons' to them), finished getting ready, climbed into the little cart, snuggled into his coat, shook up the haysack, snuggled down again, untangled the reins, snuggled down even deeper into his coat, like a person of quality, and set off on his journey.

His little boy Mishka ran out on to the steps and insisted on being given a ride. The lisping Masha wanted a 'lide' too, because she was 'thtill warm even without the theepthkin'. Polikey reined Drum in, smiling his weak smile, while Akulina put the children on board, leaned over to him and reminded him in a whisper that he had promised not to drink anything on the journey. Polikey took the children as far as the smithy, made them get down, wrapped himself up again, straightened his cap again, and set off alone at a slow steady trot, with his cheeks wobbling at every jolt and his feet bouncing on the matting. As for the barefooted Masha and Mishka, they hurtled back home down the hill yelling so loudly that a stray dog from the village took one look at them and rushed off home barking, with its tail between its legs, which made the racket coming from Polikey's progeny ten times louder.

The weather was atrocious. A cutting wind lashed a mixture of snow, rain and hail intermittently into Polikey's face and bare hands, which he thrust down under his coat sleeves along with the cold reins, and into the leather cover of the horse collar, and on to Drum's old head, making him put his ears back and squint.

Then suddenly it began to ease up. The skies were soon clearing sharply, bluish snow clouds began to show themselves, and the sun seemed to be starting to peer through them, but only timidly and cheerlessly, like Polikey's own smile. Despite everything, though, Polikey was thinking pleasant thoughts. He, the man they wanted to send into exile or into the army, the man who was cursed and beaten by everybody who wasn't too lazy to do it, who was always shoved around worse and worse – he was now on his way to fetch a *summer* money, a big *summer* money, and the mistress trusted him, and here he was driving along in the steward's cart, with Drum pulling, the cart that the lady herself sometimes drove in, bowling along like some rich landowner, with proper leather straps and reins. And he sat up straighter, tucked some bits of wadding back into his cap and snuggled deeper into his wrappings.

However, if Polikey thought he looked the picture of a rich landowner, he was deluding himself. Everybody knows that traders worth a good ten thousand drive around in sledges with proper leather harnesses, but that's neither here nor there. A man with a beard drives past dressed in a long blue coat, or a black one, sitting alone on his box and driving a sleek horse; a quick glance to establish whether the horse is well fed, whether he is himself, how good the harness is, how good the tyres are, how big his belt is, will tell you whether this man deals in thousands or hundreds. Anyone who has been around a bit would take one good look at Polikey, at his hands, his face, his stubble, his waistline, at the straw scattered about the box all over the place, at skinny old Drum and the worn tyres, and see immediately that this is no trader, no cattle-dealer, no landowner worth thousands, hundreds or even dozens of roubles – this is a common serf. But Polikey wasn't thinking along those lines; he was deluding himself, and enjoying it. Three times five hundred roubles he would be bringing back tucked into his coat. If he wanted to, he could decide not to go home, turn Drum towards Odessa (which he called Odesta) and go wherever the fates took him. But he wasn't going to do that; he was going to deliver the money properly to his mistress and say that even this kind of money was nothing to him. When they came to an inn Drum started pulling on the left rein, turning away and wanting to stop but, although Polikey was carrying money for the various purchases, he gave Drum a taste of the whip and drove on. He did the same thing at the next inn and just before noon he got down from the cart, opened the gate leading to the merchant's house where people from the estate always stayed, led the horse and cart into the yard, unharnessed the horse and gave him some hay, ate his lunch with the merchant's workmen, not omitting to mention that he was there on important business, and then went off with the letter in his cap to see the head gardener.

The gardener read through the letter but, knowing Polikey, he looked dubious as he interrogated him closely to find out whether he really had been sent to collect the money. Polikey made a show of being offended, but he couldn't manage it; all he did was smile his own peculiar smile. The gardener read the letter again and handed over the money. On receiving the money, Polikey put it safely inside his coat and went back to the inn. No tavern or beer shop, nothing could tempt him. He was enjoying a warm feeling of excitement that ran through his whole being, and he stopped several times outside shops with alluring goods on display – boots, coats, caps, cotton material, food. But after a short stop he would walk on with his warm feeling: I could buy all that lot, but I'm not going to. He went on to the market to buy what people had asked for, and once he had got everything he started haggling over a tanned sheepskin coat priced at twenty-five roubles. The shopkeeper took one look at Polikey and for some reason seemed to doubt that he had the wherewithal to pay for it, but Polikey pointed to his inside pocket and told him he could buy the whole shop if he wanted to. He insisted on trying it on, fingered it, patted it, blew into the fur until its smell was all over him, and then took it off with a sigh. 'The price isn't right. If you could let it go for fifteen roubles . . .' he said. The dealer angrily threw the coat across the table and Polikey walked out feeling good, and went back to the inn. After supper he watered Drum and gave him his oats, then climbed up on to the stove and took out the envelope, examining it closely before asking a porter who knew how to read and write if he would read out the address and the other words: 'Enclosed: one thousand, six hundred and seventeen roubles in notes.' The envelope was made from ordinary paper and sealed with brown wax stamped with an anchor, with one big seal in the middle and four more at the corners and a few drops of sealing wax down one side. Polikey inspected all of this, committed it to memory and even felt the sharp edges of the banknotes. It gave him a kind of childish delight simply to know that he was the holder of this kind of money. He pushed the envelope into the hole in his cap, put the cap under his head and lay down on it, but during the night he woke up several times and groped for the envelope. And every time he found the envelope just where it should be he felt a thrill of pleasure at the idea that here he was, the much maligned Polikey, a man of bad reputation, carrying this kind of money and he could be relied upon to deliver it – he would deliver it more reliably than the steward himself.

8

It was about midnight when the innkeeper's men and Polikey were all woken up by a banging at the gate and peasants shouting. It was the party of conscripts from Pokrovskoye. There were about ten of them: Khoryushkin, Mityukhin and Ilya the nephew of Dutlov, two substitutes, the village elder, old man Dutlov and the drivers. A night light was burning and the cook was asleep on a bench under the icons. She jumped up and set about lighting a candle. Polikey woke up, too, leaned out over the stove and took a good look at the peasants as they entered. They came in crossing themselves and sat down on the benches. All of them were so perfectly calm that you couldn't tell who were the conscripts and who was delivering them. They were saying hello, chattering amongst themselves and asking for food. True, some of them were quiet and gloomy, but then there were others who were unusually merry, obviously having had a few drinks, including Ilya, who had never been a drinker before.

'Right, lads. Sleep or supper, what do you want?' asked the elder.

'Supper,' said Ilya, throwing his heavy coat open wide and settling on a bench. 'Get some vodka.'

'I'll give you vodka,' snapped the elder, turning to the others. 'Right. Have a bite of bread, lads. No need to wake everybody up.'

'Gimme some vodka,' Ilya repeated, looking at no one in particular. His voice made it clear that he would take some stopping.

The peasants did what the elder had told them; got some bread from their cart, asked for a drink of rye beer and went to lie down on the floor or on the stove.

Now and again Ilya could be heard repeating, 'Gimme some vodka. I'm telling you I want some vodka.' Suddenly he caught sight of Polikey.

'Polikushka. Hey, Polikushka! You're here, my good friend. Know something? I'm off into the army. Said goodbye to my mum and my missus – for ever. She didn't half howl! Into the army. Cooked my goose, they did. Give us some vodka.'

'Can't afford it,' said Polikey. 'Anyway, you might get rejected,' he added by way of consolation.

'No chance, old pal. I'm as clean as a birch tree. Never had no illness. Why would I get rejected? The Tsar won't find no fitter soldiers than me.'

Polikey launched into a story about a peasant lad who had slipped the doctor a note and got off.

Ilya moved over to the stove and spoke more freely.

'No, Polikushka. That's it. And I don't want to stay now. It was my uncle what cooked my goose. Do you think he couldn't have bought me out? Thinks too much of his own lad, he does – and his money. So I gets sent . . . Don't want to stay now.' (He spoke softly, confidingly, deeply moved by his own sadness.) 'I am sorry for my dear old mum, though. She was right upset! And the missus, too. They've done for her, and no reason for it. She's had it now. Soldier's wife – say no more. Better off not getting married. Why did they want me to get married? They're coming here tomorrow.'

'But why did they bring you here as early as this?' asked Polikey. 'First we heard nothing, then all of a sudden . . .'

'Well, you know how it is, they thought I might do meself an injury,' said Ilya with a grin. 'No chance. I'm not doing nothing. When I'm a soldier I won't come to no grief. But I am sorry for my mum. Why did they want me to get married?' he said, softly and sadly.

The door opened and banged to. In came old man Dutlov, shaking the wet off his cap, as always wearing bark-fibre shoes that made him look as if he had his feet stuck into great big boats.

'Afanasy,' he said, crossing himself as he turned towards the porter, 'can I have a light? I need to get some oats.'

Dutlov had not looked across at Ilya; he slowly began to light a bit of candle. His coat was neatly belted, with his mittens and whip tucked into his waistband. With his working man's face wearing its usual nice and easy expression, preoccupied with the job in hand, he looked for all the world as if he had just arrived in charge of a wagon train.

When Ilya caught sight of his uncle he stopped speaking, gloomily looked down again vaguely in the direction of the bench, and then said to the village elder, 'Yermila. Get me some vodka. I want a nice drink.'

His gloomy voice had a sharp edge to it.

'What do you want a drink for at this time of night?' said the elder, slurping from his cup. 'Look, everybody's had a bite and gone to sleep. Why are you making all this row?'

The word 'row' seemed to put him in mind of really making a row.

'Elder, I'm going to get things going if you don't get me some vodka.'

'Can't you talk him round?' said the elder, turning to Dutlov, who had lit his lantern by now but had stayed on clearly wanting to listen and see what happened. He angled a sympathetic look at his nephew, as if surprised to see him behaving like a child.

Looking down, Ilya said once again, 'Gimme a drink. I'm going to get things going.'

'Cut it out, Ilya!' said the elder sharply. 'Come on. Cut it out. You'll live to regret it.'

But these words were scarcely out of his mouth when Ilya jumped up, smashed the window with his fist and roared at them.

'If you won't listen to me, that's what you'll get!' And he rushed over to the other window to smash that one, too.

Quick as a flash, Polikey did a double roll and disappeared into the farthest recess of the stove-top, scattering all the cockroaches. The elder dropped his spoon and rushed over to Ilya. Dutlov slowly put down the lantern, undid his girdle, shook his head and walked over, tut-tutting, towards Ilya, who was by now having a go at the elder and the porter blocking his way to the window. They had grabbed him by the arms and seemed to have a good hold on him, but the moment he saw his uncle holding the girdle his strength became that of a dozen men; he tore himself free and stepped forward to challenge Dutlov, with his eyes rolling and his fists clenched.

'I'll kill you. Don't you come near me, you brute. You've done for me, you and your sons, done for me. Why did you get me married? Don't you come near me. I'll kill you!'

Ilya was a hideous sight. He was red in the face, his eyes darted about all over the place, and his young man's body shivered feverishly all over. He seemed determined to kill all three of the attacking peasants, and capable of doing it.

'You're drinking your brother's blood, you bloodsucker!'

Something flashed across Dutlov's ever-impassive face. He stepped forward.

'If you won't do it the easy way . . .' he said. Then suddenly – Heaven knows where he got the strength from – in one swift movement he grabbed his nephew, wrestled him to the floor and, with the help of the elder, set about tying his hands. The struggle lasted five minutes or so. Then Dutlov got to his feet, assisted by the peasants, disentangled Ilya's grasping hands from his coat, steadied himself, made Ilya get up with his hands tied behind his back, and sat him down on the bench in one corner.

'Told you you'd regret it,' he said, still breathless from fighting as he straightened the narrow girdle round his shirt. 'Don't be a sinner. We all have to die. Put a jacket under his head for him,' he added, turning to the porter, 'or the blood will go to his head.' Then he picked up the lantern, pulled the cord tight round his waist and set off once again to see to the horses.

Ilya, with his pale face, his hair all over the place and his shirt rumpled, was staring round the room as if he was trying to remember where he was. The porter was picking up shards of glass and stuffing a coat into the window space to keep the draught out. The village elder sat down to his bowl.

'Oh dear, Ilya! I'm sorry for you, honest I am. We can't do nothin' about it. Look at Khoryushkin. He's married, too. There's no getting out of it.'

'My uncle's a swine. He's the one that's ruined me,' he said again, his voice sharp and bitter. 'Looks after his own, he does. My mum said the steward told him to buy me out, but he wouldn't do it. Said he couldn't afford to. And we've brought plenty into that house, we have, me and my brother. Swine!'

Dutlov walked in, said a prayer in front of the icons, took his coat off and sat down next to the elder. A girl brought him some more kvass[6] and a spoon. Ilya had stopped talking; he closed his eyes and lay down with his head on the coat. The elder pointed to him without saying anything and shook his head. Dutlov waved a hand.

'Pitiful, isn't it? My own brother's son. It's no good me being sorry for him, they still has me down as a villain as far as he's concerned. Don't know whether his old woman put the idea into his head – she's still only young, but she's a sharp one, she is – that we've got the kind of money that could buy him out. Now he blames me. Still you has to be sorry for him . . .'

'Yes. He's a good lad,' said the elder.

'Well, I can't do nothing with him. I'll send Ignat over tomorrow, and his missus wanted to come too.'

'Well, send her over. That's all right by me,' said the elder, getting to his feet and climbing up on to the stove. 'What's money got to do with it? Money's just dust and ashes.'

'If the money was there, nobody wouldn't grudge it,' said one of the innkeeper's men, looking up.

'Oh, it's all money, money! A lot of evil comes from it,' said Dutlov in response. 'Nothin' in the world causes more evil than money. 'Tis said in the Scriptures.'

''Tis all said in the Scriptures,' echoed the porter. 'A chap was telling me about this merchant. Made a stack of money, and he didn't want to leave none of it behind. Loved his money so much he took it with him into his grave. When he was dying he told them to put a cushion in his coffin with him. Nobody guessed what he was up to – they just did it. Then his sons starts looking for his money. Nothin'. One of his sons guessed his money must be in the cushion. It went right up to the Tsar, but they got permission to dig him up. Guess what. They opened it up – nothing in the cushion. Just the coffin full of creepy-crawlies. So they buried him again. See? That's what money does for you.'

''Tis a known fact. A lot of evil,' said Dutlov, getting to his feet and starting to pray.

When he had finished he glanced at his nephew. He was asleep. Dutlov walked over, untied the girdle and lay down. Another peasant went out to sleep with the horses.

9

As soon as it had all gone quiet Polikey crept down sheepishly and started to get his things together. For some reason he felt awful spending the night in there with the conscripts. By now the cockerels were crowing to each other and their calls were coming faster. Drum had finished his oats and was straining towards the drinking trough. Polikey put his harness on and led him out past the peasants' carts. His cap and its contents were intact, and the wheels of his cart were soon clattering down the frozen road to Pokrovskoye. Only when he had left the town behind did Polikey begin to feel better. And even then, for some reason he kept thinking that any moment now he might hear them chasing after him, and they would stop him, tie his hands behind his back, put him in Ilya's place and take him next morning to the recruiting station. Whether from the cold or from fear he couldn't have said, but a shiver kept running down his back, and Drum felt the continual play of his whip. The first person he came across was a priest in a tall fur cap walking along with a lame workman. This made him feel even more alarmed. But once out of the town he felt this fear gradually fading. Drum slowed to a walking pace, and the road ahead became clearer. Polikey took off his cap and felt the money. He wondered whether he ought to put it inside, under his coat. No, that would mean undoing his belt. At the bottom of the next hill he would get down and sort himself out. But his cap was well sewn up at the top and nothing could fall down through the lining; no, he wouldn't take his cap off until he got home. And at the bottom of the slope Drum took it upon himself to dash on up the next hill. Polikey, who was as keen as Drum to get home, did nothing to stop him. Everything was fine now, or so he thought, and he allowed himself to dream about how grateful the mistress would be, and how she would give him five roubles, and all the family would be delighted. He took his cap off, felt the envelope and crammed the cap down harder on his head, smiling to himself. The velveteen lining was rotten and, as a direct result of Akulina carefully sewing up one torn place, it came loose at the other end, and in the darkness Polikey's attempt to shove the money deeper into the padding tore it open, leaving one corner of the envelope sticking out of the material.

It was beginning to get light and Polikey, not having slept all night, felt drowsy. As he pulled his cap further down he pushed the envelope further out and, in his sleepy state, he let his head bump against the side of the cart. He woke up near to the house. His first thought was to feel for the cap – there it was sitting nicely on his head. Confident that the envelope was still there, he didn't take it off. He gave Drum a pat, sorted out the hay, resumed his attitude of a prosperous peasant and swaggered off towards the house.

There was the kitchen, there was the building the house serfs called their 'quartels'. There was the carpenter's wife carrying some cloth, there was the office, there was the mistress's house, where quite soon Polikey would show himself to be an upright and reliable man – anybody can have bad things said about them, as he would say – and the mistress would say, 'Well now, I'm most grateful to you, Polikey. Please take these three . . .' or maybe five, even ten roubles, and she would tell them to bring him some tea, perhaps even a drop of vodka. Wouldn't go amiss in this cold weather. With ten roubles they could enjoy the holiday, buy some boots and give Nikita his four and a half roubles back. Nothing to be done about that – he'd been going on about them. When he was about a hundred paces from the house Polikey wrapped his coat around himself again, straightened his belt and his collar, took off his cap and tidied his hair and felt into the lining with no sense of hurry. His hand scrabbled about in the cap, faster and faster; he thrust his other hand into the same place. The colour slowly drained from his face as one hand went right through . . . Polikey dropped to his knees, stopped the horse and took a good look round the cart, searching through the hay and the things he had bought, feeling under his coat and inside his baggy trousers. The money was nowhere to be found.

'My godfathers! What does this mean? What's going to happen now?' He let out a roar and clutched at his hair.

But then, realizing that he could be seen, he turned Drum round, put the cap back on his head and drove the surprised and unhappy animal back down the road.

'I can't stand going out with Polikey,' Drum must have been thinking. 'For once in my life he's not going to be late feeding and watering me, but it's all a cruel trick. Ran my heart out running back home, I did. Dead tired, and as soon as I get within smelling distance of our hay he's driving me out again.'

'Damn you, you old bag of bones!' Polikey yelled at him through his tears, standing up in the cart, jerking the reins back into Drum's mouth and cracking him with the whip.

10

All that day Polikey was not to be seen in Pokrovskoye. After dinner the mistress asked after him several times, and Aksyuta flew off to see Akulina. But Akulina said he wasn't back yet. He'd obviously been held up by the dealer, or maybe there was something wrong with the horse. 'He's not gone lame, has he?' she asked. 'Last time it took Maxim a day and a night to get back. Had to walk all the way, he did!' So Aksyuta sped off home, swinging her pendulums, and Akulina was left thinking up excuses for her husband being late and trying – without success – to keep calm. With a heavy heart she went on with the preparations for tomorrow's holiday, but nothing went right. She was particularly worried by what the carpenter's wife claimed to have seen. 'A man who looked like Polikey drove up to the avinoo[7] and then turned round and went back again.' The children were also waiting anxiously and impatiently for their daddy to come home, though for different reasons. Anyutka and Masha had been left without the sheepskin and the coat that normally gave them the chance to go outside at least one after the other, and had been reduced to going out in their indoor clothing and running around in circles at top speed near to the house, which was no minor inconvenience to anybody going in and out of their 'quartels'. On one occasion Masha had careered into the legs of the carpenter's wife who was carrying some water and, even though she burst out crying in anticipation as she crashed into the woman's knees, she got a smack round the head that made her cry all the louder. And when she managed not to crash into anybody she would fly straight in through the door and climb on to a tub to get up on to the stove. Akulina and the mistress were the only people who were really bothered about Polikey; the children were only worried about what he was wearing. As for Yegor Mikhaylovich, when he was reporting to the mistress and she asked him whether Polikey was back yet, and where he could be, he just smiled and replied, 'I wouldn't know', obviously pleased to see that his suspicions were being justified. 'Should have been back by lunchtime,' he added meaningfully.

All that day there was neither sight nor sound of Polikey. Only afterwards did it become known that some peasants who lived nearby had seen him without his cap on running down the road and saying to everybody, 'You haven't found an envelope, have you?' Another man had seen him asleep by the roadside next to a tied-up horse and cart. 'I just assumed he was drunk,' said this fellow, 'and his horse hadn't been fed nor watered for a couple of days judging by the hollows in his sides.' Akulina spent a sleepless night listening out for him, but Polikey didn't come back. If she had been on her own, or had kept a cook and a maid, she would have been even more miserable, but as soon as the cocks started crowing and the carpenter's wife was up and about she had to get up and see to the stove. It was the holiday morning – before sunrise she had to get the bread out, make the kvass, bake some cakes, milk the cow, iron the frocks and shirts, get the children washed, fetch some water and make sure her neighbour didn't take up most of the oven. Akulina set to work, still listening. Daylight came, the bells were ringing, the children were up; still no Polikey. The day before, winter weather had covered the fields, roads and rooftops with patchy snow; this morning the weather was beautiful, fair, sunny and frosty, real holiday weather. You could see and hear things miles away. But Akulina was at the oven with her head thrust in through the door, and she was so busy with the cakes that she didn't hear Polikey arrive; it was only when the children called out that she knew her husband was back.

Anyutka, the eldest, had greased her hair and got dressed all by herself. She was wearing a new pink cotton dress, rather crumpled, a present from the mistress; it stuck out like a piece of stiff bark and was the envy of all the neighbours. Her hair was all shiny – she had smeared it with half a candle. Her shoes were not exactly new, but they were nice and slim. Masha was wearing the old jacket and was still covered in mud; Anyutka wouldn't let her come anywhere near for fear of getting dirty. Masha was outside when her father drove up carrying a sack. 'Daddy's here!' she yelled, hurtling in through the door right past Anyutka and dirtying her dress. Anyutka, no longer worried about getting dirty, gave Masha a good slap. Akulina couldn't tear herself away from her work; all she could do was scream at them, 'Stop it, you two. I'll smack the pair of you!' and look round at the door. Polikey, still carrying his sack, came in through the doorway and walked over to his *corner*. Akulina thought he looked pale. His face had something about it – he seemed to have been crying or laughing, but she hadn't time to work out which.

'Hello, Polikey. Everything all right?' she asked from down by the stove.

Polikey muttered something she couldn't understand.

'You what?' she called out. 'Have you been to see the mistress?'

Polikey was sitting in his *corner* staring about him with a wild look, and smiling his usual smile, which made him a picture of guilt and abject misery. For a long time he didn't respond.

'Well? Why don't you answer?' came Akulina's voice.

'Yes, Akulina. I've given the mistress her money. She couldn't thank me enough,' he said suddenly, but he looked even more anxious as he looked around, still smiling. His staring eyes, restless and feverish, were focused on two objects in particular: the cords attached to the cradle, and the baby. He walked over to the cradle and soon his slender fingers were busy untying the knotted rope. Then his eyes settled on the baby, but at that moment Akulina came into the *corner* carrying cakes on a tray. Polikey quickly hid the rope under his shirt and sat down on the bed.

'Polikey, what's wrong with you? You don't look right,' said Akulina.

'Haven't had any sleep,' he replied.

Suddenly there was a flash of something outside the window and, swift as an arrow, in flew the girl 'from up at the big house', Aksyuta.

'The mistress orders Polikey to come to her right now,' she said. 'Right now, orders Avdotya Nikolayevna . . . right now.'

Polikey looked from Akulina to the girl.

'I'm on my way. What else does she want?' he said, so straightforwardly that Akulina was reassured. 'Maybe she wants to give me a reward. Tell her I'm on my way.'

He got to his feet and went out. Akulina picked up the wash-tub, put it on the bench and filled it with water from buckets by the door and also from the hot cauldron on the stove. Rolling up her sleeves, she tested the water.

'Here, Masha. Time for your wash.'

The lisping little girl went into a tantrum, and howled.

'Come here, you little minx. I want you to have a clean shirt on. Don't mess me about. I've still got your brother to bath.'

Meanwhile, Polikey was not following the girl up to the big house; he went somewhere else. In the passageway by the wall there was a ladder leading up into the loft. Polikey walked out into the passageway, glanced round to check that no one was there, bent down and nipped nimbly up the ladder, almost running.

'Still no Polikey. What does it mean?' said the mistress impatiently to Dunyasha, who was combing her hair. 'Where *is* he? Why doesn't he come?'

Aksyuta flew down to the serfs' quarters again, ran in through the passageway again and asked for Polikey to come and see the mistress.

'But he went ages ago,' answered Akulina, who had finished washing Masha, had sat her little baby in the tub and was ignoring his cries as she wetted his thin streaks of hair. The little boy was crying, scowling and trying to catch hold of something with his helpless little hands. Akulina was holding him with one big hand behind his soft, plump and dimpled little back while she washed him with the other.

'Check that he's not gone to sleep somewhere,' she said, looking round anxiously.

Meanwhile the carpenter's wife, with her hair all over the place, her bosom exposed and her skirts hitched up, was on her way up into the loft to get her dress that had been drying. Suddenly a cry of horror rang down from the loft, and the carpenter's wife came flying down the ladder like a mad woman, with her eyes shut, scrabbling on all fours, more sliding than running.

'It's Polikey!' she screamed.

Akulina let go of the baby.

'He's hung himself!' roared the carpenter's wife.

Akulina, unaware that the baby had rolled over backwards like a ball, cocked his little legs up and gone headfirst underwater, rushed out into the passageway.

'On a rafter . . . hanging there,' said the carpenter's wife, but she stopped when she saw Akulina.

Akulina raced up the ladder and got to the top before anyone could hold her back, only to give a terrible cry and fall back down like a corpse, which would have killed her if the people who had rushed over from every corner had not been there and managed to support her.

II

Several minutes passed before anything could be made out in the general confusion. People came rushing in endlessly, everybody shouting, everybody talking, children and old women crying, with Akulina lying there in a dead faint. Eventually the men, the carpenter and the steward who had run in, went up the ladder, while the carpenter's wife told her story for the twentieth time. 'I had gone to get my dress without a thought in my head, and looked round, like this . . . and I saw this man stood there . . . I looked . . . there was his cap, inside out. I looked again . . . his feet was swinging. I went cold all over! Not very nice, is it? A man hangs himself and I has to see it! How I come clatterin' down I'll never know. 'Tis a miracle how God saved me. Not very nice, is it? Real steep it was, and that high up! Could have killed meself.'

Those who climbed up told the same story. Polikey, in his shirt and trousers, was hanging from the beam on the rope he had taken from the cradle. There was his cap, turned inside out, and next to it his coat and sheepskin, neatly folded. His feet touched the floor, but all signs of life had gone. Akulina came round, and made as if to climb the ladder, but they wouldn't let her.

'Mummy, the baby's tsoked!' The sudden cry came from the lisping child back in their *corner*. Akulina tore herself free again and rushed across to the *corner*. The baby lay quite still on his back in the tub; his little legs were not moving. Akulina snatched him up, but the child wasn't breathing or moving. Akulina threw him down on the bed, put her hands on her hips and burst out laughing; the ghastly sound was so sharp and loud that little Masha also gave a kind of half-laugh and then covered her ears and rushed out into the passageway crying. The people were crowding into the corner, weeping and wailing.

The child was carried out and massaged, but it was no good. Akulina was rocking about on the bed, still laughing and laughing; the laughter horrified everyone who heard it. Now for the first time, the sight of this motley crowd of married people, old folk and children who had come crowding into the passageway made it clear how many people, and what different kinds, lived in the serfs' 'quartels'. Everybody was on the move, everybody was talking, many were weeping, nobody was doing anything. The carpenter's wife kept finding new people who hadn't yet heard her story, and off she went again about the effect on her sensitive feelings of seeing such a shocking thing, and how God had saved her from falling down the ladder. An aged footman wearing a woman's jacket was telling them about a woman who had drowned herself when the old master was still alive. The steward sent word to the priest and the constable, and put someone on guard. The girl from the big house, Aksyuta, stared up wide-eyed into the loft trap, and although there was nothing to be seen she couldn't tear herself away to go back to the mistress. Agafya, who had been lady's-maid to the old mistress, wept as she asked for some tea to settle her nerves. Grannie Annie was laying out the little body on the table, with her practised, plump hands covered in olive oil. Other women stood by Akulina and looked at her in silence. The children shrank back into their corners, peeped out at the mother and cried, then they would stop, peep out again and shrink back even further. Boys and men crowded round the steps, looking in at the doors and windows with frightened faces, seeing nothing, understanding nothing, wondering amongst themselves what was wrong. One said the carpenter had chopped his wife's leg off with an axe. Another said the laundrywoman had had triplets. A third said the cook's cat had gone berserk and bitten several people. But gradually the truth got round, and eventually it reached the ears of the mistress. And seemingly no one prepared her for it; Yegor, clumsy oaf that he was, came straight out with it, and upset the mistress so much that she didn't recover for quite some time. By now the crowd was beginning to settle. The carpenter's wife lit the samovar and made some tea, which meant that the outsiders, who hadn't been invited, thought it wasn't right for them to stay on. The boys had started fighting by the steps. Now, everyone knew what had happened. They were beginning to disperse, making the sign of the cross, when the word went up, 'The mistress! The mistress!', at which they all crowded back and squeezed together to let her through, though they all wanted to see what she was going to do. The mistress, looking pale and tear-stained, went down the passage, crossed the threshold and walked over to Akulina's *corner*. Dozens of heads came together to look in at the door. One pregnant woman got squashed so much that she cried out, and without further ado she took her chance to get a place at the front. Who wouldn't want to get a look at the mistress in Akulina's *corner*? For the house serfs it was like fireworks at the end of a show. It meant a lot when they lit the fireworks; it meant a lot when the mistress, dressed in her silks and lace, walked into Akulina's *corner*. The mistress went over to Akulina and took her hand, but Akulina snatched it away. The old house serfs shook their heads in disapproval.

'Akulina!' said the mistress. 'You have your children. You must look after yourself.'

Akulina gave a laugh, and got to her feet.

'My children are all silver, all silver . . . I don't deal in notes,' she muttered, gabbling. 'I told my Polikey, "Don't you take no notes," and they've smeared tar all over him, all that tar. Tar and soap, madam! You got bad skin, that'll cure it.' And she laughed again, louder.

The mistress turned round and sent for the doctor's boy and some mustard.

'Get me some cold water.' And she looked round for some herself. But when she saw the dead child and Grannie Annie standing there, the mistress turned away and everyone saw her bury her face in a handkerchief and burst into tears. Grannie Annie herself – it's a pity the mistress didn't see this, she would have appreciated it, and it was done for her – covered the baby with a linen cloth, put his little arm straight with a movement of her plump, nimble hand, then shook her head, pursed her lips and winced in such a way, with such a deep sigh, that everyone could see how good-hearted she was. But the mistress did not see it; she couldn't see anything. She gave a sob, went into hysterics and was taken away, supported under the arms, first out to the passage, and then back home. 'Did what she could,' thought many of the people as they went their separate ways. Akulina was still laughing and gabbling nonsense. She was taken into another room, where she was bled and covered with mustard poultices, with ice on her head, but she couldn't take anything in and instead of weeping she went on laughing, talking and behaving so oddly that the kind people who were looking after her lost control and laughed along with her.

12

In Pokrovskoye the holiday was not a happy occasion. It may have been a fine day, but people didn't go out to enjoy themselves, the girls didn't come together to sing their songs, the factory lads who had walked out from the town didn't play their concertinas or balalaikas, and played no games with the girls. They all sat around in corners and, if they spoke at all, it was in soft tones as if there was a bogeyman about who might overhear them. It wasn't too bad during the day, but in the evening, when darkness came down and the dogs began to howl, and as ill luck would have it the wind got up and howled down the chimneys, the people who lived there were so scared that anyone who had a candle lit it in front of an icon, anyone left alone in a *corner* went over and asked if he could spend the night with his neighbours, where there was a bit more company, and anyone who had to go to one of the out-houses didn't go, and didn't worry about leaving the cattle without fodder for a night. And all the holy water that everyone kept in little bottles was used up in the course of that night. It was even said that many people heard heavy footsteps going up and down in the loft that night, and the blacksmith saw a serpent fly up there. There was no one in Polikey's *corner*; the children and the demented woman had been taken off elsewhere. Only the little dead body lay there along with two old grandmothers and a pilgrim woman who took it upon herself to read through the

Psalms not just for the baby but to mark the whole calamity in general. It was what the mistress had wanted. Even the pilgrim woman and the old grannies heard something – a creaking rafter and somebody groaning immediately after the reading of a passage from the Psalter. And when the words 'Let God arise' were read, everything went quiet again. The carpenter's wife invited a friend over and during the night the pair of them went through a week's supply of tea. They too heard the rafters creaking up top, and the sound of something like sacks falling down. The peasants stationed as guards gave some courage to the house serfs, who would have died of fear that night without them. The menfolk spent the time in the passageway lying on some hay, and later on they would claim to have heard wonderful things up in the loft, though during the night itself they had a nice cosy chat about the 'cunscription', chewing bread, scratching themselves and filling the passage with that special men's smell – it was so bad that the carpenter's wife, as she walked past them, spat on the floor and called them 'peasant louts'. Be that as it may, the dead man was still dangling up in the loft, and it was as if the evil one himself had overshadowed their 'quartels' that night with his vast wing, showing them his power and coming closer to these people than ever before. Or so they felt, at the very least. I don't know whether they were right or not. I'm inclined to think they weren't right at all. I think that if one of them had been bold enough that terrible night to take a candle or a lantern, making the sign of the cross for himself, or not crossing himself, and go up into the loft, looking ahead and slowly dispelling the horror of the night with his candle and lighting up the rafters, the sand, the flue pipe covered with cobwebs and the bits of washing forgotten by the carpenter's wife, and gone right up to Polikey, and if he had controlled his fear enough to lift the lantern up to his face, he would have seen the same skinny body with its feet touching the floor (the rope had stretched), leaning lifelessly to one side, with its shirt collar undone and no cross showing, and its head slumped down over its chest, the kindly unseeing eyes, the sheepish, guilty smile, and over it all a harsh sense of calm and quiet. It is certainly true that the carpenter's wife, huddled up on the corner of her bed, with her hair all over the place and fear in her eyes, telling people she can hear sacks falling down is much more gruesome and horrible than Polikey, even though his cross has come off and lies there on the rafter.

Up there – which means in the mistress's house – the same horror reigned as in the house serfs' 'quartels'. The mistress's room smelt of eau-de-Cologne and medicine. Dunyasha was melting yellow wax and getting ready to drop it in water. Exactly what she was dropping it in for I can't say; all I know is, they always dropped wax in water when the mistress was ill. And at present she was so upset she had made herself ill. Dunyasha's aunt had come over for the night to keep her spirits up, so there were four of them including the little girl, and they sat there in the maids' room talking in low voices.

'Who's going for the oil?' asked Dunyasha.

'I'm not going, Dunyasha. Nothing would make me,' said the second maid decisively.

'Nonsense. You can take Aksyuta with you.'

'I'll go on my own. I'm not scared,' said Aksyuta, but she immediately faltered.

'Off you go, then. You're a clever girl. Get some from Grannie Annie – a glassful. Bring it back here, and don't spill it,' Dunyasha said to her.

Aksyuta lifted up her skirt with one hand and, although this meant that she couldn't swing both arms, she swung one of them twice as hard across her line of flight as she sped away. She was frightened, and she felt that if she saw or heard anything at all, even her own mother's living figure, she would drop dead with fright. She flew down the familiar pathway with her eyes screwed up tight.

13

'Is the mistress asleep or awake?' came a question in the deep voice of a peasant man suddenly close to Aksyuta. She opened her eyes, which had been screwed up tight, and saw the figure of a man which appeared to her taller than the 'quartel'. She gave a scream and hurtled back so fast her skirt couldn't keep up with her. In a single bound she was up on the verandah, and another one took her into the maids' room, where she flung herself on to her bed wailing like a wild thing. Dunyasha, her auntie and the second maid nearly died of fright, but before they could blink an eye slow, heavy, hesitant footsteps could be heard coming along the passage to the door. Dunyasha leapt towards her mistress, dropping her melted wax, the second maid hid away under some skirts hanging on the wall, while the auntie – more decisive – made as if to hold the door shut, but it opened and in came a peasant. It was Dutlov, wearing his boat-like shoes. Ignoring the terror-stricken girls, he directed his eyes to search for an icon, but, not noticing the little image hanging in the left-hand corner, he crossed himself in front of a cupboard where teacups were kept, put his cap down on the windowsill, thrust one arm so far down into his coat that it looked as if he was scratching himself under the other armpit, and pulled out a letter with five brown seals stamped with an anchor. Dunyasha's auntie clutched at her bosom, finding it hard to speak.

'You gave me such a scare, Semyon. I c . . . can hardly get a w . . . word out. I thought my time had come.'

'Did you have to do it like that?' said the second maid, peering out from behind the skirts.

'You've upset the mistress, too,' said Dunyasha, coming out of her mistress's door.

'What do you mean creeping in through the maids' entrance without permission! Typical peasant!'

Dutlov, making no apology, insisted that he must see the mistress.

'She's not well,' said Dunyasha.

At this point Aksyuta snorted with such loud and uncouth laughter that she had to push her head back down into the pillows on the bed, and she couldn't take it out for a good hour, despite threats from Dunyasha and her auntie, for fear of erupting again – as if she was bursting inside her pink print bosom and red cheeks. She found it so funny that they had all been so scared; again, she buried her head and scraped her foot along the floor, and her whole body shook with what looked like convulsions.

Dutlov stopped, looked closely at her as if he was trying to work out what was wrong with her, but failing to do so he turned back and went on speaking.

'What I want to say is, it's something very important,' he said. 'Just tell her a peasant has found the letter with the money in it.'

'What money?'

Before reporting to her mistress Dunyasha read the address and asked Dutlov where and how he had found the money that Polikey ought to have brought back from town. Once she knew all the details, she shoved the errand girl out into the passageway because she wouldn't stop snorting, and went in to see the mistress, but, to Dutlov's surprise, the old lady refused to see him and said nothing to Dunyasha that made any sense.

'I know nothing about it, and I don't want to know about any peasant or any money,' said the mistress. 'I cannot and will not see anybody. Tell him to leave me alone.'

'So what am I supposed to do?' said Dutlov, turning the envelope over. 'It's a decent sum of money. What's this writing say?' he asked Dunyasha, who read the address out to him again.

Dutlov seemed as if he couldn't quite believe what he was hearing. He was hoping the money didn't belong to the mistress and he had been given the wrong address. But Dunyasha had confirmed it again. He gave a sigh, put the envelope into his bosom and made as if to go.

'S'pose I'll have to hand it in to the policeman,' he said.

'Wait a minute. I'll have one more try. I'll tell her again,' said Dunyasha, stopping him. She had watched closely as the envelope had disappeared into this peasant's bosom. 'Give me the letter.'

Dutlov found it again, but he hesitated before handing it over into Dunyasha's extended hand.

'Tell her it was found on the road by Semyon Dutlov.'

'All right. Let me have it.'

'I thought it was just any ole letter, but a soldier read it and said it's got money inside.'

'Well, let me have it then.'

'I didn't dare go home first, to, er . . .' Dutlov began again, still not parting with the valuable envelope. 'Right. You go and tell her.'

Dunyasha took the envelope and went back in to see her mistress again.

'Oh, for goodness' sake, Dunyasha,' said the mistress reproachfully, 'please don't talk to me about that money. All I can think about is that little boy . . .'

The mistress opened up the envelope and shuddered the moment she saw the money. She stopped and thought.

'Horrible money! It does so much evil!' she said.

'It's Dutlov, madam. Do you want him to come in, or will you be kind enough to come out to see him? Is it all there?' asked Dunyasha.

'I don't want this money. It's horrible money. Look what it's done. Tell him he can have it if he wants it,' said the mistress in a sudden outburst, reaching for Dunyasha's hand. 'Yes, yes, yes,' she repeated to an amazed Dunyasha. 'Let him take it all and do what he wants with it.'

'Fifteen hundred roubles,' commented Dunyasha with a gentle smile as if she was dealing with a child.

'Let him take it all,' said the mistress impatiently. 'Can't you understand what I'm saying? This money is bad luck. Don't mention it again. He can take it, the peasant who found it. Go on, get out of here.'

Dunyasha went out to the maids' room.

'Is it all there?' asked Dutlov.

'You can count it yourself,' said Dunyasha, handing him the envelope. 'I've been told to give it to you.'

Dutlov put his cap under his arm, leaned forward and started to count the money.

'You haven't got an abacus?'

Dutlov thought the mistress was too stupid to count and had told him to do it.

'Count it at home. It's yours. It's your money,' snapped

Dunyasha. 'Madam says she doesn't want to see it. She said give it to the man who found it.'

Dutlov, still leaning forward, settled his eyes on Dunyasha.

Dunyasha's auntie threw her hands in the air.

'Heavens above! It's your lucky day! Heavens alive!'

The second maid couldn't believe her ears.

'Dunyasha, this is a joke, isn't it?'

'I'll give you a joke! She told me to give it to this peasant . . . Well, go on, then. Take your money, and go,' said Dunyasha, not hiding her irritation. 'Bad luck for some, good luck for others.'

'Some joke! Fifteen hundred roubles,' said the auntie.

'More than that,' said Dunyasha by way of confirmation. 'Well, you'll be able to afford a penny candle for St Nicholas,' she added contemptuously. 'Well, pull yourself together . . . This could have done some good to a poor man. He's got plenty of his own.'

At last Dutlov got the point – this was no joke. He set about collecting the notes, having spread them out for counting, and put them into the envelope, but his hands were trembling and he kept his eyes on the girls to make sure they weren't laughing at him.

'You see? He can't pull himself together. He's too happy with himself,' said Dunyasha, implying scorn for the man and his money. 'Let me put it in for you.'

And she would have taken hold of it, but Dutlov wouldn't let her. He crammed the notes together, pushed them further in and took up his cap.

'Are you happy now?'

'I don't know what to say! It's like . . .'

He couldn't finish what he wanted to say, so he just waved his hand, gave a crooked smile and walked out almost in tears.

The mistress rang.

'Well? Have you given it to him?'

'Yes, I have.'

'And? Is he happy with that?'

'He went absolutely crazy.'

'Go and call him back. I want to ask him where he found it. Bring him here. I can't possibly go out.'

Dunyasha ran off and caught up with the peasant in the passageway. He still hadn't put his cap on, but he had taken his purse out and he was leaning forward as he untied the strings, holding the money between his teeth. It was almost as if he didn't think the money was his while ever the money stayed outside his purse. When Dunyasha called to him he was shaken.

'Du . . . Dunyasha, what do you want? Does she want it back? Couldn't you put a word in for me? I'll bring you some nice honey.'

'Huh! That would be the first time.'

The door was opened again and the peasant was taken to the mistress. He did not look happy. 'Oh dear, she's going to take it back!' he was thinking. As he walked through the rooms, he stepped as high as he could and tried not to press down with his bark-fibre shoes, as if he was going through tall grass. He took in nothing of his surroundings. He was going past a mirror, he saw some flowers and a peasant in bark-fibre shoes stepping high, a painting of the master with a monocle, a sort of green tub and something in white . . . Then he looked again. The something in white was speaking to him – it was the mistress. He couldn't make out a word. He just goggled, not knowing where he was. Everything came at him through a mist.

'Dutlov, is that you?'

'Yes, madam. It's all there. I haven't touched nothing,' he said. 'I wasn't happy with it, as God's my judge. And I haven't half worked my horse . . .'

'Lucky you,' she said with a kind but derisive smile. 'You have it. It's yours.'

All he did was roll his eyes.

'I'm happy that it came to you. Let's hope some good may come of it. Well then, are you happy now?'

'You bet I am! Real happy, madam. I'll pray for you always! . . . I'm real happy – thank God our mistress is alive. Only it wasn't my fault.'

'How did you find it?'

'Well, what I mean is, we've all tried our honourable best for the mistress, and it's not . . .'

'He's not making any sense, madam,' said Dunyasha.

'I was taking me nephew off to the army, I come back on the same road and I found it. Polikey must have dropped it.'

'Very well. Off you go, my dear man. I'm happy.'

'Me too, milady!' said the peasant.

Then he realized he hadn't said thank you – he hadn't known how to go about it. The mistress and Dunyasha smiled as he strode off again as if he was stepping over grass. He was forcing himself to hold back to avoid breaking into a trot. Even then, he couldn't get it out of his head that they would stop him any moment now and take it off him . . .

14

Out in the fresh air again Dutlov stepped off the road and walked under the lindens, where he completely undid his belt to get at his purse and began putting the money away. His lips were trembling, moving in and out even though he wasn't making any sounds. Once the money had been put away and his belt was done up, he crossed himself and walked on staggering down the road like a drunk, his mind reeling under all the thoughts that had flashed into his head. Suddenly he saw the figure of a man coming towards him. He called out. It was Yefim, stick in hand, patrolling the servants' quarters.

'Well, if it's not good old Semyon,' said Yefim, full of good cheer, as he approached. (Yefim was frightened of being out on his own.) 'Have you seen the recruits off, old lad?'

'Yes, they've gone. What are you up to?'

'I'm on patrol guarding Polikey after he's hung himself.'

'Where's he done that?'

'Up in the loft. Still hanging there by all accounts,' said Yefim, pointing with his stick in the darkness over towards the roof of the serfs' quarters.

Dutlov followed the direction of his hand and, although he couldn't see anything, he frowned, screwed up his eyes and shook his head.

'Policeman's come,' said Yefim, 'according to the driver. They'll be taking him down now. Horrible at night-time, isn't it, old lad? You wouldn't get me going up there at night, not even under orders. Yegor Mikhaylovich could have me put to death and I still wouldn't go.'

'It's a sin, it is. A wicked sin,' said Dutlov over and over again. It was obviously the decent thing to say, but he wasn't thinking at all about what he was saying, and he wanted to walk on. But he was stopped by the sound of Yegor Mikhaylovich's voice.

'Hey, watchman! Come over here,' came the voice from the steps.

Yefim called back.

'Who's that man stood with you?'

'Dutlov.'

'Oh, Semyon. You come, too.'

When he got near, into the light of the lantern carried by the driver, Dutlov looked closely at Yegor Mikhaylovich and a little official in a greatcoat and a cap with a badge on it – the policeman.

'Look, this old man'll come with us,' said Yegor Mikhaylovich when he saw him.

This jarred on the old man, but there was no avoiding it.

'Yefim, be a good lad. Nip up into the loft where he's hung himself and put the ladder straight so His Honour can get up there all right.'

Earlier Yefim would have given anything not to go over to the serfs' quarters, but now he positively ran, with his bark-fibre shoes clattering like falling logs.

The police officer struck a light and lit his pipe. He lived barely a mile away and since he was fresh from a severe reprimand from his boss for drunkenness he was at his most zealous. Arriving at ten o'clock at night, he wanted to lose no time in seeing the dead man. Yegor Mikhaylovich wanted to know from Dutlov what he was doing there. As they walked, Dutlov told the steward how he had found the money and what the mistress had done about it. He said he had come to get Yegor's approval. Dutlov was horrified when he asked for the envelope and took a good look at it. The policeman also took hold of the envelope and, in sharp, terse tones, asked for details.

'The money's gone now,' thought Dutlov, and he began to justify himself. But the policeman handed it back.

'Bit of luck for a clodhopper like you,' he said.

'Come in handy, that will,' said Yegor Mikhaylovich. 'He's just taken his nephew off for conscription. He can buy him out now.'

'Aha!' said the policeman, and he walked on.

'You'll be buying him out, your Ilya, won't you?' said Yegor Mikhaylovich.

'What do you mean buying him out? Might not be enough money. Might be too late now.'

'It's up to you,' said the steward, and they walked on together behind the policeman.

They went to the serfs' quarters, where malodorous watchmen stood waiting with a lantern. Dutlov brought up the rear. The watchmen had a shifty look about them, which could only have related to the smells they had made because they hadn't done anything wrong. None of them spoke.

'Where is he?' asked the policeman.

'He's up there,' whispered Yegor Mikhaylovich. 'Yefim, be a good lad. You go first with the lantern.'

Yefim had already been up and straightened a plank at the top of the ladder, and now he seemed to have lost all fear. He went up two or three rungs at a time, leading the way with a cheerful look on his face, only turning round to light the way for the policeman. After the constable, up went Yegor Mikhaylovich. When they had disappeared Dutlov put one foot on the first rung, gave a sigh and stopped. A couple of minutes went by, and the footsteps up top went quiet. They had clearly gone over to the body.

'Semyon, you're wanted up here!' Yefim called down.

Dutlov climbed up. The upper bodies of the policeman and Yegor Mikhaylovich could be seen in the light of the lantern on the other side of a beam. Beyond them stood someone else with his back to Dutlov. It was Polikey. Dutlov clambered over the beam and stopped there, crossing himself.

'Turn him round, lads,' said the policeman.

Nobody moved.

'Yefim, be a good lad,' said Yegor Mikhaylovich.

The 'good lad' stepped over a beam, turned Polikey round and stood at his side. With a most cheerful look on his face he glanced first at Polikey, then at the arm of the law, like a showman displaying an albino girl or a Julia Pastrana,[8] keeping one eye on the public and another on his exhibit, and ready to oblige the audience in any way.

'Turn him round again.'

Polikey was turned round again, with a gentle swing of his arms and his feet dragging on the sandy floor.

'Get hold of him, and cut him down.'

'Shall we cut the rope, sir?' asked Yegor Mikhaylovich. 'Get me a hatchet, lads.'

The watchmen and Dutlov needed to be told twice before they came forward. But then the 'good lad' shouldered Polikey like a sheep's carcass, the rope was cut and the body was taken down and covered up. The policeman said the doctor would be coming in the morning, and he let them all go.

15

Dutlov went home, with his lips still trembling. At first he felt sickened, but the nearer he got to his village the more this feeling began to go, and a feeling of gladness gradually came into his heart. In the village he could hear people singing and drunken voices. Dutlov had never been a drinker, and he went straight home. It was late when he walked into his hut. His old wife was asleep. His eldest son and grandsons were asleep on the stove-top, and the second son outside in the store-room. Ilyushka's wife was the only one awake; she sat there bare-headed on a bench dressed in her dirty working smock, whining. She hadn't come out to greet her uncle, and now, as he came in, she started whining again and railing against her fate louder still. In the old woman's opinion she was pretty good at railing against her fate, even though she was so young she couldn't have had much practice at it.

The old woman got up and prepared some supper for her

husband. Dutlov sent Ilyushka's wife away from the table. 'That's enough of that,' he said. Aksinya got to her feet and went to lie on another bench, but she didn't stop wailing. The old woman laid the table and cleared it afterwards, all in silence. The old man also said not a word. He said grace, gave a good belch, washed his hands, took the abacus down from a nail on the wall and went out into the store-room. There, he and wife exchanged a few whispered words, then she went out, leaving him clicking on the abacus. Eventually he closed the lid of a chest with a bang, and went down into the cellar. He rummaged around for quite some time in both places, up in the room and down in the cellar. When he came back inside the hut it was quite dark and the little torch had gone out. The old woman, who by day was so placid and silent, lay flat out on the sleeping-bench, and her snoring filled the hut. Ilyushka's noisy wife was also asleep; her breathing made no sound. She had gone to sleep on the bench just as she was, still in her daytime clothes, with nothing to rest her head on. Dutlov prayed for a while, then looked at Ilyushka's wife, shaking his head, put the light out, gave another belch, climbed on to the stove and settled down next to his little grandson. In the darkness he lobbed his bark-fibre shoes down on to the floor and lay on his back looking up at a barely visible cross-beam over the stove and listening to the cockroaches scrabbling up the wall, the sighing and the snoring and the rubbing of one foot against another, and the sounds of the cattle outside.

He couldn't sleep. The moon rose, bringing more light into the hut. He could see more – there was Aksinya in the corner, and something he couldn't quite make out. Was it a jacket forgotten by his son, or a tub that the women had been using, or was that somebody standing there? He may have dropped off, or maybe not, but when he peered into the darkness again . . . it was all too clear: the dark spirit that had made Polikey do that awful thing – the house serfs had felt it with them yesterday evening – that spirit had winged its way to their village, to Dutlov's hut where the money was, the money that *he* had used to destroy Polikey. At least, Dutlov could sense *him* there. Dutlov squirmed – he couldn't sleep and he couldn't get up. His glimpse of something unidentifiable had reminded him of Ilyusha with his hands tied behind his back, Aksinya's face and her deliberate whining, and Polikey with his dangling hands. Suddenly – the old man could have sworn he saw someone walk past the window. 'What's that? Couldn't be the elder coming round to see us as early as this, could it?' he thought. 'How did he open the door?' wondered the old man as he heard footsteps in the passage. 'Maybe my old woman didn't put the bar across when she went down the passage.' A dog howled in the yard, and *he* walked up to the entry, and *he* seemed to be looking for something – as the old man said when he told the tale afterwards – looking for the door, and *he* walked past it, started groping at the wall again, only *he* fell over a tub and made it clatter. Then *he* was at it again, groping – must have been feeling for the latch. Then *he* grabbed at the latch. The old man felt his flesh creep. Then *he* lifted the latch and came in, taking on human form. But Dutlov knew it was *him*. He tried making the sign of the cross, but he couldn't. *He* walked over to the table, which had a cloth on it, tore it off, threw it on the floor and climbed up on the stove. The old man knew what it was – *him*, in the form of Polikey. He was grinning and his arms were dangling. He clambered up on to the stove, collapsed on top of the old man and started to strangle him.

'It's my money,' Polikey forced out.

'Let go. I'm not going to . . .' Semyon tried to say, but couldn't.

Polikey was pressing down on him with all the weight of a mountain of stone. Dutlov knew that if only he could say a prayer *he* would let go, and he knew which prayer to say, but he couldn't get it out. His grandson was sleeping at his side. The little boy cried out and burst into tears. His grandfather had shoved him up against the wall. The child's cry unlocked the old man's lips. 'Let God arise,' Dutlov managed to say. *He* eased up a little. 'And his enemies be scattered . . .' spluttered Dutlov. *He* got down from the stove. Dutlov heard both his feet bang down on the floor. He prayed and prayed, saying all the prayers he knew one after another. *He* walked to the door, went past the table and slammed the door with a bang that shook the whole hut. But everyone slept on except the grandson and grandfather. The grandfather, still praying, was shaking in every limb; the grandson, weeping, clung to his grandfather but went back to sleep. Soon it was quiet again. Grandfather lay still. A cock crew through the wall right by Dutlov's ear. He could hear the hens stirring; a young cockerel made an attempt at crowing like the old one, but couldn't manage it. Something stirred at the old man's feet. It was the cat. She jumped down from the stove-top on her soft paws, and now she was miaowing at the door. Grandfather got up and raised a window. It was dark and muddy outside. The cart was still there, standing by the window. Crossing himself, he went outside in his bare feet to see to the horses. You could tell that *he* had been there, *the master*. The mare, standing under the eaves at the end of the building, had caught her foot in the bridle and spilt her chaff all over the place; she was waiting for her master, with one foot raised and her head turned round. Her foal lay sprawling across a heap of manure. Grandfather stood him up, disentangled the mare, sorted out her feed and went back into the hut.

The old woman got up and lit a torch.

'Get the boys up,' he said. 'I'm going into town.' And, lighting a little wax taper from in front of the icons, he took it with him down into the cellar. By the time he came back up his wasn't the only candle to have been lit – there were lights in all of the neighbours' huts. The boys were up and ready to go. The womenfolk were coming and going, carrying buckets or tubs of milk. Ignat was harnessing the horse to one cart; the second son was greasing the wheels of another one. The young wife hadn't started whining yet. She had tidied herself up and put a scarf round her head; now she was sitting on a bench in the hut, waiting until it was time to go into town and say goodbye to her husband.

The old man had a particularly harsh look about him. He hadn't a word to say to anybody as he put on his best long coat and tied the belt before walking over to Yegor Mikhaylovich, with all Polikey's money stuffed in his bosom.

'Don't hang about!' he roared at Ignat, who was busy rotating the wheels jacked up on the newly greased axle. 'I'll be back in a minute. Be ready.'

The steward had only just got up, and he was having a drink of tea. He too was going into town to hand over the conscripts.

'What do you want?' he asked.

'I want to buy him out, Yegor Mikhaylovich, our lad. Do me a favour. T'other day you said you had a volunteer. Tell me what to do. We'm not well schooled.'

'Had second thoughts, have you?'

'Yes I have. I'm sorry for him. My brother's boy. Don't matter what he's turned out like. I'm sorry for him. Lot of evil it's caused, this 'ere money. Do me a favour. Tell me what to do,' he said, giving a low bow.

As always on these occasions, Yegor Mikhaylovich champed his lips for quite some time, thinking things over and saying nothing. Then, having considered the matter, he wrote two notes and told the old man what to do in town, and how to go about it.

When Dutlov got back home the young wife was already on the road with Ignat. The fat-bellied grey mare stood fully harnessed at the gate. He broke a switch off from the hedge, wrapped himself in his coat, got up on the box and whipped the horse up. Dutlov drove the mare so fast that her fat sides were sucked in, and Dutlov looked away so as not to feel sorry for her. He was tormented by the thought that for one reason or another he might be too late for the conscription, Ilyusha might go off to be a soldier and he would be left holding the devil's money.

I shall not go into all the details of what Dutlov managed to get through that morning. Suffice it to say that it really was his lucky day. The master to whom Yegor Mikhaylovich had written one of his notes did have a volunteer who was ready and waiting; in debt to the tune of twenty-three roubles, he had already been accepted by the recruitment board. His master wanted four hundred roubles for him, and a wealthy buyer who had been after him for the last three weeks was sticking out for three hundred. Dutlov fixed things with a few short words. 'Three twenty-five. All right?' he said, holding his hand out, but it was immediately obvious from the way he looked that he was prepared to go higher. The master withdrew his hand and insisted on four hundred. 'Three twenty-five, no good?' said Dutlov, taking the owner's right hand with his left, ready to smack it with his own right hand. 'No good? . . . Damn you!' he suddenly said, whacking his hand into the master's as hard as he could and turning his whole body away. 'That's it, then. Make it three fifty. I want a *deceipt*. Bring the lad here. You'll need a deposit. Two tenners all right?'

Dutlov was already undoing his belt to get at the money.

The master did not withdraw his hand, but something seemed to be holding him back from accepting the deposit. He was going on about wetting the bargain and giving the volunteer some sort of treat.

'Don't be a sinner,' said Dutlov, pressing the money on to him. 'We all have to die.' His tone was so gentle, assured and convincing that the master said, 'Oh, all right then,' before whacking his hand again and saying a prayer. 'God be with you.'

They woke the volunteer, who was still sleeping off the previous day's binge, examined him for no obvious reason and left *en masse* to see the authorities. The volunteer was in good cheer. He asked for rum – the hair of the dog that had bitten him – and Dutlov gave him the money to get some. He was all right until the moment they set foot in the entrance to the recruiting board, when his courage failed him. They stood there for some time, the old man, the master in his dark blue cloak and the volunteer in his short sheepskin coat, with his eyebrows raised and his eyes staring. For some time they carried on a whispered conversation; they kept asking to be taken somewhere, to see someone; for some reason or other they doffed their caps at every passing clerk, and they bowed as they listened with profound concentration to any ruling handed down by a clerk known to the master. It wasn't long before any hope of settling the matter that day had vanished, and the volunteer was showing signs of cheering up and making merry, when Dutlov caught sight of Yegor Mikhaylovich and immediately latched on to him, bowing and asking for help. Yegor Mikhaylovich was so effective in his assistance that by three o'clock the volunteer, much to his own surprise and dissatisfaction, was taken before the board, accepted as a recruit and – in an atmosphere of all-round celebration which somehow affected everybody from doorman to chairman – undressed, shaved, dressed again and taken outside. Five minutes later Dutlov was counting out the money. He got his receipt, said goodbye to the master and the volunteer, and went over to the house where the Pokrovskoye recruits were staying. Ilya and his young wife were sitting in a corner of the merchant's kitchen and, as soon as the old man came in, they stopped talking and stared at him with an expression of resignation tinged with hostility. As always, the old man said a prayer, then he undid his belt, took out some sort of paper and called for his eldest son, Ignat, and Ilya's mother, who was out in the yard, to come inside.

'Don't you be a sinner, Ilya,' he said, going across to his nephew. 'Last night you said some bad things to me . . . Do you think I'm not sorry for you? I remember my brother and how he left you in my care. If I'd had what it took, do you think I'd have given you away? God has sent me some good luck, and I'm not grudging you. Look, here it is, this paper.' As he spoke he put the receipt down on the table and carefully smoothed it out with his stiff, unbending fingers.

All the men from Pokrovskoye, the merchant's work people and a number of outsiders came into the hut. They had all guessed what was going on, but not one of them interrupted the solemnity of the old man's speech.

'There it is, your note. Cost me four hundred. Don't speak bad of your uncle.'

Ilya got to his feet in silence, not knowing what to say. His lips were quivering with emotion. His old mother made as if to go over and throw herself sobbing on his neck, but the old man waved her away gently but firmly, and continued to speak.

'Yesterday you said some bad things to me,' he repeated, 'and them bad things cut me to the heart. Your father left you to me on his deathbed, and you've been like my own son to me, and if I've done you wrong, well, we'm all sinners. Isn't that right, good Christian folk?' He turned to the peasants standing around him. 'Here's your mother and your young wife, and here's your *deceipt*. Never mind the money! Just say you forgive me, for the love of Christ.'

And then, folding back the skirts of his coat, he got slowly to his knees and bowed down at the feet of Ilya and his wife. It was no good the youngsters trying to hold him back; he wouldn't get up until he had touched the floor with his head, and then he shook his clothes straight and sat down on a bench. Ilya's mother and wife were howling with joy. Voices of approval murmured in the crowd. 'Truly, 'tis God's work, oh yes,' said one. 'What good is money? Money won't buy you a young lad,' said another. 'There's happiness for you,' came a third. 'Good man he is, that's for sure.' The only ones not speaking were the men being sent as recruits, who walked out in silence.

Two hours later two carts with the Dutlovs in them were driving through the outskirts of the town. In the first one, pulled by the pot-bellied grey mare with a sweaty neck, sat the old man and Ignat. Bouncing along behind them in the wagon were some little pots tied together and some cakes. In the second cart, with no one holding the reins, sat the young wife and her mother-in-law with scarves over their heads, dignified and happy figures. The younger woman was clutching a bottle of vodka under her apron. Ilya, crumpled up with his back to the horse and very red in the face, jolted against the front of the cart, munching a roll and talking nineteen to the dozen. The speaking voices, the carts rumbling along the road and the horses snorting – it all merged into a single happy sound. The horses swished their tails and trotted along faster and faster, sensing the way home. It was a happy family group that was bound to catch the eye of people passing by, driving or on foot.

On the very edge of the town the Dutlovs caught up with a party of recruits. They were standing in a group outside a tavern. One of the recruits, with the strange look that comes from having the front of the head shaven and a grey cap pushed well back, was strumming away at a balalaika. Another one, not wearing a cap, clutched a bottle of vodka in one hand as he cavorted in the middle of the ring. Ignat stopped his horse and got down to tighten the traces. All the Dutlovs looked on with curiosity, approval and amusement as the man did his dancing. The recruit seemed not to notice anyone, but he could sense his admiring audience getting larger, and this added to his energy and agility. He was giving it all he had. His brows were knitted, his red face showed no movement, his mouth was set in a fixed smile long devoid of meaning. His strength of spirit seemed to be totally focused on the placing of one foot behind the other as fast as possible, toes then heels. Now and again he would come to a sudden stop and wink at the balalaika-player, who would then thrum on all his strings faster than ever and rap his knuckles on the body of his instrument. The recruit would come to a stop, but even as he stood there motionless he seemed to be still dancing. Suddenly he would drop into a slow movement, shaking his shoulders, and then leap up, twisting in the air, before flying down, yelling out and squatting as he kicked out one leg after the other. Little boys laughed, women nodded, men smiled their approval. An old sergeant stood near the dancing recruit with a look on his face that said, 'You think it's marvellous. It's nothing to us.' Visibly tiring, the balalaika-player took a lazy look round, gave a discordant strum and rapped on the woodwork. The dancing was over.

'Hey, Alyokha!' said the balalaika-player to the dancer. 'There's your sponsor!'

'Where? My dear old friend!' cried Alyokha. It was the recruit who had been bought by Dutlov, and now he walked towards their cart, staggering forwards on his weary legs and holding a vodka bottle over his head.

'Misha! Give us a glass!' he cried. 'Master! My dear old friend! All happy now, aren't we?' he called out, his drunken head flopping over into the cart, and he offered his vodka round to the men and the women. The men had a swig; the women refused. 'All friends and family . . . what can I give you?' he shouted out, hugging the old women.

A woman selling snacks stood in the crowd. Alyokha caught sight of her, grabbed hold of her tray and scattered its contents all over the cart.

'Don't you worry. Damn it, I'm paying!' he wailed through choking tears. He pulled a purse out of his baggy trousers and threw it to Misha.

He stood there with his elbows on the cart and his watering eyes looked at the people sitting in it. 'Who's the mother here?' he asked. 'Is it you? Must give you a little treat.'

He thought for a moment, dived into his pocket and got hold of a new, neatly folded handkerchief, then a bit of towelling that he wore round his waist underneath his greatcoat and finally he took a red scarf from around his neck, rolled them all together and shoved them on to the old woman's knees.

'There you are. Present from me,' he said, his voice softening all the time.

'Why me? Thank you, dearie! What a nice lad!' said the old woman, turning towards old Dutlov, who was walking across to their cart.

Alyokha had stopped talking. There was a dreamy look in his eyes, as if he was falling asleep, and his head drooped lower and lower.

'I'm going, to save you. I'm a dead man, to save you!' he forced out. 'That's why I'm giving you things.'

'Chances are, he's got a mother, too,' said a voice in the crowd. 'Such a nice lad! It's a shame!'

Alyokha looked up.

'Yes, I have,' he said. 'And a father, too. Finished with me, they have. You listen to me, old woman,' he went on, taking Ilya's mother by the hand. 'I've given you some presents. Listen to me, for Christ's sake. Get down to my village – Vodnoye. Ask for old woman Nikonova. *She's* my mother. You follow me? Tell this old woman, old woman Nikonova, third hut from the end, where that new well is . . . Tell her . . . Alyokha, it's your son . . . He's . . . Know what I mean? . . . Music man! Get playing!' he shouted.

And he set off dancing again, still muttering, hurling his bottle to the ground with some vodka still in it.

Ignat climbed into the cart, and was about to get going.

'Goodbye. God go with you!' said the old woman, sinking into her coat.

Alyokha stopped suddenly. 'The devil go with you!' he shouted. 'Get fucking gone!'

'Oh, Lord above!' she said, making the sign of the cross.

Ignat urged the mare on, and the carts rumbled down the road.

Alyokha the recruit stood there in the middle of the road with his fists clenched, fury written on his face, swearing at the peasants as loud as he could.

'What are you looking at? Get lost! Devils! Cannibals!' he roared. 'I'll get you! Devils! Peasant scum!'

At this words failed him, and he fell where he stood full length on the ground.

It didn't take long for the Dutlovs to get out into the open fields, and when they looked back there was no sign of the crowd of recruits. They went on at walking pace for two or three miles, then Ignat got down, leaving the old man fast asleep, and walked along at the side of Ilya's cart.

They shared the bottle of vodka they had brought with them from town. After a while Ilya got going with a few songs, and the women sang along, too. Ignat shouted merrily at the horse, keeping time with the singing. A mail cart galloped merrily towards them. The driver bawled at his horses as he drove past the two celebrating carts, and the postman glanced across at the red faces of the peasants, the men and the women as they bounced along in their cart singing a happy song.

THE DEATH OF IVAN ILYICH

I

In the large law court building, during an adjournment of the Melvinsky trial, the members of the Bench and the public prosecutor had come together in the office of Ivan Yegorovich Shebek, and the conversation touched on the celebrated Krasovsky case. Fyodor Vasilyevich argued vehemently that it was beyond their jurisdiction, Ivan Yegorovich had his own view and was sticking to it, while Pyotr Ivanovich, who had kept out of the discussion at the outset and was still not contributing, was perusing a copy of the *Gazette* which had just been delivered.

'Gentlemen!' he said. 'Ivan Ilyich is dead.'

'Is he really?'

'Here you are. Read it yourself,' he said to Fyodor Vasilyevich, handing him the paper, fresh off the press and still smelling.

There was an announcement within a black border: 'It is with profound sorrow that Praskovya Fyodorovna Golovina informs family and friends that her beloved husband, Ivan Ilyich Golovin, Member of the Court of Justice, passed away on the 4th of February this year, 1882. The funeral will take place on Friday at 1 p.m.'

Ivan Ilyich had been a colleague of the gentlemen assembled there, and they had all liked him. He had been ill for several weeks, and the word was that his illness was incurable. His post had been kept open for him, but there was an understanding that in the event of his death Alexeyev would step into his place, and Alexeyev's place would be taken by either Vinnikov or Shtabel. So, the first thought that occurred to each of the assembled gentlemen on hearing the news of his death was how this death might affect his own prospects, and those of their acquaintances, for transfer or promotion.

'I'm sure to get Shtabel's job now, or Vinnikov's,' thought Fyodor Vasilyevich. 'They promised me ages ago, and a promotion like that would give me another eight hundred roubles a year, plus expenses.'

'I must apply to have my brother-in-law transferred from Kaluga,' thought Pyotr Ivanovich. 'My wife will be delighted. She won't be able to tell me I never do anything for her people.'

'I had a feeling he wasn't going to get better,' said Pyotr Ivanovich. 'It's sad.'

'What was actually wrong with him?'

'The doctors couldn't decide. Well, they could, but they all decided differently. The last time I saw him I thought he was going to come through it.'

'And I haven't been to see him since Christmas. I kept meaning to go.'

'Was he all right financially?'

'His wife had a bit of money, I think. Nothing very much.'

'Well, we'll have to go and see her. They live an awfully long way away.'

'For you they do. Where you live, everywhere's a long way away.'

'Look at that. He can't forgive me for living across the river,' said Pyotr Ivanovich, smiling at Shebek. The conversation turned to the long distances between the different parts of the city, and then they walked back into session.

Apart from the speculations aroused in each of them by this death, concerning the transfers and possible changes that this death might bring about, the very fact of the death of someone close to them aroused in all who heard about it, as always, a feeling of delight that he had died and they hadn't.

'There you have it. He's dead, and I'm not' was what everyone thought or felt. But his closest acquaintances, Ivan Ilyich's so-called friends, couldn't help thinking that they would now have to fulfil some tedious social obligations such as attending the funeral and calling on the widow to express their condolences.

Closest of all were Fyodor Vasilyevich and Pyotr Ivanovich.

Pyotr Ivanovich was an old friend from law school, and he felt indebted to Ivan Ilyich.

Over dinner he told his wife about the death of Ivan Ilyich and the mooted possibility of her brother being transferred to their district, and then, dispensing with his usual nap, he put on a dress-coat and set off for Ivan Ilyich's house.

At the entrance stood a carriage and two cabs. Downstairs in the entrance hall, next to the coat stand, a coffin lid with silk brocade, tassels and gold braid that had been powdered and polished stood propped against a wall. Two ladies in black were taking off their fur cloaks. He knew one of them, Ivan Ilyich's sister, but not the other. His colleague Schwartz was at the top of the stairs about to come down, but when he saw Pyotr Ivanovich he stopped and gave him a wink that seemed to say, 'Ivan Ilyich has messed things up – not what you or I would have done.'

Schwartz's face, with its English sidewhiskers and his lean figure in formal dress, exuded, as always, an air of elegant solemnity and, although the solemnity belied his playful personality, it was particularly poignant here, or so it seemed to Pyotr Ivanovich.

Pyotr Ivanovich allowed the ladies to pass on ahead, and slowly followed them upstairs. Instead of coming down, Schwartz stood waiting at the top. Pyotr Ivanovich knew why; he clearly wanted to arrange a game of whist somewhere that evening. The ladies proceeded upstairs to see the widow, but Schwartz pursed his lips tightly with all seriousness, though his eyes had a mischievous look as he twitched his eyebrows, directing Pyotr Ivanovich off to the right and into the room where the dead man lay.

Pyotr Ivanovich entered the room, and hesitated, as people always do on these occasions, not knowing precisely what to do. The only thing he was certain of was that in this situation you couldn't go wrong if you made the sign of the cross.

Whether or not you should bow at the same time he wasn't sure, so he went for a compromise, crossing himself as he walked in and giving a bit of a bow as he did so. At the same time, as far as hand and head movements permitted, he glanced round the room. Two young persons, nephews apparently, one of them a schoolboy, were crossing themselves as they left the room. A little old woman was standing there motionless. And a lady with curiously arched eyebrows was whispering to her. A church reader in a frock-coat – a hearty character of considerable spirit – was reading something out in a loud voice and a tone that brooked no contradiction. Gerasim, the peasant who waited at table, darted ahead of Pyotr Ivanovich, sprinkling something on the floor. Seeing this, Pyotr Ivanovich instantly recognized a slight smell of decaying flesh. When he had visited Ivan Ilyich for the last time he had seen this peasant in Ivan Ilyich's room, acting as a sick nurse, and Ivan Ilyich had had a special fondness for him.

Pyotr Ivanovich kept on crossing himself, and aimed a slight bow midway between the reader, the coffin and the icons on the corner table. Then, when the business of crossing himself seemed to be going on too long, he paused and took a close look at the dead man.

The dead man lay as all dead men lie, unusually heavy with his dead weight, with rigid limbs sinking into the soft lining of the coffin and his head bowed for eternity on the pillow, and he displayed what dead people always display, a waxen yellow forehead (with bald patches over his hollow temples) and a protruding nose that seemed to be pressing down hard on his upper lip. He had changed a good deal; he was even thinner than he had been when Pyotr Ivanovich had last seen him, but, as with all dead bodies, his face had acquired greater beauty, or, more to the point, greater significance, than it had had in life. Its expression seemed to say that what needed to be done had been done, and done properly. More than that, the expression contained a reproach, or at least a reminder, to the living. The reminder seemed out of place to Pyotr Ivanovich, or at least he felt it didn't apply to him personally. But an unpleasant feeling came over him, and he crossed himself again, hurriedly – too hurriedly, he thought, the haste was almost indecent – before turning and heading for the door.

Schwartz was waiting for him in the next room with his feet planted wide apart and both hands fiddling with the top hat held behind his back. One glance at his mischievous, immaculately elegant figure and Pyotr Ivanovich felt restored. He could see that Schwartz was above all this, and would be impervious to anything that might have been depressing. His very appearance spoke volumes: in no way would the occasion of Ivan Ilyich's funeral serve as a reason for cancelling their usual session; in other words, nothing would prevent them from breaking open a new pack and riffling through the cards that evening while a servant set up four new candles. There was, in fact, no reason to think that this occasion should stop them having a good time that very evening. He said so in a low voice to Pyotr Ivanovich as he walked past, proposing that they meet for a game at Fyodor Vasilyevich's.

But Pyotr Ivanovich was clearly not destined to play whist that evening. Praskovya Fyodorovna, a short, plump woman whose body expanded from the shoulders down despite her best efforts to the contrary, done out in black, with a lace shawl over her head and the same curiously arched eyebrows as the lady facing the coffin, emerged from her chambers with some other ladies, showed them to the door of the dead man's room, and said, 'The service is about to begin. Do go in.'

Schwartz made an indeterminate bow, and stood there without accepting or rejecting this invitation. Praskovya, recognizing Pyotr Ivanovich, gave a sigh, went straight up to him, took him by the hand, and said, 'I know you were a good friend to Ivan Ilyich . . .' And she looked at him, anticipating a suitable response. Pyotr Ivanovich knew that just as he had had to cross himself in there, out here it was necessary to squeeze her hand and say with a sigh, 'Believe me . . .' And that's what he did. Having done it, he felt that the desired effect had been achieved – he had been touched, and she had been touched.

'Let's go in before they get started. I must have a word with you,' said the widow. 'Give me your arm.'

Pyotr Ivanovich offered an arm and they made their way

into the inner rooms, walking past Schwartz, who gave Pyotr Ivanovich a gloomy wink. 'No whist for you, then. You won't mind if we find another partner. We might make up a fivesome when you can get free,' said his mischievous glance.

Pyotr Ivanovich sighed even more deeply and plaintively, and Praskovya showed her gratitude by squeezing his hand. Proceeding into her drawing-room, which was done out in pink cretonne and lit by one dismal lamp, they sat down near to a table, she on a sofa, he on a low pouffe with broken springs that wobbled unevenly as he sat on it. Praskovya had wanted to warn him off into another chair, but a warning like that did not seem appropriate in the circumstances, so she thought better of it. As he sat down on his pouffe, Pyotr Ivanovich remembered the time when Ivan Ilyich had been decorating this room and had asked his advice about this pink cretonne with the green leaves. On her way past the table to sit down on the sofa – the room was crammed with furniture and knick-knacks – Praskovya snagged the black lace of her black shawl on the carved edge of the table. Pyotr Ivanovich rose slightly to disentangle it, thus releasing the pouffe, which quivered and pushed up at him. The widow began disentangling the lace herself, so Pyotr Ivanovich sat down again, crushing the rebellious pouffe back into submission. But the widow had not finished disentangling herself, so Pyotr Ivanovich rose again, and so did the pouffe, rebellious and even creaking. When this was all over, she took out a clean cambric handkerchief and burst into tears. But Pyotr Ivanovich had cooled somewhat after the episode with the lace and the battle with the pouffe, and he sat there with a scowl on his face. The embarrassment was broken when Sokolov, Ivan Ilyich's footman, came in to report that the plot which Praskovya had chosen in the cemetery was going to cost two hundred roubles. She had stopped weeping, and she looked at Pyotr Ivanovich with a victimized air as she told him in French how hard things were for her. Pyotr Ivanovich made a silent gesture to acknowledge his absolute conviction that it could not be otherwise.

'Do smoke if you would like to,' she said in a tone of voice that was magnanimous yet flat with defeat, and she went on to discuss the cost of the plot with Sokolov. As he lit his cigarette, Pyotr Ivanovich heard that she had made detailed enquiries about the cost of various plots of land before settling on the one she wanted. That was not all: once the plot had been ordered, she went on to make arrangements for the choir. Then Sokolov left.

'I'm doing everything myself,' she told Pyotr Ivanovich, pushing aside some albums on the table. Noticing that the table was under threat from the cigarette, she swiftly moved an ashtray across and spoke again. 'I think it would be hypocritical to claim that I cannot manage practicalities because of my grief. On the contrary, if anything can . . . I won't say console me, but . . . take my mind off things, it's seeing to what has to be done about him.' She took out her handkerchief again as if on the verge of tears, but suddenly she seemed to get a grip on her feelings, snapped out of it and spoke calmly. 'But there is one thing I would like to discuss with you.'

Pyotr Ivanovich bowed his head. The springs shifted under him, but he did not let them have their way.

'He suffered terribly those last few days.'

'Did he really?' asked Pyotr Ivanovich.

'Oh yes, terribly. The last few minutes, no, hours really, he never stopped screaming. He screamed for three solid days without stopping for breath. It was unbearable. I don't know how I got through it. You could hear him three rooms away. Oh, I've been through it all right!'

'And was he conscious?' asked Pyotr Ivanovich.

'Yes,' she whispered. 'To the very end. He said goodbye a quarter of an hour before he died, and he was still asking us to take Volodya away.'

For all the disagreeable awareness of hypocrisy, his own and hers, the thought of the suffering endured by a man he had known so well, first as a happy young lad, then as a schoolboy, then as an adult colleague, left Pyotr Ivanovich with a feeling of horror. Once again he could see that forehead, the nose pressing down on the upper lip, and he felt a pang of fear for himself.

'Three days and three nights of horrible suffering, and then death. Just think, it could happen to me any time, now,' he thought, and he felt that momentary pang of fear. But immediately he was saved, without knowing how, by the old familiar idea that this had happened to Ivan Ilyich, not him, and it could not and would not happen to him, and that kind of thinking would put him in a gloomy mood, for which there was no need, as Schwartz's face had clearly demonstrated. Pursuing this line of thought, Pyotr Ivanovich calmed down and began to show a close interest in the details of Ivan Ilyich's death, as if death was a chance experience that may have applied to Ivan Ilyich but certainly didn't apply to him.

After giving a detailed account of the truly horrendous physical agony that Ivan Ilyich had endured (details that Pyotr Ivanovich learned only in terms of the distressing effect they had had on Praskovya), the widow clearly saw that it was now necessary to get down to business.

'Oh, Pyotr Ivanovich, it's dreadful, absolutely dreadful.' She burst into tears again.

Pyotr Ivanovich gave a sigh, and waited for her to blow her nose. When she had blown her nose, he said, 'Believe me . . .' Then she spoke out again, and told him what must have been the main reason for consulting him: it was all a matter of using the death of her husband to get some money from the Treasury. She made it seem as if she was asking Pyotr Ivanovich's advice about getting a pension, but he could see that here she knew more than he did, she knew the finest details of this subject down to the last penny that could be screwed out of the Treasury in terms of death benefits. What she wanted to know was whether there might be some way of screwing a bit more out of them. Pyotr Ivanovich tried to think of some way of doing this but, having given it some thought and doing the decent thing by cursing the government for being so stingy, he said he thought there was no more to be had. Upon which she gave a sigh, and made no bones about getting rid of her visitor. He got the message, stubbed his cigarette out, stood up, shook hands, and went out into the hall.

In the dining-room with the clock that Ivan Ilyich had prided himself on having acquired in an antique shop, Pyotr Ivanovich came across a priest and a number of people that he knew, here for the funeral, and he saw a pretty young lady whom he also knew, Ivan Ilyich's daughter. She was all in black. Her tiny waist looked tinier than ever. She looked gloomy, assertive, almost truculent. She bowed to Pyotr Ivanovich in a way that suggested he was to blame for something. Behind the daughter stood a wealthy young man, also known to Pyotr Ivanovich, who looked no less offended – he was an examining magistrate, her fiancé by all accounts. Pyotr Ivanovich gave a gloomy bow in their direction and was about to walk through into the dead man's room when Ivan Ilyich's schoolboy son, the image of his father, appeared from behind the stairwell. This was the little Ivan Ilyich that Pyotr Ivanovich remembered from law school. His tear-filled eyes were those of a twelve- or thirteen-year-old boy who has lost his innocence. Seeing Pyotr Ivanovich, he looked embarrassed and scowled morosely. Pyotr Ivanovich gave him a nod and walked into the dead man's room. The funeral service was soon under way – candles, moaning, incense, tears, sobbing. Pyotr Ivanovich stood there with a frown on his face, staring at the legs of those in front of him. Not once did he look at the dead man or succumb to any feelings of weakness; he was one of the first to leave. There was no one in the hall. Gerasim, the servant of peasant stock, darted out of the dead man's room, and sorted through all the fur coats with his big strong hands before finding Pyotr Ivanovich's coat and handing it over.

'Gerasim. How are you feeling, my boy?' said Pyotr Ivanovich, who had to say something. 'A bit sad?'

''Tis God's will, sir. 'Twill come to us all,' said Gerasim, displaying an even white row of peasant's teeth, and then, with the air of a man with a lot of work to do, he wrenched the door open, called the driver up and sprang back to the porch steps, wondering what else needed to be done.

Pyotr Ivanovich found it particularly pleasant to inhale the fresh air after the incense, the corpse and carbolic.

'Where to, sir?' asked the coachman.

'It's still quite early. I think I'll drop in on Fyodor Vasilyevich.'

And that's where he went. And there they were, sure enough, finishing the first rubber. He was just in time to make up a fifth.

2

The past history of Ivan Ilyich's life had been straightforward, ordinary and dreadful in the extreme.

Ivan Ilyich had died at forty-five, a member of the Court of Justice. He was the son of an official who had worked his way through various ministries and departments in Petersburg, carving out the kind of career which brings people to a position from which, despite their obvious incapacity for doing anything remotely useful, they cannot be sacked because of their status and long years of service, so they end up being given wholly false and fictitious jobs to do for which they receive salaries that are anything but fictitious, anything from six to ten thousand a year, and this enables them to live on to a ripe old age.

Such a man was Ilya Yefimovich Golovin, Privy Councillor, superfluous member of various superfluous institutions.

He had three sons. Ivan Ilyich was the second son. The eldest had carved out the same career as his father but in a different ministry, and was now near to achieving the kind of seniority that confers sinecure status. The third son was a failure. He had gone through a series of jobs, ruining his prospects in all of them, and he now worked for the railways. His father, his brothers and especially their wives not only hated meeting him but forgot his existence unless compelled to do otherwise. Their sister had married Baron Greff, a Petersburg official cut from the same cloth as his father-in-law. Ivan Ilyich was what they called *le phénix de la famille*. He was neither as cold and starchy as the elder brother nor as profligate as the younger. He was halfway between – an intelligent, lively, personable and decent man. He had attended law school along with his younger brother. The younger brother didn't finish the course; he was expelled in the fifth grade, whereas Ivan Ilyich passed with honours. As a student he was already the kind of person he remained for the rest of his life, a capable man, cheerful and kind, sociable and convinced of the need to follow the path of duty – duty being anything so designated by higher authority. Boy and man he had avoided toadyism, but from his earliest years he was like a moth to the flame in being drawn towards people in authority, he assumed their mannerisms along with their philosophy of life, and he was on good terms with them. All the distractions of childhood and youth has passed him by leaving scarcely a trace; he had succumbed to both sensuality and vanity, and then in the top classes to liberal thinking, but always within limits unerringly set by his own instinctive feelings.

In his student days he had done things that at first he thought of as utterly revolting, things that made him feel disgusted with himself even as he was doing them, but in later life, noticing that the same things were being done by people of high standing without a qualm, although he couldn't quite bring himself to think they were good, he did manage to dismiss them, and he felt no pangs of remorse when he recalled them.

When he graduated from law school, qualifying for the tenth grade of the civil service, and received enough money from his father to buy his basic necessities, Ivan Ilyich ordered a new set of clothes from Scharmer's,[1] hung a medallion on his watch chain inscribed with the words *Respice finem*,[2] said goodbye to the prince and principal, dined at Donon's[3] with his friends, and set off for one of the provinces with his fashionable luggage, linen, clothes, shaving tackle, toiletries and travelling rug, all ordered and purchased from the very best shops, to take up a position arranged for him by his father as special assistant to the governor.

In the provinces it did not take Ivan Ilyich long to arrange a lifestyle that was as easy and agreeable as the one he had enjoyed at law school. He did his work, pursued his career and at the same time discreetly enjoyed himself. He went off now and then on official visits to country districts, cutting a dignified figure with superiors and inferiors alike, and he prided himself on carrying out his duties, especially in matters concerning religious dissidents, with scrupulous fairness and incorruptibility.

In his official duties, despite his youth and an attitude of some frivolity, he was exceedingly conservative, bureaucratic and even forbidding, but on the social side he was often amusing and witty, and always pleasantly polite – what the governor and the governor's wife called a *bon enfant*, and with them he was like one of the family.

In the provinces he had an affair with a lady only too keen to liaise with a smart young lawyer. There was also a milliner, and there were drinking sessions with visiting aides-de-camp, as well as after-dinner excursions to a certain street on the outskirts. There was a need to work on the governor and even the governor's wife in order to win them over. But all of this bore the stamp of high respectability to such an extent that no one could have called it by a bad name; all of it was catered for by what the French describe as 'youth having its fling'. All of it was conducted with clean hands, in clean linen, in French phrases, and – what mattered most – at the highest level of society, which meant with approval from those in authority.

Ivan Ilyich spent five years in this kind of service, but the time came for a career change. New legal institutions were opening up; new men were needed.

Ivan Ilyich became one of the new men.

Ivan Ilyich was offered the post of examining magistrate, and he took it, even though it meant moving to a new province, dropping all his old contacts and establishing new ones. Ivan Ilyich was given a send-off by his friends, who presented him with a silver cigarette case; they had a group photograph taken, and off he went to his new job.

As an examining magistrate Ivan Ilyich was just as *comme il faut* and respectable, just as capable of separating official duty from private life and earning respect as he had been when working as a special assistant to the governor. The new work itself struck Ivan Ilyich as far more interesting and rewarding than his earlier job. Before, he had quite liked strutting about in his Scharmer uniform, sauntering past anxious petitioners and envious officials and walking straight into the governor's office, where he would sit down for a cup of tea and a smoke. But not many people had been under his authority – only the rural police chiefs and the religious dissidents that he came across on his assignments – and he loved to treat these dependent people with a courteous, almost comradely spirit, he loved to let them feel that although he had the power to crush them he was being straight with them, treating them like friends. There had not been many of them then, but now that Ivan Ilyich was an examining magistrate he felt that everyone without exception was in his power, even the most important and self-satisfied of people; at a stroke from his pen on headed notepaper any important or self-satisfied person could be brought before him as a defendant or witness to answer questions and be kept on his feet if Ivan Ilyich chose not to let him sit down. Far from abusing this power, he did his best to play it down, but his consciousness of that power and the very chance to play it down were what gave his new job its interest and appeal. In the work itself, the process of investigation, Ivan Ilyich soon mastered the technique of distancing himself from all irrelevancies and reducing the most complicated cases to a version that could be set down on paper in objective outline, excluding any personal opinion on his part, while observing all the necessary formalities, which was what mattered most. This was the new way of working, and he was one of the first men to implement the reformed Legal Code of 1864.[4]

Ivan Ilyich's transfer to a new town and the post of examining magistrate meant meeting new people and making new contacts; he also struck a new attitude, and slightly changed his tone. The new attitude involved distancing himself somewhat from the provincial authorities while cultivating the best circles among the judiciary and the wealthy gentry of the town, and the new tone entailed mild dissatisfaction with the government, a degree of liberalism and a civilized man's sense of public duty. At the same time, without compromising the fastidiousness of his dress sense, in his new situation he left his chin unshaven, allowing his beard to grow as and where it wanted.

In his new town, too, Ivan Ilyich set himself up very nicely. The section of society opposed to the governor was friendly and agreeable, his pay had gone up, and one thing that made his life particularly pleasurable was the playing of whist, which he now took to with the enjoyment of a skilled card-player, astute, quick-thinking and almost invariably a winner.

After two years working in the new town Ivan Ilyich met his future wife. Praskovya Fyodorovna Mikhel was the most attractive, intelligent and colourful young lady in the social circle frequented by Ivan Ilyich. To the list of other distractions and relaxations from his work as an examining magistrate Ivan Ilyich added a mild flirtation with Praskovya.

When he had been an assistant on special commissions Ivan Ilyich had been quite a dancer, but now he was an examining magistrate he took to the floor much less frequently. When he danced it was only as if to say, 'Look, I may be part of the reformed system, and I've got as far as Grade 5, but if you want to see me on the floor I can show you that even in dancing I can be the best.' So, just occasionally, he would take to the floor with Praskovya at the end of an evening, and it was actually while dancing like this that he won her heart. She fell in love with him. Ivan Ilyich had no clear and definite plans for marriage, but once the girl fell in love with him he began to wonder. 'When all's said and done, why shouldn't I get married?' he asked himself.

This young woman, Praskovya Fyodorovna, belonged to a good family, and she was quite attractive. She also came with a little money. Ivan Ilyich might have held out for a more brilliant partner, but she was herself a decent catch. Ivan was earning good money, and he could count on something similar from her. It would be a good match – she was a nice girl, quite pretty and a thoroughly decent young woman. To claim that Ivan Ilyich got married because he was in love with his bride, and saw in her someone who shared his outlook on life, would have been no more justifiable than to say that he married because the match met with the approval of the society that he moved in. Ivan Ilyich married for both reasons. He was pleasing himself by acquiring such a wife, but at the same time he was appealing to his superiors and their sense of propriety.

So, Ivan Ilyich got married.

The process of getting married, and the early days of married life, with conjugal caresses, new furniture, new crockery, new linen, everything up to his wife's pregnancy, went very smoothly, to the extent that Ivan Ilyich was beginning to think that marriage would not disrupt his easy, agreeable and enjoyable lifestyle, which was decency itself, approved of by society and something that Ivan Ilyich considered to be part of life itself – and it might even improve it. But it was at this stage, during the first months of his wife's pregnancy, that something happened, something new, unexpected, unpleasant, difficult and disgusting, something that could not have been anticipated and could not in any way be got rid of.

For no reason that Ivan Ilyich could fathom, other than what he called *gaîté de coeur*, his wife did begin to disrupt the pleasant and decent run of his life. She became jealous of him for no apparent cause, demanded his closest attention, laid into him and started arguments that were unpleasantly vulgar.

At first Ivan Ilyich hoped to escape the unpleasantness of his new situation by relapsing into the same carefree but respectable way of life that had stood him in good stead before – he tried to ignore his wife's moodiness and carry on in the easy, agreeable way that he had formerly enjoyed, inviting friends round for a game of cards and trying to get out and drive round to the club or visit people close to him. But there came a time when his wife started shouting at him so furiously, using such foul language, determined to keep on yelling at him when he failed to do what she wanted, obviously with every intention of keeping it up until he came to heel, stayed in and went through the same anguish that she felt, that Ivan Ilyich was horrified. He realized that married life – at least with his wife – didn't always mean enjoyment and decency, but, on the contrary, it often disrupted them, and it was therefore necessary to guard against such disruptions. And Ivan Ilyich began to seek ways of doing this. His work was the one thing that impressed Praskovya, and it was through work and the commitments associated with it that he took on his wife and asserted his own independence.

When the baby was born, with the various difficulties with feeding, the real and imaginary illnesses of mother and child, which demanded his sympathetic involvement even though he understood nothing about them, the need for Ivan Ilyich to safeguard his independence became even more urgent.

As his wife grew more and more irritable and demanding, Ivan Ilyich gradually shifted his life's centre of gravity on to his work. He loved his work more and more, and became more ambitious than he had been.

It didn't take him long – no more than a year after his wedding – to realize that although married life did provide some conveniences, it was actually rather a complex and difficult business, and the path of duty, which meant leading a decent life approved of by society, called for a clearly defined attitude, as at work.

And Ivan Ilyich managed to establish such an attitude towards his married life. He required of it whatever domestic conveniences it could provide in terms of meals on the table, a good household and a bed and, most important, the outward show of respectability that society required. Beyond this, he required some enjoyment and pleasure, and if he found this he was very thankful, but if he was met with rejection and crabbiness he immediately took himself off into his own separate, carefully guarded world, the world of work which gave him pleasure.

Ivan Ilyich was considered a good colleague, and within three years he was promoted to assistant chief prosecutor. His new responsibilities, the importance that they entailed, the opportunity of bringing people before the court and sending them to prison, the publicity given to his speeches, and the success enjoyed by Ivan Ilyich in these matters – all of this made his work seem even more enjoyable.

Other children were born. His wife was becoming more and more bad-tempered and crabby, but the new attitude established by Ivan Ilyich towards his home life made him all but impervious to her crabbiness.

After serving for seven years in the same town Ivan Ilyich was transferred to another province, as public prosecutor. They moved, they were short of money, and his wife didn't like the town they had moved to. His salary had gone up, but so had their living expenses. On top of that, two of their children died, and family life became even more unpleasant for Ivan Ilyich.

Praskovya blamed her husband for all the setbacks they were suffering in their new place of residence. Most of the topics of conversation between husband and wife, especially about bringing up the children, led to questions that reminded them of past arguments, and new arguments were liable to flare up at any moment. They were left with a few short periods of amorousness that came over them as husband and wife, but these did not last long. These were nothing more than little islands where they could anchor for a while, only to plunge back into a sea of hidden hostility as they grew further and further apart. This growing apart might have upset Ivan Ilyich if he had thought there was anything wrong with it, but now not only did he consider this state of affairs to be quite normal, he saw it as the whole point of his role in the family. His role was to distance himself increasingly from all the unpleasantness and give it an air of harmless respectability; this he achieved by spending less and less time with the family, and when he was forced to be with them he sought to safeguard his own position by ensuring the presence of others. But the main thing was that Ivan Ilyich did have his work. It was in the world of his work that the whole interest of his life came into focus. And this interest absorbed him totally. The knowledge of the power that he wielded, the possibility of ruining anyone that he fancied ruining, the gravitas (even if it was all outward show) which could be sensed as he walked into court or dealt with his subordinates, the success that he was enjoying with his superiors and subordinates alike, and, above all, his masterly handling of the cases – all of this gave him pleasure, and, along with chit-chat with colleagues, dinners and whist, filled his life to the full. And so, life in general proceeded for Ivan Ilyich just as he thought it should proceed – pleasantly and respectably.

He lived like this for about seven years. Their daughter, the eldest child, was now sixteen, another child had died and their one remaining son was the subject of strong disagreement. Ivan Ilyich wanted to send him to law school, but Praskovya had defied him by putting him down for the high school. The daughter was being educated at home, and was developing nicely; the boy too was doing quite well at his studies.

3

This was the course that Ivan Ilyich's life had taken during the seventeen years that followed his wedding. He was now a senior public prosecutor who had turned down several transfers in the hope of securing an even more desirable position, but then suddenly an unpleasant circumstance arose which looked like completely disrupting the peaceful progress of his life. Ivan Ilyich was expecting an appointment as presiding judge in a university town, but Hoppe pipped him at the post and got the job. Ivan Ilyich was livid, and he made some insinuations, taking issue with Hoppe himself and his immediate superiors. He was met with a chill rebuff, and was overlooked again when the next appointment came up.

This was in 1880. That year was the hardest he ever lived through. It was a year in which it transpired, for one thing, that they couldn't make ends meet financially, and, for another, that he was a forgotten man and, whereas he saw himself as the victim of an outrageously cruel injustice, everyone else thought it was just the way things went. Even his father saw it as no duty of his to help out. He felt deserted by everyone; they all thought that his situation, with a salary of three thousand five hundred roubles, was perfectly normal, even fortunate. He was the only person who knew that, with all the injustices that had been visited upon him, with nothing but nagging from his wife, and the debts that were now mounting up because he was living beyond his means – he was the only one who knew that his position was anything but normal.

That summer, in order to cut costs, he took leave of absence and went with his wife for a country holiday at her brother's place. In the country, with no work to occupy him, Ivan Ilyich had his first experience of not just boredom but unbearable anguish. He decided he couldn't go on like this – definite steps must be taken.

During a sleepless night, the whole of which he spent pacing the terrace, he decided he would go to Petersburg and make representations; he would get his own back on *those men* who had underestimated him, by changing ministries. Next morning he defied all the remonstrations from his wife and brother-in-law, and left for Petersburg.

He went with one aim in mind: to get himself a position that would bring in five thousand a year. By now he had no allegiance to any particular ministry, faction or function. All he needed was a job, a job that would bring in five thousand a year, in administration, in one of the banks, with the railways, in one of the charitable institutions set up by the Dowager Empress Maria,[5] even in the customs service; all that mattered was five thousand a year and an immediate transfer from the ministry where he was so undervalued.

And his trip was crowned with unexpected, unbelievable success. At Kursk, an acquaintance of his, F. S. Ilyin, got into his first-class carriage, sat down and told him that the governor of the province had just received a telegram informing him of a reshuffle in the ministry – Pyotr Ivanovich was being replaced by Ivan Semyonovich.

The proposed reshuffle, whatever its impact on Russia at large, meant something special to Ivan Ilyich: the emergence of Pyotr Petrovich, and also apparently his friend, Zakhar Ivanovich, was very good news for him. Zakhar Ivanovich was a colleague and friend.

The new development had been confirmed in Moscow; now, arriving in Petersburg, Ivan Ilyich looked up Zakhar, who promised him a definite position in his former department, the Ministry of Justice.

Within a week he was able to send the following telegram to his wife: *Zakhar replaces Miller. Appointment mine with first report.*

Because of this change of staff Ivan Ilyich had suddenly achieved a position in his former ministry which put him two grades higher than his colleagues, with five thousand a year plus three thousand five hundred roubles removal expenses. All the acrimony that he had felt towards his enemies and the ministry in general was forgotten, and Ivan Ilyich was a happy man.

He returned to the country feeling in high spirits, more

contented than he had been for a long time. Praskovya's spirits had also picked up, and a truce was declared between the two of them. Ivan Ilyich described how honoured he had been in Petersburg, how his former enemies had been put to shame and were now licking his boots, how people envied him his new position, and, most of all, how popular he had been in Petersburg.

Praskovya listened to all of this, pretending to believe it and not querying anything, but her real interest was only in sketching out the new way of life that they would lead in the city to which they were moving. And Ivan Ilyich was delighted to see that her plans were his plans, they were together as one, and that his life, having hit a bad patch, was now getting back to its old way, its true path of happy enjoyment and respectability.

Ivan Ilyich had not come back for long. He had to take up his duties on the 10th of September, and before that he had to settle into new surroundings, have all his things brought in from the provinces, buy in and order up many more items – in other words he had set up home just as he had worked things out in his own mind, which was almost exactly as Praskovya had worked things out in her own heart.

And now that everything had been set up so successfully, and he and his wife were agreed in their aims, having lived together so little of late, they came together more closely than at any time since they were first married. Ivan Ilyich had intended to move his family in straightaway, but at the insistence of his sister-in-law and brother-in-law, who were suddenly all over Ivan Ilyich and his family, it was arranged for him to go on alone.

Ivan Ilyich set out on his journey. The happy feelings brought on by his success and a rapprochement with his wife, each intensifying the other, never left him. He found a delightful place, a dream apartment for him and his wife. The spacious, high-ceilinged reception rooms with their old-fashioned décor, the gracefully appointed and comfortable study, the rooms for his wife and daughter, the classroom for his son – all of it seemed to have been designed with them in mind. Ivan Ilyich took it upon himself to organize the fittings and furnishings; he chose the wallpaper, purchased furniture, predominantly of the old-fashioned style which he considered to be *comme il faut*, the upholstery . . . and the whole thing grew and grew, approaching the ideal that he had set himself. Even halfway through the refurbishment, the whole thing exceeded his expectations. He could see how elegant it would all be, quite *comme il faut* and devoid of vulgarity, when it was completed. As he went to sleep he would imagine what the large reception room was going to look like. When he glanced into the half-finished drawing-room he could envisage the fireplace, the screen, the whatnot and the little chairs dotted about the room, the plates and dishes on the walls and the bronze pieces, everything in its proper place. He enjoyed the thought of surprising Pasha and Lizanka,[6] who were not without taste themselves. This was beyond their expectations. He had been particularly successful in tracking down antiques and buying them at bargain prices; they now gave the whole place an air of distinction. He deliberately understated everything in his letters home so that they would be surprised. He was so taken up with all of this that the work he loved so dearly interested him less than he had thought it would. In court he found his mind wandering; he would be miles away, wondering whether to have plain or moulded cornices with his curtains. He became so involved that he often did the work himself, rearranging the furniture and rehanging the curtains. On one occasion, climbing a stepladder to show a dull-witted upholsterer how to hang the draperies, he slipped and fell, though he was strong and agile enough to hold on, and all he did was bump his side on a window-frame knob. The bruised place hurt for a while but it soon passed off. And all this time Ivan Ilyich felt particularly well and in the best of spirits. 'I seem to have shed fifteen years,' he wrote home. He had hoped to get it all finished by the end of September, but things dragged on until mid-October. Still, it was magnificent, and he wasn't the only one to say so – everybody did.

But these were essentially the accoutrements that appeal to all people who are not actually rich but who want to look rich, though all they manage to do is look like each other: damasks, ebony, plants, rugs and bronzes, anything dark and gleaming –

everything that all people of a certain class affect so as to be like all other people of a certain class. And his arrangements looked so much like everyone else's that they were unremarkable, though he saw them as something truly distinctive. When he met his family at the railway station, brought them home and ushered them into his well-lit furnished apartment and a footman wearing a white tie opened the door into the entrance hall decorated with flowers, and then they went into the drawing-room and the study, ooh-ing and ah-ing with delight, he was a very happy man, showing them around everywhere, revelling in their praise and beaming with delight. That evening, as they took tea, when Praskovya asked him casually about his fall he gave a laugh and demonstrated how he had gone flying and given the upholsterer a scare.

'It's a good job I'm athletic. Any other man would have killed himself, but all I did was bruise myself a bit here. It hurts when you touch it, but it's getting better. It is only a bruise.'

And so they began life in their new abode, where, as always happens with people who have recently settled in, they found themselves just one room short, and their new income wouldn't quite run to it, though it was only a matter of five hundred roubles or so. Still, they were very nicely off, especially during the early days when not everything was finished and work was still to be done – things had to be bought, ordered, rearranged, adjusted. There were one or two disagreements between husband and wife, but both of them were so satisfied and so busy that everything resolved itself without serious arguments. When there was nothing more to be finished off they developed a feeling of dullness and a sense of something missing, but by this time they had got to know new people and formed new habits. Their lives had filled out.

Ivan Ilyich would return for lunch after a morning in court and in those early days he tended to be in a good mood; any slight distress that he suffered came from the apartment itself. (The slightest stain on a tablecloth or upholstery, or a loose cord on the draperies annoyed him; he had put so much effort into the furnishings that the slightest disturbance upset him.) But, all things considered, Ivan Ilyich's life went along, as he saw it, just as life ought to go – easily, pleasantly, decently. He rose at nine, drank some coffee, read the newspaper, then put on his uniform and went to court. There, the collar that he worked in had been worn into shape and he soon found that it fitted him well – the petitioners, the enquiries received, the office, the public sessions and the administrative meetings. In all of this the trick was to eliminate the element of crude everyday life that always disrupts the smooth flow of official business; no relationships should be entered into beyond the official ones, the reason behind any relationship had to be strictly official and the relationship itself had to be strictly official. Say, for example, a person arrives wanting to know something. This is not the responsibility of Ivan Ilyich; he can have no relationship with such a person. But if this person were to approach him in his capacity as a member of the judiciary and in a relationship that can be set down on letterhead paper, within the terms of that relationship Ivan Ilyich will do anything he can, and do it decisively, while maintaining a semblance of friendly human relations – nothing more than common courtesy. At the point where an official relationship breaks off, everything else breaks off, too. The skill of compartmentalizing the official side of things and keeping that apart from his own real life was one that Ivan Ilyich possessed in the highest degree; long practice and natural talent had enabled him to refine it to such a degree that now he could act like a virtuoso performer, occasionally allowing himself to mix human and official relationships by way of a joke. He allowed himself this liberty because he felt strong enough whenever necessary to reinstate the distinction between the official and the human by discarding the latter. This was more than just an easy, pleasant and decent thing for Ivan Ilyich to do – he was acting like a virtuoso performer. During his breaks he would have a smoke, drink tea and chat, exchange a word or two about politics, current affairs and cards, and a whole lot more about who was in and who was out. And he would go home tired, but feeling like a virtuoso performer, a first violin in the orchestra, who has given of his best. At home his daughter and his wife would either have been out visiting or would have entertained someone at home, while his son, back from school, would have had a session with his private tutors and gone on to cram whatever it is they teach in schools. Everything was fine. After dinner, if there were no guests, Ivan Ilyich sometimes read a book that people were talking about, and later in the evening he sat down to do some work, reading through papers, studying the law, comparing depositions and sorting them by statute. This neither bored nor amused him. He found it boring when he might have been playing whist, but if whist was off it was better than just sitting there on his own or with his wife. What gave Ivan Ilyich real pleasure, though, was having little dinner parties to which he would invite ladies and gentlemen of good social standing and passing the time with them precisely as such people invariably do pass the time, in the way that his drawing-room was exactly like all the others.

One day they held an evening party with dancing. Ivan Ilyich enjoyed it and everything went swimmingly, except for a big row between him and his wife over the cakes and sweets. Praskovya had had her own ideas, but Ivan Ilyich had insisted on bringing in an expensive caterer who had provided too many cakes; the leftovers had caused the row when the caterer's bill came to forty-five roubles. The row was a big one, very nasty, and it ended with Praskovya calling him a stupid fool while he clutched his head and muttered something about divorce. But he still enjoyed the party. The best people were there and Ivan Ilyich danced with Princess Trufonova, whose sister had famously founded the charity known as 'Take Away My Sorrow'. Pleasure derived from work was self-indulgence, pleasure derived from socializing tickled his vanity, but real pleasure came to Ivan Ilyich only from playing cards. He was prepared to admit that, at the end of the day, with any amount of unpleasantness behind him, the one pleasure that outshone all others like a beacon was to sit down and play whist with quiet-mannered partners, good players, always in a foursome (sitting out was such a bore when there were five, and you had to pretend not to mind), and playing seriously and playing well (when you got a decent hand) before going on to supper with a glass of wine. And after a game of cards, especially if he had won a small amount (big winnings were not nice), Ivan Ilyich would go to bed in the very best of spirits.

This was how they lived. They moved in the best of circles, receiving people of quality, and the younger set.

In their attitude towards the circle of their acquaintances husband, wife and daughter were of one mind. Without collusion, each of them in the same way shrugged off and discarded all the shabby friends and relatives who flocked around fawning on them in the drawing-room with the Japanese plates on the walls. It wasn't long before the shabby friends stopped flocking around and left the Golovin family to the best people in society and no one else. Young men were attracted to their little Liza and one examining magistrate by the name of Petrishchev, the son of Dmitriy Ivanovich Petrishchev and his sole heir, became so attentive towards her that Ivan Ilyich mentioned this once or twice to Praskovya and wondered whether they ought perhaps to take them out for a ride in a troika or set up some private theatricals. This was how they lived. This was how things went, nothing changed, and everything was fine.

4

They were all in good health. The fact that Ivan Ilyich sometimes complained of a strange taste in his mouth and a funny feeling in his left side didn't count as ill health. But as it happened this funny feeling began to get worse and turned into, if not pain exactly, a constant dragging sensation in his side, which put him in a bad mood. And this bad mood, which got worse and worse, began to spoil the pleasant, easy-going and respectable way of life that the Golovins had just set up for themselves. There were more and more quarrels between husband and wife, the pleasant, easy-going way of life lapsed, and they were hard put to keep up an appearance of decency. Once again scenes became more and more frequent. They were left once again with nothing more than those little islands, all too few of them, on which husband and wife could come together without an explosion.

And now Praskovya began to say, not without justification, that her husband was a hard man. With her usual capacity for exaggeration she claimed that he had always been horrible like that and only her good nature had enabled her to put up with it for twenty years. It was true that all the arguments now began on his side. His jibes always started just as they sat down to dinner, often over the soup. There was always something – if it wasn't chipped crockery or something wrong with the food, he would go on about his son putting his elbow on the table or his daughter's hair. And it was always Praskovya's fault. To begin with, Praskovya would take issue with him and say something nasty, but on a couple of occasions he flew into such a rage at the beginning of dinner that she realized this was a pathological condition brought on by consuming food, so she bit it all back, stopped objecting and got on with her dinner as fast as she could. Praskovya took great pride in biting things back. Convinced that her husband was a horrible man who had made her life a misery, she was now sorry for herself. And the sorrier she became, the more she hated her husband. She began to wish he was dead, and then not to, because without him there would be no income. All of which made her even more exasperated with him. She felt thoroughly miserable at the thought that not even his death could rescue her. She was exasperated, though she hid it, but her hidden exasperation served only to strengthen his exasperation.

After one scene during which Ivan Ilyich had been particularly unfair and after which, by way of explanation, he had admitted being exasperating but claimed he was ill, she told him that if he was ill he needed treatment and insisted that he must go and see a famous doctor.

He did. The whole thing turned out just as he had expected, and as it always does. He was made to wait, the doctor was full of his own importance – an attitude he was familiar with because it was one that he himself assumed in court – then came all the tapping and listening, the questions with predetermined and obviously superfluous answers, the knowing look that seemed to say, 'Just place yourself in our hands and we'll sort it out, we know what we're doing, there's no doubt about it, we can sort things out the same way as we would for anyone you care to name.' It was just like being in court. The way he looked at the accused in court was exactly the way he was being looked at now by the famous doctor.

The doctor was holding forth. Such-and-such demonstrates that in your inside there is such-and-such, but if this is not confirmed by our tests on this-and-that then you will need to go on to such-and-such. And if you go on to such-and-such, then . . . and so on. As far as Ivan Ilyich was concerned there was only one question that mattered: Is this condition life-threatening or not? But the doctor treated this question as irrelevant, and ignored it. From the doctor's point of view it was a pointless question not worthy of discussion; the only thing was a balancing of probabilities – floating kidney, chronic colitis, problem with the blind gut.[7] The question of Ivan Ilyich living or dying didn't arise; there was just this conflict between the floating kidney and the blind gut. And before his very eyes the doctor resolved the conflict at a brilliant stroke in favour of the floating kidney, with the sole proviso that new evidence might emerge from the urine test, and if that happened the case would have to be reviewed. All of it from start to finish was precisely what Ivan Ilyich himself had done to the accused a thousand times and with no less brilliance. Brilliant indeed was the doctor's summing-up of the situation as he looked in triumph bordering on delight over his glasses at his own prisoner in the dock. From the summary Ivan Ilyich drew only one conclusion: he was in a bad way and the doctor didn't care, nobody cared probably, but he was in a bad way. And this conclusion left Ivan Ilyich with a sickly feeling, filling him with self-pity and great animosity towards the doctor who showed so much indifference to such an important question.

But he said nothing about it. He got up, laid his money on the table and said, with a sigh, 'I'm sure that when we're ill we ask a lot of pointless questions. But, er, is it life-threatening or not . . . ?'

The doctor glared at him through one eye over his glasses as if to say, 'Prisoner in the dock, if you will not confine yourself to answering the questions put to you I shall have to arrange for you to be removed from the courtroom.'

'I have already told you what I consider necessary and appropriate. Anything further will be determined by the tests.' The doctor bowed.

Ivan Ilyich walked out slowly, climbed gloomily into his sledge and drove home. All the way back he kept going over in his mind everything the doctor had said, trying to translate his confusingly complex technicalities into everyday speech and find in them an answer to one question: am I in a bad way, a really bad way, or is it nothing to worry about just now? And it seemed to him that the message from all that the doctor had said was yes, you're in a very bad way. Ivan Ilyich thought the streets looked dismal. The drivers looked dismal, the houses looked dismal, and so did the pedestrians and the shops. And in the light of the doctor's confusing pronouncements the pain, that dull, nagging pain that never went away, was taking on a new and more serious significance. It was with a new feeling of dejection that Ivan Ilyich focused on it.

He reached home and started to tell his wife. His wife listened closely, but halfway through his account their daughter came in wearing a little hat – she and her mother were on their way out. She made an effort to sit down and listen to his boring story, but she couldn't contain herself for long and her mother gave up listening.

'Well, I'm very pleased,' said his wife. 'And now, you listen to me. Make sure you take your medicine properly. Give me the prescription and I'll send Gerasim to the chemist's.' And she went off to get dressed.

He had hardly paused for breath while she was in the room, and when she went out he gave a deep sigh.

'Oh well,' he said. 'Maybe that's right. Nothing to worry about just now . . .'

He started taking his medicine and following the doctor's instructions, though these were changed once the urine test results were in. But at this point it turned out that there was some confusion over the test itself and what was supposed to follow it. Without getting at the doctor, it was becoming clear that what was going on was not what the doctor had said. He must have overlooked something, or he had been telling lies, or he was hiding something.

Nevertheless, Ivan Ilyich started to follow his instructions, and from the process of doing so he derived some comfort for a while. Since his visit to the doctor Ivan Ilyich had made it his main preoccupation to follow all instructions to the letter in matters of hygiene, the taking of medicine, focusing on his pain and monitoring all his bodily functions. His main interests were in human sickness and human health. When he overheard anyone talking about people who had fallen ill, died or recovered, especially if the illness sounded like his own, he tried to hide his agitation but he listened closely, asked lots of questions and applied what he heard to his own illness.

The pain was not getting any less, but Ivan Ilyich made every effort to make himself believe he was feeling better. And he was able to delude himself as long as nothing upset him. But the moment he fell out with his wife, or something went wrong at work or he got a bad hand at whist, he felt the full force of his illness. Before this he had been able to withstand setbacks like these, expecting to put things right before long, to win through, succeed again, come out with a grand slam. But now the slightest setback cut the ground from under him and left him in despair. He would say to himself, 'Look at that. I was just starting to get better and the medicine was just beginning to work, and now this damn thing comes up, this rotten luck . . .' And he raged against his misfortune or against those people who were causing his problems and killing him off; he sensed that it was his own rage that was killing him and he couldn't control it. It ought to have been obvious to him that raging against his situation and the people around him was only feeding his illness and, because of that, he ought to ignore any unpleasant developments, but he thought the exact opposite: he told himself he needed peace of mind so he had to get on to anything that disrupted his peace of mind, and the slightest disruption left him exasperated. His situation was made worse by the fact that he had taken to reading medical books and consulting doctors. The decline was so gradual that he was able to delude himself by comparing one day with another and seeing little difference. But the moment he consulted a doctor he thought he was going downhill, and fast. Yet, despite this, he kept on consulting the doctors.

That month he went to see another celebrity. This celebrity told him more or less the same as the first one, but put things differently. And the consultation with this celebrity served only to reinforce Ivan Ilyich's doubts and fears. A friend of a friend – a very good doctor – diagnosed something entirely different and, even though he swore he would get better, his questions and assumptions confused Ivan Ilyich even more and deepened his suspicions. A homeopath produced yet another diagnosis and gave him some medicine, which Ivan Ilyich took for a week or so without telling anyone. But by the end of the week, feeling no better and losing faith in every treatment that had been prescribed so far including that one, he felt more despondent than ever. One day a lady of his acquaintance talked to him about the curative powers of icons. Ivan Ilyich caught himself listening closely to what she was saying, and beginning to accept it as fact. This scared him. 'Am I really going weak in the head?' he wondered. 'Nonsense. It's all rubbish! I'm not falling for stupid ideas like that. I'd rather pick one doctor and stick to what he says. That's what I'm going to do. That's it. I'm going to stop thinking about it, and follow the treatment to the letter until the summer. Then we'll see. No more shilly-shallying.' This was easy to say but impossible to do. The pain in his side went on wearing him down and seemed to be getting worse, nagging incessantly, while the taste in his mouth got more and more peculiar and he began to think that his breath smelt awful, and his appetite and strength fell away. The time for fooling himself was over: something new and dreadful was going on inside Ivan Ilyich, something significant, more significant than anything in his whole life. And he was the only one who knew it; the people around him didn't know, or didn't want to know – they thought that everything in the world was going on as before. This was what tormented Ivan Ilyich more than anything. He could see that his family – especially his wife and daughter, whose visiting season was in full swing – had no inkling; it annoyed them that he was not much fun and asked so much of them – as if he was to blame. Despite their best efforts to hide it, he could see that he was in their way. His wife had developed an attitude to his illness and she was sticking to it whatever he might say or do. Her attitude went like this: 'You know what it's like,' she would say to her friends. 'Ivan Ilyich can't be like other people. He won't stick to his treatment. One moment he takes his drops and eats what he's supposed to, and goes to bed when he should; the next day, if I'm not watching him, he doesn't take his medicine, he eats sturgeon – which he's not allowed – and he stays up playing whist until one in the morning.'

'Oh, come on,' says Ivan Ilyich. 'I did that once, with Pyotr Ivanovich.'

'What about yesterday, with Shebek?'

'It made no difference. I couldn't sleep with all that pain . . .'

'Well, it doesn't matter why. Only you'll never get better like that, and it's getting us down.'

Praskovya's attitude towards Ivan Ilyich's illness, of which she made no secret to other people or to him, was that it was all his fault; he was making his wife's life a misery yet again. Ivan Ilyich felt she was doing this unconsciously, but that didn't make things any easier for him.

In court Ivan Ilyich noticed, or thought he noticed, the same strange attitude towards him. There were times when he thought people were watching him closely like a man who was about to give up his job; at other times his associates would make friendly little jokes about the way he worried over his health, as if this ghastly, fearful, unheard-of thing that had got going inside him and was now incessantly gnawing at him and inexorably taking him away was a good subject and a laughing matter. The one who infuriated him most was Schwartz, with his playfulness, *joie de vivre* and all-round respectability which recalled the Ivan Ilyich of ten years before.

His friends have come round for a game of cards. They take their places and deal, softening the new cards. He sorts his diamonds – seven of them. His partner bids no trumps and supports him with two diamonds. Couldn't be better. This should be a wonderful, joyous moment – a grand slam is on. But suddenly he feels that gnawing pain, that taste in his mouth, and he is struck by the barbarity of rejoicing in a grand slam.

He glances across at his partner, Mikhail Mikhaylovich, who is tapping the table with an eager hand, politely and graciously holding back from grabbing the tricks and pushing them towards Ivan Ilyich so that he can enjoy the pleasure of raking them in without having to make any effort or reaching very far. 'Does he think I'm too weak to reach out?' thinks Ivan Ilyich, forgetting what are trumps and overtrumping his partner with his own, which leaves them three tricks short of a grand slam. And worst of all, he can see how upset Mikhail Mikhaylovich is, and he doesn't care. And it is awful to think why he doesn't care.

They can all see that he is distraught, and they say to him, 'We can stop if you're feeling tired. Why don't you have a rest?' Rest? No, he's *not tired*. They finish the rubber. They are all gloomy and silent. Ivan Ilyich senses that he has caused the gloom, and he cannot dispel it. They have supper and go home, and Ivan Ilyich is left there alone with the knowledge that his life has been poisoned and is poisoning other people's lives, and the poison is not wearing off, it is working its way deeper and deeper into his very being.

And he has to take this knowledge to bed with him, along with the physical pain and the terror, often to spend a near-sleepless night because of the pain. And next morning he has to get up again, put on his clothes, go to court, talk, write or, if he doesn't go out, stay in with every one of those twenty-four hours that make up a day and a night, each one of them an agony. And he has to live like this on the edge of destruction, alone, with nobody at all to understand and pity him.

5

One month passed like this, then another. His brother-in-law came to their town to stay with them for the New Year celebrations. Ivan Ilyich was in court when he arrived. Praskovya was out shopping. On his return Ivan Ilyich walked into his study and found his brother-in-law already there, a strong, fit young man, busy unpacking his own suitcase. He looked up when he heard Ivan Ilyich approaching and stared at him in silence for a moment. That stare told Ivan Ilyich everything. His brother-in-law opened his mouth to exclaim, but managed to restrain himself. That movement confirmed everything.

'I've changed, haven't I?'

'Well . . . you have rather.'

And after this, however hard Ivan Ilyich tried to raise the subject of his appearance, his brother-in-law wouldn't say a word. Praskovya arrived home and her brother went to see her. Ivan Ilyich locked the door and went to have a good look at himself in the mirror, full face, then in profile. He picked up a photograph of himself with his wife and compared his likeness with what he now saw in the mirror. The difference was enormous. Then he pulled his sleeves up, looked at his arms, pulled his sleeves back down and sat down on an ottoman, looking blacker than night.

'No, no. I mustn't,' he told himself. He jumped up and went to his desk, where he opened a file and began to read, but he couldn't go on. He opened the door and went out into the hallway. The door into the drawing-room was shut. He tiptoed over to it and started to listen.

'No, you're exaggerating,' Praskovya was saying.

'What do you mean, exaggerating? You can't see it. He's a dead man. Look at his eyes – there's no light in them. What is it he's got exactly?'

'Nobody knows. Nikolayev [yet another doctor] said something, but I don't know what it was. Leshchetitsky [the celebrity] said the exact opposite . . .'

Ivan Ilyich walked away back into his room, lay down and started to think things over. 'Kidney, a floating kidney . . .' He could remember everything the doctors had told him about it becoming detached and starting to wander. With an effort of his imagination he tried to catch the kidney, stop it moving and fix it strongly. It seemed to take so little effort. 'No, I'm going back to Pyotr Ivanovich [the friend who was the doctor's friend].' He rang the bell, ordered the carriage and prepared to go out.

'*Jean*,[8] where are you going?' asked his wife, looking very gloomy but uncharacteristically kind.

The uncharacteristic kindness infuriated him. He gave her a dark look. 'I've got to go and see Pyotr Ivanovich.'

He went to see the friend with the friend who was the doctor, and on with him to the doctor himself, who was in. They had a long talk.

Going through the details of anatomy and physiology in terms of what the doctor considered to be happening in his insides made everything quite clear to him.

There was a little bit of something, a tiny little thing, in his blind gut. It could all be put right. By raising the energy level in one organ and lowering the activity of another, absorption could be achieved and everything would be all right. He was a little late for dinner. He talked cheerfully after dinner, but for some time he couldn't bring himself to go to his room and work. Eventually he did go off to his study and he got straight down to it. He worked at the files for a while, but he couldn't shrug off the awareness that he had some important unfinished personal business that would have to be attended to in the end. When he had finished the files he remembered that this personal business meant thinking about his gut. But instead of giving in to this he went to take tea in the drawing-room. They had guests – there was conversation, piano-playing and singing – and among them was the examining magistrate who was such a good match for his daughter. As Praskovya remarked, he enjoyed the evening more than usual, but never for a minute did he forget that he had some important unfinished thinking to do, about his gut. At eleven o'clock he said goodnight and went to his room. He had been sleeping alone since his illness began, in a tiny little room next to his study. He went in, undressed and took up a Zola novel, but instead of reading it he lapsed into thought. And in his imagination the longed-for healing of his blind gut took place; absorption was followed by evacuation and its proper function was restored. 'Yes, that's how it goes,' he said to himself. 'All you have to do is give nature a helping hand.' He remembered his medicine, eased himself up and took it, then lay on his back focusing on the good that the medicine was doing and the way it was getting rid of the pain. 'Keep taking it regularly and avoid anything harmful. I feel a bit better already, a lot better.' He felt his side – no pain to the touch. 'No, there's no feeling there. It really is getting a lot better.' He put out the candle and lay on his side . . .

Absorption; the blind gut was curing itself. Then suddenly he could feel the same old dull gnawing pain, quiet, serious, unrelenting. The same nasty taste in his mouth. His heart sank and his head swam. 'O God! O God!' he muttered. 'It's here again, and it's not going away.' And suddenly he saw things from a completely different angle. 'The blind gut! The kidney!' he said to himself. 'It's got nothing to do with the blind gut or the kidney. It's a matter of living or . . . dying. Yes, I have been alive, and now my life is steadily going away and I can't stop it. No. There's no point in fooling myself. Can't they all see – everybody but me – that I'm dying? It's only a matter of weeks, or days – maybe any minute now. There has been daylight; now there is darkness. I have been *here*; now I'm going *there*. Where?' A cold shiver ran over him; he stopped breathing. He could hear nothing but the beating of his heart.

'When I'm dead, what happens then? Nothing happens. So where shall I be when I'm no longer here? Is this really death? No, I won't have it!' He jumped up, tried to light the candle, fumbling with trembling hands, dropped the candle and the stick on the floor and flopped back down on to his pillow. 'Why bother? It doesn't make any difference,' he said to himself, staring into the darkness with his eyes wide open. 'Death. Yes, it's death. And not one of them knows, or wants to know. They have no pity for me. Too busy playing.' (Through the door he could hear the distant sounds of a singing voice and the accompaniment.) 'They don't care, but they're going to die, too. Fools! Me first, then them, but they've got it coming to them. And they're enjoying themselves! Animals!' He was choking with spite. And he felt a wave of agonizing, unbearable misery. It surely wasn't possible that everybody everywhere should be condemned to this awful horror. He sat up.

'Something's not right. I've got to calm down and think it through from the beginning.' And he began to think. 'Yes, the beginning of the illness. I banged my side, but I felt just the same that day and the next. A bit of discomfort, then a bit more, then doctors, depression, worry, more doctors, and all the time I was getting nearer and nearer to the edge. Less and less strength. Nearer and nearer. And I've been wasting away. No light in my eyes. Death is here, and I've been worrying about my gut. Worrying about getting my gut better, and this is death. Is it really death?'

Horror swept over him again, he gasped for breath, bent over and groped for the matches, leaning with one elbow on the bedside table. It was in his way, hurting him; he lost his temper with it, pressing down on it even harder in exasperation, and knocked it over. Breathless and in despair, he flopped down on to his back, expecting to die at any moment.

By this time the guests were leaving. Praskovya was seeing them out. She heard something fall, and came in.

'What's the matter?'

'Nothing. I just dropped something.'

She went out and came back with a candle. He lay there, puffing and panting heavily like a man who has just run a mile. His eyes settled on her.

'What's the matter, *Jean*?'

'No-thing. I . . . dropped it.' ('No use talking to her. She won't understand,' he thought.)

And she didn't. She picked up the candle and lit it for him, then she hurried out of the room to say goodnight to another guest.

When she came back he was still lying there on his back, staring upwards.

'What's wrong? Are you feeling worse?'

'Yes.'

She shook her head and sat down.

'Listen, *Jean*. I think perhaps we ought to ask Leshchetitsky to visit you at home.'

This meant asking the celebrated doctor to come to them, whatever the expense. He gave her a vitriolic smile and said no.

She sat there for a while, then came over and kissed him on the forehead.

He hated her with every fibre of his being while she was kissing him, and it took all his strength not to push her away.

'Goodnight. God willing, you'll soon go to sleep.'

'Yes.'

6

Ivan Ilyich could see that he was dying, and he was in constant despair.

In the depths of his soul Ivan Ilyich knew he was dying but, not only could he not get used to the idea, he didn't understand it, couldn't understand it at all.

All his life the syllogism he had learned from Kiesewetter's logic[9] – Julius Caesar is a man, men are mortal, therefore Caesar is mortal – had always seemed to him to be true only when it applied to Caesar, certainly not to him. There was Caesar the man, and man in general, and it was fair enough for them, but he wasn't Caesar the man and he wasn't man in general, he had always been a special being, totally different from all others, he had been Vanya with his mama and his papa, with Vitya and Volodya, with his toys, and the carriage-driver, then little Katya,[10] with all the delights, sorrows and rapture of childhood, boyhood and youth. Did Caesar have anything to do with the smell of that little striped leather ball that Vanya had loved so much? Was it Caesar who had kissed his mother's hand like that, and was it for Caesar that the silken folds of his mother's dress had rustled the way they did? Was he the one who had rebelled at law school over the provision of snacks? Had Caesar been in love like him? Could Caesar chair a session like him?

Yes, Caesar is mortal and it's all right for him to die, but not me, Vanya, Ivan Ilyich, with all my feelings and thoughts – it's different for me. It can't be me having to die. That would be too horrible.

These were the feelings that came to him.

'If I had to be like Caesar and die, I would have been aware of it, an inner voice would have told me, but there hasn't been anything like that on the inside. I've always thought – and all my friends have, too – that we're not the same as Caesar. And now look what's happened!' he said to himself. 'It can't be. It can't be, but it is. How can it be? What's it all about?'

He couldn't understand, and he tried to banish the idea – it was false, wrong and morbid – and replace it with proper, healthy thinking. But the same thought – it wasn't just a thought but something that seemed like reality – kept coming back and facing him.

And in order to dispel these thoughts he started calling up different thoughts one after another, hoping to get support from them. He tried to get back to his earlier ways of thinking which had once protected him from thinking about death. But, strange to say, everything that once had protected him by hiding and eliminating any awareness of death was unable to perform that function now. In these latter days Ivan Ilyich spent most of his time trying to get back to the earlier ways of feeling that had protected him from death. He would say to himself, 'I must get down to some work. When all's said and done it's what I've been living for.' And he would go off to court banishing all his doubts, get into conversation with his colleagues and casually take his seat as he had done so many times before, contemplating the crowd before him with a pensive air and resting his wasted hands on the oaken arms of his chair, leaning over in his usual way to exchange whispered words with a colleague while toying with a file before raising his eyes suddenly and sitting up straight in order to go through the familiar words and begin the proceedings. But then suddenly there it was, the pain in his side, irrespective of where they had got to in the proceedings, and it was beginning to gnaw at him. Ivan Ilyich focused on it, drove the thought of it away, but it continued to make itself felt. *It* kept coming back, facing him and looking at him, while he sat there rigid, the fire went out of his eyes and he began to wonder whether *It* was the only truth. And his colleagues and subordinates looked on in distress, amazed that he, a man of such brilliant and subtle judgement, was getting confused and making mistakes. He would pull himself together, try to bring himself round and somehow bring the session to a conclusion, only to return home sadly aware that his judicial work could no longer hide him, as it once had done, from what he wanted to conceal, that he could not use his judicial work to rid himself of *It*. And the worst thing was that *It* was distracting him not in order to make him do something but only to get him to look *It* straight in the eye, just look at *It* and do nothing but suffer beyond words.

And in order to escape from this situation Ivan Ilyich sought other forms of consolation, other ways of screening it off; other screens appeared and for a while they seemed to be the saving of him, but immediately they were not so much destroyed as shone right through; it was as if *It* could penetrate anything, no defence being any good.

Sometimes in these latter days he would go into the drawing-room that he had furnished – the very room where he had had his fall, the room which (it was bitterly amusing to reflect) he had given his life to furnish, because he knew his illness had started with that bruise – he would go in and notice a scratch on a lacquered table top left behind by something sharp. Looking for the cause he would find it in the decorative bronzework on an album with one edge bent up. He would pick up the album, an expensive one which he had compiled with loving care, annoyed at the carelessness shown by his daughter and her friends – it was torn in places and some of the photographs were upside down. He would go to a lot of trouble sorting it out and bending the bronzework back into place.

Then it would occur to him to move this entire *établissement* of albums over into a corner near the flowers. He would call the footman. Either his wife or his daughter would come to help. They wouldn't agree, they would take issue with him, he would argue and lose his temper – but none of this mattered because he had stopped remembering *It*. *It* was nowhere to be seen.

But once, when he was moving something himself, his wife said, 'Let the servants do that. You'll hurt yourself again,' and suddenly *It* flashed through the screen – he saw *It*. *It* flashed at him and, even as he longed for *It* to disappear, he couldn't help focusing on his side – still there, the same ache that would not be ignored, and *It* was staring straight at him from behind the flowers. What was it all about?

'And that's the truth of it – I've lost my life here on this curtain, my battleground. Have I really? How horrible and how stupid! It can't be! It can't be, but it is.'

He would go into his study, lie down and find himself alone again with *It*. Face to face with *It*. Nothing to be done about *It*. Only stare at *It* and go cold.

7

How it came about in the third month of Ivan Ilyich's illness no one could have said, because it came on imperceptibly, by stages, but it happened that all of them – his wife, and daughter, and son, and the servants, and their friends, and the doctors, and most importantly he himself – everybody knew that the only interesting thing about him now was whether it would take him a long time to give up his place, finally release the living from the oppression caused by his presence, and himself be released from his suffering.

He slept less and less. He was given opium and injected with morphine, but this brought no relief. To begin with, the dull feeling of anguish which he experienced in his semi-conscious state gave him a sense of relief simply by being something new, but then it became just as agonizing as the raw pain, perhaps more so.

They gave him special food cooked from recipes provided by the doctors, but the food became more and more tasteless, more and more repulsive.

For the call of nature he also had special arrangements, and each time it was agonizing. The agony came from the dirtiness, the unseemliness, the smell and also the knowledge that someone else had to be involved in it.

But this most unpleasant business brought one consolation to Ivan Ilyich. The person who came to take things away was Gerasim, the peasant servant who waited on them at table.

Gerasim was a clean, fresh peasant lad, always bright and cheerful, who had fattened up on city food. To begin with, Ivan Ilyich was embarrassed to watch him, always so neatly dressed in his Russian costume, performing such a distasteful service.

One day as he got up from the chamber pot not strong enough to pull up his own trousers he collapsed into a soft armchair and looked down in horror at his bared puny thighs with their starkly protruding muscles.

Who should come in but Gerasim, wearing his thick boots and exuding both their nice tarry smell and that of the fresh winter air, Gerasim with his light but firm tread, sporting a clean hessian apron and a clean cotton shirt, with his sleeves rolled up his bare strong young arms, and without a glance at Ivan Ilyich – to spare the sick man's feelings he was clearly suppressing the joyful vitality that shone from his face – he walked over to the pot.

'Gerasim,' said Ivan Ilyich feebly.

Gerasim started, clearly worried that he might have done something wrong, and in one swift movement he presented to the sick man his fresh, kind, open young face which was showing the first traces of a beard.

'Yes, sir?'

'This is not very nice for you, is it? You'll have to forgive me. I can't help it.'

'Please don't worry, sir.' And Gerasim's eyes flashed as he bared his young white teeth. 'It's no trouble. You're a sick man.'

And with his quick strong hands he did his usual thing and walked out with a light step. And five minutes later with the same light step he came back in.

Ivan Ilyich was still sitting there in his armchair.

'Gerasim,' he said, when the lad had replaced the clean, freshly washed chamber pot, 'would you mind helping me? Over here.' Gerasim came across. 'Lift me up, please. I can't manage it on my own, and I've sent Dmitriy away.'

Gerasim came over. In one movement that was as easy as his way of walking, he put his strong arms gently round Ivan Ilyich, lifted him up and held him with one hand, pulled up his trousers with the other, and tried to settle him down. But Ivan Ilyich asked to be taken across to the sofa. Effortlesly and apparently without tightening his grip, Gerasim took him, almost carried him, to the sofa and settled him down there.

'Thank you. You do everything so . . . nicely. So well.'

Gerasim gave another smile and made as if to leave the room. But Ivan Ilyich felt so comfortable with him that he didn't feel like letting him go.

'That's better . . . Would you mind moving that chair over here? No, that one. Under my legs. It feels easier when my legs are up high.'

Gerasim brought the chair over, set it squarely on the floor without banging it down, and lifted Ivan Ilyich's legs up on to it. Ivan Ilyich felt an easing of the pain as Gerasim raised his legs.

'I feel better when my legs are up,' said Ivan Ilyich. 'Would you put that cushion under me?'

Gerasim did so. He raised his legs again and put the cushion under them. Again Ivan Ilyich felt better when Gerasim was holding his legs. When he lowered them he felt worse.

'Gerasim,' he asked, 'are you busy just now?'

'Not in the slightest, sir,' said Gerasim, who had learned from the townspeople how to speak to the masters.

'What do you have on at the moment?'

'What do I have on? I've done everything there is to do – except chop the firewood for tomorrow.'

'Well, I'd like you to hold my legs up. Would you mind?'

'Of course not. I don't mind.' Gerasim held his legs up, and Ivan Ilyich could have sworn that in this position he couldn't feel any pain.

'But what about the firewood?'

'Don't you worry about that, sir. We'll manage.'

Ivan Ilyich told Gerasim to sit down and hold his legs up. He struck up a conversation and, strangely enough, he seemed to feel better with Gerasim holding his legs.

After that Ivan Ilyich would send for Gerasim now and then and have his legs held up on his shoulders. He liked it when they talked to each other. Gerasim did all of this easily, willingly and with a kindliness that Ivan Ilyich found moving. Health, strength and vitality in all other people were offensive to Ivan Ilyich; only Gerasim's strength and vitality gave him comfort rather than distressed him.

Ivan Ilyich's worst torment was the lying – the lie, which was somehow maintained by them all, that he wasn't dying, he was only ill, and all he had to do was keep calm and follow doctor's orders and then something good would emerge. Whereas he knew that, whatever was done to him, nothing would emerge but more and more agony, suffering and death. And this lie was torture for him – he was tortured by their unwillingness to acknowledge what they all knew and he knew; they wanted to lie to him about his terrible situation, and they wanted him – they were compelling him – to be a party to this lie. All this lying to him, lie upon lie, on the eve of his death, lying that was inexorably reducing the solemn act of his death to the same level as their social calls, their draperies, the sturgeon for dinner . . . it was all a terrible torment for Ivan Ilyich. And strangely enough, on many occasions when they were acting out this farce in front of him, he was within a hair's breadth of screaming at them, 'Stop all this lying! You know and I know that I'm dying, so the least you can do is stop lying to me.' But he never quite had the nerve to do it. He could see that the awful, terrible act of his dying had been reduced by those around him to the level of an unpleasant incident, something rather indecent (as if they were dealing with someone who had come into the drawing-room and let off a bad smell), and this was done by exploiting the very sense of 'decency' that he had been observing all his life. He could see that no one had any pity for him because no one had the slightest desire to understand his situation. Gerasim was the only one who did understand his situation, and he was sorry for him. This was why Ivan Ilyich felt comfortable only with Gerasim. It was a comfort to him when Gerasim, sometimes for nights on end, held his legs up and refused to go to bed, saying, 'Please don't worry about it, Ivan Ilyich. I'll catch up on my sleep.' Or else he would suddenly address him in familiar language and add, 'It'd be different if you weren't ill, but with things the way they are why shouldn't I help you out?' Gerasim was the only one who didn't lie to him; everything showed that he was the only one who understood what was going on and saw no need to hide it. He just felt sorry for his weak and emaciated master. Once, when Ivan Ilyich was dismissing him, he put it quite bluntly: 'We've all got to die one day. Why shouldn't I give you a hand?' This was to say there was a good reason for not making a fuss about helping out: he was doing it for a dying man and he hoped that when his time came someone would help him out in the same way.

Apart from all this lying, or perhaps because of it, the most tormenting thing of all for Ivan Ilyich was the fact that no one showed him any pity in the way that he wanted them to. There were some moments, after long periods of suffering, when what Ivan Ilyich wanted more than anything else – however embarrassed he would have been to admit it – what he wanted was for someone to take pity on him as if he were a sick child. He wanted to be kissed and cuddled and have a few tears shed over him in the way that children are cuddled and comforted. He knew he was a big man and something of a greybeard, which made this impossible, but nevertheless that is what he wanted. And his relationship with Gerasim offered something close to this, which was why the relationship with Gerasim gave him comfort.

Here is Ivan Ilyich wanting to weep, wanting to be cuddled and have tears shed over him, when in comes his colleague Shebek and, instead of weeping and getting some tenderness, Ivan Ilyich puts on a solemn and serious face, looks thoughtful and from sheer habit not only comments on the significance of a decision handed down by the Court of Cassation,[11] but goes on to defend it strongly.

It was this living a lie, all around him and within him, that did most to poison the last days in the life of Ivan Ilyich.

8

It was morning. It was morning only because Gerasim had gone and Pyotr the servant was there, putting out the candles, opening one curtain and quietly tidying up. Morning or evening, Friday or Sunday – it didn't matter, it was all the same – grinding, agonizing pain, never for a moment relenting; an awareness of life hopelessly slipping away but not yet gone; the same terrible, relentless approach of hateful death, the only reality; and still all that lying. With all of this, what did the days, weeks and hours matter?

'Can I get you some tea, sir?'

'He likes good order. The masters must have their tea in the morning,' he thought, but all he said was, 'No.'

'Would you care to move over to the sofa, sir?'

'He wants to tidy the room, and I'm in the way. I am dirt and disorder,' he thought, but all he said was, 'No. Leave me alone.'

The servant went about his work again. Ivan Ilyich stretched out one hand. Pyotr came over ready to help.

'What can I do for you, sir?'

'My watch.'

Pyotr took the watch, which was lying nearby, and handed it over.

'Half-past eight. Are they still in bed?'

'No, sir, they're not. Master Vasily [his son] has gone to school and madam asked me to wake her if you wanted her. Shall I do that?'

'No. Don't bother.' Ivan Ilyich wondered whether to try some tea. Yes. 'Bring me some tea.'

Pyotr moved towards the door. Ivan Ilyich felt terrified at the thought of being left alone. How could he stop him leaving? Oh yes, medicine. 'Pyotr, would you give me my medicine?' Well, why not? The medicine might help. He took a spoonful and swallowed it. No, it wouldn't help. It was all rubbish. Just pretending. He felt sure of this as the old familiar taste returned, sickly and beyond hope. No, his faith was gone. And the pain, the pain, why couldn't it ease up just for a minute? He gave a groan. Pyotr came back in.

'No, carry on. Get me some tea.'

Pyotr left the room. Ivan Ilyich groaned, not really from the pain, however terrible that was, but from anguish. It was the same thing all the time, day and night, with no end to it. Make it soon. Make *what* soon? Death, darkness. No, no. Anything was better than death!

When Pyotr came back in with the tea tray Ivan Ilyich looked at him distractedly for some time, unable to work out who he was or what he was doing there. Pyotr was embarrassed by the long look. The embarrassment brought Ivan Ilyich to his senses.

'Yes,' he said. 'Tea . . . Good. Leave it there. But I'd like you to help me get washed and put a clean shirt on.'

And Ivan Ilyich began to wash himself. With pauses for rest he washed his hands and face, cleaned his teeth, combed his hair and then took a look in the mirror. He was horrified. The most horrible thing was the limp way his hair stuck to his pallid forehead.

As he had his shirt changed he knew it would be more horrible still to glance down at his body, so he looked away. At last it was done. He put on his dressing-gown, wrapped a rug around himself and sat down in the armchair with his tea. For one moment he felt refreshed, but at the first drink of tea there it was again, the same taste, the same pain. He forced the tea down, then lay back and stretched out his legs. He lay down and told Pyotr he could go.

The same thing again. One glittering drop of hope followed by a raging sea of despair, and nothing but pain, more pain, more anguish, always the same thing. It was depressing to be left alone, and he felt like calling somebody in, but he knew in advance that to have other people there would be even worse. Oh, for another dose of morphine – he might lose himself in that. He must tell that doctor to think of something else. 'I can't go on like this. I can't.'

An hour goes by like this, then another. The bell rings in the hall – could it be the doctor? Yes, it is the doctor, fresh and cheerful, fleshy and hearty, with a look on his face that seems to say, 'Well now, you seem to have had a bit of a fright, but we'll soon sort you out.' The doctor knows that this look is out of place here, but he has assumed it once and for all and he can't get rid of it any more than a man who has gone out visiting can get rid of the frock-coat he put on that morning.

The doctor rubs his hands cheerfully, reassuringly.

'Chilly out there. Thick frost. Give me a minute to get warmed up.' His manner of speaking implies that he won't take long, he just needs to warm up and once he is warmed up he'll put everything right.

'Right then. How are you feeling?'

Ivan Ilyich senses that the doctor feels like saying, 'How's tricks?' but even he can see that this won't do, so he says, 'What sort of night did you have?'

Ivan Ilyich fixes the doctor with a look that seems to ask whether anything would ever make him feel too ashamed to go on lying. The doctor does not wish to understand.

So Ivan Ilyich says, 'No change. Terrible. The pain won't go. It's there all the time. There must be something you can do!'

'Yes, it's normal for patients like you to say that sort of thing. Right then. I think I'm warm enough now. Your good lady is a stickler for these things, but even she wouldn't say I was too cold. So. Good morning to you . . .' And the doctor shakes him by the hand.

And now, dropping all the banter, the doctor adopts a serious attitude and begins to examine the patient – pulse, temperature, tapping and listening.

Ivan Ilyich knows full well – it is beyond doubt – that this is all nonsense, an empty sham, but when the doctor goes down on his knees, reaches across him, applies his ear higher up and lower down, and then with the gravest look on his face performs a selection of gymnastic contortions, Ivan Ilyich accedes to this just as he once acceded to speeches from lawyers even when he was well aware that they were lying, and why they were lying.

The doctor is still kneeling on the sofa, busily tapping away, when from the doorway comes the rustling of a silk dress and Praskovya can be heard reproaching Pyotr for not letting her know the doctor has arrived.

She comes in, kisses her husband and immediately begins to make it clear that she has been up for some time and only a little misunderstanding has prevented her from being there when the doctor arrived.

Ivan Ilyich looks at her searchingly, resenting everything about her, the whiteness, fullness and cleanliness of her arms and neck, the sheen of her hair and the light in her eyes that are so full of life. He loathes her with every fibre of his being. Physical contact with her is agony for him because it brings on a surge of loathing.

Her attitude towards him and his illness is still the same. Just as the doctor has worked out an attitude towards his patients which he cannot now get rid of, she has worked out a particular attitude towards him – he is failing to do something he ought to do, and it's his fault, and she lovingly reproaches him for it – and she has not been able to rid herself of this attitude towards him.

'He just won't do as he's told! He forgets to take his medicine. And the worst thing is he will lie there in a position that must be bad for him – with his legs up.'

She described how he got Gerasim to hold his legs up for him.

The doctor gave a sweetly condescending smile. 'Can't be helped,' he seemed to be saying. 'These sick people do sometimes have silly ideas. We can't blame them.'

When the examination was over the doctor consulted his watch and then Praskovya informed Ivan Ilyich that, like it or not, she had invited a celebrated specialist to visit them that day and, along with Mikhail Danilovich (the name of the regular doctor), he would conduct an examination and consultation.

'Now please don't argue with me. I'm doing this for myself,' she said sarcastically, implying that she was doing it all for him and this alone deprived him of any right to refuse. He scowled and said nothing. He felt that the lies that enveloped him were now so messy that he could hardly make sense of anything.

Everything she did for him she was doing for herself, and she told him she was doing for herself what she was actually doing for herself, but she made it sound so implausible that he was forced to assume the opposite.

Sure enough, at half-past eleven, the celebrated specialist arrived. More soundings and grave consultations both in his presence and in the next room concerning the kidney and the blind gut, with questions and answers expressed with such an air of gravity that, instead of the real life-and-death question which was the only one staring him in the face, up came the question of his kidney and blind gut, which were not doing quite what they should and which would shortly be set upon by Mikhail Danilovich and made to work properly.

The celebrated specialist took his leave looking serious but not hopeless. And in answer to the question put to him diffidently by Ivan Ilyich, whose eyes were glistening with fear and hope, as to whether there was any possibility of recovery, he replied that nothing could be guaranteed but there was a possibility. The look of hope on Ivan Ilyich's face as he watched the doctor leave was so pathetic that when she saw it Praskovya actually burst into tears as she walked out of the study to give the celebrated specialist his fee.

The lifting of his spirits induced by the doctor's words of encouragement was short-lived. It was still the same room, the same pictures, curtains, wallpaper, medicine bottles, and the same body, his body, still suffering, racked with pain. And Ivan Ilyich began to moan, so they gave him an injection and he lapsed into unconsciousness.

When he came to, it was getting dark. They brought him his dinner. He forced down a little thin soup, then it was the same again, with another night coming on.

When dinner was over, at seven o'clock, Praskovya came in dressed for going out, with her ample breasts well supported and traces of powder on her face. That morning she had reminded him that they were going to the theatre. Sarah Bernhardt[12] was in town, and they had a box which they had taken at his insistence. By now he had forgotten this, and he was offended to see her dressed up. But he hid his feelings when he remembered having insisted that they reserve the box and go, this being an aesthetic experience of educational value for the children.

As she came in Praskovya had looked pleased with herself, if rather guilty. She sat down on the edge of a chair and asked how he was feeling, though he could see that she was asking for the sake of asking rather than to find out, since she knew there was nothing to find out, and then she launched into what she felt she had to say, that nothing would have induced her to go out tonight, but the box had been reserved, Hélène and her daughter were going and so was Petrishchev (their daughter's fiancé, the examining magistrate), and they couldn't be allowed to go alone. But for that, she would have preferred to stay in with him. And he must be sure to follow the doctor's orders while she was out.

'Oh yes, and Fyodor [the fiancé] would like to come in. Do you mind? And Liza.'

'Let them come in.'

In came his daughter, dressed up to the nines, an exposed young body – while his body was causing him so much suffering. And she was flaunting it. Healthy and strong, obviously in love, she had no time for the illness, suffering and death that were marring her happiness.

In came Fyodor Petrovich, also in evening dress and sporting an *à la Capoul* hairstyle.[13] The veins stood out on his long neck which was squeezed into its tight collar over a vast expanse of white shirtfront, and his narrow black trousers were tightly stretched over his strong thighs. One of his hands wore a close-fitting white glove and he carried an opera hat.

Creeping in unobtrusively behind him came the schoolboy, wearing a new uniform and gloves, poor chap, with terrible dark blue rings under his eyes, the meaning of which was not lost on Ivan Ilyich.

He had always felt sorry for his son. And his frightened, compassionate look was dreadful to behold. Apart from Gerasim, Ivan Ilyich thought, Vasya was the only one who understood and felt sorry for him.

They all sat down and asked how he was feeling. Then for a while no one spoke. Liza asked her mother whether she had the opera glasses. Mother and daughter had a little argument about who had put them where. It ended nastily.

Fyodor asked Ivan Ilyich whether he had ever seen Sarah Bernhardt. At first Ivan Ilyich didn't quite catch what the question was, but then he said, 'No. Have you?'

'Yes. In *Adrienne Lecouvreur*.'[14]

Praskovya mentioned something she had been particularly good in. Her daughter demurred. They were off into a conversation about her charm and naturalism as an actress, the same old conversation that everybody else has.

In the midst of it Fyodor looked across at Ivan Ilyich and suddenly broke off. The others looked, and they stopped, too. Ivan Ilyich was staring straight ahead, his eyes glittering, and he was obviously furious with them. Things had to be put right, but there was absolutely no way of putting things right. Somehow the silence had to be broken. No one made a move, and everyone was becoming terrified that the living lie demanded by propriety would somehow be shattered and seen by everyone for what it was. It was Liza who made the first move. She broke the silence. She wanted to cover up what everyone was feeling, but by speaking out she revealed it.

'Oh well, if we're *going* it's time we got started,' she said, glancing at her watch, a present from her father, and she smiled almost imperceptibly at her young man to convey something known only to the two of them as she got up, rustling her skirts.

They all got up, took their leave and drove off.

When they had gone Ivan Ilyich seemed to feel easier; the lie had gone, gone away with them – but the pain was still there. That same pain, that same feeling of dread made sure that nothing was harder, nothing easier. Everything was worse.

Once again the minutes passed one after another, then the hours one after another; it was always the same, endlessly, and the inevitable end itself was all the more horrible.

'Yes, send Gerasim in,' he said in reply to a question from Pyotr.

9

It was late at night when his wife returned. She tiptoed into the room, but he heard her; he opened his eyes and rapidly closed them again. She wanted to dismiss Gerasim and sit with him herself. He opened his eyes and said, 'No. You go.'

'Are you in a lot of pain?'

'It doesn't matter.'

'Take some opium.'

He consented, and drank some. She went away.

Until about three in the morning he was in a state of excruciating pain and delirium. He dreamt that somehow he was being forced, along with his pain, into the depths of a narrow black sack, being forced further and further in and not quite getting there. It was a harrowing, agonizing process. And he was scared, he wanted to get through and out, he was struggling, trying to help. Then suddenly he lost his hold and fell, and woke up. Gerasim was still there, sitting at the foot of the bed, dozing quietly, patiently. And he himself was lying there with his withered stockinged legs raised up on Gerasim's shoulders. The same candle was there, with its shade, and the same unremitting pain.

'Go away, Gerasim,' he whispered.

'I don't mind, sir. I'll just sit here for a bit longer.'

'No, you go away.'

He lowered his legs, turned sideways on to one arm and felt sorry for himself. He waited only for Gerasim to go out into the next room, and then he could restrain himself no longer: he burst into tears like a child. He was weeping because of his own helpless state, and his loneliness, and other people's cruelty, and God's cruelty, and God's non-existence.

'Why hast Thou done all of this? Why hast Thou brought me to this point? Why oh why dost Thou torture me like this? . . .'

He was not expecting any answers; he was weeping because there were not and could not be any answers. The pain struck him again, but he didn't move and didn't call out. He said to himself, 'Here it comes again. Hit me then! But what's it for? What have I done to Thee? What is it for?'

Then he fell silent, and not only stopped crying, he stopped breathing. Suddenly he was all ears; he seemed to be listening not to a voice speaking in words but to the voice of his soul, the thoughts welling up in his mind.

'What do you want?' was the first expressible concept that came to him. 'What do you want? What do you want?' he repeated to himself. 'What is it?'

'No more pain. Staying alive,' came the answer.

And once again his concentration became so intense that not even the pain could distract him.

'Staying alive? How?' asked the voice of his soul.

'Oh, life like it used to be. Happy and good.'

'Life like it used to be? Happy and good?' came the voice.

And in his imagination he started to run through the best times of his happy life. But what was strange was that all the best times of his happy life no longer seemed anything like what they had been before. Nothing did – except the first recollections of his childhood. There, in his childhood, there was something truly happy that he could have lived with if it returned. But the person living out that happiness no longer existed; it was like remembering someone quite different.

At the point where he, today's Ivan Ilyich, began to emerge, all the pleasures that had seemed so real melted away now before his eyes and turned into something trivial and often disgusting.

And the further he was from childhood, the nearer he got to the present day, the more trivial and dubious his pleasures appeared. It started with law school. That had retained a little something that was still really good: there was fun, there was friendship, there was hope. But in the last years the good times had become more exceptional. Then, at the beginning of his service with the governor, some good times came again: memories of making love to a woman. Then it became all confused, and the good times were not so many. After that there were fewer still; the further he went the fewer there were.

Marriage . . . an accident and such a disappointment, and his wife's bad breath, and all that sensuality and hypocrisy! And the deadliness of his working life, and those money worries, going on for a year, two years, ten, twenty – always the same old story. And the longer it went on the deadlier it became.

'It's as if I had been going downhill when I thought I was going uphill. That's how it was. In society's opinion I was heading uphill, but in equal measure life was slipping away from me . . . And now it's all over. Nothing left but to die!

'So what's it all about? What's it for? It's not possible. It's not possible that life could have been as senseless and sickening as this. And if it has really been as sickening and senseless as this, why do I have to die, and die in agony? There's something wrong. Maybe I didn't live as I should have done?' came the sudden thought. 'But how can that be when I did everything properly?' he wondered, instantly dismissing as a total impossibility the one and only solution to the mystery of life and death.

'So, what *do* you want now? To live? Live how? To live as you do in court when the usher yells out, "The Court is in session!"' 'Court in session, sessions in court,' he repeated to himself. 'Here comes judgement! But I'm not guilty,' he cried out angrily. 'What is this for?'

And he stopped crying, turned to face the wall and let his mind dwell on one single question: 'Why all this horror? What's the reason for it?'

But, for all his dwelling on it, he could find no answer. And whenever the thought occurred to him – which it often did – that all this was happening to him because he had been living the wrong kind of life, he would instantly remember how proper his life had been and dismiss such a bizarre notion.

10

Another two weeks went by. Ivan Ilyich no longer rose from his sofa. He didn't care to lie in bed, so he lay on the sofa. And lying there, almost invariably facing the wall, he endured all the inexplicable agony in solitude, and in solitude he brooded on the same inexplicable question: 'What is this? Can it really be death?' And an inner voice would reply, 'Yes, that's what it is.' 'What is this torture for?' And the voice would reply, 'It's just there. It's not for anything.' Above and beyond this there was nothing.

From the very onset of his illness, since the first time he had driven round to see the doctor, his life had divided itself into two opposite and alternating moods: either despair and the anticipation of a horribly incomprehensible death, or hope accompanied by an obsessive fascination for the workings of his body. He had eyes for only two things: either a kidney or blind gut that had temporarily stopped doing what it should do, or a horribly incomprehensible death, which there was no way to avoid.

These two moods alternated in him from the very outset of his illness, but the further the illness progressed the more dubious and preposterous his notions of a kidney became, and the more realistic was his awareness of impending death.

All he had to do was remember what he had been like three months before and what he was now, remember how steadily he had gone downhill, and any possibility of hope was shattered.

In his last days of solitude, when he found himself lying there facing the back of the sofa, solitude in the midst of a populous city and his own friends and family – a solitude more complete than anything anywhere, at the bottom of the sea or in the bowels of the earth – in these last days of terrible solitude Ivan Ilyich lived only by recreating the past. Images of his past life came back to him one after another. This process always began with the most recent ones and proceeded back to the most remote, to childhood, and there it lingered. If Ivan Ilyich remembered the stewed prunes he had been offered for dinner that day he would remember the raw and wrinkly French prunes of his childhood, their special taste and how his mouth watered when he got down to the stone, and along with the memory of that taste would come a whole series of further memories of that time: his nurse, his brother, his toys. 'No, don't, not that. It's too painful,' Ivan Ilyich would say to himself, transporting himself back to the present: there it was – a button of the back of the sofa, creases in the morocco. 'Morocco is expensive, and it doesn't wear well. It started an argument. But that was different morocco and a different argument – when we tore father's briefcase and got punished, and mother brought us some tarts.' Once again his thoughts were settling on his childhood, and again they were too painful for Ivan Ilyich, so he tried to drive them away and think of something else.

And once again, along with this train of recollections, another train of recollections troubled his spirit – the way in which his illness had grown and got worse. Here, too, the further back he went the more life there was. More goodness in life, more of life itself. The two things were merging. 'It's like the pain getting worse and worse – all of my life has been getting worse and worse,' he thought. There was one point of light back there at the beginning of life, but after that everything had been getting blacker and blacker. 'In inverse proportion to the square of the distance from death,' he thought. And this image of a stone accelerating as it flies down imprinted itself on his soul. Life, a series of increasing sufferings, flies ever faster towards its end, the most terrible suffering. 'I'm flying somewhere . . .' He would shiver and shudder, trying to resist, but he knew by now that resistance was impossible, and he would turn his eyes to the back of the sofa, eyes that were weary of looking, but couldn't stop looking, at what lay ahead. And he was waiting, waiting for that terrible fall, shock and annihilation. 'Resistance is impossible,' he would say to himself. 'But if only I could see what it's all about! No, that's impossible, too. There would be an explanation if I could say I've been wrong in the way I've lived my life. But you couldn't say that. It's not possible,' he would tell himself, recalling how fastidious he had been about the propriety and respectability of his life. 'You can't say that. It's not possible,' he would tell himself, twisting his lips into a smile as if someone might see it and be taken in by it. 'There is no explanation. Agony and death . . . What for?'

11

Two weeks went by like this. During those two weeks an event took place that Ivan Ilyich and his wife had been hoping for: Petrishchev made a formal proposal. It happened one evening. The next morning Praskovya came in to see her husband, wondering how best to break the news of Fyodor's proposal, but during that night Ivan Ilyich's condition had taken another turn for the worse. Praskovya found him on the same sofa, but in a different position. He was lying flat on his back, moaning and staring ahead with a fixed look.

She started talking about his medicine. He transferred his gaze to her. She didn't finish what she had started to say; there was so much enmity in that gaze, and it was levelled straight at her.

'For Christ's sake, let me die in peace!' he said.

She made as if to leave the room, but at that moment in walked their daughter, who came over to say good morning. He gave her the same look he had directed at his wife, and in response to her enquiries about his health he said drily that soon he would no longer be a burden to them. Both of them sat on for a while, saying nothing, and then they left.

'What have we done wrong?' Liza asked her mother. 'Anyone would think it was our fault. I'm sorry for Papa, but why do we have to suffer?'

The doctor arrived at his usual time. Ivan Ilyich responded to him with a yes and no, fixing him with a malevolent look, and finally he said, 'Look, you know you can't help me. Just leave me alone.'

'We can ease the pain,' said the doctor.

'You can't. Leave me alone.'

The doctor went out into the drawing-room and told Praskovya that things were very bad. Only one thing could help – opium. That might ease the pain, which must be dreadful.

The doctor said that the physical pain must be dreadful, which was true. But more dreadful than the physical pain was the suffering in spirit, his greatest agony.

His spiritual suffering took the form of a thought that had suddenly struck him that night as he looked at Gerasim's sleepy-eyed, good-natured face with its high cheekbones. 'What if I really have been *wrong* in the way I've lived my whole life, my conscious life?'

It occurred to him that what had once seemed a total impossibility – that he had not lived his life as he should have done – might actually be true. It occurred to him that the slight stirrings of doubt he had experienced about what was considered good by those in the highest positions, slight stirrings that he had immediately repudiated – that these misgivings might have been true and everything else might have been wrong. His career, the ordering of his life, his family, the things that preoccupied people in society and at work – all of this might have been wrong. He made an attempt at defending these things for himself. And suddenly he sensed the feebleness of what he was defending. There was nothing to defend.

'But if it's like that,' he said to himself, 'and I am leaving this life knowing I have ruined everything I was given, and it can't be put right, what then?' He lay on his back and started to go through his whole life again in a different way. Next morning, when he saw his servant, then his wife, then his daughter, then the doctor – their every movement and every word bore out the terrible truth that had been revealed to him during the night. In them he saw himself and all he had lived by, and he could clearly see that it was all wrong; it was all a gross deception obscuring life and death. This knowledge exacerbated his physical suffering, making it ten times worse. He moaned and writhed, and clutched at his clothing, which seemed to be choking and stifling him. And he hated them for it.

After being given a heavy dose of opium he lost consciousness, but by dinner time it had all begun again. He sent everyone away and lay there tossing and turning.

His wife came to him and said, '*Jean*, darling, please do this for my sake.' (For *her* sake?) 'It can't do any harm, and it often helps. Look, it's nothing much. Even healthy people . . .'

He opened his eyes wide.

'What? Take communion? What for? I'm not doing that . . . Oh, I don't know . . .'

She burst into tears.

'All right, my dear? I'll send for our priest. He's such a nice man.'

'All right. That's fine,' he said.

When the priest came and heard his confession, Ivan Ilyich relaxed, feeling some relief from his doubts and therefore from his suffering, and he experienced a moment of hope. His mind turned again to his blind gut and the possibility of a cure for it. When he took communion there were tears in his eyes.

When he was laid down after taking communion he felt better for a while; there was hope that he might live on. His thoughts turned to the operation that he had been offered. 'I want to live. I do want to live,' he said to himself. His wife came in to greet him after communion. She said the usual things, and then added: 'You really do feel better, don't you?'

'Yes,' he said, looking away.

Her clothes, her figure, the look on her face, the sound of her voice – all said the same thing to him: 'This is wrong. Everything you have lived by, and still do, is a lie, a deception that hides life and death away from you.' And the moment this thought occurred to him, his hatred welled up, and along with the hatred came physical suffering and agony, and along with the agony came awareness of the inevitable destruction that was now so close. There was something different about it: a twisting, shooting pain, and constricted breathing.

The look on his face as he said 'Yes' had been dreadful. When he had got the word out, looking straight at her, he wrenched himself over face down remarkably quickly for one so weak, and roared at her: 'Get out! Go away! Leave me alone!'

12

From that moment on the screaming began. It went on unbroken for three days, so terrible that people two rooms away were horrified to hear it. At the moment when he had answered his wife he had realized he was done for, there was no way back, the end was here, the absolute end, and his unresolved doubts would remain as doubts.

'Oh! Oh! Oh!' he cried, varying the tone. He began by crying out, 'Oh no!' and went on screaming the letter 'o'. Throughout the three days, during which time had ceased to exist for him, he struggled with the black sack into which he was being crammed by an invisible, unstoppable force. He resisted like a condemned man resisting his executioner, knowing that he is not going to be spared, and with every minute that passed he sensed that, despite all his fighting and struggling, he was getting nearer and nearer to the thing that terrified him. He sensed that the pain came from being thrust into that black hole and, what was worse, not being able to get through. What was preventing him from getting through was his insistence that his life had been a good one. This vindication of his lifestyle was holding him down, preventing him from moving on, and causing him the greatest suffering.

Suddenly he felt a strong jolt in his chest and side, and a further constriction of his breathing. He was into the hole, and there at the end of the hole a kind of light was shining. What was happening to him was like when he had been in a railway carriage and you think you are going forwards but you are really going backwards, and suddenly you know what the right direction is.

'Yes, it's all been wrong,' he told himself, 'but that doesn't matter. It's possible to do the right thing. But what is the right thing?' he wondered, and suddenly he was calm.

It was nearing the end of the third day, an hour before his death. At that very moment his schoolboy son crept in to see his father and came over to his bed. The dying man was still screaming desperately and waving his arms about. His hand happened to catch the boy's head. The boy took hold of it, pressed it to his lips and burst into tears.

This was the very moment when Ivan Ilyich had fallen through and seen a light, and it was revealed to him that his life had not been what it should have been, but that it could still be put right. He was wondering what the right thing was, and he had calmed down, listening. Now he could feel someone kissing his hand. He opened his eyes and looked at his son. He felt sorry for him. His wife came over. He looked at her. With her mouth open and the tears not wiped away from her nose and cheek she was looking at him in despair. He felt sorry for her.

'Yes, I'm hurting them,' he thought. 'They feel sorry for me, but they'll be all right when I'm dead.' He wanted to tell them this, but he wasn't strong enough to get the words out. 'Anyway . . . no good talking. Must *do* something.' He looked at his wife, motioned to their son and said: 'Take him away . . . sorry for him . . . and you . . .' He tried to say, 'Forgive me,' but it came out as, 'For goodness . . .' Too weak to correct himself, he waved his hand knowing that he who needed to would understand.

And suddenly everything was clear to him: what had been oppressing him and would not go away *was* now going away, all at once, on two sides, ten sides, all sides. He felt sorry for them, and he must do something to stop hurting them. Set them free, and free himself from all this suffering. 'So nice, and so simple,' he thought. 'But what about the pain?' he wondered. 'Where's it gone? Hey, pain, where are you?'

He listened and waited.

'Oh, here it comes. So what? Bring on the pain.'

'What about death? Where is it?'

He was looking for his earlier, accustomed fear of death, but he couldn't find it. Where was death? What death? There was no fear whatsoever, because there was no death.

Instead of death there was light.

'So that's it!' he said suddenly, out loud. 'Oh, bliss!'

All of this happened to him in a single moment, and the meaning of that moment was not going to change. For those present, his agony went on for another two hours. There was a rattling in his chest. His wasted body shook. Then the rattling and the wheezing dwindled away.

'He's gone!' said someone over him.

He caught these words and repeated them in spirit. 'Death has gone,' he told himself.

'It's gone.'

He took in some air, stopped halfway through a deep breath, stretched out, and died.

AFTER THE BALL

A Tale

'What you're all saying, you see, is that on his own a person can't distinguish the good from the bad, that it all depends on his environment, that a person's a prey to his environment. But the way I see it is that it's all up to chance. Listen, I'll tell you something that happened to me personally . . .'

This was how our universally respected Ivan Vasilyevich began to address us after a discussion we had been having on the subject of whether all that was necessary in order to achieve individual perfection was to alter the conditions under which people lead their lives. It should be pointed out that none of us had actually said that on his own a person cannot tell the good from the bad, but Ivan Vasilyevich had a peculiar way of answering questions of his own that had occurred to him in the course of the discussion, and of making these the pretext for tales concerning episodes in his own life. Quite often he would completely forget the point from which he had started, and would get carried away by his stories, all the more so since he told them with a high degree of sincerity and truthfulness.

It was no different on this occasion.

'I'll tell you what happened to me. The whole of my life's been like this; it hasn't been influenced by my environment, but by something else entirely.'

'What?' we all wanted to know.

'Oh, it's a long story. It'll take quite a bit of telling if you're really to understand.'

'That's all right, go ahead and tell us.'

Ivan Vasilyevich thought for a moment, and then nodded his head.

'Yes,' he said. 'The whole of my life changed as a result of one night, or rather one morning.'

'But what happened?'

'What happened was that I'd fallen deeply in love. I've fallen in love many times, but this was my deepest love. It's all an age ago now: she's got married daughters nowadays. The girl's name was B—, yes, Varenka B—. [Ivan Vasilyevich mentioned the family's name.] Even at fifty she was a remarkably attractive woman. But when she was young, eighteen years old, she was stunning: tall and graceful, with a lovely figure – majestic, truly majestic. She always maintained an unusually erect posture, as though she could not do otherwise, with her head thrown slightly back, and this, together with her beauty and her tall stature, and in spite of her thin, almost bony physique, gave her a queenly appearance which would have been intimidating had it not been for her lovely, joyous smile, her beautiful, shining eyes and her overall charm and youthfulness.'

'I say, hark at Ivan Vasilyevich's description!'

'No description could possibly tell you what she was really like . . . but that's not important. The events I'm going to tell you about took place in the 1840s. In those days I was a student at a provincial university. I don't know whether it was a good thing or a bad one, but at the time I was there our university contained no circles or theories of any kind. We were simply young and we lived as the young do: pursued our studies and enjoyed ourselves. I was a very jolly, lively fellow, and I had money, too. I owned a magnificent pacer, went tobogganing with the young ladies (skating had not yet come into fashion), and lived it up with my companions (in those days we never drank anything but champagne; if we were out of money we didn't drink at all, and never turned to vodka, as students do nowadays). But what I enjoyed most were the soirées and balls. I was a good dancer, and was tolerably good-looking.'

'Come, come, you needn't be so modest,' said one of the ladies in our company. 'We know what you look like in your daguerreotype, don't we? You weren't just tolerably good-looking, you were handsome!'

'That's as may be, but it's not important, either. The important thing was that during this time, when my love for her was reaching its highest point – the last day of Shrovetide, it was – I went to a ball at the house of the local marshal of nobility,[1] a good-natured old man who was well off, liked throwing parties and was a gentleman-in-waiting at the court. The guests were received by his wife, who was also very good-natured, wearing a velvet dress, a diamond *ferronière* on her forehead, her white, puffy, aged shoulders and breast exposed, as in the portraits of the Empress Elizabeth Petrovna. It was a wonderful ball: a fine big reception room, with choirs, an orchestra, famous in those days, composed of the serfs of a landowner who was also an amateur musician, a magnificent buffet and a veritable ocean of champagne. Although I was fond of champagne, I didn't drink any, as I was already drunk, without need of wine, drunk on love; on the other hand, I danced until I dropped: quadrilles, waltzes, polkas, all as far as possible with Varenka, of course. She wore a white dress with a pink sash, white kid gloves that reached almost to her thin, pointed elbows, and white satin shoes. I had the mazurka poached from me by a really terrible fellow called Anisimov, an engineer – I still haven't forgiven him to this day. He had asked her for this dance at the very moment she had arrived, while I had been delayed by having had to go back to the barber's to fetch the gloves I had left there by mistake. So instead of getting to dance the mazurka with Varenka, I had as my partner a young German girl I'd once run after. I'm afraid I wasn't very considerate to her that evening, hardly spoke to her or looked at her and only had eyes for that tall, shapely figure in the white dress with the pink sash, for her flushed, radiant face with its dimples, and for her tender, affectionate eyes. I wasn't the only one: everyone was looking at her and admiring her, men and women alike, even though she put them all in the shade. It was impossible not to admire her.

'Officially, so to speak, I had another partner for the mazurka, but in reality I danced most of the figures with her. Without the slightest embarrassment she would walk the whole length of the room and come straight up to me, I would jump to my feet, not waiting to be asked, and she would thank me with a smile for my quick-wittedness. When we were led before her to choose one of us, she would give her arm to another gallant, unable to guess my quality, shrug her thin shoulders and smile to me as a sign of regret and consolation. When the figures of the mazurka were being danced as a waltz, I waltzed with her for a long time and, smiling and breathing fast, she said: "*Encore*!" And I waltzed and waltzed, until I was no longer conscious of my body at all.'

'What do you mean you weren't conscious of it? I bet you were very conscious of it when you had your arm around her waist, not only of your body but of hers as well,' said one of the guests.

Ivan Vasilyevich suddenly turned a deep red and in his anger almost shouted: 'Yes, there you are, there's the youth of today for you! You don't see anything apart from the body. It wasn't like that in our day. The more deeply I fell in love, the more disembodied she became for me. Nowadays you study their legs, their ankles and a bit more besides; you undress the women you're in love with. But for me, as Alphonse Karr[2] used to say (he was a good writer, by the way), the object of my love was always dressed in vestments of bronze. It wasn't just that we didn't undress our women mentally; like the good sons of Noah, we tried to conceal their nakedness. Well, you wouldn't understand . . .'

'Don't pay any attention to him. Carry on with the story,' said one of us.

'Yes, all right. Well, there I was dancing with her, and I completely lost track of the time. The musicians were strumming away at the same old mazurka tune with a sort of desperate weariness – you know how it is at the end of a ball – the mamas and papas had already risen from the card tables and were waiting for supper to be served, the manservants were running to and fro, carrying things. It was already after two a.m. I would have to make the most of the last few minutes. Yet again I asked her to dance with me and for the hundredth time we sailed through the ballroom together.

'"May I have the quadrille after supper?" I asked her, as I took her back to her seat.

'"Of course, if they haven't taken me home by then," she said with a smile.

'"I won't let them," I said.

'"Give me back my fan," she said.

'"It breaks my heart to do even that," I said, as I returned her inexpensive white fan to her.

'"Well, here you are, so your heart doesn't break," she said, plucking a feather from her fan and giving it to me.

'I took the feather, and was only able to express my joy and gratitude by the way I looked at her. I was not merely light of heart, contented; I was blissfully happy, I overflowed with goodness, I was no longer myself but some unearthly being that had no knowledge of evil and was capable only of doing good. I hid the feather in my glove and remained standing there, unable to summon up the strength to leave her.

'"Look, they're trying to get Papa to dance," she said, pointing out the tall, stately figure of her father, a colonel in silver epaulettes who was standing in the doorway with the hostess and some other ladies.

'"Varenka, come over here," we heard the hostess, with her diamond *ferronière* and empress shoulders, call in a loud voice.

'Varenka went over to the doorway. I followed her.

'"*Ma chère*, do try to talk your father into taking a round of the floor with you. Come along now, please, Pyotr Vladislavych," said the hostess to the colonel.

'Varenka's father was a very tall, stately, handsome, well-preserved old man. His face had a rubicund complexion, he had a white, curly moustache *à la Nicolas*[3] which joined a pair of sidewhiskers, also white, and his hair was combed forwards over his temples. A happy, affectionate smile like that of his daughter played in his brilliant eyes and around his lips. He was magnificently built, with his broad chest thrown forwards, military style, and adorned with a tasteful clutch of medals, his powerful shoulders and his long, elegant legs. He was a military commander with the bearing of an old campaigner from the days of Nicholas I.

'As we approached the doorway, the colonel was on the point of refusing, saying that he had forgotten how to dance; none the less, smiling and reaching with his right arm for his left side, he drew his sword from its scabbard, gave it to an obliging young man and, putting a suede glove on his right hand – "Everything according to regulations," he said, smiling – led his daughter out on to the dance floor, made a quarter turn and waited for the mazurka tempo to begin.

'When it did, he stamped one foot smartly on the floor, put the other one forward, and his tall, stout figure began, now quietly and smoothly, now noisily and impetuously, to move around the ballroom with a thudding of boot soles and of foot against foot. Beside him floated Varenka's graceful figure, imperceptibly lengthening or shortening the steps her small feet took in their white satin shoes. All who were present in the room followed each and every movement of the couple. Not only was I lost in admiration as I watched them, I was filled with a moved, ecstatic feeling. I was particularly moved by the colonel's boots, which were fastened by foot-straps – they were good, calf-leather boots, though not of the pointed, fashionable kind, but with the old-style square toecaps and without heels, obviously the work of a regimental cobbler. "In order to bring out his favourite daughter and set her off he hasn't bought fashionable boots but is just wearing his ordinary, homemade ones," I thought, and those square toecaps continued to move me. It was evident that he had once been an excellent dancer; now he had grown stout, however, and his legs were no longer supple enough for the swift, elegant dance steps he was trying to perform. All the same, he managed to make two rounds of the floor with considerable dexterity. And when he swiftly planted his feet apart and then rejoined them and fell to one knee, albeit somewhat heavily, and when she, smiling and patting her skirt where he had caught it, circled him gracefully, everyone burst into loud applause. Getting to his feet again with a certain amount of effort, he embraced his daughter tenderly and affectionately by the ears and, kissing her forehead, led her over to where I stood, thinking that I was dancing with her. I told him that I was not her escort.

' "Well, never mind, you take her for this dance,' he said, smiling kindly and putting his sword away in its scabbard.

'Just as a single drop poured from a bottle is followed by the gushing-forth of the entire contents, so my love for Varenka released the entire amorous capacity of my soul. At that moment I embraced the whole world with my love. I loved the hostess with her *ferronière* and Empress Elizabeth bust, I loved her husband, her guests, her manservants and even Anisimov, the engineer, who was now giving me a rather cool look. As for her father, with his regimental boots and his affectionate smile that was like hers, for him I felt an emotion that was composed of enthusiasm and tenderness.

'The mazurka came to an end, the host and hostess asked the guests to come in to supper, but Colonel B— refused, saying that he had to get up early next morning, and he took his leave of them both. I was beginning to worry that Varenka too would have to go, but she remained with her mother.

'After supper I danced the quadrille with Varenka, as she had promised, and, although my happiness already seemed infinite, it continued to grow and grow. We said nothing on the subject of love. I did not ask her, any more than I asked myself, whether she loved me. And the only thing I was afriad of was that something might spoil my happiness.

'When I got home I undressed and thought about sleep, and then realized that sleep was quite out of the question. I was still holding the feather from her fan and one of her gloves which she had given me as she had been leaving (I had helped both her and her mother to get into their carriage). I looked at these objects and, without closing my eyes, saw her before me, now as she had been at the moment when, choosing between two escorts, she had tried to guess which quality I represented, and I had heard her charming voice say, "*Pride?* Yes?" – and had joyfully given me her hand; and now as she had been at supper, taking little sips from her goblet of champagne and looking at me with affectionate mistrust. But most clearly of all I saw her together with her father, circling around him and surveying the admiring spectators with pride and joy both at him and at herself. And I found myself linking them both in a single emotion of tender rapture.

'At that time I was living with my brother, who is dead now.

In general, my brother wasn't much disposed towards society life and didn't go to balls; just then he was studying for his final-year university exams and was leading a very regular life. He was asleep. As I looked at his head, buried in the pillow and half-covered by a flannel blanket, I felt sorry for him in a brotherly sort of way, sorry that he neither knew nor shared the happiness I was experiencing. Our household serf Petrusha came to meet me with a candle and wanted to help me undress for bed, but I sent him away. I found the sight of his sleepy face and tousled hair charmingly touching. Trying not to make any noise, I went into my room on tiptoe and sat down on the bed. It was no good, I was too happy, I would never be able to sleep. What was more, I found the heated rooms far too warm and, without taking off my uniform jacket, I went quietly into the hallway, put on my overcoat, opened the front door and went out on to the street.

'It had been after four a.m. when I had left the ball; since my arrival home two hours had passed, which I had spent sitting about; thus it was already light when I emerged on to the street. It was real Shrovetide weather – there was a fog, patches of snow saturated with water were melting on the roads, and there was a steady dripping from the roofs. In those days the B—s lived on the outskirts of town near a large field, at one end of which there was a Shrovetide fair, and at the other an institute for young ladies. I walked down the deserted lane outside our house and came out on to the main road; here, even at this hour, I began to meet pedestrians and draymen with firewood on their sledge carts that grazed the road surface with their runners. Everything – the horses rhythmically swaying their sopping heads under the glossy shaft-bows, the cab-drivers, their shoulders covered in bast matting, trudging along beside their cabs in enormous boots and, on either side of the streets, the houses, which in the fog seemed extraordinarily tall – for me it was all charged with a peculiar fascination and significance. When I came to the field where their house was situated, I saw at its opposite end, near the fairground, something large and black; I could hear the sound of a fife and drum coming from over that way. My head was still full of music, and every now and then I had been silently hearing the tune of the mazurka. What filled my ears now, however, was another kind of music, harsh and unpleasant.

'"I wonder what that is?" I thought, and made my way along the slippery path that had been trampled across the middle of the field in the direction the sounds were coming from. When I had gone about a hundred yards or so, I began to be able to make out through the fog a large number of people dressed in black. They were obviously soldiers. "They must be on manoeuvres," I thought and, together with a blacksmith in a dirty apron and dirty sheepskin coat who was walking in front of me, carrying something, I went closer. Black-uniformed soldiers were standing perfectly still in two rows, their rifles at rest. Behind them stood a drummer and a fifer who kept playing the same shrill, unpleasant melody over and over again.

'"What are they doing?" I asked the blacksmith, who had stopped beside me. "Giving a Tartar a hiding for desertion," said the blacksmith gruffly, his eyes trained on the far end of the rows of men.

'I followed his gaze and, between the rows, saw something terrifying coming towards me. It was a man stripped to the waist and tied to the rifles of the two soldiers who were escorting him. Beside him, in an overcoat and peaked cap, walked a tall colonel who looked familiar to me. His whole body twitching, his feet slapping on the melting snow, the man who was being punished was moving towards me under a hail of blows that descended on him from all sides, now throwing himself backwards – whereupon the NCOs who were dragging him along on their rifles would push him forwards – now falling forwards – whereupon the NCOs would pull him backwards in order to keep him upright. And by his side, with a firm, slightly quivering step, walked the tall colonel. It was her father, with his rubicund face and his white moustache and sidewhiskers.

'Each time he was struck, the man who was being punished turned his face, which was contorted with suffering, in the direction from which the blow had come, as if in surprise, and, baring his teeth, kept repeating the same words. It was only when he was quite close to me that I was able to make out what they were. In a voice that was more of a sob, he was mouthing: "Have mercy on me, lads. Have mercy on me, lads." But the lads were not having any mercy on him and, when the procession drew level with me, I saw the soldier standing opposite me take a determined step forwards and bring his stick whistling down on the Tartar's back with a violent slash. The Tartar convulsed forwards, but the NCOs restrained him, and another, similar blow landed on him from the other side; this was followed by another from the side I was on, then by a further one from the other side, and so it went on. The colonel maintained his accompanying presence and, looking now at his feet and now at the man who was being punished, he took deep gulps of air, blowing out his cheeks and letting the air escape through his protruding lips. When the procession had gone past me, I caught a glimpse of the Tartar's back through the ranks of men. It looked so lurid, wet and unnaturally red that I could hardly believe it was a man's back.

' "Oh, Christ," said the blacksmith, who was standing beside me.

'The procession began to move off into the distance, the blows continued to rain down from both sides on the stumbling, writhing man, the drum went on beating and the fife went on shrilling, and the tall, stately figure of the colonel continued to move alongside the Tartar with its firm step. Suddenly the colonel stood still. Then he went up to one of the soldiers.

' "I'll teach you to miss the mark," I heard him say in an angry voice. "Going to miss the mark, were you? Going to miss it, eh?"

'And I saw his powerful, suede-gloved hand strike a puny, frightened little soldier in the face for not bringing his stick down on the Tartar's back hard enough.

' "Give them fresh sticks!" he shouted, and as he looked round he caught sight of me. Pretending not to know me, he wasted no time in turning away, frowning angrily and menacingly as he did so. I was so embarrassed that, not knowing where to look, as though I had been caught red-handed in the most shameful misdeed, I lowered my eyes and hurried off home. All the way back I could hear either the beating of the drum and the shrilling of the fife and the man sobbing, "Have mercy on me, lads," or the self-assured, angry voice of the colonel shouting, "Going to miss the mark, were you? Going to miss it, eh?" And all the while I was filled with an almost physical anguish that rose in me to the point of nausea, and so powerfully that several times I had to stand still and thought I was going to vomit up all the horror that this spectacle had aroused in me. I don't even remember how I managed to reach home and get into bed. But no sooner had I fallen asleep than I heard and saw it all over again, and I leapt out of bed.

'"He obviously knows something that I don't," I said to myself, thinking of the colonel. "If I'd known what he knows, I'd have understood what I was seeing and it wouldn't have upset me." But no matter how hard I tried, I couldn't imagine what it was the colonel knew, and it was not until that evening that I was able to fall asleep, and even then only after I had gone to the house of a friend and got completely drunk with him.

'Well, do you suppose I made up my mind then that what I had seen was something sickening? Not a bit of it. "If it was done with such assurance and everyone thought it was necessary, then they must have known something I didn't," was what I thought, and I tried to find out what it was. But I couldn't, no matter how hard I exerted myself. And since I couldn't, I couldn't join the army as I'd planned to, and not only did I not join the army, I couldn't find a place for myself anywhere in society, and ended up being no good for anything, as you can see.'

'Oh yes, we know all about how you're no good for anything,' said one of us. 'But tell us: how many men would be no good for anything if it weren't for the likes of you?'

'Oh, come, that's just plain stupid,' said Ivan Vasilyevich with unfeigned irritation.

'Well, and what about that love of yours?' we asked.

'My love? Oh, from that day on it started to fade. Whenever she grew pensive, with that smile on her face, as she often did, I'd immediately find myself thinking about the colonel on the field, and I'd feel awkward and unwell; so I started to see her less often. And my love for her just disappeared. That's the way it is with some affairs, and those are the sort of events that change the course of a man's entire life. But you say . . .' he concluded.

THE FORGED COUPON

Part One

I

Fyodor Mikhailovich Smokovnikov, the head of a government tax department, a man of incorruptible integrity and proud of it, a gloomy liberal who was not only a free-thinker but also a hater of every manifestation of religious tendencies, which he considered a throwback to the superstitions of earlier times, had come home from his office in a very sour frame of mind. He had just received a most stupid memo from the governor, and from it the inference could be drawn that Fyodor Mikhailovich had acted in a dishonest fashion. Bitterly angry, Fyodor Mikhailovich had immediately written the governor a stinging and caustic reply.

When he got home it seemed to him as if everything were going against him.

It was five to five. He had expected dinner to be served as soon as he made his appearance, but it wasn't ready yet. Fyodor Mikhailovich banged the door and stalked off to his study. There was a knock. 'Who the devil is it now?' he wondered, and he shouted: 'Who is it now?'

Into his study came a fifth-form grammar school boy, his fifteen-year-old son.

'What do you want?'

'It's the first of the month today.'

'Money, is it?'

They had an arrangement whereby on the first day of each month the father gave his son an allowance of three roubles to cover the cost of entertainments. Fyodor Mikhailovich made a sour face, took out his wallet, searched inside it and extricated from it a two-and-a-half-rouble bond coupon;[1] then he fished out his small change and counted out another fifty kopecks. His son said nothing and did not take the money.

'Papa, please let me have some more in advance.'

'What?'

'I don't like to ask you, but I borrowed some money and promised on my word of honour to pay it back. As a man of integrity, I can't . . . I have to have another three roubles, really I do, I wouldn't ask you, or at least, well . . . Please, Papa.'

'You were told . . .'

'I know, Papa. Look, it's just this once . . .'

'You get an allowance of three roubles, and still it's not enough. When I was your age I didn't even get fifty kopecks.'

'All my friends get more than I do now. Petrov and Ivanitsky get fifty roubles a month.'

'And I'm telling you that if you go on like this you'll end up as a swindler. That's it, now, I've told you.'

'So what if you have? You'll never be able to put yourself in my shoes; now I've got no alternative but to be a swindler. It's all right for you.'

'Get out of here this instant, you idle good-for-nothing! Get out!'

Fyodor Mikhailovich leapt to his feet and rushed towards his son.

'Out! You ought to be given a good whipping!'

His son was overtaken by fear and a sense of bitter resentment; his resentment, however, was greater than his fear. Bowing his head, he walked quickly to the door. Fyodor Mikhailovich had no intention of laying a finger on him, but he was enjoying his fit of anger, and he continued to hurl abuse at his son for some considerable time, until the latter had disappeared.

When the maid came in to say that dinner was served Fyodor Mikhailovich rose to his feet.

'At last,' he said. 'I don't even feel hungry now.' And with a black scowl on his face he went to have dinner.

At the dinner table his wife started to talk to him, but so

angrily did he bark out his replies that she fell silent. His son, too, said nothing, keeping his eyes steadily fixed on his plate. In silence they continued to eat, and silently they rose from the table and went about their separate tasks.

After dinner the grammar school boy went back to his room, where he took the coupon and change out of his pocket and threw them on to his writing desk; then he removed his school tunic and put on a jacket. After he had spent some time poring over a tattered Latin grammar, he got up, closed the door and fastened its hook, then swept the money off the desk top and into a drawer. From the same drawer he took some Russian cigarette papers with their cardboard holders, stuffed a quantity of tobacco into one of them using a piece of cotton wool and started to smoke.

He continued to pore over his grammar and his exercise books for a couple of hours without taking anything in. Then he stood up and began to pace to and fro in his room, stamping his heels as he recalled the scene he had had with his father. All his father's abusive talk and, in particular, the malevolent expression there had been on his face, came back to him as clearly as if it had all just been a moment ago. 'You idle good-for-nothing! You ought to be given a good whipping!' And the more of the scene he remembered, the more his anger at his father grew. He remembered his father saying to him: 'It's easy to see what you'll end up as – a swindler. Just you wait.' 'He said I'd end up as a swindler if I went on like this. It's all right for him. He's forgotten what it's like to be young. Anyway, what crime have I committed? All I did was go to the theatre and because I didn't have any money I borrowed some off Petya Grushetsky. What's wrong with that? Anyone else would have shown some sympathy and given the matter some consideration, but all he could do was bellow at me and think of himself. When he hasn't got something he wants he shouts the whole house down, but I'm a swindler. No, even though he is my father, I don't like him. Maybe all fathers are like he is, but I still don't like him.'

The maid knocked at his door. She had brought a note for him. 'You're to reply to it at once,' she said.

The note read: 'This makes three times now that I've asked you to return the six roubles you borrowed from me, but you always try to get out of it. Men who are honest don't behave like that. Please send the money at once via bearer. I'm really broke myself. Surely you can get it for me? Your – depending on whether or not you give me my money back – respectful or contemptuous friend, Grushetsky.'

'I don't believe it. The greedy pig, he can't wait. I'll have another go.'

Mitya went to see his mother. This was his last hope. She had a kind heart and was never able to refuse him anything, and she would probably have helped him on this occasion, too, except that she was in an anxious state about the illness of two-year-old Petya, her youngest boy. She was angry at Mitya for coming in and making a noise, and she turned down his request point-blank.

He muttered something to himself under his breath, and went out of the room. His mother immediately felt sorry for him and called him back.

'Wait, Mitya,' she said. 'I haven't got it right now, but I'll get it for you tomorrow.'

But Mitya was still burning with resentment against his father.

'What's the good of waiting till tomorrow, when I need it today? I may as well tell you that I'm going to ask one of my friends to lend me it.'

He went out, finally this time, banging the door behind him.

'There's nothing else for it. At least he'll be able to tell me where I can pawn my watch,' he thought, fingering the watch in his pocket.

Mitya took the coupon and the change out of the desk drawer, put on his coat and set off to visit his friend Makhin.

2

Makhin was a fifth-former with a moustache. He played cards, knew women and always had money. He lived with his aunt. Mitya knew that Makhin was a ne'er-do-well, but when he was with him he unconsciously let him take the upper hand. Makhin was at home, getting ready to go to the theatre: his grimy little room smelt of scented soap and eau-de-Cologne.

'That's too bad,' said Makhin, after Mitya had related his woes to him, shown him the coupon and the fifty kopecks, and told him he needed nine roubles more. 'You can pawn your watch, of course, but you can do better than that,' said Makhin, giving him a wink.

'How do you mean, better?'

'It's very simple.' Makhin took the coupon. 'If you insert a 1 before the 2 r. 50 it'll read 12 r. 50.'

'But do coupons for that amount exist?'

'Of course they do, on thousand-rouble bonds. I put one of them into circulation myself once.'

'I don't believe it!'

'All right then, shall we do it?' said Makhin, taking a pen and smoothing out the coupon with the index finger of his left hand.

'But it's not right.'

'Rubbish.'

'He was right,' thought Mitya, remembering the things his father had shouted at him. 'A swindler. I'll be a swindler now.' He looked Makhin in the face. Makhin was watching him with a quiet smile.

'Well then, shall we?'

'All right.'

Makhin painstakingly wrote in a figure 1.

'Right, now we'll go to a shop. There's one on the corner here that sells photographic supplies. It just so happens that I need a frame for this lady.'

He produced a photograph of a round-eyed girl with vast tresses of hair and magnificent breasts.

'How do you fancy her, eh? Eh?'

'Yes, yes. But how . . . ?'

'It's very simple. Come on.'

Makhin put on his coat, and they left the house together.

3

The bell in the entrance to the photographic supply shop gave a tinkle. The two grammar school boys went inside and looked around the deserted shop with its shelves of photographic equipment and its counters on which stood showcases. From a doorway at the back of the shop a plain woman with a kindly face emerged. Taking up her position behind the counter, she asked them what they wanted.

'A nice frame, miss.'

'How much do you want to spend?' asked the lady, running the swollen-jointed fingers of her mittened hands swiftly and deftly over various types of frames. 'Those are fifty kopecks each, but these are a little more expensive. This one here is very nice, it's a new line, priced at a rouble twenty.'

'All right, I'll take that one. But wouldn't you let me have it for a rouble?'

'All our prices are fixed,' said the lady, with dignity.

'Oh, all right then,' said Makhin, putting the coupon down on one of the glass showcases. 'But please hurry up and let me have my change. I don't want to be late for the theatre.'

'Oh, you're in plenty of time,' said the lady, and she began to examine the coupon with eyes that were obviously short-sighted.

'She'll look stunning in that frame, won't she?' said Makhin, turning to Mitya.

'Haven't you any other money with you?' asked the shop lady.

'That's just it, I'm afraid I haven't. My father gave me this and told me to get it changed.'

'Are you sure you haven't got a rouble twenty on you?'

'I've got fifty kopecks. Anyway, what's the matter, are you afraid we're trying to pass a forgery off on you?'

'No, nothing like that.'

'Then give me the coupon back, please. We'll have it changed somewhere else.'

'How much change do I have to give you?'

'Well, let's see, it works out at eleven something.'

The shop lady flicked the beads on her abacus, unlocked the till, took out a ten-rouble note and, running her hands through the change, raked together six twenty-kopeck pieces and two five-kopeck bits.

I'd like it wrapped up, please,' said Makhin, taking the money in a leisurely fashion.

'It won't take a moment.'

The shop lady wrapped the frame and tied the parcel up with string.

Mitya only dared to breathe again after the entrance bell had tinkled and they were out on the street once more.

'All right, here's ten roubles for you; let me keep the rest. I'll give you it back.'

And Makhin went off to the theatre, while Mitya visited Grushetsky and settled his debt.

4

An hour after the two grammar school boys had left the shop, the proprietor returned and started to count his day's takings.

'Oh, you idiot of a woman! You idiot!' he shouted at his wife when he saw the coupon and immediately spotted the forgery. 'And what are you doing accepting coupons, anyway?'

'But I've seen you accept them, Zhenya, twelve-rouble coupons exactly like this one,' said his wife, who was by now confused, upset and on the point of tears. 'I don't know how they managed to fool me,' she said. 'Grammar school boys, they were, too. One of them was such a handsome young man, he seemed so *comme il faut*.'

'I'll *comme il faut* you, you idiot!' shouted her husband, keeping up a steady stream of abuse at her as he continued to count the takings. 'When I accept a coupon I make sure I know what's printed on it, but you, all you can see is those boys from the grammar school with their ugly mugs.'

This was too much for his wife, and she too flew into a rage.

'There's a man for you! All you can do is put the blame on other people; I suppose losing fifty-four roubles at cards is neither here nor there?'

'That's something else entirely.'

'I'm not going to waste any more breath on you,' said his wife, and she went off to her room. There she started to remember how reluctant her family had been to consent to her marriage, as they had considered that her husband belonged to a lower social class than theirs, and how she had had to insist; she remembered the child she had had who had died, and her husband's indifference to this loss, and she felt such hatred for him that she wished it had been him that had died. This thought frightened her, however, and she quickly put on her coat and went out. When her husband got back to their apartment, she was gone. Without waiting for him, she had taken her coat and set off alone for the house of a teacher of French who had invited them to a soirée that evening.

5

At the home of the teacher of French – a Russian Pole – there was a gala tea with sweet pastries. After it was over, everyone sat down at several tables to play bridge.

The photographic supplier's wife shared a table with the host, an officer, and a deaf old lady in a wig who was the widow of a music shop owner and had a passion for cards, which she was very good at. This particular game seemed to be going in favour of the photographic supplier's wife; twice now she had made a grand slam. Beside her was a plate that contained a bunch of grapes and a pear, and she was in the best of spirits.

'What's keeping Yevgeny Mikhailovich?' asked the hostess from another table. 'He's supposed to be our fifth hand.'

'Oh, he's probably still doing his accounts,' said Yevgeny

Mikhailovich's wife. 'Today's the day he always pays the grocery and firewood bills.'

And, remembering the scene she had had with her husband, she frowned, and her mittened hands trembled with resentment towards him.

'Talk of the devil,' said the host, turning to greet Yevgeny Mikhailovich, who had just walked in. 'What held you up?'

'Oh, various bits of business,' replied Yevgeny Mikhailovich cheerfully, rubbing his hands. Then, much to his wife's astonishment, he went over to her and said: 'You remember that coupon? Well, I've managed to pass it on.'

'You have?'

'Yes, I gave it to a *muzhik*[2] for some firewood.'

And with great indignation Yevgeny Mikhailovich proceeded to tell everyone the story of how some dishonest grammar school boys had tricked his wife, while his wife supplied the details.

'Right, now let's get on with it,' he said at last, sitting down at the table when his turn came and shuffling the cards.

6

Yevgeny Mikhailovich had indeed managed to pass the coupon on: he had persuaded a peasant named Ivan Mironov to accept it in exchange for some firewood.

Ivan Mironov made his living by buying up single loads of firewood in the wood yards and then carting them for sale around the town; he split the loads into five, and sold each part for what a quarter-load cost at the wood yards. Early on the morning of this day that was to prove so unlucky for him, Ivan Mironov had carted out an eighth-load and, having quickly sold it, had brought out another eighth in the hope of selling it, too. This time, however, he could not find a customer, and spent all day until evening carting the load around in search of someone who might possibly buy it. He kept running across canny townsfolk who were wise to all the sharp practices of *muzhik* firewood salesmen, and were not so credulous as to believe that he had brought the wood in from the country, as he said he had. He was thoroughly famished, and felt chilled to the bone in his worn sheepskin jacket and his ragged undercoat; by evening the temperature had dropped to minus twenty; his horse, which he had been driving without mercy, since he was about to sell it to the knacker, refused to go any further. Ivan Mironov was even thinking of selling the firewood at a loss when he encountered Yevgeny Mikhailovich, who had gone out to buy some tobacco and was now on his way home.

'Would you like to buy some firewood, sir? I'll sell it to you cheap. My horse won't go any further.'

'Tell me where you're from first.'

'From the country, sir. The wood's all my own. It's good, dry stuff.'

'I know your sort. Well, what do you want for it?'

Ivan Mironov named an exorbitant price, then started to reduce it, and finally parted with the firewood at his normal price.

'Just for you, sir, seeing it's not far to deliver,' he said.

Yevgeny Mikhailovich did not make too much fuss about the price. He was pleased at the thought that now he would be able to pass on the coupon. Pulling the cart along by his own efforts, Ivan Mironov somehow managed to manoeuvre the firewood into the yard; he unloaded it and stacked it in the shed himself. The yard-keeper was not on duty. At first Ivan Mironov was unwilling to accept the coupon, but Yevgeny Mikhailovich was so persuasive and seemed to be such an important gentleman that in the end he agreed to take it.

As he entered the servants' room through the tradesmen's entrance, Ivan Mironov crossed himself, wrung the icicles from his beard and, turning back the lapel of his sheepskin jacket, produced a leather purse from which he counted out eight roubles and fifty kopecks change. He handed the money over, took the coupon, rolled it up in a piece of paper and put it in his purse.

Having proffered his thanks, in a manner befitting the conclusion of a transaction with a gentleman, Ivan Mironov proceeded to set the legs of his doomed, frost-encrusted horse in motion, not with the lash of his whip now, but with its handle, forcing it to drag the empty cart as far as the local inn.

At the inn Ivan Mironov ordered eight kopecks' worth of tea and vodka. Once he had thawed out and even begun to perspire a bit, his mood became thoroughly amiable, and he got into conversation with the yard-keeper, who was sitting at his table. He really warmed to the conversation and told the yard-keeper that he came from the village of Vasilevskoye, some twelve versts[3] outside town, that he had been given his share of the family fortune and now lived independently of his father and brothers with his wife and two sons, the elder of whom was undergoing professional training and so was not yet able to help him out. He told the yard-keeper that while he was in town he was staying in lodgings, and that tomorrow he was going to the knacker to sell his old jade, and might possibly buy a new horse. He said he had now managed to save up the sum of twenty-five roubles and that half of the money was in the form of a coupon. He took out the coupon and showed it to the yard-keeper. The yard-keeper could neither read nor write, but he said he had changed money like that for the tenants, that it was all right, but that there were forgeries around and, for that reason, he advised him to play safe and have it changed at the bar. Ivan Mironov gave the coupon to the waiter and asked him to bring him the same amount in ready cash. The waiter went off but did not return. Instead, the inn's bald-headed, shiny-faced manager appeared, clutching the coupon in his pudgy hand.

'Your money is no good,' he said, indicating the coupon but not returning it.

'It's perfectly good. I was given it by a gentleman.'

'No, my fine fellow. This coupon's been tampered with.'

'Give it back to me, then.'

'No, my fine fellow. You'll have to be taught a lesson. You forged this coupon yourself, you and your swindler friends.'

'Give me my money back; you've got no right to do this.'

'Sidor! Call the police!' said the barman to the waiter.

Ivan Mironov was slightly the worse for the drink he had had. And being slightly the worse for drink, he was also getting rather agitated. He seized the manager by the collar and shouted: 'Give me it back, I'll go and see the gentleman. I know where he lives.'

The manager tore himself free of Ivan Mironov's grip, but as he did so his shirt began to split.

'Oh, so that's how you want to play it! Take him!'

The waiter seized hold of Ivan Mironov and, at that very instant, the local policeman appeared. As master of the situation, he listened to both sides of the story and then brought the whole episode to a speedy conclusion.

'You've got to come down to the station!'

The policeman put the coupon into his own wallet, and then escorted Ivan Mironov and his horse to the police station.

7

Ivan Mironov spent the night in the cells at the police station, together with the drunks and the pickpockets. Not until around noon the following day was he summoned to appear before the station chief. The station chief asked him a lot of questions and then told the policeman to take him along for an interview with the proprietor of the photographic supply shop. Ivan Mironov could remember the name of the street and the number of the house.

When the policeman knocked on Yevgeny Mikhailovich's front door and confronted him with the coupon and with Ivan Mironov, who confirmed that this was the gentleman who had given him the coupon, Yevgeny Mikhailovich's expression of astonishment was quickly replaced by one of grim severity.

'What? Have you taken leave of your senses? I've never seen this man before in my life.'

'Master, be sure your sins will find you out. One day we all must die,' said Ivan Mironov.

'What's the matter with him? You must be dreaming. It was someone else you sold your firewood to,' said Yevgeny Mikhailovich. 'In any case, wait a moment, I'll go and ask my wife if she bought any firewood yesterday.'

Yevgeny Mikhailovich went off and immediately summoned the yard-keeper. The yard-keeper was a very strong, handsome, agile fellow who seemed to be perpetually in a good mood, gave himself airs and went by the name of Vasily. Yevgeny Mikhailovich instructed him that if anyone should ask him where the last load of firewood had come from he was to say they had got it from the wood yards, and that they never bought firewood from the *muzhiks*.

'There's a *muzhik* here claiming I gave him a forged coupon. He's a stupid nitwit, talking a lot of nonsense, but you're an intelligent chap. You tell him we only ever buy our firewood at the wood yards. Oh, by the way, I'd been meaning to give you this towards a new jacket,' Yevgeny Mikhailovich added, giving the yard-keeper a five-rouble note.

Vasily took the money and his eyes flashed from the note to Yevgeny Mikhailovich's face; he tossed back his hair and gave a little smile.

'It's common knowledge they're a stupid lot. Uneducated. Don't you worry, sir, I know what to say to the likes of him.'

No matter how tearfully Ivan Mironov beseeched Yevgeny Mikhailovich to admit that the coupon was his, and the yard-keeper to confirm that this was so, both men stuck to their story: they never bought firewood off carts. And the policeman took Ivan Mironov back to the police station, where he was charged with forging a coupon.

It was only by following the advice of his cell-mate, a drunken office clerk, and slipping the station chief a five-rouble note, that Ivan Mironov was able to procure his release from detention. Now he was minus the coupon and had only seven roubles left out of the twenty-five he had had the day before. Ivan Mironov spent three of these seven roubles on drink. Dead drunk, looking utterly crushed, he crept back to his wife.

His wife was in the last stages of a pregnancy and she was feeling ill. She started to shout at her husband, he pushed her away, and she began to pummel him with her fists. Making no attempt at retaliation, he lay face down on the plank bed of the lodging house and wept loudly.

Not until the following morning did his wife discover what

had happened; believing her husband's story, she spent a long time cursing the fraudulent gentleman who had tricked her Ivan. And Ivan, who was now sober, remembered what the factory hand with whom he had been drinking the night before had advised him, and decided to find a lawyer and lodge a complaint.

8

The lawyer agreed to take on the case, not so much for any money he could hope to receive as because he believed Ivan's story and was angry that anyone should so shamelessly defraud a poor *muzhik*.

Both parties attended the hearing, at which the yard-keeper Vasily was the sole witness. The hearing was a repetition of all that had gone before. Ivan Mironov made allusions to God, and to the fact that one day we all must die. Yevgeny Mikhailovich, though troubled by an awareness of what he was doing as both shabby and dangerous, was unable now to go back on the testimony he had already given, and he continued to disclaim all responsibility with an appearance of outward calm.

Vasily the yard-keeper pocketed another ten roubles and calmly asserted that he had never set eyes on Ivan Mironov in his life before. And when he was summoned to be sworn in, even though he quailed inwardly, he none the less repeated the words of the oath after the old priest who had been specially brought in for the occasion, and swore on the crucifix and the Holy Gospel that he would tell the whole truth and nothing but the truth.

The court proceedings ended with the judge rejecting the action brought by Ivan Mironov and making him forfeit court costs to the tune of five roubles, which Yevgeny Mikhailovich magnanimously paid for him. Discharging Ivan Mironov, the judge cautioned him to be more careful in future about bringing accusations against decent, law-abiding citizens, and told him he should be grateful to the defendant for paying his court costs for him, instead of prosecuting him for slander, an offence for which he could have been sent to prison for at least three months.

'I thank your honour kindly, sir,' said Ivan Mironov, and he left the chamber, shaking his head and sighing.

The whole episode seemed to have ended well for Yevgeny Mikhailovich and Vasily the yard-keeper. But that was only the way it looked on the surface. No one perceived what had really happened – something far more grave than what could be discerned by human eyes.

It was getting on for three years now since Vasily had left his village and gone to live in the town. With every year that passed he gave less and less of what he earned to his father, and he had not sent for his wife, since he did not need her. Here in the town he could have as many women as he wanted, and they were no useless old hags like her. With every year that passed Vasily forgot more and more of the country laws and customs, and adapted himself more and more to the ways of the town. Back there, life had been crude, cheerless, impoverished and messy; here it was tasteful, comfortable, clean and luxurious – everything had been taken care of. Increasingly he had grown convinced that those countryfolk lived blindly, like beasts in the forest, while all the real people were here. He read books by good authors, novels and went to stage performances at the People's House.[4] One could never see anything like that in the country, not even in one's dreams. In the village he had come from the old men had used to say: 'Live with your wife according to the law, work hard, don't eat too much, don't give yourself airs.' But here people were clever, educated – that meant they knew what the real laws were – and they enjoyed life. Everything was just perfect. Until the hearing concerning the coupon, Vasily had refused to believe that the upper classes had no laws to govern the conduct of their lives. He had thought they did have laws, but that he, Vasily, did not know what they were. But after the hearing, and in particular his perjury, which in spite of all his fears had had no negative consequences for him and had indeed resulted in his being ten roubles better off, he became fully persuaded that there were no laws and that all one was supposed to do was to enjoy life. This he did and this he continued to do. At first he merely fiddled a bit of money on the purchases he made for the tenants, but this was not enough for all his expenses, and he started, whenever he got the chance, to pilfer money and valuables from the tenants' apartments; once he even tried to steal Yevgeny Mikhailovich's wallet. Yevgeny Mikhailovich caught him in the act, but did not bring proceedings against him in court: instead, he saw to it that Vasily got the sack.

Vasily did not find the idea of going back to his village particularly appealing, and he stayed on in Moscow with his mistress, looking for work. He found a low-paid job as yard-keeper to the proprietor of a small shop. Vasily started in the job, but in the very second month of his employment he was caught stealing sacks. His employer did not make an official complaint against him, but gave him a beating and drove him off the premises. After that it was impossible for Vasily to find work, his money was all spent, soon he had pawned most of his clothes and in the end all he had left was a tattered coat, a pair of trousers and some ragged footwear. His mistress left him. But Vasily did not lose his cheerful, high-spirited disposition, and when spring came round he set off home for his village on foot.

9

Pyotr Nikolayevich Sventitsky, a thick-set little man who wore smoked glasses (he had trouble with his eyes and was threatened by total blindness), got up before dawn, as was his custom, and, after he had had a glass of tea, put on his knee-length fleece coat, trimmed with lambskin, and set off to make the rounds of his estate.

Pyotr Nikolayevich had been a customs officer and had managed to save some eighteen thousand roubles of what he had earned. Almost twelve years previously he had gone into retirement, not quite voluntarily, and had bought the poky little estate of a young landowner who had squandered his fortune. Pyotr Nikolayevich had married while he had still been on government service. His wife was the poor orphan of an old aristocratic family, a plump, attractive woman who had borne him no children. Pyotr Nikolayevich was, in all his dealings, a man of persistence and thoroughness. The son of a Polish gentleman, he had known nothing about agriculture, yet so skilful at it had he proved to be that the ramshackle, three-hundred-desyatina[5] estate had, within the space of ten years, become a very model of perfection. All the structures he put up, from the house itself to the granary and the shelter over the firehose, were solid and reliable, covered by sheet iron and given a coat of fresh paint whenever they needed it. In the implement shed there was an orderly collection of carts, harrows and wooden and iron ploughs. The horses' harness was kept properly greased. The horses themselves were medium-sized animals, nearly all from the same stud – well-fed, sturdy greys, matched in pairs. The threshing machine was operated in its own covered barn, the feed was kept in a special shed, and the liquid manure flowed into a pit with a paved base. The cows were likewise all of the same stock, medium-sized, but giving a high milk yield. The pigs were the 'English' variety. There was a poultry yard with several breeds of hen notable for their laying properties. The fruit trees in the orchard were sprayed and coated, and new ones had been planted. Wherever one looked there were signs of thrift, reliability, cleanliness and good order. Pyotr Nikolayevich drew a great deal of satisfaction from his estate, and was proud of the fact that he had achieved all this not by making his peasants' lives a misery but, on the contrary, by exercising the most scrupulous fairness in their regard. Even when mixing with the local nobility he tended to hold to a middle-of-the-road point of view, one that was closer to a liberal rather than a conservative position, and he always defended the common people to the advocates of serf ownership. 'Be good to them and they'll be good to you' was his motto. It was true that he would not tolerate slips and blunders on the part of those who worked for him, and sometimes he would urge them along himself; he demanded that they work hard for him, but on the other hand the accommodation and the food he offered them were of the very highest quality, their wages were always paid on time, and on holidays he treated them to vodka.

Stepping carefully over the melting snow – this was in February – Pyotr Nikolayevich made his way past the farm hands' stable to the *izba*[6] where the farm hands lived. It was still dark; the fog made it even darker than it might have been, but light was visible in the windows of the *izba*. The farm hands were getting out of bed. His intention was to hurry them up: this morning six of them were supposed to be taking the cart over to the thicket to gather in the rest of the firewood.

'What's this?' he thought, suddenly noticing that the door of the stable was open.

'I say, who's in there?'

There was no answer. Pyotr Nikolayevich went into the stable.

'Who's in here, I say?'

Still there was no answer. It was dark, the ground under his feet felt soft, and there was a smell of manure. A pair of young greys occupied a stall to the right of the door. Pyotr Nikolayevich stretched out his hand – but there was nothing there. He moved his foot forward. Perhaps they had lain down. His foot met empty air. 'Where have they taken them?' he wondered. They couldn't have been taken for harness, the sleigh was still out there. Pyotr Nikolayevich went back outside and shouted, loudly: 'Hey, Stepan!'

Stepan was the head farm hand. He was just coming out of the *izba*.

'I hear you!' Stepan shouted back in a jovial voice. 'Is that you, Pyotr Nikolayevich, master? The lads are just coming.'

'Why is the stable door open?'

'The stable door? I don't know, sir. Hey, Proshka, give us a lantern.'

Proshka came running with a lantern. They went into the stable. Stepan knew at once what had happened.

'It's thieves, Pyotr Nikolayevich. The lock's been smashed.'

'Never!'

'They've taken them, the villains! Mashka's not here. Neither's Yastreb. No, here's Yastreb. It's Pyostry that's missing. And Krasavchik.'

Three of the horses were missing. Pyotr Nikolayevich said nothing. He was frowning and breathing heavily.

'Just wait till I get my hands on them. Who was supposed to be keeping watch?'

'It was Petka, sir. Petka fell asleep.'

Pyotr Nikolayevich reported the theft to the police. He told the chief constable about it, informed the leader of the *zemstvo*[7] and sent his men to comb the entire neighbourhood. The horses were not found.

'Filthy peasants!' said Pyotr Nikolayevich. 'Look what they've done to me. As if I hadn't been good to them. Just you wait. Thugs and villains, the lot of you. From now on I'm going to deal with you rather differently.'

10

But meanwhile the horses – three greys – had been taken away to the outlying districts. The raiders sold Mashka to the gypsies for eighteen roubles, bartered Pyostry for the horse of a *muzhik* in a village forty miles away, and rode Krasavchik until he dropped from exhaustion and then slaughtered him, selling his hide for three roubles. The man who organized the raid was Ivan Mironov. He had worked for Pyotr Nikolayevich in the past, and knew his way around the estate, and he had decided to recoup his losses by doing a little horse-stealing.

After his misfortune with the forged coupon, Ivan Mironov had spent a long time drowning his sorrows, and indeed he would have drunk away everything he possessed, had his wife not hidden his horse-collars, his clothes and everything else he could have sold to buy vodka. During his drunken binge Ivan Mironov never for a moment ceased to think not only about the gentleman who had wronged him, but also about all the gentlemen and not-so-gentle men who lived by milking his fellow peasants. On one occasion Ivan Mironov happened to be drinking with some *muzhiks* from the area around Podolsk. As they journeyed along, the *muzhiks* told him the story of how they had made off with the horses that had belonged to one of their number. Ivan Mironov began to chide these horse thieves for wronging a *muzhik* in this manner. 'It's a sin,' he said. 'A horse is like a brother to a *muzhik*, yet you took all his horses from him. If you're going to steal horses, then steal them from the higher-ups. Those sons of bitches deserve it.'

As the conversation developed, the *muzhiks* from Podolsk said that you had to be pretty crafty to be able to steal horses from the gentry. You had to know your way around, and you needed the help of someone on the inside. Then Ivan Mironov remembered about Sventitsky, on whose estate he had once lived and worked as a farm hand; he remembered that Sventitsky had once deducted one and a half roubles from his wages as compensation for a broken coupling bolt, and he remembered the greys he had used in his farm work.

Ivan Mironov went to call on Sventitsky, making it appear as though he wanted Sventitsky to hire him, but really in order to spy out the terrain and to familiarize himself with Sventitsky's arrangements. Once he had seen that there was no nightwatchman, and that in the stable the horses were kept in separate stalls, he summoned the thieves and the deed was done.

After he had split the proceeds with the *muzhiks* from Podolsk, Ivan Mironov went home to his village with five roubles in his pocket. At home there was no work he could do: he had no horse. And from that time onwards, Ivan Mironov began to associate with horse thieves and gypsies.

II

Pyotr Nikolayevich Sventitsky spared no effort in attempting to track down the thieves. He knew that the raid would not have been possible without the connivance of one of his own employees. So he regarded them all with suspicion, and tried to find out if any of them had been away from the farm on the night in question. He discovered that there was one such peasant. This was Proshka Nikolayev, a young lad who had just come back from his military service. He was a handsome, agile fellow, and Pyotr Nikolayevich employed him in place of a coachman, to look after the horses and carriages and drive them on occasion. The chief constable was a friend of Pyotr Nikolayevich's, as were the district police inspector, the leader of the local *zemstvo* and the investigating magistrate. Each year all four were invited to Pyotr Nikolayevich's name-day festivities, and they were well acquainted with his delicious liqueurs and pickled mushrooms – white, honey-agaric and milk-agaric. Now they were sympathetic to him and tried to help him.

'You see, that's what you get for taking the side of the *muzhiks*,' said the chief constable. 'I wasn't making it up when I told you they were worse than wild animals. You won't get anywhere with them if you don't use the whip and the rod. So you think it was Proshka, do you, the chap who works as coachman for you?'

'Yes, it's him.'

'Let's have him in here, then.'

Proshka was summoned, and they began to question him.

'Where were you that night?'

Proshka shook his hair back, and his eyes flashed. 'At home, sir.'

'What do you mean, at home? All the farm hands say you weren't.'

'As you please, sir.'

'What I please has nothing to do with it. Where were you?'

'At home, sir.'

'All right, then. Constable, take this man into custody.'

'As you please, sir.'

The reason why Proshka would not say where he had been on the night of the theft was that he had spent it at the house of his girlfriend Parasha, and had promised not to get her into trouble. There was no evidence, and Proshka was released from custody. But Pyotr Nikolayevich was convinced he had been responsible for the raid, and he conceived a hatred for him. Once, when he had taken his carriage out with Proshka as driver, he sent him off to buy some fodder. Proshka did what he usually did and bought two measures of oats at a wayside inn, giving one and a half measures to the horses and exchanging the remaining half for vodka. Pyotr Nikolayevich found out about it, and made a complaint to the local JP. The JP sentenced Proshka to three months' imprisonment.

Proshka was a man of self-esteem. He considered himself a cut above the rest, and had a degree of personal pride. His spell in prison was a humiliating experience for him. No longer could he strut with pride before his fellows, and his spirits sank at once.

Proshka went home from prison embittered not so much against Pyotr Nikolayevich as against the whole world.

Everyone said the same thing: after he came out of prison, Proshka went to pieces. He grew too lazy to work, took to drink, and was soon caught stealing clothes from the tradesman's wife. Once again he ended up in prison.

As for the horses, all Pyotr Nikolayevich could find out about them was that someone had discovered the hide of a grey-coated gelding which he was subsequently able to identify as once having belonged to Krasavchik. To an ever-increasing degree, he was infuriated by the thieves' impunity. Now he could not set eyes on a *muzhik* without a sense of anger. The very mention of them was enough to make his blood boil, and he tried whenever he could to make their lives a misery for them.

12

In spite of the fact that, once he had passed it on, Yevgeny Mikhailovich had stopped thinking about the coupon, his wife, Marya Vasilevna, could neither forgive herself for having been taken in, nor her husband for all the unkind things he had said to her, nor – and this was what rankled most – the two young louts for having so skilfully deceived her.

From the day she had been tricked onwards, she kept a watchful eye on every grammar school boy who came along. On one occasion she encountered Makhin, but failed to recognize him because when he saw her he distorted his features in a way that completely altered his appearance. When, however, some two weeks after the event, she ran smack into Mitya Smokovnikov on the street, she recognized him immediately.

She allowed him to go by and then, turning round, she set off in pursuit. When she reached the entrance of the apartment where he lived, she took a note of his parents' name. Next day she went to the grammar school. In the vestibule she encountered Mikhail Vvedensky, the school's religious instructor. He asked her if he could help. She said she wanted to see the headmaster.

'I'm afraid the headmaster isn't here today; he's unwell. Perhaps I can deal with your inquiry, or at least take a message for him?'

Marya Vasilevna decided to tell the religious instructor everything.

Father Vvedensky was a widower, a traditionalist and a man of considerable personal vanity. The year before, he had met Smokovnikov's father at a soirée and had had a difference with him during a conversation on the subject of religion, in the course of which Smokovnikov had outmanoeuvred him on all counts and had made a laughing stock of him. Father Vvedensky had resolved to single out the son of this man for special attention. When he discovered that the son showed the same indifference to religion as that displayed by his infidel father, he began to persecute him and even failed him in an exam.

Father Vvedensky could not help feeling a certain satisfaction when he heard from Marya Vasilevna what the young Smokovnikov had done, as he saw in the incident a confirmation of his hypotheses concerning the immorality of those who did not follow the guidance of the Church. He decided that he would make use of the incident in order, as he tried to persuade himself, to highlight the risk run by all who stray from the Church and its teachings. His real reason for doing so was, however, to take revenge on a man whom he considered to be a proud and self-opinionated atheist.

'Yes, very sad, very sad,' said Father Mikhail Vvedensky, smoothing with one hand the smooth edges of the confessional crucifix he wore at his chest. 'I'm so glad you've told me about this. As a servant of the Church I shall of course endeavour not to leave the young man without guidance; but I'll also try to make his edification as painless as possible.'

'Yes, I shall act in accordance with my vocation,' said Father Mikhail to himself, in the belief that he had completely forgotten the hostility of Smokovnikov senior and desired nothing but the welfare and salvation of the son.

During the Scripture lesson the following day Father Mikhail told his pupils the whole episode of the forged coupon, and said this had been done by one of the boys at the grammar school.

'It was a vile, wicked thing to do,' he said. 'But not to own up is even worse. I don't believe it was one of you; but if it was, that boy had better own up now and not try to hide behind others.'

As he said this, Father Mikhail gave Mitya Smokovnikov a fixed look. The other pupils, following his gaze, turned round to look at Mitya, too. Mitya turned red and began to sweat; at last he burst into tears and ran from the classroom.

When Mitya's mother learned of this, she made her son tell her the whole story, and then hurried off to the photographic supply shop. She paid the supplier's wife back the twelve roubles fifty, and made her promise to keep quiet about the grammar school boy's identity. She instructed her son to deny everything, and on no account to make a confession to his father.

And indeed, when Fyodor Mikhailovich found out what had happened at the grammar school, and his son, on being interviewed, denied all knowledge of the matter, he went to see the headmaster and laid the facts of the case before him, saying that the religious instructor had behaved in a most reprehensible manner and that he, Fyodor Mikhailovich, was not going to let the affair rest there. The headmaster sent for the religious instructor and a heated exchange of opinions ensued.

'First a stupid woman makes insulting and damaging accusations against my son, and then withdraws them, yet all you can do is blacken the name of an honest, truthful boy.'

'I have blackened no one's name, and I will not permit you to talk to me like that. You forget my vocation.'

'I spit on your vocation.'

'Your mistaken ideas,' said the religious instructor, his chin quivering so that his beard trembled, 'are familiar to the whole town.'

'Gentlemen, gentlemen,' remonstrated the headmaster, trying to pacify the two adversaries. This, however, proved to be impossible.

'My holy calling imposes upon me the duty of concerning myself with the moral and religious upbringing of the young.'

'That's enough of your hypocrisy. Do you think I don't know you've got no more religion than a common heathen?'

'I consider it beneath my dignity to continue holding a conversation with an individual such as yourself,' said Father Mikhail, who had taken particular offence at Smokovnikov's last remark, as he knew it was perfectly correct. He had gone through the complete course at the theological academy, and so had long ago ceased to believe what he practised and preached. All he believed now was that it was everyone's duty to compel themselves to believe the things he had compelled himself to believe.

Smokovnikov was less incensed by the religious instructor's behaviour than he was by this illustration of the way the influence of the clergy was beginning to manifest itself in Russian society, and he told all his friends and acquaintances about this incident.

Father Vvedensky, on the other hand, saw in it yet one more manifestation of the nihilism and atheism which were becoming established not only among the younger generation, but among older people as well, and which he believed it necessary to combat. The more he censured the unbelief of Smokovnikov and of those like him, the more convinced he was of the unshakeable solidity of his own faith, and the less he felt the need to put that faith to the test or to make himself live in accordance with it. His faith, recognized as it was by the world at large, was his principal weapon in his struggle against its repudiators.

These thoughts, engendered in him by his confrontation with Smokovnikov, and by the unpleasant events at the grammar school that had followed in the wake of that confrontation – namely the reprimand and black-marking he had received from the school authorities – finally induced him to do something that had been enticing him for a long time, ever since the death of his wife, in fact: to become a monk, and thus embark upon a career already chosen by several of his fellow students at the academy, one of whom was already an archbishop, and another of whom was the father superior of a monastery, in line for appointment as a diocesan.

At the end of the academic year, Vvedensky relinquished his post at the grammar school, took monastic vows and the name 'Misail', and was very soon given the rectorship of a theological seminary in a town on the Volga.

13

Meanwhile Vasily the yard-keeper had set out on foot down the high road to the south.

By day he tramped, and at night a local gendarme would show him to the lodgings that were always reserved for travellers. Wherever he put in he was given bread, and sometimes people would invite him to sit down at table and have supper with them. In one village in the province of Oryol where he spent the night he was told that a merchant who had leased an orchard from the local landowner was looking for able-bodied nightwatchmen. Vasily had by this time had enough of the beggar's existence he had been leading. He did not, however, want to return to his village, so he went to see the merchant who had leased the orchard and got himself taken on as a nightwatchman for a wage of five roubles a month.

Vasily found life in his watchman's hut very pleasant, particularly when the sweet apples had been picked, and the other watchmen brought enormous bundles of straw that had been gathered from under the threshing-machine in the master's shed. He could lie all day long on the fresh, fragrant straw beside the even more fragrant heaps of spring and winter windfall apples, and all he had to do was keep a lookout to see that none of the young lads tried to steal the apples that were on the trees, whistle, and sing songs, which he was very good at, since he had a fine singing voice. The peasant women and girls would come up from the village in quest of apples. Vasily would tease them a bit, giving apples to the ones that caught his fancy, or exchanging lesser or greater quantities of apples for eggs, say, or a few kopecks – and then he would lie back again, only getting up in order to have his breakfast, dinner and supper.

Vasily only possessed the one shirt: it was made of pink cotton and was full of holes. On his feet he wore nothing at all, but his body was strong and healthy and, when the pot of *kasha*[8] was removed from the fire, Vasily would eat enough for three men, to the perpetual astonishment of the old head watchman. Vasily never slept at night, and either whistled or called out from time to time in order to keep himself awake; he could see a long way in the dark, like a cat. One night some big lads from the village started climbing the trees and shaking the apples to the ground. Vasily crept up and pounced on them; they tried to escape, but he knocked them all to the ground, and then took one of them back to his hut and handed him over to the master.

Vasily's first hut was at the far end of the orchard, but his second, into which he moved when the sweet apples were picked, was situated only forty yards or so from the master's house. Vasily found life in this hut even more pleasant. All day long he could see the gentlemen and young ladies playing games, going out for drives or taking walks together; and later on, when it got dark, he would observe them playing the violin or the piano, singing or dancing. He would see the students and the young ladies sitting in the windows fondling one another, and later, some of them walking together in the dark avenues of the lime trees, where the moonlight only filtered through in stripes and patches. He would see the servants running to and fro with refreshments, and would note how the cooks, the laundresses, the managers, gardeners and coachmen were all working for the sole purpose of supplying their masters and mistresses with food, drink and entertainment. Sometimes the young gentlefolk would drop by to see him in his hut, and he would pick out the best, juiciest and reddest apples and give them to them; the young ladies would munch them on the spot, praising them and saying a few words in French – Vasily would understand that they were about him – and they would insist that he sing for them.

Vasily viewed this way of life with admiration and, as he thought back to the life he himself had led in Moscow, more and more did he grow convinced that what mattered most of all in life was to have money.

Vasily began to spend more and more time trying to think how he could quickly get his hands on a large sum of money. He remembered how he had fiddled bits of money for himself on the side, and he decided that that was not the way to go about it; it was not enough simply to attempt to grab whatever lay in temptation's way – one had to plan things in advance, observe the lie of the land, and do the deed neatly, leaving no loose ends.

When it was nearly Christmas, the last of the winter apples were picked. The fruit-grower had made a handsome profit, and he paid off and thanked all the watchmen, including Vasily. Vasily put on the coat and hat the fruit-grower had given him, but he did not go home – the mere thought of that brutish, peasant existence was enough to make him feel positively ill. Instead, he went back to the town in the company of the drunken ex-conscripts who had worked as watchmen with him. Once there, he decided he would break into and burgle the shop where he had once worked as yard-keeper, and whose proprietor had given him a beating and driven him off the premises without giving him his wages. He knew the place inside out, including where the money was kept. He stationed one of the ex-conscripts outside the shop as a guard, smashed a window at the rear, climbed inside and took all the money. It was all so skilfully managed that no one was ever able to find out who had done it. Vasily got away with three hundred and seventy roubles. He gave a hundred to the man who had helped him, and took the rest to another town, where he spent it on a wild binge with his mates and girlfriends.

14

Meanwhile, Ivan Mironov had become a skilled, fearless and successful horse thief. Afinya, his wife, who previously had been critical of him for his 'bungling', as she called it, was pleased with her husband and proud of him because he now owned a sheepskin coat with a hood, and she had a shawl and a new fur coat.

Everyone in the village and the surrounding district knew that there was not one local instance of horse-stealing in which he was not somehow involved, but they were all afraid to give evidence against him, and so whenever the finger of suspicion pointed at him he came out as clean as a whistle. His most recent raid had been on the night-grazing over at Kolotovka. So far as he was able, Ivan Mironov tried to choose the people he stole from, and his favourite victims were landowners and merchants. It was also, however, more difficult to steal from them. So when their horses seemed out of reach, he stole the *muzhiks'* horses instead. Thus, from the night-grazing at Kolotovka he stole as many as he could get his hands on. He didn't do the thieving himself, but employed a smart young lad by the name of Gerasim to do it for him. Not until daybreak did the *muzhiks* realize that their horses were missing; then they took to the roads in a mad rush to look for them. By that time, however, the horses were standing in a deep ravine in the middle of the State forest. Ivan Mironov intended to keep them hidden there until the following night, and then take them to a yard-keeper he knew in a village forty versts away. Ivan Mironov visited Gerasim in the forest, brought him pie and vodka, and then went home again by a forest path on which he hoped he would not meet anyone. He was unlucky enough to encounter one of the forest watchmen, an ex-conscript.

'Been looking for mushrooms, have you?' asked the ex-conscript.

'I can't find any today,' replied Ivan Mironov, pointing to the basket he had taken along with him just in case he did happen to find any mushrooms.

'Aye, it's not the mushroom season yet,' said the ex-conscript. 'They only start coming up after Lent.' And he walked past.

The ex-conscript was aware that something here was not as it should be. Ivan Mironov had no business to be walking through a State forest that early in the morning. The ex-conscript went back the way he had come and began to probe around in the forest. Near the ravine he heard the snorting of horses. Silently he crept up to the place it had come from. The floor of the ravine had been trampled by hooves, and there were horse droppings everywhere. A little further off sat Gerasim, eating something, and two horses stood tethered to a tree trunk.

The ex-conscript ran off to the village and fetched the elder, the constable and two men to act as witnesses. From three sides they approached the place where Gerasim was sitting, and then seized him. Gerasim made no attempt to protest his innocence; being drunk, he immediately confessed to everything. He told them that Ivan Mironov had plied him with drink and put him up to the whole thing, and that he had said he would come to the forest to fetch the horses that day. The *muzhiks* left Gerasim and the horses in the forest, and set an ambush for Ivan Mironov. When night fell, a whistle was heard. Gerasim whistled back. As soon as Ivan Mironov started to come down the slope, the *muzhiks* rushed at him and took him to their village.

The next morning a crowd assembled in front of the elder's *izba*. Ivan Mironov was led out and questioned. Stepan Pelageyushkin, a tall, stooping, long-armed *muzhik* with an aquiline nose and a dour expression was the first to question him. Stepan had done his military service and now lived independently with his wife and children. It was only very recently that he had moved out of his father's house; just when he had been starting to find his own feet, his horse had been stolen. By working for two years in the mines he had managed to buy two new horses. Both had now been stolen.

'Tell me where my horses are,' said Stepan, pale with anger, staring from the ground to Ivan's face and back at the ground again.

Ivan Mironov said he knew nothing about it. Then Stepan

struck him in the face, breaking his nose, from which blood began to trickle.

'Tell me or I'll kill you.'

Ivan Mironov said nothing, and inclined his head. Stepan struck him once with his long arm. Then he struck him again. Ivan still would not say anything, but merely swung his head from side to side.

'Everyone stone him!' said the elder.

And they all began to stone him. Ivan fell silently to the ground, and then shouted: 'Barbarians, devils, stone me to death! I'm not afraid of you!'

Then Stepan took a stone from the pile he had ready and smashed Ivan Mironov's skull with it.

15

Ivan Mironov's murderers were brought to justice. Stepan Pelageyushkin was among those put on trial. The charge brought against him was more serious than those that were brought against the other men, because they all testified that he had been the one who had smashed Ivan Mironov's skull with a stone. Stepan made no attempt to conceal anything at his trial. His explanation was that when his pair of horses had been stolen he had gone to the police station to report the matter – it would probably have been possible to track the horses down with the help of the gypsies – but the constable had refused to see him, and had made no effort to look for the animals.

'What were we supposed to do with a man like him? He'd ruined us.'

'Why were you the only one to stone him?' asked the prosecutor.

'I wasn't. We all stoned him; the *mir*[9] had sentenced him to death. I just finished him off. What was the point of making him suffer unnecessarily?'

The judges were shocked by Stepan's expression of utter calm as he told of what he had done, of how they had stoned Ivan Mironov, and how he had finished him off.

Stepan really did not consider that the murder he had committed was such a terrible act. During his military service he had taken part in a firing squad, and then as now he had seen nothing wrong in this type of killing. If you killed a man, you killed him. Today it was his turn; tomorrow it might be yours.

Stepan was let off lightly. He was given one year in prison. His *muzhik*'s clothes were taken away from him and locked away in the prison stores under a numbered tag, and he was given a convict's overall and boots to wear.

Stepan had never had a great deal of respect for authority, but now he was fully convinced that all the powers that be and all the nobility except the Tsar, who alone took pity on the common people and was just in his dealings with them, were nothing but robbers and bandits, sucking the life blood of the poor. The stories of the deportees and hard labour convicts with whom he associated in the prison confirmed him in this view. One man had been sentenced to hard labour for exposing the pilfering of some local officials, another for striking an official because he had unlawfully confiscated the property of peasants, yet a third for forging banknotes. The gentry and the merchants could get away with anything, it seemed, while the poor *muzhiks* were sent to feed the lice in prison for the slightest misdemeanour.

During the time that Stepan spent in prison he received visits from his wife. Things had been bad enough for her with him gone from home, but now she had become completely destitute and had had to go begging with her children. His wife's misfortunes made Stepan even more embittered. He was viciously aggressive towards everyone in the prison, and on one occasion he nearly killed one of the prison cooks with an axe, for which he was given another year. During the course of that second year he learned that his wife had died, and that his household had ceased to exist . . .

When Stepan's term was up, he was summoned to the stores and his *muzhik*'s clothes were taken down from the shelf and handed back to him.

'Where am I to go now?' he asked the quartermaster-sergeant as he put his own clothes on again.

'Home, of course.'

'I haven't got a home any more. I suppose I'll just have to take to the road and rob folk.'

'If you rob folk you'll be back to see us again.'

'Well, that's as may be.'

And Stepan went away. In spite of what he had said, he set off in the direction of his home. There was nowhere else for him to go.

On his way there he stopped to spend the night at a roadside inn and drinking house he knew.

The innkeeper was a fat tradesman from Vladimir. He knew Stepan, knew that he had gone to prison as a result of misfortune, and agreed to let him stay the night.

This rich tradesman had run off with the wife of a *muzhik* in the neighbourhood, and she now lived with the tradesman both as spouse and employee.

Stepan knew all about the episode – how the tradesman had injured the *muzhik*'s honour, how this vile woman had left her husband and then grown fat from overeating. Just at that moment she was treating her sweaty personage to tea; charitably, she asked Stepan if he would like some. There were no other guests at the inn. Stepan was allowed to sleep the night in the kitchen. Matryona cleared away the dishes and went off to her room. Stepan lay down on top of the stove, but he couldn't sleep, and kept snapping beneath his weight the lengths of kindling that had been placed on the stove to dry. He could not for the life of him get the tradesman's fat belly out of his head; in his mind he saw it bulging from the waist of his cotton shirt, which had been washed and rewashed so many times that it had grown faded. Again and again the thought recurred to him of slashing that belly with a knife and letting out the fatty intestines. And of doing the same to the woman, as well. One moment he would say to himself: 'Oh, to hell with them, I'll be gone tomorrow,' and the next he would remember Ivan Mironov and start thinking once again about the tradesman's belly and Matryona's white, sweaty throat. If he was going to kill, he'd better kill them both. The second cockcrow sounded. If he was going to do it, he had better do it now, or it would be daylight. The night before he had spotted a knife and an axe that had been left lying out. He climbed down from the stove, took the axe and the knife, and went out of the kitchen. Out in the hall he heard the latch click on the other side of the door. The tradesman opened the door and came out. This was not the way Stepan had been planning it. The knife would be no good now, so he swung the axe and split the tradesman's head in two. The tradesman fell against the lintel and slumped to the floor.

Stepan went into Matryona's room. Matryona leapt up and stood on her bed, dressed in nothing but her nightshirt. With the same axe Stepan killed her, too.

Then he lit a candle, took the money from the till and fled.

16

In the chief town of a country district lived an old man who had once been a civil servant, but had now taken to drink. He owned the house in which he lived with his two daughters and son-in-law, and which stood some way from the other buildings in the town. The married daughter also drank and led a disreputable life, and it was the elder, widowed daughter, Maria Semyonovna, a wrinkled, emaciated woman of fifty, who kept them all on her pension of two hundred and fifty roubles a year. The entire family lived on this money. Maria Semyonovna also did all the housework. She looked after her drunken, enfeebled old father and her sister's baby, she cooked the meals and did the laundry. And, as always happens in such cases, they each of them unloaded all their wants and requirements on to her, yet never ceased to shout abuse at her; the son-in-law would even beat her when he was drunk. She endured it all in silence and humility and, as is also usual in such cases, found that the more she was compelled to do, the more she was able to do. She even offered assistance to the poor, leaving herself short; she gave away her clothing and helped to look after the sick people in the neighbourhood.

On one occasion Maria Semyonovna hired the services of a crippled, one-legged country tailor. He altered her father's long overcoat and re-covered her fur-lined jacket with new cloth so that she could wear it when she went to market in winter.

The crippled tailor was an intelligent, observant man who had come across a lot of people in the course of his work and whose disability had compelled him to spend much of his life sitting down, and thus predisposed to reflection. He had stayed for a week in Maria Semyonovna's household, and had been lost in wonderment at the life she led. Once she came into the kitchen, where he did his sewing, in order to wash some towels, and as she did them she talked to him about his life – how badly his brother had treated him and how he had taken his patrimony and left to live on his own.

'I thought it would be better, but I'm poor just the same as I was before.'

'It's better not to change, but to live in the way you've always lived,' said Maria Semyonovna.

'That's what I find so wonderful about you, Maria Semyonovna: you're always putting yourself out for others, yet you seem to get precious little good back from them in return.'

Maria Semyonovna did not say anything.

'You must have decided that it's true what the Good Book says, and you'll get your reward in the world to come.'

'We know nothing of that,' said Maria Semyonovna. 'All I know is that it's better to live that way.'

'And is that what the Book says?'

'Yes, it is,' she said, and out of the Gospels she read him the Sermon on the Mount. The tailor began to reflect. Even after he had been paid and had set off home, he still continued to reflect on what he had observed in the house where Maria Semyonovna lived, and on what she had told him and read to him.

17

Pyotr Nikolayevich had changed his attitude towards the common people, and the common people had changed their attitude towards him. Within the space of barely a year the local *muzhiks* had felled twenty-seven of his oak trees and burned down a threshing-barn that had not been insured. Pyotr Nikolayevich decided he could not go on living among people such as these.

At about this time, a family called the Liventsovs were looking for a manager to run their estate, and the marshal of nobility had recommended Pyotr Nikolayevich as being the best farmer in the district. The Liventsov estate was enormous, but it was failing to yield any profit and the peasants were helping themselves to the land. Pyotr Nikolayevich undertook to put everything to rights. He leased out his own estate and went with his wife to live in the remote Volga province where the Liventsov holdings were situated.

Pyotr Nikolayevich had always been a stickler for law and order, and this made him all the more determined that these wild, uncivilized *muzhiks* were not to be allowed to take illegal possession of land and property that did not belong to them. He was glad of this opportunity to teach them a lesson, and he set about his task with severity. He had one peasant sent to prison for stealing timber, and another he flogged personally and without mercy for not getting out of the way and doffing his cap when he was supposed to. As for the meadows which were in dispute, and which the peasants regarded as theirs, Pyotr Nikolayevich let it be known that if they allowed their cattle on to them he would have the beasts impounded.

Spring came, and the peasants, as they had done in previous years, let their cattle out on to the manorial meadows. Pyotr Nikolayevich called all the farm hands together and instructed them to drive the cattle into the manorial stockyard. The *muzhiks* were out ploughing, and so, in spite of the warning cries of the peasant women, the farm hands were able to round up the cattle. When the *muzhiks* came back from work, they gathered together and came over to the manorial stockyard to demand the return of their animals. Pyotr Nikolayevich came out to meet them with a rifle slung across his shoulder (he had just come back from making a round of inspection) and told them he would only give them back their cattle upon payment of a fine of fifty kopecks per cow or steer and ten kopecks per sheep. The *muzhiks* began shouting that the meadows were theirs, that they had belonged to their fathers and their grandfathers before them, and that he had no right to impound other people's cattle.

'Give us our cattle or it'll be the worse for you,' said one old man, advancing towards Pyotr Nikolayevich.

'What did you say?' exclaimed Pyotr Nikolayevich, his face drained of colour. He went up to the old man.

'Give us them back if you don't want trouble, shark.'

'What?' howled Pyotr Nikolayevich, and he struck the old man in the face.

'You wouldn't dare fight us. Lads, take the cattle by force.'

The crowd advanced. Pyotr Nikolayevich attempted to make his escape, but they would not let him. He tried to force his way through, and his rifle went off by accident, killing one of the peasants. A riot ensued, in the process of which Pyotr Nikolayevich was crushed to death. Five minutes after it was all over, his disfigured corpse was dragged down into the ravine.

The murderers were tried by a military tribunal, and two of them were sentenced to death by hanging.

18

In the village the crippled tailor hailed from, five of the well-to-do peasants leased from the local landowner a hundred and five desyatinas of rich, arable land as black as tar and distributed it among the other *muzhiks* in exchange for payments of eighteen and fifteen roubles per allotment. None of the allotments changed hands for less than twelve roubles. So the well-to-do peasants made a good profit. They each took five desyatinas for themselves, and these allotments cost them nothing. One of these *muzhiks* died, and the others asked the crippled tailor if he would like to come in on the deal with them.

When they began to divide the land up among themselves, the tailor refused to drink vodka with them, and when they got round to discussing who should get how much land, the tailor said he thought that everyone should receive the same amount, and that no charge should be made, but that everyone should receive according to his need.

'Whoever heard of such an arrangement?'

'Otherwise we won't be acting as Christians. That's all very well for the higher-ups, but we're peasants. We have to do things God's way. Follow the law of Christ.'

'Where's it written down, this law?'

'In the Good Book, in the Gospels. Here, I tell you what, you come over to my place on Sunday; I'll read you a bit of it, and then we can discuss it.'

Most of the peasants did not bother to go to the tailor's house on Sunday. Three, however, did, and the tailor began to read to them.

He read them five chapters of the Gospel according to St Matthew. When he had finished, they proceeded to discuss what they had heard, but only one man, a peasant called Ivan Chuyev, thought it made any sense. So bowled over by it was he that he began to do everything according to God's law, and all his family followed suit. He refused to accept the extra land and would only take what was his proper share.

Other people began visiting Ivan and the tailor, and gradually they too were won over. They gave up smoking, drinking and swearing, and started trying to help one another. They also stopped going to church, and they took down their icons and gave them back to the village priest. Eventually seventeen households – comprising sixty-five people in all – were involved in this movement. The village priest was frightened, and reported the matter to his bishop. The bishop wondered what he should do, and finally decided to send for Father Misail, the former grammar school religious instructor.

19

The bishop asked Father Misail to sit down, and began to tell him about the strange new goings-on in his diocese.

'It's all caused by ignorance and spiritual weakness. You're a man of learning. I'm relying on you. I want you to go down there, call them all together and get the matter sorted out.'

'With Your Grace's blessing, I shall try,' said Father Misail. He was glad of this assignment, as he always was whenever he was given an opportunity to demonstrate his faith. Converting others was the best means he knew of persuading himself that he did in fact believe.

'Please do the best you can. I'm really awfully worried about my little flock,' said the bishop, accepting in leisurely fashion a glass of tea from the lay brother, with his white, pudgy hands.

'Why have you only brought one sort of jam? Bring some others,' he told the lay brother. 'I'm really most, most upset,' he went on, addressing Father Misail.

Father Misail was glad of this chance to show the stuff he was made of. Being a man of modest means, however, he asked that his expenses be paid and, anticipating the opposition he would encounter on the part of the uncultured peasants, he also requested that the governor of the province should instruct the local police to give him assistance in case of need.

The bishop made all the necessary arrangements for him, and when Father Misail had, with the help of the lay brother and the cook, got together the hamper and provisions that were so essential when travelling to the back of beyond, he set off for his destination. As he set off on this mission, Father Misail had a pleasant sense of the importance of his vocation; at the same time he ceased to have any doubts concerning his own faith, and was on the contrary quite swept away by a conviction of its authenticity.

His thoughts centred not on the substance of his faith – that he considered an axiom – but on the refutation of these objections that were being made to its outer forms.

20

The village priest and his wife gave Father Misail a most respectful welcome, and the day after his arrival they called all the peasants together in the village church. Father Misail, attired in a new silken surplice, wearing a confessional crucifix at his chest, his hair neatly combed, walked up into the ambo.[10] Standing by his side was the priest; a little further away stood the deacons and the choirboys; a number of policemen were stationed by the side doors. Some of the sectarians had also arrived; they were dressed in dirty, ragged sheepskin coats.

After the public prayer, Father Misail delivered a sermon in which he exhorted the apostates to return to the bosom of the Mother Church, threatening them with the torments of hell and promising absolution to those who repented.

The sectarians fell silent. When they were actually questioned, however, they did make some reply.

To the question why they had broken away from the Church, they replied that it had been because what people worshipped in the churches were wooden, manmade gods; not only was this not indicated by the Holy Scriptures, the prophecies actually forbade it. When Father Misail asked Chuyev whether it was true that they called the holy icons 'boards', Chuyev replied: 'Well, you just turn any old icon round and see for yourself.' When it was inquired of them why they didn't recognize the priesthood, they replied that in the Scriptures it was written: 'Freely ye have received, freely give', whereas the priests would only offer their holy grace in exchange for money. All Father Misail's attempts to support his arguments by Holy Scripture were met with the calm but firm rejection of Ivan and the tailor, who referred to that same Scripture, which they knew inside out. Father Misail grew angry and threatened them with the secular authorities. To this the sectarians replied that the Scriptures said: 'They will persecute you, even as they persecuted me.'

Thus it all came to nothing, and all would have passed off peacefully, had not Father Misail delivered, at Mass the following day, a sermon about the harmful influence of false witnesses in which he said that they deserved every form of punishment. As the peasants were shuffling out of the church afterwards, they started talking about what they could do to teach the atheists a lesson and prevent them from stirring up any more trouble among the village folk. And that very day, at the same time as Father Misail was nibbling smoked salmon in the company of His Holy Reverence and an inspector who had arrived from a nearby town, a riot broke out in the village. The orthodox believers had gathered together in a crowd outside Chuyev's *izba* and were waiting for the sectarians to come out so they could beat them up. There were about twenty sectarians, men and women. Father Misail's sermon and now this assemblage of orthodox believers with their threatening taunts had aroused a malevolent spirit in the sectarians, one that had not been there before. Evening approached, and it was time for the peasant women to go and milk the cows, but the orthodox believers continued to stand outside and wait. When a young lad ventured out of the *izba*, the crowd started to lay about him and drove him back inside. The sectarians discussed what they should do, but were unable to reach any agreement among themselves.

The tailor said they ought just to put up with it and not fight back. Chuyev, on the other hand, said that if they didn't do anything they would all be beaten up, and he grabbed a poker and went out into the street. The orthodox believers hurled themselves upon him.

'All right then, let's do things according to the law of Moses!' he shouted, and started to lay about the orthodox believers with the poker, putting one man's eye out in the process. The rest of the sectarians, meanwhile, slipped out of the *izba* and went back to their homes.

Chuyev was brought before the court for false witness and blasphemy, and was sentenced to deportation.

Father Misail, on the other hand, received a reward and was made an archimandrite.[11]

21

Two years before all this happened, an attractive girl of healthy, oriental appearance called Katya Turchaninova arrived in St Petersburg from the territory of the Don Cossacks in order to take up her studies at the university. There she met the son of the leader of the *zemstvo* in Simbirsk province, a student by the name of Tyurin. Her love for him was not the ordinary kind of female love that expresses itself in the desire to become a man's wife and the mother of his children, but was rather a comradely affection which drew most of its strength from the couple's shared sense of outrage and hatred where the established social order was concerned, from a similar animus towards the representatives of that order, and from a consciousness of their own intellectual, educational and moral superiority to them.

Turchaninova was a capable student. She had no difficulty in memorizing her lecture notes and thus passed her examinations, managing at the same time to devour enormous quantities of the most recently published books. She was quite certain that her calling lay not in the bearing and nurturing of children – she looked upon such a vocation with disgust and contempt – but in destroying the existing social order, which put shackles on the finest aspirations of the common people, and in showing men and women the new way of life that had been revealed to her by the most modern European writers. Full of figure, fair-skinned, red-cheeked and attractive, with flashing black eyes and a thick tress of black hair, she aroused in men feelings she did not intend to arouse and indeed had no time for, so immersed was she in her labour of agitation and propaganda. Nevertheless, she liked the fact that she aroused these feelings and, although she never dressed to kill, she did not neglect her appearance either. She liked the fact that she appealed to men, as it meant she was able to show that she despised that which was held in such esteem by other women. In her views on the methods to be used in the struggle with the established order she went further than Tyurin and the majority of her friends, maintaining that the end justified any means whatsoever, including murder. Yet this same revolutionary, Katya Turchaninova, was also a truly kind-hearted and self-effacing woman who was forever putting herself out for the sake of other people's advantage, enjoyment and well-being, and who was always genuinely glad of an opportunity to do favours, whether for children, old people or animals.

Turchaninova spent the summer months in the principal

town of one of the Volga districts, where she stayed with a friend of hers who was a country schoolmistress. Tyurin also spent the summer in this district where his father owned a house. Turchaninova, her friend, Tyurin and the local doctor often met, exchanged books, argued with one another and got generally worked up about social issues. The Tyurins' estate bordered on the Liventsov holding where Pyotr Nikolayevich was now manager. As soon as Pyotr Nikolayevich arrived and started to set the place in order, young Tyurin, noticing that the Liventsovs' peasants seemed to have acquired a spirit of independence and a firm resolve to uphold their rights, began to take an interest in them and often walked down to the village to talk to them, trying to promote the theory of socialism among them, with particular regard to the nationalization of the land.

When Pyotr Nikolayevich was murdered and the district sessions arrived, the circle of revolutionaries in the district town had a marvellous pretext for agitation in court, and they spoke out their opinions in no uncertain terms. Unfortunately, however, Tyurin's walks to the village and his conversations with the peasants were alluded to during the court proceedings. His house was searched, some revolutionary pamphlets were discovered, and he was arrested and taken away to St Petersburg.

Turchaninova followed him to St Petersburg and went to the prison to try to see him, but was not permitted to have a private interview with him; instead, she had to come on the public visitors' day, and could only catch a glimpse of him through two iron gratings. This meeting increased her sense of outrage still further. Her indignation finally reached its limit when, remonstrating with a handsome young officer of the gendarmes, she discovered that he was willing to offer her some concessions if she would agree to certain proposals he wished to make to her. This sent her into a violent rage against representatives of authority. She went to the chief of police in order to file a complaint. The chief of police repeated what the gendarme had said, that there was nothing they could do and that it was all in the hands of the Minister of the Interior. She sent a petition to the minister, requesting an interview with Tyurin; it was refused. Then she decided she would commit an act of desperation, and bought a revolver.

22

The minister received his visitors at the hour he usually set aside for this purpose. Three of his petitioners he avoided; he had a few words with the governor of a province and then went up to a pretty, dark-eyed young woman who was standing with a document in her left hand. A lecherous glint appeared in the minister's eyes at the sight of such an attractive petitioner but, remembering his status, he assumed a serious countenance.

'What can I do for you?' he asked, drawing closer to her.

Without replying, she quickly produced her revolver from under her cape and, pointing it at the minister, fired, but missed.

The minister tried to grab her arm, but she stumbled backwards and fired a second shot. The minister took to his heels. The woman was trembling all over, unable to say a word; then, suddenly, she burst into hysterical laughter. The minister escaped without even a scratch.

It was Turchaninova. She was thrown into a cell to await trial. Meanwhile the minister, who had received the compliments and commiserations of those in the very highest places and even from the Tsar himself, appointed a commission to investigate the plot that had led to this attempt on his life.

There was, of course, no plot; but officials of both the civil and the secret police forces zealously applied themselves to the search for all the threads of the non-existent conspiracy, conscientiously earning their salaries and their keep. Getting up early in the morning, before it was light, they conducted search after search, copied documents and books, read diaries and personal letters and made extracts from these in beautiful handwriting on beautiful paper; they cross-examined Turchaninova any number of times, confronting her with witnesses and endeavouring to make her tell them the names of her accomplices.

The minister was a kindly man at heart and was really sorry

for this healthy, attractive Cossack girl, but he told himself that he had grave responsibilities to the state which he must discharge, however painful they might be. And when an old friend of his, who knew the Tyurin family, met him at a court ball and started to ask him about Tyurin and Turchaninova, the minister shrugged his shoulders, crinkling the red ribbon that traversed his white waistcoat, and said: '*Je ne demanderais pas mieux que de lâcher cette pauvre fillette, mais vous savez – le devoir*.'

And all the while Turchaninova was sitting in her cell awaiting trial, exchanging tapped signals with her fellow prisoners from time to time and reading the books she had been given. On occasion, however, she would suddenly give way to rage and despair, hammering on the walls, screaming and laughing.

23

One day, when Maria Semyonovna was on her way home from collecting her pension at the paymaster's office, she met a teacher she knew.

'Hello, Maria Semyonovna, did you get your pension all right?' he shouted to her from the opposite side of the street.

'Yes, thank you,' replied Maria Semyonovna. 'It'll be enough to fill a few cracks, anyway.'

'Well, you've got enough there, you can fill the cracks and still have some over,' said the teacher, and with a goodbye he walked on.

'Goodbye,' said Maria Semyonovna. As she watched him depart, she ran straight into a tall man with very long arms, whose face wore a stern expression. Approaching her house, she was surprised to see this same long-armed man again. He watched her as she went into her house, stood around for a while outside and then turned on his heels and left.

At first Maria Semyonovna felt a sensation of fear, but this soon gave way to one of melancholy. None the less, once she was inside and had given sweets to the old man and her scrofulous little nephew Fedya and made a fuss over the dog Treasure, who yelped with joy to see her return, she felt all right again and, giving the pension money to her father, resumed the household chores with which she was never done.

The man she had bumped into had been Stepan.

After he had murdered the yard-keeper at the wayside inn, Stepan had not gone home to Moscow. It was a strange thing: the recollection of the murder was in no way disagreeable to him; indeed, he thought about it several times a day. He liked the idea that he could do something of this nature so cleverly and skilfully that no one would ever find him out or prevent him from doing the same again to other people. As he sat in an eating-house in a provincial town sipping tea and vodka, he looked at all the customers with one thought in his head: how to murder them. He went to the house of a man who came from his village and worked as a drayman in order to ask him for a bed for the night. The drayman was out. Stepan said he would wait, and sat talking to the drayman's wife. Then, when she turned her back to him, leaning over the stove, he had the idea of killing her. Surprised at himself, he gave his head a shake, then took his knife from his bootflap, threw the woman to the ground and cut her throat. The children started to cry, so he killed them too and left the town that same night. Once he was out of town he found a village and slept the night at its inn.

The following day he came back to the market town, and while he was walking along the street he overheard Maria Semyonovna's conversation with the teacher. Her gaze frightened him, but all the same he decided he would break into her house and steal the money she had drawn. That night he broke the lock and entered an upstairs room. The younger, married daughter was the first to hear him. She cried out. Stepan immediately cut her throat. The son-in-law woke up and grappled with him. He seized Stepan by the throat and struggled with him for a long time, but Stepan was too strong for him. When he had dealt with the son-in-law, Stepan, agitated now and aroused by the fighting, went behind the partition. In bed behind the partition lay Maria Semyonovna. She sat up and looked at Stepan with meek, frightened eyes and made the sign of the cross over herself. Once again Stepan found her gaze intimidating. He lowered his eyes.

'Where's the money?' he asked, without looking up.

She did not say anything.

'Where's the money?' Stepan repeated, showing her the knife.

'What are you doing? You can't do this.'

'Oh, can't I?'

Stepan moved closer to her, getting ready to seize her arms so that she could not stop him, but she offered no resistance and did not raise her arms, merely pressed them to her bosom, gave a deep sigh and said repeatedly: 'Oh, what a terrible sin! What are you doing? Have mercy on yourself. You think you're harming others, but it's your own soul you're ruining . . . O-oh!' she screamed.

Stepan could stand her voice and her gaze no longer, and with a cry of 'I'm not going to waste my breath on you!' he slashed her throat with his knife. She sank back on to the pillows and began to wheeze, soaking one of the pillows in blood. He turned away and walked through the upstairs rooms, gathering the valuable items together. When he had taken what he wanted, he lit a cigarette, sat down for a while in order to brush down his clothes, and then left the house. He had thought that this murder would pass off with ease, as the previous ones had done, but before he had reached the place where he intended to lodge for the night he suddenly felt so exhausted that he could hardly move a limb. He lay down in a ditch and stayed there for the rest of that night, all the following day and all the next night.

Part Two

I

As he lay in the ditch, Stepan kept seeing Maria Semyonovna's meek, emaciated and frightened face, and hearing her voice. 'You can't do this,' it kept saying in that peculiar, lisping, plaintive way. And each time it spoke he relived what he had done to her all over again. He began to grow really afraid, and he closed his eyes and flailed his head from side to side in an effort to shake these thoughts and memories out of it. For a moment he would succeed in freeing himself from the memories, but they would be replaced first by one black devil, then by another, followed in turn by yet more black devils, with glowing red eyes, making dreadful faces, and all saying the same thing: 'You killed her – now kill yourself, or we won't give you any peace until you do.' And he would open his eyes and see her again and hear her voice, and he would start feeling sorry for her and experiencing fear and revulsion at himself. Once more he would close his eyes – and once more the devils would appear.

Towards the evening of the second day he got up and walked to a nearby inn. With much effort he got there, and began drinking. But no matter how much he drank, he could not get drunk. He sat at a table in silence, knocking back glass after glass of vodka. The village policeman entered the inn.

'Who might you be, then?' asked the policeman.

'Oh, I'm the one who slit everybody's throats up at Domotvorov's place the night before last.'

They bound him hand and foot. After he had been held for

day in the local police station, he was sent to the chief town f the province. The warden of the prison there, recognizing im as the unruly inmate he had once had to deal with in the ast, gave him a sour reception.

'You'd better not play any tricks on me now, mind,' the arden said hoarsely, knitting his eyebrows and making his wer jaw protrude. 'At the first sign of it I'll have you flogged death. You won't escape from my prison.'

'What would I be doing trying to escape?' retorted Stepan, oking at the ground. 'I gave myself up of my own free will.'

'Don't answer back when I'm around. And look up at a perior when he's addressing you,' shouted the warden, and ave him a sock on the jaw.

Just then Stepan was thinking once more about Maria emyonovna and hearing her voice inside his brain. He had not eard a word the warden had been saying.

'What?' he asked, brought back to his senses with a start by e sudden blow on his chin.

'Come on, come on. Forward march. None of your nonsense, ow.'

The warden had been expecting disorderly behaviour, machiations with other convicts, escape attempts. But of all this ere was none. Whenever the orderly or the warden himself oked in through the peephole in the door of Stepan's cell, ey would see him sitting on a sack that had been stuffed with raw, his head propped in his hands, constantly whispering mething to himself. When he was questioned by the court vestigator he again behaved differently from other prisoners. e seemed absent-minded, seemed not to hear the questions he as asked or, if he did take them in, was so truthful in his plies that the examining magistrate, who was used to battling ith ingenuity and subterfuge on the part of the defendants ho appeared before him, now experienced a feeling akin to at of someone climbing a flight of stairs in the dark and ddenly putting his foot into empty space. Knitting his eyerows and fixing his eyes straight in front of him, Stepan consed to all the murders he had committed in the most naffected, business-like tone of voice, doing his utmost to remember all the details: 'He came out,' said Stepan, describing the first murder, 'without any shoes or socks on, and stood in the doorway, so I gashed him once, and he croaked, and then I went straight to work on his missus . . .' – and so it went on. When the public procurator made his rounds of the prison cells and asked Stepan if he had any complaints to make or if there was anything he lacked, Stepan answered that he had everything he wanted and that no one had mistreated him. The procurator, having gone a few steps down the stinking corridor stopped for a moment and asked the warden who was accompanying him what the behaviour of this convict was like in general.

'He baffles me,' replied the warden, gratified that Stepan had praised the treatment he had received. 'He's been with us nearly two months now, and he's been a model of good behaviour. All I'm scared of is that he's got something up his sleeve. He's a plucky chap, and incredibly strong.'

2

For the first month he spent in prison Stepan was incessantly tormented by the same thing: he saw the grey wall of his cell heard the sounds of the prison – the buzz of voices in the communal cell below him, the footsteps of the sentry in the corridor, and the ticking of the clock – and in addition he saw *her*, with her meek gaze, the gaze that had vanquished him the first time he had encountered her in the street, with her scraggy, wrinkled throat which he had cut with his knife, and her sweet, plaintive, lisping voice saying: '*You think you're harming others, but it's your own soul you're ruining. You can't do this!*' Then the voice would die away and the three black devils would reappear. They would reappear irrespective of whether his eyes were open or closed. When they were closed the devils appeared more distinctly. When they were open, the devils would fuse with the doors and the walls and gradually disappear, only to re-emerge from three different directions making leering faces and saying over and over again: 'Kil yourself, kill yourself. You can make a noose, you can start a fire.' At this point Stepan would begin to shiver, and he would start reciting what prayers he knew – 'Ave Maria' and 'Our Father' – and initially this seemed to help. As he said these prayers, he would begin to remember his past life: he would remember his father and mother, his village, Wolf the family dog, his grandfather lying on top of the stove, the upturned benches on which he had tobogganed in the snow with the other boys; then he would remember the girls and their songs, and then the horses, and how they had been stolen, how they had caught the horse thief and how he, Stepan, had finished him off with a stone. And then his first prison term would come back to him, and he would remember the fat yard-keeper, the drayman's wife and her children, and then again he would remember *her*. And he would feel hot all over, he would throw off his prison dressing-gown, leap up from his bunk and begin to pace up and down his cramped cell with rapid strides, like a wild beast in a cage, turning abruptly whenever he reached the damp, sweating walls. And again he would recite his prayers, only now they were to no avail.

On one of those long, autumn evenings, when the wind was howling and whistling in the chimneys, he sat down on his bunk, having had enough of pacing his cell, and knew that it was no use struggling any longer, that the devils had won, and he submitted to them. For a long time now he had had an eye on the stovepipe. If he were to wind some thin twine or thin strips of cloth round it, it would hold. But it would have to be done cleverly. He set to work and spent two days cutting long strips of cloth from the sack he slept on (when the orderly came in he covered the bed with his dressing-gown). He tied the strips together in double knots so that they would support the weight of his body. While he was engaged in this task, his mental anguish ceased. When everything was ready he made a noose, put it round his neck, climbed on to the bed and hanged himself. But his tongue had only just started to protrude when the strips of cloth broke and he fell to the ground. The noise brought the orderly running in. The medical orderly was sent for, and Stepan was taken away to the hospital. By the next day he had fully recovered, and he was discharged from hospital and taken, not to his solitary cell, but to the communal one.

In the communal cell he lived with twenty other prisoners as if he were alone: he saw no one, spoke to no one and suffered again from his former mental anguish. He suffered particularly when all the men were asleep except for him, and he would see her again as of old, hear her voice, and then witness once again the appearance of the black devils with their terrible eyes, mocking and tormenting him.

Once again, as formerly, he said his prayers, and once again they were to no avail.

On one occasion when, after he had prayed, she appeared to him again, he began to pray to her instead; he prayed to her soul, begging it to let him go, to forgive him. And when, towards morning, he collapsed on to his tattered sack, he fell fast asleep, and as he slept she appeared to him again in his dreams with her scraggy, wrinkled, cut throat.

'Please forgive me.'

She looked at him with her meek gaze and said nothing.

'Won't you forgive me?'

Three times he begged her to forgive him. But she said nothing, and finally he woke up. From that time on he started to feel better, and it was as if his eyes had been opened: he looked around him and for the first time he began to make friends with his cell mates and to talk to them.

3

One of the men in Stepan's cell was Vasily, who had been caught stealing again and been sentenced to deportation; another was Chuyev, who had also been sentenced to forcible settlement. Vasily spent his time either singing songs in his magnificent voice or telling his cell mates the story of his exploits. Chuyev, on the other hand, either worked, mended some article of outer clothing or underwear, or read the Gospels and the Psalms.

To Stepan's query as to why he was being deported Chuyev replied that it was because he was a true believer in Christ, because the deceiving priests could not tolerate the strength of spirit of those who lived according to the Gospels and thus laid bare their own sinfulness. When Stepan asked him what the law of the Gospels was, Chuyev explained to him that it consisted in not praying to manmade gods, but rather in worshipping in spirit and in truth. And he described how they had learned this true faith from a one-legged tailor when they had been dividing up the land.

'All right, so what's the punishment for evil-doing, then?' asked Stepan.

'It's all written in the Gospels.' And Chuyev read to him:

'"When the Son of man shall come in His glory, and all the holy angels with Him, then shall He sit upon the throne of His glory:

'"And before Him shall be gathered all nations: and He shall separate them one from another, as a shepherd divideth his sheep from the goats:

'"And He shall set the sheep on His right hand, but the goats on the left.

'"Then shall the King say unto them on His right hand, Come, ye blessed of my Father, inherit the kingdom prepared for you from the foundation of the world:

'"For I was an hungred, and ye gave me meat: I was thirsty, and ye gave me drink: I was a stranger, and ye took me in:

'"Naked, and ye clothed me: I was sick, and ye visited me: I was in prison, and ye came unto me.

'"Then shall the righteous answer Him, saying, Lord, when saw we Thee an hungred, and fed Thee? or thirsty, and gave Thee drink?

'"When saw we Thee a stranger, and took Thee in? or naked, and clothed Thee?

'"Or when saw we Thee sick, or in prison, and came unto Thee?

'"And the King shall answer and say unto them, Verily I say unto you, Inasmuch as ye have done it unto one of the least of these my brethren, ye have done it unto me.

'"Then shall He say also unto them on the left hand, Depart from me, ye cursed, into everlasting fire, prepared for the devil and his angels:

'"For I was an hungred, and ye gave me no meat: I was thirsty, and ye gave me no drink:

'"I was a stranger, and ye took me not in: naked, and ye clothed me not: sick, and in prison, and ye visited me not.

'"Then shall they also answer Him, saying, Lord, when saw we Thee an hungred, or athirst, or a stranger, or naked, or sick, or in prison, and did not minister unto Thee?

'"Then shall he answer them, saying, Verily I say unto you, Inasmuch as ye did it not to one of the least of these, ye did it not to me.

'"And these shall go away into everlasting punishment: but the righteous into life eternal."' (Matthew 25:31–46)

Vasily, who had squatted down on the floor opposite Chuyev in order to listen to the Scripture reading, nodded his stately head in approval.

'That's right,' he said, emphatically. '"Go ye accursed into eternal torment, you never fed a poor man, but filled your own bellies instead." That's what they deserve. Here, give me the book, I want to read a bit, too,' he added, anxious to show off his reading ability.

'But won't there be any forgiveness?' asked Stepan, silently lowering his shaggy head to listen.

'Hang on a minute, and shut up,' Chuyev said to Vasily, who was still going on about how the rich had neither fed the poor wanderer nor visited him in prison. 'Hang on, will you?' said Chuyev again, leafing through the copy of the New Testament. When he found the place he wanted, Chuyev smoothed out the pages with a large, strong hand that had gone white from his long-term in prison.

'"And there were also two other malefactors, led with him" – with Christ, that is,' Chuyev began, '– "to be put to death.

'"And when they were come to the place, which is called Calvary, there they crucified him, and the malefactors, one on the right hand, and the other on the left.

'"Then said Jesus, Father, forgive them; for they know not what they do. And they parted His raiment, and cast lots.

'"And the people stood beholding. And the rulers also with

them derided Him, saying, He saved others; let him save himself, if he be Christ, the chosen of God.

'"And the soldiers also mocked him, coming to him, and offering him vinegar.

'"And saying, If thou be the king of the Jews, save thyself.

'"And a superscription also was written over him in letters of Greek, and Latin, and Hebrew, THIS IS THE KING OF THE JEWS.

'"And one of the malefactors which were hanged railed on him, saying, If thou be Christ, save thyself and us.

'"But the other answering rebuked him, saying, Dost not thou fear God, seeing thou art in the same condemnation?

'"And we indeed justly; for we receive the due reward of our deeds: but this man hath done nothing amiss.

'"And he said unto Jesus, Lord, remember me when Thou comest into Thy kingdom.

'"And Jesus said unto him, Verily I say unto thee, Today shalt thou be with me in paradise."' (Luke 23: 32–43)

Stepan said nothing, but sat reflecting and, although he appeared to be listening, he heard no more of what Chuyev was reading.

'So that's what the true faith is,' he thought. 'It's only the people that feed the poor and visit the prisoners who'll be saved, all the rest'll go to hell. All the same, the thief didn't repent until he was on the cross, and he went to heaven.' He saw no contradiction here. The one circumstance seemed rather to confirm the other: the merciful would go to heaven and the unmerciful would go to hell, and that meant that everyone had better be merciful; the fact that Christ had pardoned the thief meant that Christ too was merciful. All this was completely new to Stepan; he only wondered why it had all been previously concealed from him. And he spent all his free time with Chuyev, asking him questions and listening to Chuyev's replies. As he listened, the truth came home to him. The overall meaning of the doctrine – that all men were brothers and that they ought to love and have compassion for one another, and that then everyone would be all right – was revealed to him. As he listened, he perceived as something forgotten and familiar everything that confirmed the overall meaning of this doctrine, and simply let slip past his ears everything that did not confirm it, ascribing it to his lack of understanding.

And from that time onwards, Stepan became a different man.

4

Even before this, Stepan Pelageyushkin had been a docile prisoner; but of late, with the change that had taken place in him, he had become a source of amazement to the warden, the orderlies and the other prisoners. Without being told to, even when it was not his turn, he performed all the most difficult and unpleasant tasks, including the emptying and cleaning of the night pail. But in spite of this obedience, his cell mates feared and respected him, knowing his will power and his great physical strength; this was particularly so after an incident involving two vagrants who attacked him, but whom he repulsed, breaking the arm of one of them. These vagrants had set out to beat a well-to-do young prisoner at cards, and had fleeced him of every penny he owned. Stepan had interceded for him and had managed to get back from them the money they had won. The vagrants had started to curse him and had then tried to beat him up, but he had overpowered them both. When the warden made an inquiry as to the cause of the quarrel, however, the vagrants claimed it had been Stepan who had tried to beat them up. Stepan had made no attempt to protest that he had been in the right, and had meekly accepted his punishment, which had consisted of three days in the punishment block and transfer to a solitary cell.

He found solitary confinement irksome because it separated him from Chuyev and the Gospels, and also because he feared a return of his hallucinations involving Maria Semyonovna and the devils. But the hallucinations did not come back. His soul was entirely filled with a new, joyful radiance. He would have been glad of his solitude if only he had been able to read and had possessed a New Testament. The prison authorities would have given him the latter, but he was unable to read.

As a boy he had begun to learn the alphabet in the old-fashioned way – *az, buki, vedi*[12] – but because of his slow-wittedness he had got no further than learning the individual letters, had never been able to understand the way words were put together, and had remained illiterate. Now, however, he resolved to try again, and he asked the orderly for a New Testament. The orderly brought him one, and he set to work. He could recognize the individual letters, but he could not for the life of him work out how they were put together. No matter how hard he struggled to understand the composition of the words, he could make no sense of it at all. He was unable to sleep at nights, spent all his time thinking about this problem, even went off his food. In the end he grew so depressed that he had an attack of lice and could not get rid of them.

'How's it going then? Still can't make it out, eh?' the orderly asked him one day.

'No.'

'I tell you what, do you know "Our Father"?'

'Yes.'

'Well, look, here it is; now you say it. There you are.' And the orderly showed him the text of the Lord's Prayer in the New Testament.

Stepan began to recite the Lord's Prayer, fitting the familiar letters together with the familiar words. And suddenly the mystery of words was revealed to him, and he began to read. He was overjoyed. And from that day forth he continued to read, and the meaning that little by little emerged from the words which he composed with difficulty acquired even greater import.

Stepan's solitude was no longer a burden to him – it was a joy. His whole life was filled with his task, and he was dismayed when he was transferred back to the communal cell so that his solitary cell could be made available to house one of the newly arrived political prisoners.

5

Now it was often Stepan, not Chuyev, who read aloud from the Gospels in the communal cell, and while some of the prisoners sang bawdy songs, others would listen to what he read and what he had to say about it. There were two men in particular who paid attention in this way: Makhorkin the executioner, who was doing hard labour for murder, and Vasily, who had been caught stealing and was being held in this prison while he awaited trial. On two occasions during his stay in the prison, Makhorkin had carried out his duties as an executioner, both times in other towns where no one could be found to carry out the sentences imposed by the judges. The peasants who had murdered Pyotr Nikolayevich had been tried by a military tribunal, and two of them had been sentenced to death by hanging.

Makhorkin was ordered to go to Penza to act as executioner in the prison there. On previous occasions such as this, possessing a degree of literacy that was above the average, he had immediately written a letter to the governor, explaining that he had been called away to Penza to carry out his duties and requesting the chief of the province to grant him a regulation daily maintenance allowance; this time, however, he declared, much to the astonishment of the warden, that he would not go and said he would never carry out his official duties ever again.

'Have you forgotten the whip?' shouted the warden.

'The whip's as may be, but killing's against the law.'

'Been talking to our prison prophet Pelageyushkin, have you? Just you wait.'

6

While all this was going on, Makhin, the grammar school boy who had shown his friend how to forge a coupon, had left school, gone to university and taken a degree at the Faculty of Law. Thanks to his success with women, and in particular with an ex-mistress of an aged cabinet minister with whom he was friendly, he had, at a remarkably early age, become an examining magistrate. He was a dishonest man who cheated on his debts, a seducer of women and a gambler, but he was also clever and keen-witted, and had a retentive memory and a shrewd eye for a case.

He was the examining magistrate in the district where Stepan Pelageyushkin was being tried. Even at the first examination he was taken aback by the simplicity, truthfulness and calm of Stepan's replies to his questions. Makhin sensed unconsciously that this man who stood before him in fetters and shaven-headed, and who had been escorted to the prison and placed under lock and key by two soldiers, was endowed with a perfect freedom, and existed at a superior moral level that was inaccessible to him, Makhin. So as he examined him, he had constantly to keep rallying his spirits and egging himself on, so as not to lose face and be put off his mark. He was astonished by the way Stepan talked about what he had done as though it were something that had happened long ago, and as though it had not been him but someone else who had been involved.

'And didn't you feel sorry for them?' asked Makhin.

'No. I didn't understand in those days.'

'Well, how do you feel about them now?'

Stepan smiled sadly.

'I wouldn't do it now even if you were to roast me on the fire.'

'Why not?'

'Because now I know all men are brothers.'

'What, do you mean to say you think I'm your brother?'

'Of course I do.'

'What, I'm your brother, and yet I'm having you put away?'

'You're only doing that because you don't understand.'

'What don't I understand?'

'You don't understand, otherwise you wouldn't be having me put away.'

'Oh all right, let's get on with it. So where did you go after that?'

Makhin was astonished most of all by what the prison warden

told him about Pelageyushkin's influence on the executioner Makhorkin, who, at the risk of receiving a flogging, had refused to carry out his official duties.

7

At a soirée in the house of the Yeropkin family, where there were two rich marriageable daughters, both of whom Makhin was courting, the singing of romances had just come to an end. Makhin was musically gifted, and he particularly excelled in the performance of romances, being both a fine singer and a fine accompanist. After the singing was over, Makhin gave a very objective, faithful and detailed account – he had an excellent memory – of the story of the strange criminal who had converted an executioner to Christ. Makhin was able to remember and describe everything so exactly because he was always totally uninvolved with the people he had to deal with. He neither entered into nor knew how to enter into the emotional condition of others, and this was why he had such a good memory for all the things that happened to people, all the things they said and did. Pelageyushkin, however, had awoken his interest. He did not attempt to put himself in Stepan's shoes, but he found himself asking himself the question: 'What's going on inside his head?' Although he was unable to come up with any answer, he none the less had a feeling that it must be something interesting, so at the soirée he related the entire case: the executioner's conversion, the warden's stories about Pelageyushkin's strange behaviour, his reading of the Gospels, and the powerful influence he exerted on his fellow convicts.

Everyone took an interest in Makhin's story; most interested of all, however, was the Yeropkins' younger daughter, Liza, who was eighteen years old and had just completed her studies at a ladies' institute. It was only recently that she had woken up from the darkness and narrowness of the false surroundings in which she had been reared, and had burst like a swimmer to the surface, gulping in the fresh air of life. She began to question Makhin about the details of the story, about how and why it was that such a change had taken place in Pelageyushkin. Makhin informed her of what Stepan had told him about his most recent murder, and about how the meekness and docility of this extraordinarily kind-hearted woman, who had known no fear of death but who had been his victim none the less, had vanquished him and opened his eyes, and how the reading of the Gospels had done the rest.

It took Liza Yeropkina a long time to get to sleep that night. For several months now a struggle had been going on inside her between the fashionable social life her sister had been trying to get her interested in, and her love for Makhin, which in her was connected with a desire to reform him. And now it was this latter pull that took over. She had already heard something of the woman before she had been murdered. Now, however, in view of the terrible manner of her death and what Makhin had told her about the things Pelageyushkin had said, she inquired after all the details of Maria Semyonovna's history and was quite shaken at what she learned.

Liza passionately longed to be another Maria Semyonovna. She was rich, and she was afraid that Makhin was only interested in her for her money. And so she decided she would give all her land away, and told Makhin of her intention.

Makhin was glad of this opportunity of showing how disinterested he was, and he told Liza that her money had nothing to do with his love for her and that her decision, which he thought a very magnanimous one, had touched him deeply. Meanwhile a struggle had developed between Liza and her mother – the estate had been given to her by her father – who would not allow her to give the land away. Makhin went to Liza's aid. And the more he acted in this way, the more he came to understand this new world of spiritual aspiration, which he perceived in Liza and which until now had been a complete mystery to him.

8

In the communal cell, all had grown quiet. Stepan was lying in his berth on the plank bed, not yet asleep. Vasily went across to him and tugged his foot, winking to him as a signal to get up and come over to where he was standing. Stepan clambered down from the plank bed and approached Vasily.

'Now, my friend,' said Vasily. 'You see if you can't help me.'

'How can I help you?'

'Escaping is what I have in mind.'

And Vasily told Stepan that he had made all the arrangements for an escape.

'Tomorrow I'll start a bit of trouble with them' – he pointed to the prisoners lying asleep – 'and they'll complain to the orderlies. They'll take me to the cells upstairs, and from then on it'll be plain sailing. Only you'll have to help to get me out of the mortuary.'

'All right, then. But where'll you go?'

'I'll go where fortune leads me. Do you think there's any shortage of villains out there?'

'That's true, Vasily, but it's not for us to judge them.'

'Well, I mean, it's not as if I was a murderer, is it? I've never killed a person in my life, and what's stealing? What's wrong about it? Don't they rob us poor blighters?'

'That's their business. They'll have to answer for it.'

'Well, and are we supposed to just stand still and watch? Look, I burgled a church once. What harm did that do anyone? What I want to do now is make one really big haul – not just break into some little shop or other – and give the money away to them that need it.'

Just then one of the convicts sat up on the plank bed and began to eavesdrop. Stepan and Vasily went their separate ways.

On the following day Vasily carried out his plan. He began complaining about the bread, saying it was mouldy, and egged on the convicts to send for the warden and make an official complaint. The warden arrived, showered them with abuse and, discovering that Vasily was the ringleader, ordered him to be locked up separately in one of the solitary cells upstairs.

This was exactly what Vasily had wanted.

9

Vasily was well acquainted with the upstairs cell into which he had been put. He knew how its floor was constructed and, as soon as he arrived there, he started to take the floorboards up. When he was able to wriggle under the floor, he prised open the planks on the ceiling of the room that lay directly below, and jumped down. This room was the prison mortuary; that day there was only one corpse on the mortuary table. It was in this mortuary that the sacks used for making the convicts' straw mattresses were kept. Vasily knew this and was counting on it. The padlock on the door of the room had been unlocked and pushed inside. Vasily opened the door and went out along the corridor to its far end, where a new latrine was under construction. In this latrine there was a hole leading from the third floor down to the basement. Feeling for the door, Vasily went back into the mortuary, removed the shroud from the ice-cold corpse (his hand touched it as he pulled the shroud away), then took some sacks, tied them together with the shroud so as to make a long rope, and lowered the rope into the latrine hole; then he tied the rope to a cross-beam and climbed down it. The rope was not long enough to reach all the way down. How much of a gap was left, he did not know, but there was nothing to be done about it now, so he hung down as far as he could, and then jumped. He hurt his legs, but was able to continue walking. There were two windows in the basement. They were wide enough for him to crawl through, but were fitted with iron gratings. One of the iron gratings would have to be dislodged. What could he use to do that? Vasily began to rummage about. Lying in the basement were some sections of boards. He found one section that had a pointed end and began using it to force the bricks that held the grating in place. This work took a long time. Second cockcrow came, but still the grating held. At last one side of it came loose. Vasily shoved his pointed section of board into the gap and heaved; the grating came away, but a brick fell to the floor, making a noise. The sentries might hear. Vasily froze. All was quiet. He climbed out of the window. He would have to scale the prison wall in order to make his escape. In a corner of the yard stood an outhouse. He would have to climb on to the roof of this outhouse and get over the wall that way. He would have to take a section of board with him, for otherwise he would not be able to get on to the roof. He climbed back through the window, came out again with a section of board and froze, listening for the sentry. As he had been counting on, the sentry was marching on the other side of the courtyard square. Vasily went over to the outhouse, placed his piece of board against it, and started to climb. The board slipped and fell. Vasily was wearing socks, but no shoes. He took off his socks so as to get a better grip with his feet, positioned the board again, leapt on to it and seized the roof gutter with his hand. 'Oh God, don't let me fall, keep me up,' he prayed. He hung on to the roof gutter, and then managed to get up on to the roof by one knee. The sentry was coming. Vasily lay down and froze. The sentry did not notice anything and continued on his rounds. Vasily leapt to his feet. The iron roofing clattered under his feet. He took one step, two. Then he was at the wall. He could reach it easily with his hand. One hand first, and then the other, he stretched up, and there he was, on the wall. All he had to do now was to be careful and not hurt himself as he jumped down. He turned round, hung by both hands, stretched to his full length, lowered one arm, then the other and – praise the Lord! – he was on the ground. It was soft ground, too. His legs were unharmed, and off he ran.

When he reached his house in the suburbs, Malanya opened the door for him, and he crawled under the warm, patchwork quilt that was steeped in the smell of sweat.

10

Pyotr Nikolayevich's large and attractive wife, childless, forever placid, and plump as a dry cow, stood at the window and watched her husband being killed by the peasants and his body being dragged away somewhere into the fields. The feeling of terror Natalya Ivanovna (such was the name of Pyotr Nikolayevich's widow) experienced at the sight of this bloody deed was – as is generally the case – so powerful that it blotted out all other feelings in her. When, however, the crowd of peasants had disappeared from sight behind the garden fence and the hubbub of voices had died away, and Malanya, the barefoot girl who worked as a servant for them, came rushing in with her eyes sticking out of her head as though she were about to relate some joyous event, to say that Pyotr Nikolayevich had been murdered and his body thrown in the ravine, Natalya Ivanovna's feeling of horror was gradually supplanted by another emotion: a sense of joy at her liberation from the despot in the smoked eyeglasses who had kept her in slavery these past twelve years. She was deeply shocked by this feeling, and tried not to acknowledge it to herself, and even more not to tell anyone else about it. When his yellow, hairy, disfigured corpse was washed and dressed and laid in its coffin, she was filled with horror, and she wept and sobbed. When the examining magistrate with special responsibility for serious cases interrogated her as a witness, he confronted her, right there and then in his office, with two peasants in fetters who had been charged with being the principal culprits. One of them was quite old, with a long, white curling beard and a face that was calm, stern and handsome; the other was of gypsy appearance and was somewhat younger, with shining black eyes and curly, dishevelled hair. Natalya Ivanovna thereupon testified that to the best of her knowledge these were the same two men who had been the first to seize Pyotr Nikolayevich by the arms, and even though the peasant who looked like a gypsy flashed and darted his eyes under his flickering eyebrows, and said reproachfully: 'It's a sin, ma'am! We'll all die some day, you know' – even in spite of this, she did not feel in the slightest sorry for them. On the contrary, during the investigation a hostile feeling rose up in her, coupled with a desire to take revenge on the murderers of her husband.

But when a month later the case, which had been transferred to a military tribunal, ended in eight men being sentenced to penal servitude and the two ringleaders – the white-bearded old man and the swarthy 'gypsy' as he was called – being sentenced to be hanged, she experienced an unpleasant sensation. This soon disappeared, however, under the influence of the solemn ritual of the court. If this was what the higher authorities considered to be necessary, then it must be all right.

The executions were to be carried out in the village. And, returning from Mass one Sunday, Malanya, wearing a new dress and new shoes, told her mistress that a gallows was being put up, that an executioner was expected to arrive from Moscow on Wednesday, that the two men's relatives were wailing without cease, and that the noise could be heard all over the neighbourhood.

Natalya Ivanovna stayed indoors so as not to see the gallows or the people, and wished only for one thing: for it all to be over as soon as possible. She took thought only for herself, and not for the condemned men or their families.

II

On the Tuesday, the chief constable, who was a friend of Natalya Ivanovna's, dropped in to see her. Natalya Ivanovna treated him to vodka and her own pickled mushrooms. When the chief constable had sampled both, he told her that there was to be no execution the following day.

'What? Why is that?'

'It's an odd story, really. We can't find a hangman. There was one in Moscow, but my son was telling me that he started reading the Gospels and now says killing's against his conscience. He got hard labour for the murders he committed, but now all of a sudden he says he can't kill even if he's got the law behind him. He was told he'd be whipped. Whip me, he says, but I still won't do it.'

Natalya Ivanovna suddenly blushed, and her thoughts even started to make her perspire.

'But can't they be pardoned now?'

'How can they be pardoned when they've been found guilty by a court of law? Only the Tsar can pardon them.'

'But how will the Tsar ever find out about them?'

'They have the right to appeal for mercy.'

'Anyway, it's for my sake that they're being executed,' said Natalya Ivanovna, who was not very intelligent. 'And I forgive them.'

The chief constable laughed. 'Why don't you put in a petition for them?'

'Can I?'

'Of course you can.'

'But won't it be too late now?'

'You can send a telegram.'

'To the Tsar?'

'Of course, you can send a telegram even to the Tsar.'

The discovery that the executioner had refused to do his job and was prepared to suffer rather than kill anyone caused a sudden upheaval within Natalya Ivanovna; the sense of horror and compassion which had already surfaced a few times in her now broke through and took possession of her.

'Dear Filipp Vasilyevich, please write the telegram for me. I want to ask the Tsar to show mercy to them.'

The chief constable shook his head. 'What if we were to be punished for it?'

'I'll take the responsibility. I won't mention you at all.'

'There's a kind woman,' thought the chief constable. 'A really kind woman. If my wife was like her I'd be in clover now.'

And the chief constable wrote a telegram to the Tsar: 'To His Imperial Majesty the Sovereign Emperor. Your Imperial Majesty's loyal subject, the widow of the collegiate assessor Pyotr Nikolayevich Sventitsky, murdered by peasants, prostrating herself at the sacred feet of Your Imperial Majesty [the chief constable was especially proud of this passage in the telegram] begs you to have mercy on the condemned men, the peasants so-and-so, of such-and-such a village, *volost*,[13] district and province.'

The chief constable dispatched the telegram himself, and Natalya Ivanovna began to feel much happier. She felt that if she, the widow of the murdered man, forgave his murderers and asked for mercy for them, the Tsar could not refuse to grant her request.

12

Liza Yeropkina was living in a state of continuous exaltation. The further she progressed along the Christian way of life that had been revealed to her, the more convinced she became that this was the only true way, and her heart grew lighter and lighter.

Now she had two immediate objectives: the first was to convert Makhin, or rather, as she put it privately, to return him to himself, to his good and beautiful nature. She loved him, and by the radiance of her love she saw into the divine nature of his soul, which is common to all human beings, seeing in this universal principle of life, however, a goodness, tenderness and exaltedness that were peculiar to him alone. Her other objective was to cease being rich. She wanted to get rid of all her land, in the first place in order to put Makhin to the test, and secondly for her own good, for the good of her soul – and she wanted to do this according to the letter of the Gospels. She began by dividing up the land and announcing her intention of giving it away, but she was prevented from carrying out this plan in the first instance by her father, but even more effectively by the deluge of personal and written applications that flooded in on her. Then she decided to turn to an elder who was noted for the holy life he had led, and asked him to take her money and do with it whatever he thought fitting. When her father found out about this, he was furious, and in the course of a heated conversation with her called her a madwoman and a psychopath, and said he was going to take steps to protect her from herself.

Her father's angry, irritable tone of voice had its effect on her and, before she was aware of it, she burst into resentful tears and said insulting things to him, calling him a despot and even a shark.

She begged her father to forgive her; he said he was not angry, but she could see that he was hurt and had not really forgiven her. She was reluctant to tell Makhin about what had happened. Her sister, who was jealous of her because of Makhin, shunned her completely. She had no one to talk to about her feelings, no one to whom she could confide.

'It's God I must confide in,' she told herself, and since it was Lent she decided she would fast and take holy communion, and that during confession she would tell the father confessor everything and ask his advice as to what her future actions should be.

Not far from the city was the monastery where the elder lived, the one who was renowned for his way of life and for the teachings, prophecies and cures that were ascribed to him.

The elder had had a letter from Yeropkin senior, warning him of his daughter's arrival and of the abnormal, hysterical state of mind she was in; the letter expressed his confidence that the elder would be able to put her on the right track, the way of moderation and of the good, Christian life, in harmony with existing circumstances.

Tired after a long succession of visitors, the elder received Liza and quietly began to impress upon her the importance of moderation and obedience to the existing circumstances of her life and to her parents. Liza blushed, perspired and said nothing, but when he had finished she began to remind him, timidly at first, with tears in her eyes, that Christ had said: 'Leave thy father and thy mother, and follow me,' and then, with an increasing degree of animation, went on to explain her entire conception of Christianity. At first the elder just smiled and made some routine points of dogma, but then he grew silent and began to sigh, muttering 'Oh God!' to himself now and again.

'Well, all right, then, come to me for confession tomorrow,' he said, and blessed her with his wrinkled hand.

The following day he heard her confession and, without continuing their conversation of the day before, he sent her away, curtly refusing to take upon himself the disposition of her property.

The purity of this girl, her fervour and complete subservience to the will of God had made a deep impression on the elder. He had long wanted to turn his back on the world, but the monastery needed his services, as they brought in money. And so he had agreed to stay on, although he had a vague awareness of the falsity of the position he was in. He had been turned into a saint and worker of miracles, while really he was just a weak man who had been carried away by his own success. And the soul of this girl, which she had just revealed to him, had opened to him a revelation of his own soul. He had seen how far he was from what he wanted to be and from what his heart was drawing him towards.

Soon after Liza's visit, he went into a retreat and it was not until three weeks later that he came out into the church, conducted the service and after it delivered a sermon in which he reproached himself and castigated the world for its sinfulness and called it to repentance.

Every two weeks he delivered a new sermon. Each time they were attended by more and more people. His fame as a preacher spread further and further afield. There was something unique, bold and sincere about his sermons, and this was the reason for the powerful effect he had on other people.

13

Meanwhile Vasily had been doing exactly as he pleased. One night with some companions he broke into the house of Krasnopuzov, a rich man. He knew that Krasnopuzov was miserly and debauched, and he broke open the writing desk and took thirty thousand roubles from it. And he did what he pleased. He even stopped drinking and gave the money away to poor girls who wanted to get married. He provided dowries, paid off debts and kept a low profile. All he worried about was how to distribute the money fairly. He even gave some of it to the police, who as a result did not spend much time looking for him.

His heart rejoiced. And when in the end he was arrested none the less and brought to trial, he laughed and boasted, saying that the pot-bellied Krasnopuzov's money had been lying idle, that its owner had not known its true value, while he, Vasily, had put it into circulation and had used it to help good folk.

And indeed, so good-humoured and kind-hearted was his defence that the jury almost acquitted him. He was sentenced to deportation.

He thanked the judge and told him in advance that he was going to escape.

14

Sventitsky's widow's telegram to the Tsar produced no result whatsoever. It was decided by the petitions office not even to report the matter to His Majesty. One day, however, when the Tsar was having lunch, the Sventitsky affair came up in the course of the table talk, and the director of the petitions office, who was present, told him about the telegram that had been received from the murdered man's wife.

'*C'est très gentil de sa part*,' said one of the ladies of the Imperial family.

The Tsar merely sighed, shrugged his epauletted shoulders, and said: 'The laws's the law.' Then he set up his glass, into which the valet poured some sparkling Moselle. Everyone pretended to be overwhelmed by the wisdom of the Tsar's words. And after that there was no more mention of the telegram. The two *muzhiks* – the older man and the younger fellow – were hanged with the help of a cruel and bestial murderer, a Tartar executioner who had been summoned especially from Kazan.

The old man's widow had wanted to dress her husband's corpse in a white shirt, white foot-cloths and new shoes, but they would not let her, and both men were buried in a common grave outside the wall of the cemetery.

*

'Princess Sofya Vladimirovna was telling me he's the most marvellous preacher,' said the Tsar's mother, the Dowager Empress, to her son one day: '*Faites le venir. Il peut prêcher à la cathédrale.*'

'No, it'd be better to have him preach at home,' said the Tsar, and gave orders that elder Isidor was to be summoned to court.

All the generals assembled in the court chapel. A new and out-of-the-ordinary preacher was, after all, something of an event.

A little, grey-haired, emaciated old man came out and looked everyone over: 'In the name of the Father, and of the Son, and of the Holy Ghost,' he said, and began his sermon.

It started off all right, but the longer it went on, the worse it became. '*Il devenait de plus en plus aggressif*' was how the Empress described it afterwards. He fulminated against everything and everyone, spoke of the death sentence and ascribed its necessity to bad government. Can it really be permissible, he asked, to kill people in a country that is supposed to be Christian?

Everyone looked at one another, and everyone thought only of the impropriety and of how displeased the Tsar must be, but no one said anything. When Isidor said 'Amen', the Metropolitan approached him and asked him to come and have a word with him.

After a talk with the Metropolitan and the Chief Procurator of the Synod, the old man was immediately sent off to a monastery – not his own, this time, however, but the one at Suzdal, where the Father Superior and prison commandant was Father Misail.

15

Everyone pretended that there had been nothing untoward about Isidor's sermon, and no one made any mention of it. Even the Tsar felt that the elder's words had left no impression on him, although a couple of times during the day he did find himself thinking about the execution of the peasants, and

Sventitsky's widow's telegram of intercession for them. There was a parade that afternoon, followed by a drive through the streets, then there was a reception of ministers, dinner, and in the evening he went out to the theatre. As usual, the Tsar fell asleep as soon as his head touched the pillow. That night he was awoken by a terrible dream: in a field stood a gallows with corpses dangling from it; the corpses' tongues were protruding, sticking out further and further. And someone was shouting: 'It's all your doing, it's all your doing!' The Tsar woke up in a sweat and started to think. For the first time in his life he began to think about the responsibility that rested with him, and he remembered everything the old man had said . . .

But he could see the human being in himself only from afar, and he could not give himself up to the demands of the human being because of all the demands that are made on a tsar from every side; as for admitting that the demands of the human being might be more binding than the demands made on him as a tsar – he did not have the strength to do that.

16

Proshka, that high-spirited, dandified, proud young lad came out from his second term in prison completely broken. When he was sober he merely sat around and did nothing, and, no matter how much his father shouted at him, he lived as a parasite and did no work – not only that, he was in the habit of stealing things and taking them down to the public house to sell for drink. He slouched around, coughed, hawked and spat. The doctor he visited auscultated his chest and shook his head.

'What you need, my friend, is something you haven't got.'

'I know, it's what I've always needed.'

'Drink plenty of milk and don't smoke.'

'But it's Lent, and anyway we haven't got a cow.'

One night that spring he was unable to sleep; he felt depressed and wanted to drink. There was no drink in the house. He put on his fur hat and went out, making his way along the street until he came to the houses where the clergy lived. There was a harrow leaning against the fence outside the deacon's house. Proshka went over, slung the harrow over his shoulder and carried it off to Petrovna at the drinking house. 'Maybe she'll give me a bottle of vodka for it.' He had not gone far when the deacon came out on to his porch. It was already broad daylight, and he could see that Proshka had taken his harrow.

'Hey, what do you think you're doing?'

The deacon's servants came out, seized Proshka, and threw him in the lock-up. The Justice of the Peace sentenced him to eleven months in prison.

Autumn came. Proshka was transferred to the prison hospital. He could not stop coughing, his chest was nearly bursting, and he could not keep warm. Some of the patients must have been fairly healthy, for they at least were not shivering. But Proshka shivered by day and by night. The warden liked to economize on firewood, and did not start heating the hospital until November of each year. Proshka suffered physical agonies, but spiritually he suffered even worse. Everything disgusted him, he hated everyone: the deacon, the warden who refused to heat the hospital, the orderly and even one of the patients near him who had a red, swollen lip. He also conceived an intense dislike of the new convict who had just been brought in. This was Stepan. He had caught an inflammation of the head, had been transferred to the hospital and had been put in a bed next to Proshka. Although Proshka hated him at first, he subsequently grew so fond of him that all he cared for was the chance of talking to him. It was only after his conversations with him that Proshka's intense depression ever lifted.

Stepan was forever telling the other patients about his most recent murder and about the effect it had had on him.

'She didn't yell or scream or anything,' he would say. 'She just said: "Go on, then, cut my throat. It's not me but yourself you ought to feel sorry for," she said.'

'Yes, I know, it's a terrible business killing anything. I once killed a sheep, but I wasn't proud of myself for doing it. And here I am, I haven't killed a soul, but they've gone and ruined me anyway, the rats. I've never harmed a living soul in all my life . . .'

'Never mind, it'll all be counted in your favour.'

'Where, might I ask?'

'What do you mean, where? Where's your faith in God?'

'You don't see much of Him, somehow; you know, I don't believe in Him. I think you just die and the grass grows over you. That's all.'

'How can you say that? I've killed that many folk, but she was kind, all she did was help people. Do you think we'll get the same treatment, she and I? No, you wait and see . . .'

'So you think that when you die your soul stays alive?'

'What else? It stands to reason.'

Death was not coming easily to Proshka, and he was gasping for breath. But at the very last moment he suddenly felt at ease. He called to Stepan.

'Well, brother, farewell. I see it's time for me to die now. I was that scared, but now I can see there's nothing to it. I just want it to be over as soon as possible.'

And Proshka died in the hospital.

17

Meanwhile the affairs of Yevgeny Mikhailovich were going from bad to worse. He had had to mortgage his shop. Business was bad. Another photographic supply shop had opened in the town. The interest on his mortgage was due. He had to borrow more money in order to pay off the interest. And the upshot of it all was that the shop was earmarked for sale, and all the goods in it as well. Yevgeny Mikhailovich and his wife ran all over town, but nowhere could they raise the four hundred roubles they needed in order to save their business.

They had had a faint hope that the merchant Krasnopuzov, whose mistress was friendly with Yevgeny Mikhailovich's wife, might help them. But by now the whole town knew that an enormous amount of money had been stolen from Krasnopuzov. It was said that the sum amounted to half a million.

'And who do you think stole it?' said Yevgeny Mikhailovich's wife. 'It was Vasily, our old yard-keeper. They say he's throwing the money around like anyone's business, and he's even bribed the police with it.'

'He never was any good,' said Yevgeny Mikhailovich. 'Perjured himself as easy as blinking that time, he did. I'd never have believed it of him.'

'They say he called by at our place one day. The cook said it was him. She says he paid the dowries for fourteen poor girls who wanted to get married.'

'Yes, well, people do make things up, you know.'

Just then a strange-looking elderly man in a woollen jacket came into the shop.

'What can I do for you?'

'There's a letter for you.'

'Who's it from?'

'It says on it.'

'Well, they'll want a reply, won't they? Wait a moment.'

'I can't.'

And having handed over the envelope, the strange-looking man left in a hurry.

'Funny.'

Yevgeny Mikhailovich tore open the fat envelope and could hardly believe his eyes: it contained hundred-rouble notes. There were four of them. What on earth was this? And there was a badly spelled letter addressed to Yevgeny Mikhailovich, which read: 'The Gosspels tell us to render good for evil. You cauzed me a lot of truble with that cupon and a lot of truble to that *muzhik* as well, but I feel sory for you. Here's four undred for you, and remember your old yard-keeper Vasily.'

'Well, isn't that extraordinary!' said Yevgeny Mikhailovich; he said it both to his wife and to himself. And whenever he remembered this subsequently or mentioned it to his wife, the tears would come to his eyes and her heart would be filled with joy.

18

In the prison at Suzdal there were fourteen clergymen who had all been sent there in the first instance for apostasy; this was where Isidor too had been sent. Father Misail received Isidor according to the instructions he had been given and, without interviewing him, ordered him to be put in a solitary cell, as befitting a serious criminal. In the third week of Isidor's stay in the prison, Father Misail made the rounds of the inmates. Going into Isidor's cell, he asked if there was anything he required.

'There are a lot of things I require, only I can't tell you what they are in front of the other men. Let me have a private talk with you.'

They looked at each other, and Father Misail saw that he had nothing to fear. He ordered Isidor to be brought to his retreat and, when the two of them were alone, he said: 'All right, go ahead, then.'

Isidor fell on his knees.

'Brother!' said Isidor. 'What are you doing? Have mercy on your own soul. You're the worst villain alive, you've spat on everything that's holy . . .'

A month later Father Misail filed documents for the release, on the grounds of penitence, not only of Isidor but also of seven other men, with a request that he himself be allowed to retire to a monastery.

19

Ten years went by.

Mitya Smokovnikov had graduated from the technical institute and was now an engineer on a large salary; he was engaged in gold prospecting in Siberia. It was necessary for him to make an exploratory tour of the area. The director of the project suggested that he take the convict Stepan Pelageyushkin along with him.

'One of the hard labour men? Won't that be rather dangerous?'

'He'll not be any trouble. He's a holy man. Ask anyone you like.'

'What's he in for?'

The director smiled. 'He murdered six people, but he's a holy man. I promise you.'

And so Mitya Smokovnikov agreed to take Stepan, who was now a balding, emaciated, weather-beaten old man, along with him, and they set off together.

On the journey Stepan looked after Smokovnikov as if he were his own child, and told him his whole story, and all the whys and wherefores of his present existence.

And it was a strange thing. Mitya Smokovnikov, who until that time had lived only in order to eat, drink, play cards and chase women, now thought about life for the very first time. And these thoughts gave him no peace; indeed, they gradually turned his soul upside down. He was offered a very advantageous position. He turned it down and decided to use the money he had in order to buy some property, get married and serve the common people as best he could.

20

And that was what he did. But first he went to see his father, with whom he had been having difficulties on account of his father's new family. Now, however, he decided to make it up with his father. And so he did. And his father, surprised, laughed at him at first, but later recalled the many times he had been guilty with regard to him.

Notes

THE RAID

1. *Description of War*: More exactly, *Description of the Patriotic War of 1812*. Tolstoy used material from this well-known book for *War and Peace*.
2. *dhzigiting*: '*Dhzigit*' means 'brave' in Kalmuck. Translated into Russian, 'to dhzigit' means 'to put on a brave show'. [*Tolstoy*]
3. *Mullah Nurs*: *Mullah Nur* (1836) was an exotic novel by Aleksandr Bestuzhev-Marlinsky, set in the Caucasus. Marlinsky was at one time exceedingly popular for his Byronic tales of adventure. He was killed at the age of forty in a skirmish with Circassians under mysterious circumstances.
4. *Heroes of Our Time*: Mikhail Lermontov's famous novel *A Hero of Our Time* (1839) is set in the Caucasus.
5. *Varangians*: These were Norsemen who in the ninth century raided the eastern shores of the Baltic, penetrated into the interior and established the great trade route to Byzantium along the river Dnieper. According to legend the East Slavs invited them to rule Russia, and thus the dynasty of the Ruriks began. It would appear that Tolstoy is poking fun at Rosenkrantz here.
6. *call of frogs*: Frogs in the Caucasus make a noise quite different from the croaking of Russian frogs. [*Tolstoy*]
7. *in full spate at this time of year*: In the Caucasus rivers tend to overflow in July, [*Tolstoy*]
8. *Shamil*: Shamil (1797–1871) was the religious and political leader of the north Caucasian Muslim tribes in their resistance to Russian expansion. In 1859 he surrendered at Gunib and was taken to central Russia. He died in Mecca.
9. *him*: The collective noun by which soldiers in the Caucasus indicate the enemy. [*Tolstoy*]

THE WOODFELLING

1. *Great Chechnya District*: Part of the north Caucasus, with a mainly Muslim population. During the 1830s and 1840s the Russian army was engaged in numerous campaigns, leading to the eventual subjugation and colonization of the region.
2. *filka*: A soldier's card game. [*Tolstoy*]
3. *Mount Kizbeck*: Mount Kazbek, one of the highest mountains in the Caucasus.
4. *Unicorn*: Field gun with a unicorn engraved on it.
5. *Anna or Vladimir medal*: The order of St Anne was awarded for civil and military distinction and was worn around the neck. The order of St Vladimir was originally awarded for meritorious civil achievements but later for valour on the field of combat.
6. *Passek*: Major-General D. V. Passek, who served with distinction in the Caucasus.
7. *Sleptsov*: General N. P. Sleptsov, a hero of the war in the Caucasus and an extremely popular commander.
8. *Yermolov*: A. P. Yermolov – Russian general, commander-in-chief in Georgia and, before that, in command of a corps in the Caucasus.
9. *riabko*: Soldier's food of soaked rusks and lard. [*Tolstoy*]
10. *Dargo*: A mountain stronghold captured by Count Vorontsov, Viceroy of the Caucasus, in 1845. It was the scene of fierce fighting.
11. *Indian Mountain*: This is a soldier's corruption of Andiysky. Andiysky Mountain is a spur of the main Caucasus range (i.e. the soldier thinks it is Indiysky).

POLIKUSHKA

1. *Conscription for military service*: This was a serious business since many of the young men sent for service never returned and those who did could be away for twenty years or more. Estate owners had the right to excuse anyone from being conscripted, but this would involve finding a substitute or paying a large sum of money. The draft fell first on families with three adult males other than the head, then families with two. Families with one son were often able to show that he was needed for support at home.
2. *Feast of Pokrov*: The Intercession of the Virgin, 1 October.

3. *Glauber's salt*: The German-born chemist Johann Rudolph Glauber (1604–70) was the discoverer of hydrochloric acid and sometimes known as 'the father of chemistry'. His 'Glauber's salt' (sodium sulphate) had some therapeutic value, but rather less than he claimed.
4. *lye*: A product derived from scalding wood ash which the women used for washing.
5. *come to no harm*: It was not uncommon for young men to cut off their trigger finger or mutilate themselves in some other way in order to avoid conscription.
6. *kvass*: A refreshing, non-alcoholic Russian peasant drink derived from rye bread.
7. *avinoo*: A mispronunciation of 'avenue'. The Russian word *prospékt* (avenue) tended to be mispronounced by the uneducated as *preshpékt*. This mistaken version, which appears also in *War and Peace* (One, iii, 3), has been affectionately bestowed as the name of an avenue and a restaurant at present-day Yasnaya Polyana, Tolstoy's estate.
8. *Julia Pastrana*: A freak-show bearded lady who toured Russia in the 1850s.

THE DEATH OF IVAN ILYICH

1. *Scharmer's*: A fashionable tailor's shop in St Petersburg.
2. *Respice finem*: 'Look Before You Leap' (Latin motto). Literally, 'Examine the End'.
3. *Donon's*: A restaurant in St Petersburg popular among the well-to-do.
4. *Legal Code of 1864*: The emancipation of the serfs in 1861 was followed three years later by sweeping changes in the Russian judicial system. These included setting up Chambers of Justice independent of the administration, the appointment of Justices of the Peace to deal with petty crime locally, public trials and trial by jury.
5. *Dowager Empress Maria*: Maria Fyodorovna was the second wife of Paul I (1754–1801). When she became the Dowager Empress in the reign of Alexander I she founded a number of charitable institutions and schools for young ladies of the gentry. Eventually these were administered by a government department.
6. *Pasha and Lizanka*: Affectionate diminutives for Praskovya (his wife) and Liza (his daughter).

7. *blind gut*: The caecum or 'blind gut' ('intestinum caecum') is a 'blind' pouch where the small intestine ends and the colon begins. The appendix is attached to it. The doctor may suspect something like appendicitis, but this term was not used until the early twentieth century.
8. *Jean*: It was common practice within a family to use Russian names in their equivalent French form.
9. *Kiesewetter's logic*: G. K. C. Kiesewetter (1766–1819) was a follower and popularizer of Kant. His textbook of logic was a standard text in Russian schools.
10. *Vitya and Volodya . . . little Katya*: Family names for Ivan Ilyich's brothers and sister, called respectively Vitaly, Vladimir and Yekaterina.
11. *the Court of Cassation*: A department of the Russian Senate which heard appeals made possible by the judicial reforms of 1864.
12. *Sarah Bernhardt*: The French classical actress (1844–1923) was the leading tragedienne of her day. She toured Russia during the winter of 1881–2.
13. *à la Capoul hairstyle*: A hairstyle with a central parting and two curls falling over the forehead after the manner of a popular French tenor, Joseph Capoul (1839–1924).
14. *Adrienne Lecouvreur*: An 1849 comedy by A. E. Scribe and E. Legouvé which depicts the life of an eighteenth-century actress. The title role was made famous by Sarah Bernhardt.

AFTER THE BALL

1. *marshal of nobility*: A representative of the Russian nobility elected to manage their affairs and represent their interests in the local government of a district or province.
2. *Alphonse Karr*: French writer and journalist (1808–90) known for a long series of witty novels, including *Geneviève* (1838) and one memorable saying, '*Plus ça change, plus c'est la même chose*', originally applied to revolutions.
3. *à la Nicolas*: In the style of Nicholas I (1796–1855), who wore his moustaches long, reaching out east and west in two impressive curls. The reference implies that the moustache is stylish, flamboyant, but two generations out of date.

THE FORGED COUPON

1. *coupon*: A detachable voucher on Tsarist government bonds, used for obtaining interest on them.
2. *muzhik*: A Russian peasant.
3. *versts*: One verst is approximately two miles.
4. *the People's House*: The People's Houses (*narodnye doma*) were the working men's clubs of pre-revolutionary Russia, places of popular entertainment, vaudeville, etc. Towards the end of the nineteenth century the People's Houses in the main urban centres also acquired an educational function, and began to contain libraries and reading rooms.
5. *desyatina*: One desyatina is 2.7 acres.
6. *izba*: Hut, small wooden dwelling.
7. *zemstvo*: Elective district council in pre-revolutionary Russia.
8. *kasha*: A dish of cooked grain or groats, similar to porridge.
9. *mir*: Village community.
10. *ambo*: Special name for the pulpit in early Christian Churches or an enclosed reading desk in the Russian Orthodox Church.
11. *archimandrite*: A senior officer in the Greek and Russian Orthodox Churches, the superintendent of a monastery (like an abbot in the Western Church) or of several monasteries.
12. *az, buki, vedi*: Mnemonic names for the first three letters of the Russian alphabet. One of Tolstoy's educational projects was a new presentation of the alphabet and a system for learning to read.
13. *volost*: Small rural district.

read more

PENGUIN CLASSICS

THE COSSACKS AND OTHER STORIES
LEO TOLSTOY

'You will see war … in its authentic expression – as blood, suffering and death'

In 1851, at the age of twenty-two, Tolstoy travelled to the Caucasus and joined the army there as a cadet. The four years that followed were among the most significant in his life, and deeply influenced the stories collected here. Begun in 1852 but unfinished for a decade, 'The Cossacks' describes the experiences of Olenin, a young cultured Russian who comes to despise civilization after spending time with the wild Cossack people. 'Sevastopol Sketches', based on Tolstoy's own experiences of the siege of Sevastopol in 1854–55, is a compelling description and consideration of the nature of war. In 'Hadji Murat', written towards the end of his life, Tolstoy returns to the Caucasus of his youth and portrays the life of a great leader, torn apart and destroyed by a conflict of loyalties: it is amongst the greatest of his shorter works.

The translations in this volume convey the beauty and power of the original pieces, while the introduction reflects on Tolstoy's own wartime experiences. This edition also includes notes and maps.

Translated with notes by David McDuff and Paul Foote
With an introduction by Paul Foote

PENGUIN CLASSICS

WAR AND PEACE
LEO TOLSTOY

'Yes! It's all vanity, it's all an illusion, everything except that infinite sky'

At a glittering society party in St Petersburg in 1805, conversations are dominated by the prospect of war. Terror swiftly engulfs the country as Napoleon's army marches on Russia, and the lives of three young people are changed forever. The stories of quixotic Pierre, cynical Andrey and impetuous Natasha interweave with a huge cast, from aristocrats and peasants, to soldiers and Napoleon himself. In *War and Peace* (1863–9), Tolstoy entwines grand themes – conflict and love, birth and death, free will and fate – with unforgettable scenes of nineteenth-century Russia, to create a magnificent epic of human life in all its imperfection and grandeur.

Anthony Briggs's superb translation combines stirring, accessible prose with fidelity to Tolstoy's original, while Orlando Figes's afterword discusses the novel's vast scope and depiction of Russian identity. This edition also includes appendices, notes, a list of prominent characters and maps.

'A book that you don't just read, you live' Simon Schama

'A masterpiece … This new translation is excellent' Antony Beevor

Translated with an introduction and notes by Anthony Briggs
With an afterword by Orlando Figes

THE STORY OF PENGUIN CLASSICS

Before 1946 … 'Classics' are mainly the domain of academics and students; readable editions for everyone else are almost unheard of. This all changes when a little-known classicist, E. V. Rieu, presents Penguin founder Allen Lane with the translation of Homer's *Odyssey* that he has been working on in his spare time.

1946 Penguin Classics debuts with *The Odyssey*, which promptly sells three million copies. Suddenly, classics are no longer for the privileged few.

1950s Rieu, now series editor, turns to professional writers for the best modern, readable translations, including Dorothy L. Sayers's *Inferno* and Robert Graves's unexpurgated *Twelve Caesars*.

1960s The Classics are given the distinctive black covers that have remained a constant throughout the life of the series. Rieu retires in 1964, hailing the Penguin Classics list as 'the greatest educative force of the twentieth century.'

1970s A new generation of translators swells the Penguin Classics ranks, introducing readers of English to classics of world literature from more than twenty languages. The list grows to encompass more history, philosophy, science, religion and politics.

1980s The Penguin American Library launches with titles such as *Uncle Tom's Cabin*, and joins forces with Penguin Classics to provide the most comprehensive library of world literature available from any paperback publisher.

1990s The launch of Penguin Audiobooks brings the classics to a listening audience for the first time, and in 1999 the worldwide launch of the Penguin Classics website extends their reach to the global online community.

The 21st Century Penguin Classics are completely redesigned for the first time in nearly twenty years. This world-famous series now consists of more than 1300 titles, making the widest range of the best books ever written available to millions – and constantly redefining what makes a 'classic'.

The Odyssey continues …